My
Taxing
Career

a novel by

F. M. Cipriano

<u>FMC Press</u>

My Taxing Career

[ISBN 978-0-9941743-3-8]
First published 2017 by FMC Press
PO Box 13179
Law Courts VIC 8010
Australia
Copyright © F. M. Cipriano 2017
Book Cover Design: Avanska Design
Editing & Proofreading: Brenda Gurr

National Library of Australia Cataloguing - in - Publication entry (pbk):
Cipriano, F. M., author.
My taxing career / F. M. Cipriano
ISBN: 9780994174338 (paperback)
Employee-management relations in government—Fiction
Civil service—Fiction
Taxation—Fiction
A823.4

Disclaimer: This book is a fact-based fiction. Names and characters are the product of the author's imagination or are used fictitiously. Any resemblance to actual persons, living or dead, is coincidental. No responsibility can be accepted by the publisher or author for any damages resulting from the misrepresentation of this work by associating any resemblances to any factual person, living or dead.
All care has been taken in the preparation of the information herein, but no responsibility can be accepted by the publisher or author for any damages resulting from the misinterpretation of this work. All contact details given in this book were current at the time of publication, but are subject to change.

Published by FMC Press

www.fmcpress.com

DEDICATION

This book is dedicated to the rare breed of people across the public service who hold one thing above all others—to be true public servants. These people are sincerely committed to their careers and to work for the community. They are not driven by personal gain or promotion but to perform an honourable, although often thankless, task. These are people who don't pay lip service to the policies and principles of their agency; they live them. I did not find these people among the senior ranks; they were usually behind the scenes. It was my privilege to have worked with these people.

TABLE OF CONTENTS

ACKNOWLEDGEMENTS

I thank my fellow workers who assisted me over the course of my 32-year career with the Australian Taxation Office (ATO).

Thanks to my family and friends who not only put up with me but also provided me with the encouragement to continue on.

My appreciation goes to Jeff Lapidos, Secretary of the Taxation Branch of the Australian Services Union, who was willing to help me when no-one else would and who gave me a level of support that no-one else could.

Special thanks to Dr Allan J. Bond, who not only attended to my health issues but who was also willing to listen to my story, show empathy to my condition and be sympathetic to my needs.

I greatly appreciate the efforts of Martin Lock, former ATO colleague and friend, who was the first person to read my manuscript and who provided me with constructive and helpful feedback.

I am eternally grateful to my dearly departed parents, Porzia and Giuseppe. They instilled in me the importance of leading a responsible and honest life, regardless of the personal sacrifice.

ABOUT THE AUTHOR

F. M. Cipriano (Frank) was born in Melbourne, Australia. He holds a Bachelor of Business, a Graduate Diploma in Accounting and a Master of Taxation.

Frank was a career public servant with the Australian Taxation Office (ATO) until he gained a voluntary redundancy, departing on 29 August 2014.

Since leaving the ATO, Frank has pursued his passion for writing. His first book, *A Bachelor's Travels*, was published in March 2015. This book, Frank's second, is a fictional book inspired by his career with the ATO.

Chapter 1 – Campus Interviews

It was a warm, spring morning when Fred Campari made his way to the meeting room for the second last of his university campus interviews. He arrived just before the scheduled time and quickly adjusted his tie before taking a seat in the waiting area. Fifteen minutes later, the interview room door opened and a man waved him inside.

The interview was with a highly rated accounting firm. Fred entered the room to be greeted by two men wearing designer suits. One of the men appeared in his mid-twenties and the other appeared of middle-age. The two men were seated at one side of the table and the older man invited Fred to take a seat at the other side of the table.

The interview commenced with some brief introductions and the interviewers proceeded to ask a number of technical questions. Fred was reasonably comfortable with his responses until the younger man spoke. "There are a number of credits among your grades," he said with a sneer.

"Yes, that's right," Fred responded.

The younger man sniggered as he asked his next question. "So what do your parents do for a living?"

"My father works for the General Post Office and my mother works in a factory," Fred instinctively responded, and then momentarily reflected on the question. He grimaced. "But how is this relevant to the job interview?"

"In assessing a candidate's suitability for our firm, we often find that an applicant's family background can provide some insight into their values and business culture," the older man said.

Fred raised his eyebrows. "So how does your firm assess a person's background where their mother and father started out with nothing and dedicated their whole lives to work hard for their family?"

There was conspicuous uneasiness as the interview was wound up and Fred was thanked for his time.

Fred had his head bowed as he made his way to the university cafeteria. He was seated at a table on his own when a fellow student, Hector Ioannou, joined him.

Fred glanced up. "Hi, Hector, how did your interview go?"

"It was with the Audit Office and I think I did okay," Hector replied.

"If you get the job, wouldn't that mean you'd have to go to Canberra?"

"That's true," Hector confirmed. "However, it seems that you can usually get back to Melbourne after the first year's training."

"One whole year in that artificial city," Fred said as he shook his head. "There's no way I'd want to spend that long in such a sterile place."

"So how did your interview go?" Hector asked.

"It was absolute crap," Fred asserted. "Not that it matters; I wouldn't want to work for those arrogant pricks."

"I'm sure you'll do better in your interview with the Tax Office," Hector said, in an upbeat voice.

Fred arrived for his last interview just before the scheduled time. He was about to take a seat in the waiting area when an elderly man approached and invited him to enter the meeting room. The man was wearing a brown sports coat with light brown elbow patches and an open-necked shirt.

Fred engaged in social conversation with the man, which seemed appropriate given his own apathetic mood, and, he felt, that of the interviewer.

After about half an hour, there was a silent pause and Fred reflected on how wishy-washy the whole interview had been.

"So, is that it from your end?" Fred asked nonchalantly.

"I think so," the elderly gentlemen answered.

Fred felt he couldn't possibly leave the interview on such a sober note. "Sir, let me say that this has been an absolute pleasure and I would be highly honoured if I could be considered to join such a fine establishment as the Tax Office." He offered the man his hand and, as the man took hold, Fred initiated an enthusiastic handshake.

The interviewer seemed genuinely inspired and Fred left the room thinking, *Now there's one place I definitely would not want to work.*

Chapter 2 – First Instalments

Fred planned to celebrate the completion of his accounting degree with a gap year that was to commence with a trip around Australia with some of his friends; however, his travelling companions pulled out. He was at a loss to know what to do when he caught up with a fellow student named Chris Economou.

"You simply have to join the Tax Office," said Chris.

"That's one place I wouldn't want to work," Fred responded.

"It's not that bad and you earn money for doing very little," Chris explained. "I plan to work through the ranks for a few years and then get into public accounting."

Fred hadn't anything else planned, so he heeded Chris's advice. He sat the public service examination and was soon called up for an interview. The interview was a mere formality and he was referred for a physical. He fronted up at the Commonwealth Centre on the corner of Spring and La Trobe Streets, Melbourne. Inspired by its colour, the building was referred to as the Green Latrine.

The medical officer didn't seem to do much more than to find a pulse and Fred was given the all clear.

It wasn't long before Fred was notified to report at 8.30 am on 17 March 1982 at the Tax Office at 350 Collins Street, Melbourne.

Fred's parents, Rosa and Michael, were ecstatic that their only son was joining the Tax Office. They were just as excited when their only daughter, Gina, became a teacher. Rosa and Michael valued positions in the public service, as they stressed the importance of having a secure job, especially during hard times.

Fred was advised that he could wear smart casual clothing but as he was mildly enthused about his first day of full-time work, he decided to wear a suit and tie. He was escorted into a room where he was soon joined by a group of scruffily dressed individuals. The last entrant was the Tax Office training representative, arriving at precisely 9.00 am.

The group underwent their induction, which included a rundown of the office's policies, practices and principles. A detailed explanation of the tax secrecy provisions was given paramount importance.

At the end of the day, the group members were told where they were to report for duty. Everyone was to report to Defaults in the same building, except for Fred. He was required to report to Instalments at 270 King Street, Melbourne.

Fred was looking resplendent in his three-piece suit, complete with briefcase and fob watch. As he exited the lift, he approached the first person he saw—a woman of generous proportions—seated at a desk.

"Excuse me, my name is Fred Campari and I'm required to report to the Officer-in-Charge, Mr Brian Quinn."

The woman was sucking from a straw inserted in a soft drink can, which she held in her right hand. Her left hand was in a packet of crisps that was poking out of her side drawer. The woman rolled her eyes and simply pointed towards a desk near a window while she continued sucking from the straw. As soon as she noticed Fred looking towards where she was pointing, she quickly re-inserted her left hand into the bag to pull out another handful of crisps.

Fred thanked the woman and approached a distinguished-looking, elderly gentleman.

"Good day, sir, my name is Fred Campari and I'm to report to the Officer-in-Charge, Mr Brian Quinn."

The man looked up with a smile. "G'day, Fred, I'm Brian. Welcome to Instalments."

Brian invited Fred to take a seat and they engaged in some small talk. As they were conversing, a number of people were progressively arriving and clocking on. It was bang on 9.30 am when a middle-aged man arrived wearing a sports coat, an open-necked shirt and designer sunglasses. Brian came to life the moment he noticed the man and called him over.

Brian introduced Fred to a manager in Instalments, Tony Webber, who was a relaxed and smooth talking gentleman. Brian then readily handed further responsibilities for Fred over to Tony.

Tony led Fred over to a desk, which faced a group of desks in grid formation. Tony provided a general explanation of the Tax Office and was in high praise of the establishment. "The working conditions here are fantastic. They provide me with the flexibility to pursue all my other interests," Tony said with a wink and, if Fred correctly read between the lines, the other interests included womanising.

As Tony was giving his spiel, a man to the side of them was chuckling after just about every comment and, every now and then, gave off intermittent grunts of approval.

"George Shipp will be your team manager," Tony advised Fred and the man to the side momentarily stopped chuckling. Tony then readily handed further responsibilities for Fred over to George.

George was in a bit of quandary as to what to do with Fred, but he soon continued with the positive spin. "Yeah, this place is great; I'm going to try to get all my kids to work here," he said.

A conspicuous rattling sound was heard, which seemed to make George very agitated and he sprang up. "Fred, you can settle into the spare desk and we can continue with our talk after tea break," George suggested, moving quickly towards the tea trolley.

There was a mad rush to make it to the tea trolley as the tea lady locked the trolley into position. It had two large metal urns, one for coffee and one for tea. There was also a selection of assorted snacks, including coffee scrolls, hot cross buns, cream buns, chips, chocolate bars and cold drinks.

"Come on you guys, have some order in the line," the tea lady called out. "Okay, who's next in line? Hurry up and make up your minds; I haven't got all day you know!"

The tea lady was stern-looking and strong-sounding, although Fred sensed that the whole affair was in good fun.

During the bustle, a young man tentatively approached Fred and introduced himself as Zane. After Fred introduced himself, Zane enthusiastically commenced a conversation.

"It's always the same guys to be first in line for the tea trolley, usually the managers," Zane explained. "The official time for tea breaks is 15 minutes, but the unofficial practice is that the time starts from when the last person is served. This usually results in morning and afternoon tea breaks of around 30 minutes or even longer."

Zane turned to the manager's desk. "There is only one telephone per team. You can use it as a contact number, but is strictly for work purposes and private emergencies."

Zane then turned to Fred's desk, which was of solid timber with a green plastic writing surface and two large drawers on either side. "Every desk is equipped with an ash tray, of course," Zane said. "You should also have pens, pencils, pads, notepaper and pins—and whatever you do, don't forget to book your pins."

What in the hell does 'book your pins' mean? Fred was left wondering as Zane strode off to buy a coffee. Fred also made his way to the tea trolley, where he was the last customer with his purchase of a coffee and a coffee scroll.

George was reluctantly making his way towards Fred when he made a beeline to a middle-aged woman and escorted her with him. "Fred, this is Esmeralda and she can show you around," George said with a smile as he readily handed further responsibilities for Fred over to Esmeralda.

Esmeralda provided some general information, with the first detail being the location of the toilets. She progressively introduced Fred to the other people on the floor and declared a lunch break of 30 minutes at 12.45 pm.

After lunch, Esmeralda provided Fred with an overview of Instalments, which formed part of the 'Pay-As-You-Earn' (PAYE) area.

"PAYE is basically the tax taken out of salary and wages that can be claimed against tax payable when taxpayers lodge their annual tax returns," Esmeralda explained. "However, in order for them to claim their credit, they need a tax stamp sheet or a group certificate. If taxpayers don't have either one when they lodge their tax return, that's where we come in. We're the Token Control Unit." Esmeralda added with a hint of pride in her voice.

Esmeralda was explaining further details of the PAYE system when there was the familiar rattle of the tea trolley at 2.30 pm and another mad scramble to be first in line, with the managers leading the way once more.

The remainder of the day was spent attending to administrative matters. Fred was allocated a clock card and it took some time to track down George, who was required to initial Fred's starting time of 8.30 am.

"Who do I see if I want to join the union?" Fred asked Esmeralda.

"Sean Green is the man to see and he should be in tomorrow," she said.

Fred clocked off at exactly 4.21 pm, which meant he clocked up seven hours and twenty-one minutes—a standard day. This made for an easy calculation for the time he banked for his first day at work, being precisely zero minutes.

As Fred was leaving, he was joined in the lift by Shirley, a thin woman in her mid-twenties with mousy blonde hair and green eyes. Shirley started to laugh.

"So, what's the joke?" Fred asked.

"You're the joke," Shirley responded. "With that get-up of a suit and tie we thought you were management from national office but you just turned out to be a Clerk Class 1."

Fred exited the building, loosened his tie and undid the top button of his shirt. *I won't have to bother wearing a suit in that area*, he thought.

The next day, Fred clocked on at 8.30 am and the first thing he did was to introduce himself to Sean Green. "I'd like to join the union," Fred said.

Sean was happy to sign up the new recruit.

Esmeralda instructed Fred with his main task, which was to fill out token credit dockets to replace a taxpayer's group certificate or tax stamp sheet where it had been lost or destroyed. The information he needed for the token either came from a letter from the employer or a statutory declaration from the employee.

As Fred got on with his work, he looked in disbelief as he witnessed a staff member coming out of a room wearing a fur overcoat.

"Is that guy all right?" Fred asked Esmeralda.

She giggled. "James is definitely not all right. However, there is some justification for the overcoat. He's coming out of the Unapplied Credits Register room, which is controlled at a cool temperature to maintain the registers."

Fred checked out the air-conditioned room, which was indeed cool, and found it packed from floor to ceiling with shelving supporting large registers.

James entered the room. "You know, there's millions of dollars worth of unapplied credits in those registers," he advised. "All one needs to do is to lodge fake tax returns with details in the registers and collect the refunds."

"That's a brilliant idea," Fred replied. "I'm amazed no-one has ever thought of it before."

"Oh, but they have," James said.

Fred raised his eyebrows. "How do you know?"

"The guy was found out and he's now in jail."

Fred continued his work, filling out the token credit dockets and, as he transcribed the figures, he remembered what he had been told. *Be extra careful with the dollar amounts as it's real money, you know.*

Fred completed a number of the dockets and commented that he was getting bored.

"It's little wonder you're getting bored. You're doing too many of them, one straight after the other," George suggested and then cried out, "Fred, you didn't book your pins!"

"Oh, I was going to ask about that," said Fred. "What does 'book your pins' mean?"

George stuck up his thumb, which had a trickle of blood. "You need to tuck the pins into the paper so the point isn't exposed and people don't puncture themselves," George advised with a frown.

*　　*　　*

Fred had been in Instalments for just over a month when positions were advertised for Clerk Class 2/3 assessors.

"Have you applied for the assessor positions?" Esmeralda asked.

"I thought it would be too soon for me to apply," Fred replied.

"Not at all," she said. "It's common for qualified people to spend only a month or two as a Clerk Class 1 before they're promoted. There have even been officers still completing their study part-time who have been promoted."

Fred lodged an application and was soon contacted for an interview. He bumped into Chris Economou who was already in Assessing and Chris filled him in with some information about the job.

"The interview should be a breeze," Chris concluded.

Fred dug out his suit for the job interview and, as Chris suggested, he found the interview to be easy. It therefore came as a surprise when he was advised that his application was unsuccessful.

"You needn't be too concerned," Esmeralda said reassuringly. "Positions are usually advertised every few months and you are sure to get promoted the next time."

Further positions were indeed advertised within a few months. Fred applied for the second time and was soon contacted for an interview. He spoke with Chris again, and was buoyed by his assurance of success. Fred completed his preparations, got suited up and approached the interview with a little more purpose. He was comfortable with the interview as, just like the first time, it was a breeze.

The promotions were published and, to Fred's astonishment, he was unsuccessful once again. For the life of him, he couldn't work it out.

Esmeralda was equally perplexed. "Fred, I'm surprised you've been unsuccessful for a second time. You may wish to contact the selection committee and request feedback."

Fred was booked for a feedback session with the two people who comprised the selection committee for both of his job applications, Dean Lewis and Jerry Martin.

"Thank you for the opportunity to meet with you," Fred said. "I've been unsuccessful in both of my applications so I'd really appreciate some feedback."

Dean was the chairperson and led the feedback session. "Fred, your application was of an acceptable standard; however, you fell down at the interviews."

Fred considered both of the interviews as being not much more than social chit-chats so he asked Dean to elaborate.

"You didn't come across as being all that interested in the job as you didn't ask too many questions," Dean explained.

"I'm certainly interested in the position, that's why I applied," Fred replied in exasperation. "As for questions, I know someone who is already in Assessing so I might be aware of information that other applicants may not. Could you give me an example of the sort of questions asked?"

"Well, one applicant asked what the pay range was for a Clerk Class 2/3," Dean responded. Fred smiled at what he thought was a joke; however, Dean maintained a serious demeanour. Jerry was just looking into space.

Anyone working in the public service would have to be aware of the salary ranges for the various levels; it's common knowledge, Fred thought. He took a breath before he commented. "Okay, if I'm successful in gaining a job interview in the future, I'll consider some questions to ask. Thank you for the feedback."

Fred was about to depart when Dean pulled him up. "You know you also have the option to lodge an appeal against the promotions," Dean said.

"But I wouldn't necessarily know the other applicants. On what basis could I appeal?" Fred asked.

"You don't have to know the other applicants. Just do what

everybody else does. Lodge an appeal and state that you are better than the other applicants," Dean suggested.

"I'd prefer to rely on the merits of my application," Fred stated.

"You'll never get anywhere in this place unless you play the game," Dean advised.

Fred gave a wry smile before he left the room.

*　*　*

During the year, Fred attended his university graduation and a reunion dinner with his fellow students. They were engaging in heated discussion when they got onto the topic of their respective salaries and went around the table to ascertain the range.

The top salary was around $18 000, with the bulk of the graduates being on around $16 000. The lower end salaries were the public servants, with Hector and Chris at around $15 000. This gained a chorus of laughter from around the table and it took some time for the laughter to die down.

Fred was smiling and looking about, being the only one who hadn't answered the question. He held off answering, hoping that they would forget about him, but they didn't. They turned their attention to Fred and one of them popped the question.

Fred was coy about answering. "Like Chris, I work in the Tax Office," he stated.

The group was obviously dissatisfied with his response and they pressed. "And exactly how much salary would that be?" asked one of them.

Fred looked around the table and all eyes were upon him. "Precisely $11 750," he blurted out.

There was a moment of silence before those at the table erupted in laughter with the graduates rolling about. The uproar took up most of the remainder of the evening.

*　*　*

Positions for Clerk Class 2/3 assessors were advertised yet again; however, the process had changed. The applicants not only had to undergo the interview, but also successfully complete a two-week assessing training school before positions were awarded.

Fred applied and was contacted for an interview. Yet again, Dean Lewis and Jerry Martin were on the selection committee. Fred had trouble formulating questions to ask and relied on information he had found on the future directions of the Tax Office in the light of recently announced legislative changes.

The interview commenced with the standard preliminaries and proceeded with a general discussion. When they stumbled on a quiet moment, Fred thought it might be a good time to raise some questions.

"I was reading about recent legislative amendments and I expect they will have an impact on the work in Assessing," he stated in a positive tone.

"I'm not aware of these legislative changes," Dean said, to Fred's amazement.

"The legislative amendments include changes to the spouse and zone rebates, the introduction of new pension and dividend rebates and the withdrawal of the zero rate tax threshold for non-residents. I expect these will require changes for Assessing," Fred suggested.

"I haven't read about these legislative changes," Dean said.

Fred was disheartened, but he made one last attempt to generate some discussion. "I expect the Tax Office's future direction toward self-assessing will provide challenges and opportunities for Assessing staff," he said.

Dean and Jerry looked at each other and made no comment.

"These were the only topics I had for discussion," Fred said in a disconsolate voice.

Fred left the interview room totally demoralised and didn't hold out much hope of success. Nevertheless, he completed the assessing training school, where he relished the opportunity to tackle technical exercises and engage in technical discussions.

Nervously awaiting the outcome of the promotions process, Fred received a letter from the Tax Office. The letter advised that he had been successful in his application as a Graduate Officer. *Graduate Officer?* Fred thought. *I didn't even apply for that position. Or did I?*

Fred rang the woman named as the contact person on the letter and queried the position.

"The offers emanate from campus interviews and candidates are being selected for the next intake," the woman advised.

"I actually already work in the Tax Office as a Clerk Class 1," Fred explained.

"I don't know anything about that. All I know is that this graduate position is available to you," informed the woman. "You will be required to undertake a two-week assessing training school and will then be automatically promoted to an Assessor Class 2/3."

Fred was unsure what to say. "I'd like to think about it; can I get back to you with my decision?" he asked.

"You can think about it but I'll need a decision by the end of the week," the woman advised.

Considering the situation to be most unusual and being uncertain as to what to do, Fred decided to contact Dean. After explaining his situation, he asked the status of the selection committee and sought his advice.

"The selection committee is still deliberating and I don't know how long the process will take," Dean advised. "In terms of your situation, I don't really care what you do."

Fred was surprised by Dean's last comment, but it did help him to make a decision. As soon as he put down the receiver, he quickly made a telephone call to the contact person and accepted the graduate position.

It was Fred's birthday on 12 January, which was also the date of the letter he received from the Deputy Commissioner, E. J. Hoover. The letter detailed that he had been appointed to the public service as a Graduate Officer on a commencing annual salary of $14 650. The permanent appointment was effective from 17 January 1983 and he was to report to 13th Floor North, 350 Collins Street. Fred read the final sentence of the letter, paused and then read it a second time.

"It is hoped that you have a long and rewarding career in the Tax Office."

Fred fronted up at precisely 8.30 am on 17 January 1983, when he commenced a career with the Tax Office for the second time.

Chapter 3 – Assessing & Quality Control

Dispensed with having to complete the one-day Tax Office induction again, Fred spent the day doing private research in the library. He then undertook the two-week assessing training school for the second time and on 10 February 1983, he was promoted to Assessing as a Clerk Class 2/3.

Fred was to report to his team manager at 350 Collins Street. It would not be such a lonely assignment, as he was to be joined by some of his fellow graduate officers.

The team manager was Frank Capri, with the other five people on the team being Sonia Tischer, Pep Carello, Jim Zissis, Michael Pantano and Anthony Fazio. Each new assessor was assigned a desk, handed a couple of purple pens and distributed an assessor's stamp with a purple ink pad. Fred's assessing stamp read:

ASSD. 4014

F.CAMPARI

......../......../........

The next thing the team members received was a bundle of tax returns: *Form S 1982 Income Tax Returns for Salary and Wages Etc.*

The assessing area was like a production line, which was little wonder as each assessor had a quota of over 300 tax returns to be assessed per day. There were banging noises coming from all directions as the experienced assessors ploughed through their returns and stamped them as they went.

Fred commenced examining his first few returns and found that some contained quite a bit of information. He took the time to review the details, ensured that all the necessary labels were filled in, made the required queries and effected adjustments where incorrect entries were made.

Jim Zissis was seated across from Fred. "What in the hell are you doing?" Jim asked.

"It's called assessing tax returns," Fred responded.

"I know that, but you don't have to do all that work; you only need to make sure the required labels are filled in and then stamp the damn thing," said Jim.

"Well, that's not really doing a proper job," Fred replied.

"Maybe not," said Jim, "but we're not given the time to do a proper job."

Fred recognised what Jim had said was right. The assessors only had a couple of minutes to complete each tax return. By lunchtime, the experienced assessors had just about completed their quota and were loafing around and socialising. Jim was on target to complete his quota by the end of the day; however, Fred had only completed 50 tax returns by midday. The harsh reality was that there was no chance of achieving quota if one was to do the job properly and this would reflect badly on an assessor and their team. It was a numbers game and the managers' priority was for their team to meet quota. In fact, the managers seemed to resent it when assessors did anything more than the bare minimum, as it required them to check more work.

By the end of the day, Frank reviewed the completed tax return numbers of the team and the scorecard showed Jim: 320, Michael: 310, Anthony: 300, Sonia: 280, Pep: 280 and Fred: 200.

"It's been a reasonable effort from the team given that you are new," Frank stated. He then pulled Fred aside. "You're dragging the team down, so you really need to pick up the pace."

"Don't worry, Frank," Fred responded. "I now know what to do and I'm sure I'll be able to get the quota from now on."

Fred soon fell into line and achieved quota every day.

*　　*　　*

During the call centre peak periods, assessors were required to relieve staff in Telephone Enquiries. Fred wasn't keen on this prospect; however, he was called upon one morning. He reluctantly made his way downstairs and his phone soon rang. He picked up the receiver. It sounded like a dear old woman, who explained how she used to front up at the Tax Office and a nice man would prepare her tax return.

"Unfortunately the Tax Office doesn't provide such a service anymore, so you may wish to engage the services of a tax agent," Fred suggested.

The woman just kept talking and it was about 20 minutes into the call when the Telephone Enquiries manager whispered for Fred to hang up, as she made a motion of cutting her throat. Fred couldn't make himself hang up on the woman but eventually managed to wind up the conversation at just over half an hour. He only ever answered that one call as it was time for a break and he was never summoned for Telephone Enquiries again.

*　*　*

The assessing teams settled into a routine that centred on a strong social clique. Fred's assessing team often went to the pub at lunchtime for a meal and a couple of drinks; however, after work at 4.00 pm on Friday was party time. The assessors mainly frequented two pubs: the Grosvenor Hotel, where they rubbed shoulders with the chartered accountants, and the London Tavern, which they called their own.

The London Tavern's front entrance was in Elizabeth Street; however, the assessors entered via the rear entrance from Equitable Place situated near 350 Collins Street. Once inside, they would alternate between the Tap Room and the Ski Bar.

Pep was the rowdiest of the party-goers and he was usually the first to order a round of drinks. The prospect of driving home drunk didn't seem to concern him.

Jim noted an assessor, Celine Diamond, among the crowd having a drink. Celine was renowned for practising singing at work. Jim already had a few drinks under his belt when he cried out to her.

"Hey, Celine, why don't you give us a bar?"

Celine automatically responded in a clear and strong voice. "Why don't you flop it out, Jim, and then I'll give you a bar!"

The men were not expecting such a reply and it left them lost for words. However, after a moment they gave her a round of applause and gained a new-found admiration for the aspiring diva.

*　*　*

The closing of the financial year meant there would soon be the avalanche of tax return lodgements. This gave the assessors the opportunity to do overtime, which was available during the weekday evenings and on Saturdays. There was a selection of the easier tax returns set aside for overtime, which was understandable as the quotas were much more demanding at over 400 tax returns per day.

On Saturday overtime, the boys usually had lunch at the Royal Arcade Hotel where veal parmigiana was the popular choice. The meals came with a complimentary salad buffet. One of the assessors was content to follow the crowd, grab a couple of rolls and stuff them with salad.

"Ever thought of actually paying for a meal?" Pep queried.

"Nah," the assessor responded. "The free salad and bread rolls are enough for me."

After a couple of months, Pep, Jim and Fred were advised that they were being transferred to QCU.

"What's QCU and why us?" Pep asked.

Frank took the three of them aside. "QCU is the Quality Control Unit. I don't know why the three of you have been chosen. However, from what I can gauge, the job tends to be given to the better operatives."

Pep, Jim and Fred found their way to QCU and reported to a jovial, middle-aged man named John Kruger. John introduced them to the three other members of the team—Charlie Ambrose, Harry Rice and Adrian Brown.

Adrian was quick to break the ice. "That's great, it was just a matter of time before you wogs made up the majority!" he exclaimed.

Pep, Jim and Fred were all slightly taken aback by the comment before Charlie responded. "Clever calculation, Skippy, and for your reward you can now go off and play with your little Joey."

This had the whole group laughing and the new recruits sensed they had found a happy home.

Harry and Charlie were the best of friends, which of course meant that they were incessantly hanging shit on one another. They also proved to be excellent instructors, as they succinctly explained the general procedures.

"Newcomers, are you ready for battle?" Harry asked.

"Ready for battle?" Fred queried. "What battle and with whom?"

Harry and Charlie led the boys out of the room, through the lift lobby and over to the opposite side of the building where the pair momentarily stopped ahead of double doors.

"Let's do it!" Charlie cried as he pushed open the doors. They burst into the area and marched inside.

"Okay, ladies, the studs have arrived!" Harry declared.

There were women lined up in teams, seated at desks and

operating computers. Their replies were loud and clear.

"Yeah, right, studs in your own mind."

"Was that studs or duds?"

"The last stud I had was at the end of my boot!"

"Who in the hell are these women?" Jim asked.

"They're DPOs and before you ask what a DPO is, it stands for Data Processing Officer. They key in the data from the tax returns," Harry explained.

"As assessors, we sit on stand-by," Charlie added. "If any errors pop up, we're supposed to fix them on the spot. If we can't fix them on the spot, we set the tax return aside to fix later."

Harry and Charlie selected their favourite DPO teams and the others were left to select from the rest.

"Which team do you usually sit on?" Fred asked Adrian.

"I'll just sit in a spot if there's one left, which I hope there isn't as I don't really like this job," Adrian confessed.

Fred couldn't understand why Adrian had such a negative attitude until he heard the vulgar comments directed at Adrian from all quarters. Adrian was like a lamb to the slaughter.

Fred sat down on an assessor's seat at the next available team. "Hello," he stated, although the women were ignoring him.

They commenced keying in data from the tax returns and one of them soon tossed a return towards Fred.

"Fix it," the woman demanded.

Fred started to intently examine the return.

"What are you doing? It just needs a zero at label R," the woman snapped at him.

Fred stared her down. "Hold on a moment—I'm the assessor here."

After a little while, Fred made an insertion on the return and communicated his determination. "There you go; it just needed a zero at label R."

Fred was in the middle of witnessing some of the most disgusting conversations he had ever heard in his life as the women were describing in detail their sexual experiences, when he was saved by the bell.

"What's that bell?" Fred queried.

"It's the bell for a tension break," one of the women replied.

"Tension break?" Fred asked. "What's that?"

"Where have you been, man?" another woman said. "There's been an epidemic of Repetitive Strain Injury or RSI. We've been complaining about it for ages; however, management refuse to believe us and do nothing about it, other than giving us a few tension breaks and reviewing our number of keystrokes. There are hundreds of cases and the union expects that management will try a test case in an attempt to get around any liability."

"So how serious is this RSI thing?" Fred queried with some concern.

The women took turns in explaining the situation. "There are numerous cases. Some of these poor girls have conditions where they feel numbness and weakness in their hands and arms. Some even have stabbing pains. Management's position is that it's all psychological and that the unions are encouraging mass hysteria."

Fred sought out Harry and Charlie to ascertain more about RSI.

"What the DPOs told you is true but management just say it's a put-on," Harry said. "However, what are the odds of hundreds of workers all making up the same story? I know some of these women. They're in real pain and it's affecting their whole lives."

"Surely management will ultimately end up having to help them?" Fred suggested.

"Get serious, Fred," Charlie stated. "Management are spending heaps of money to discredit the claims. You'll learn soon enough— management are arseholes."

*　*　*

Charlie advised that he was organising a weekend away with a few of the DPOs. Jim and Pep were excited about the prospect but Fred wasn't too keen.

"I think I'll give it a miss," he said.

However, the guys did not accept Fred's rejection and spent the rest of the week pressuring him before they convinced him to go.

The bus pick-up was in the Melbourne CBD and Fred brought a bottle of whisky for the long journey to Albury-Wodonga. They eventually arrived and checked into their hotel rooms. Fred had polished off his bottle and was feeling sick in the bathroom. He then returned to one of the rooms to the sight of two DPOs being passed from one man to the next, with the guys taking turns to give them a passionate kiss. The pair eventually arrived on Fred's lap, but he refused to kiss them.

"Are you a fag or something?" Charlie asked.

"No, I'm not a fag," Fred replied. "Maybe it's just the fact that I know where these women have been."

As Fred was recovering on the couch, Charlie announced that they were going to the pub. Fred dragged himself along and, as he wasn't into pokies, he thought he may as well have a few drinks at the bar. Arriving back at the hotel, Fred was sick for a second time.

"You'd better pull yourself together," Harry told Fred. "We're going to a nightclub."

Fred felt like a zombie as he followed the guys to catch a cab.

Arriving at the club, Fred wasn't up to dancing so he decided to have some mixed drinks in the lounge bar.

The group eventually got back to the hotel with Fred being helped along the corridor by Harry and Charlie. As they passed by Michael and Anthony's room, they saw a guy outside the room, banging on the door.

"Rhonda, please open the door, Rhonda!" the guy was crying out.

Even in his paralytic state, Fred picked up on the fact that the guy was obviously missing out on some hot action.

There was continued drinking in one of the other hotel rooms when hotel management rang and warned that the partying had to cease or they would be kicked out of the hotel.

The table was full of bottles and Fred was seated at the table, gulping down beer out of a stubby. Jim made an appearance and started parading around the room, holding a chair in the air with one hand and a stubby in the other hand. Fred noticed that the chair was about to collide with the chandelier so he thought he'd jump to the rescue. As he got up, his vision became fuzzy and he collapsed. The table tipped over, with glasses and bottles crashing to the ground, which caused the revellers to scatter.

Waking up the next morning, Fred found himself seated on the toilet with his trousers and underpants around his ankles. He slowly came to his senses, washed up and assembled with the others for the long ride back to Melbourne.

*　*　*

It was only a couple of months further into their assessing careers when Clerk Class 4 positions in Business Assessing were advertised. Fred didn't consider applying until he heard that everyone else from his assessing training school was applying.

Fred was soon called up for an interview and, after a couple of weeks, there was a bit of movement about the place as rumours were flying that the positions were coming out. The experienced assessors suggested that positions were invariably posted on a Friday afternoon.

"Posted?" the aspiring promotees queried.

"Yeah, the lists of promotions are posted on the noticeboard."

The next Friday came around and expectations heightened. At mid-afternoon, a manager holding a few sheets of paper quietly pinned them up on the noticeboard. There was a short pause before crowds emerged to try to get a look. This was followed by a number of verbal sounds.

"Oh yeah!"

"You beauty!"

Given Fred's poor record with promotions, he continued going about his work. There were pockets of small groups enjoying contained celebrations around the floor, including members of Fred's team. Jim noted Fred at his desk and approached him.

"How come you haven't checked the lists?" Jim asked.

"There's no rush," Fred commented.

"Well, to save you the time, I'll just let you know that you've been promoted along with the rest of our team," Jim advised.

"That's great," Fred stated in a blasé fashion, although he was bursting with relief inside.

Chapter 4 – Businesses, Partnerships, Companies & Trusts

The promotions were made effective on 10 October 1983. The promotees underwent the business assessing training school and were advised of their new positions.

Anthony, Pep, Michael and Fred ended up on the same Business Assessing team. They approached their new manager, Con Mathis, a tall, gangly person, who was reading the newspaper. Con was quietly spoken and seemed to move in slow motion. After the introductions, the new team members settled into their seats and Con continued to read his newspaper.

The team members collected and then commenced to work on their first bundles of business tax returns: *Form AB Income Tax Returns for Business, Professional, Investment Income Etc.*

The promotees were soon busy lodging protective appeals in respect of the promoted positions.

"Fred, have you lodged your protective appeal?" Pep queried.

"I'm not interested in the appeal system," Fred responded.

"You've got to be joking!" Pep exclaimed. "There are going to be hoards of people lodging appeals and protective appeals. You know how it works. If anyone is successful in an appeal, the Merit Agency looks to see if the person who got rolled has a protective appeal. If they do, then they go over the whole list to compare that person against the rest of the promotees to see if they can roll someone else. However, if the person hasn't lodged a protective appeal, they're gone!"

"I know how the system works and I think it stinks," Fred advised. "I prefer to just rely on the merits of my application."

"Fred, you should accept the fact that you need to play the game in this joint," Pep stated.

Fred just returned a wry smile.

After a couple of months, the results of the appeals process were publicised and a number of people got rolled. There was much suspicion, as management allowed some of the assessors who got rolled to keep their positions, while others had to revert back to their previous positions. Fred was grateful to be notified that the appeals and protective appeals against him were dismissed.

It was drawing towards the end of the year and invitations went out for an Assessing dinner. The guys were not interested, as the senior managers were expected to attend, but they soon had a change of heart when they learned that the price of the ticket included complimentary finger food and all-you-can-drink. But it wasn't enough for the guys to just roll up to the event—they thought they'd turn up in fancy dress.

"You want to turn up to a formal dinner in fancy dress?" Fred queried.

"Yeah," Harry responded. "Why, what's wrong with that?"

"There's nothing wrong with that," Fred said with a grin. "In fact, I think it's brilliant."

Harry, Charlie, Pep and Fred turned up as two sets of the Blues Brothers. They burst into the nightclub and Harry immediately blew their cover.

"Okay, ladies, the studs have arrived!"

It was a fun filled evening of dancing and drinking, with the highlight being when the DJ played a special song request of *Shake Your Tail Feather*, which had everyone dancing.

*   *   *

Fred was interested in furthering his technical knowledge, but found there was limited opportunity to do so in the Tax Office. In the first semester of 1984, he commenced a Graduate Diploma in Accounting, majoring in Taxation.

During the first half of 1984, promotions were advertised for Clerk Class 5 positions. Fred applied along with everyone else on his team and, just like the previous occasion, it wasn't long before they were called up for interviews and the positions were posted on the noticeboard. Once again, all the members of the team were successful.

Fred gained a position in Partnerships. He was the only person of his team to go there, although he did know the other assessors who had gained a position there. His position was effective on 4 April 1984 and he reported to the team manager, Kurt Grass, a short, pudgy man with a distinctive limp.

Kurt was a sociable person and Fred got on well with him, as did the other members of the team.

It wasn't long before the usual appeal process gathered pace. As always, Fred did not put in a protective appeal and was soon called up for an interview. He was happy with his performance and returned to his team in good spirits.

Members of Fred's team were discussing the appeal process as Fred listened in.

"Kurt stated that someone had apparently put him down as referee without asking him so he said he was going to teach them a lesson," one of the team members said.

"Hang on," Fred stated. "I put Kurt down as a referee, but hadn't asked him."

The team members were silent as they took a minute to consider the ramifications of what Fred had just said.

"It's customary to nominate your current manager as a referee and Kurt wasn't around at the time when I was going to ask him," Fred explained. "Surely he wouldn't do anything to ruin my chances of holding my position. Would he?"

It was just over a month later when a superior officer who was unfamiliar to Fred called him in for a meeting.

"Fred, you have been rolled and, as a result, you will be reverting back to your former position as a Clerk Class 4."

Fred was devastated as he returned to Partnerships. While he collected his belongings, Kurt approached him.

"Gee, Fred, I'm surprised that you got rolled. When they asked me about you, I backed you 100 per cent of the way."

Fred had spent several weeks back in Business Assessing when another batch of positions was advertised. He applied and was soon called for an interview. He thought the interview was going well when one of the interviewers raised an additional matter.

"Fred, we find that there were a number of adverse comments made about you by your previous manager, Kurt Grass. Do you wish to respond to these comments?"

Astounded that the selection committee would divulge this information, Fred was thankful that he was given the opportunity to respond and it was an opportunity that he wasn't going to pass up.

"Gentlemen, I thank you for your candour in raising this matter. I have never had any adverse comments made to me by Mr Grass, either in writing or to my face. It therefore comes as a complete shock to me that Mr Grass has made any disparaging remarks about me. As you can see from my written referee reports, including the referee report I received from Mr Grass, they are all consistent in their positive appraisal of me. Any inconsistency between the comments put in writing and remarks made behind my back may best be put to Mr Grass to reconcile."

The selection committee members glanced at each other before they wound up the interview. Fred left the room not knowing where he stood, but he was glad that the facts had come to light.

Fred subsequently learned that Kurt had a reputation for stabbing people he didn't like in the back. Fred not having asked Kurt to be his referee seemed to be a mere excuse for Kurt to justify his malicious act.

Within a month, the results of the promotions were placed on the noticeboard. Fred tentatively approached, viewed the list and saw his name. He had gained promotion to Partnerships for a second time.

Towards the end of 1984, Clerk Class 6 positions were advertised. Fred didn't bother asking anyone whether he should apply for a position, he just did. Everyone Fred knew was applying except for Adrian so Fred sought to find out why.

"I'm really not too fussed about progressing much further in this place," Adrian stated. "In any case, one can't be promoted to a technical position as Clerk Class 6 unless they're qualified and I'm not qualified."

"What about the managers?" Fred asked. "A number of senior managers aren't qualified."

"Management positions are usually considered non-technical positions, so they strictly don't need qualifications and those positions are generally just handed to the favourites," Adrian said. "In any case, I think that there are a lot more important things in life than getting a promotion in a place like this."

Fred gained promotion as a Clerk Class 6 in Company Superannuation. Unlike mainstream Company Assessing situated at 350 Collins Street, Company Superannuation was in a small area located at 270 King Street. Fred was to report to Mr Ben Robson on 12 November 1984.

Ben was in his late 60s and described as old school. Fred found him to be a wealth of knowledge and a perfect gentleman.

The work involved checking superannuation trust deeds, superannuation tax returns and employer superannuation contributions.

Fred was happy to have gained the promotion and even happier when he survived the appeal process.

Company Superannuation had a conspicuously large number of elderly gentlemen. This was said to be due to the period after World War II when returned servicemen had preferential treatment in being recruited into the public service and, for some reason, a large number of them ended up in Company Superannuation.

One such man was Dane Tuck. When a group of assessors was milled around the floor having a social chinwag, Dane approached them, at which time the experienced assessors dispersed. It wasn't long after that the other assessors realised why the experienced assessors scattered. Dane had performed his method of breaking up a group, which was by dropping his guts.

*　　*　　*

Approaching the end of 1984, invitations went around for the end of year assessing dinner. While some assessors were deliberating over whether they would go, the guys in the former QCU team were deliberating what they would go as. They eventually decided to dress up as construction workers.

The guys approached the entrance to the nightclub and a bouncer pulled them up.

"Sorry, guys, this is a private function," a bouncer said.

"We know that," Fred replied. "We've got tickets."

"You mean you guys work for the Tax Office?" another bouncer queried.

"Well, I don't know about work," Charlie said with a grin.

The guys gained entry and were soon sculling mixed drinks as they danced and sang on the dance floor until the early hours.

*　　*　　*

Fred was finding the work in Company Superannuation limiting and uninspiring. He therefore didn't mind it too much when, due to operational requirements, he was transferred to Trusts.

On 11 February 1985, Fred reported at 280 La Trobe Street, Melbourne, referred to as the Bourke's Building. He exited the lift and approached three men seated in managers' chairs with their backs to the windows, facing him. All three men appeared to be of similar age, in their mid-50s, although their statures ranged in order from small to large.

"Hello, are you Mr Steven Harley?" Fred asked the small man.

"No, I'm Mr Steven Hardy," the small man replied.

Fred then looked to the medium man who was just staring back at him. Fred moved closer to the medium man. "Excuse me, but are *you* Mr Steven Harley?"

"No, I'm Mr Steven Harvey," the medium man replied.

Fred then looked to the large man and expected that he would have to be Mr Steven Harley, but the large man was simply staring back at him. Fred was waiting for him to make some sort of admission; however, he remained silent.

"Excuse me, sir, but would you happen to be Mr Steven Harley?" Fred eventually asked.

"Of course I'm Steven Harley. Who else could I be?" the large man replied and the three Stevens laughed.

Having been shown to his desk, Fred was settling in when Steven Harley slowly waddled over, sat on the desk and started talking. Fred continued settling in while Steven continued talking. Fred was nodding every now and then as Steven went on and on. Steven's telephone then rang and he slowly levered himself off Fred's desk and made his way back to his desk. By the time he reached the telephone, it had rung out. Fred then heard a couple of the assessors on his team quietly giggle and one of them walked up to him.

"I'd say you owe me one," the assessor stated.

"Why is that?" asked Fred.

"Because I saved you from Steven," was the reply.

"And how did you do that?" Fred enquired.

"I was the one who rang Steven. We take turns in ringing him when he comes up to us and starts talking," the assessor explained. "Once he plonks himself down, he can go on for ages."

"My name is Fred Campari and maybe I do owe you one."

"Hi, Fred. I'm Joe Breton and the other assessor on our team is Eva Demetriou."

Fred was introduced to Eva and the three of them hit it off. They were roughly the same age, somewhat younger than the other assessors in the area, so they tended to stick together.

After a few days, Fred found that there was a lack of trust returns to assess so he asked Eva and Joe whether they had any bundles to spare, but they were both sitting on their last bundle.

Fred looked about and stumbled upon shelves that had bundles of trust tax returns for assessment. He was in the process of grabbing a couple of bundles when he heard somebody cry out.

"What the fuck do you think you're doing?"

Fred looked around. It was a manager approaching him at speed.

"I didn't have any work so I was grabbing a couple of bundles," Fred explained.

"The bundles in those pigeonholes are put aside for overtime," the manager sternly advised.

"So where do I get more work from?" Fred asked.

"I don't know and I don't care, but don't you dare touch those bundles."

Fred returned the bundles to the pigeonhole and sheepishly returned to his desk while the three Stevens looked on, chuckling.

Chapter 5 – Business Audit

Fred was advised that due to operational requirements he was to be transferred to Business Audit. He ended up back at 270 King Street where he was to report to Sam Jones on 11 July 1985.

Sam was all a flutter at the time Fred attempted to report to him. It was a condition that Fred soon learned was the norm for the scruffy, podgy manager.

Fred located a spare desk and met the rest of his team, where he was reunited with Michael Pantano and Anthony Fazio and introduced to Walter Melon and Paul Altis.

Sam organised his team under a buddy system whereby a senior auditor would take a new auditor under their wing. In the case of Fred, Walter was to be his buddy.

The Business Audit team was involved in undertaking field investigations. Fred was keen to examine his first few cases and was not impressed with what he found. They were small, family-run businesses in working class suburbs. On the other hand, the more established members of the team seemed to have been allocated more substantial business cases.

Fred was escorted by Walter on his first interview and Walter seemed highly agitated as Fred proceeded to go through the standard interview questionnaire that covered all aspects of the taxpayer's financial affairs. Walter pushed to have the interview wrapped up, so Fred took the documentation on hand with him.

Walter justified the early departure due to urgent work commitments. It was only when Walter directed Fred to take a detour that it was revealed what the work commitments were for. Walter wanted to inspect the construction of his new house.

Once Fred had obtained all the necessary information on the first two of his audits, he prepared T-Accounts, which involved recording all items of income and expenditure in order to highlight any indication of income understatement when compared to the taxable income as declared in the tax returns.

After a couple of weeks, Walter asked Fred to deliver his

recommendations on his first two cases.

"These businesses have a small turnover and seem to have limited scope for any significant understatements of income. In truth, the cases don't appear high risk and I don't know why they were selected for audit in the first place," Fred advised.

Walter didn't seem impressed. "Fred, you need to accept that your performance is gauged on how many cases you complete and how much money you bring in," Walter stated. "So, what have you actually come up with in your audits?"

"One case has only minor preliminary understatements of around $2 000 for each of three years," Fred explained. "The other case has no apparent understatements, although there are minor claims for deductions that are strictly not allowable. I would recommend that we advise that they should not claim the deductions in the future and that no further action be taken on both of these cases."

"You should be pursuing the adjustments on the understated income as well as knocking out the deductions," Walter stated aggressively. "Now I want you to get the details together, arrange the interviews and I'll come with you to show you how it's done!"

Walter and Fred travelled to the first audit interview situated at the taxpayer's home on the outskirts of Melbourne. The taxpayer was unrepresented and Walter took the initiative for the interview.

"We've calculated your income based on the information you've provided and it has revealed that you have understated your income by $2 000 each year for three years," Walter said.

The taxpayer was stunned. "That can't be right," he pleaded. "I'm sure that I disclosed all my income, although I must admit that my records could have been better maintained."

"Well, it's obvious that there have been omissions by you and that you should settle the case, otherwise we are going to have to come down hard on you with penalties," Walter threatened.

The taxpayer was shocked, but had no further defences and eventually signed a settlement, still pleading his innocence.

Walter drove back to the office bragging about what a great negotiator he was. Fred thought that Walter had conducted himself like a standover merchant and didn't say a word.

The next week, Walter directed Fred on what to do to settle his other audit case. Fred drove to the interview situated at the tax agent's office in the inner suburbs of Melbourne. In attendance at the interview were the tax agent, the taxpayer, his wife and their two children—a boy aged 14 and a girl aged 12.

"You have claimed deductions that are considered to be not allowable," Fred stated.

"I consider the deductions to be allowable," the tax agent argued. "And the amounts involved are very modest."

Fred would have been willing to let it go, but Walter had directed him otherwise. "The deductions are strictly not allowable and you should encourage your client to settle if you want any reasonable remission of penalties," Fred countered.

"Given that the taxpayers are small business people, any amount of penalties should be minimal," the tax agent contested.

Fred personally agreed with this contention, but his directive was not to be so accommodating. "The taxpayers may be small business people, but they were represented by a tax agent. The practice is not to consider this situation as a mitigating factor and the best offer for remission of penalties is if your client is willing to settle," Fred pressed.

The tax agent and the taxpayers were devastated, but felt compelled to settle. Fred observed the children watching television in the adjoining room, which made him feel sad and got him thinking. *You're despicable, Walter.*

Feeling demoralised by the time he returned to the office, Fred was quick to request a meeting with Sam.

"I'd like to be given the opportunity to maximise my chances of improving my productivity," Fred stated. "I'd appreciate being given permission to select my own cases from Case Selection and to run the audits myself."

"I'll allow you this liberty," Sam said. "But there will be no excuses if you don't achieve your quotas."

Fred was soon selecting his own cases from Case Selection, choosing the more substantial, higher risk taxpayers. It wasn't long before his audit results improved and his performance was among the best in Business Audit.

* * *

As part of the audit program, cases were gathered from various country areas and, when sufficient cases were amassed from a particular country town, a country trip would be arranged. Auditors were given the option to undertake the country trips on a form of rotation basis, although there were certain officers who seemed to monopolise the trips. The next trip was arranged and, to Fred's surprise, he was permitted to go.

There were 10 auditors travelling and they had the choice of taking a government car or their own car. Of course, everyone took their own car as they received a generous reimbursement based on the kilometres travelled.

Fred owned a yellow panel van. He didn't consider his shaggin' wagon to be the most appropriate vehicle for a Tax Office representative; however, as it was the car he owned, it was the car he'd be taking.

Len Fisher and Lee Marlin were the two team managers going on the trip. People thought it a bit odd that two team managers were required, but the two managers thought it was fine. Lee also considered it appropriate to take his wife.

Preparations were made, with the local authorities being advised of the impending visit from the Tax Office. The auditors packed their documentation and supplies, including a portable photocopier. It took most of the day to drive to the town and settle into their motel rooms. The teams then assembled in the reception area before they set off for dinner.

"Okay, whose car am I going in?" Len asked.

"How about we take your car?" Lee suggested.

"Lee, you know that once I arrive at the motel my car doesn't leave the joint," Len advised with his usual cheeky grin and Lee, who was well aware of Len's practice, laughed.

The next day was the first day of interviews. Fred was relieved when Len decided to accompany other auditors and Lee was content to stay at the motel, which left Fred free to conduct his own audits.

The auditors had two to four cases, depending on the level of complexity. Some of the audits were restricted to dividend and interest checks, while Fred was required to undertake two audits that both involved interviews, bank checks and the completion of T-Accounts. The objective was to complete the cases on the trip.

Completing one interview on the Tuesday morning, Fred conducted the bank checks that afternoon. He completed his second interview on Wednesday morning and undertook further bank checks on Wednesday afternoon.

"Everything seems to be under control and I've had enough," Len advised and he headed home.

Lee was content in the confines of the motel, enjoying the jacuzzi with his wife and was happy to stay on for the entire week.

Spending all day Thursday completing T-Accounts, Fred finalised three years' worth on one case that indicated understatements of income. He completed as much as he could on the T-Accounts for the other case; however, he required further information.

On Thursday evening, Fred was in his motel room packing away his work when the other auditors banged on his door. They had come back from the pub and were obviously drunk.

"What are you up to, Fred?" one of the auditors asked.

"Just finishing off some work," Fred replied.

"Work? Who does any work after hours?" another auditor queried. "I've already finished my three dividend and interest cases so I'm taking it easy for the rest of the week."

"Well, you're fortunate, but I've got two T-Account cases to complete," Fred advised.

"I've got two T-Account cases to do, but I don't listen to management," another auditor said. "Realistically, you can't finish two T-Account cases within a week unless you're handed all the information and don't do any checks. I just collect the information that's provided, do some checks and take it back to Melbourne where I complete the cases back there. The country trips are supposed to be for the travel perks and for fun."

The auditors headed home Friday morning, although Fred stayed behind to attend two meetings, one for each of his two cases with the respective tax agents. One tax agent provided Fred with the additional information he required, which he took away. Fred handed the second tax agent copies of the completed T-Accounts and left them with him to examine. Fred enjoyed lunch on his own at a pub before he made his way back to Melbourne.

The following week, Fred completed his forms for his travel and car reimbursements. He was heading off to hand them in to Personnel when Len gave Fred his forms to hand in. Fred noted that Len had claimed almost double the number of kilometres that Fred had claimed.

Months after, word had got around that Len had been banned from travelling on the country trips anymore. Fred suspected that it may have been the rorting of his reimbursements; however, the reasons were rumoured to be much more serious.

Sam went on leave and Walter acted in the manager's position. Fred continued with his audit work and noted that Walter was acting even more strangely than usual. Walter called Fred over to his desk and gave him a tongue lashing about his tea breaks.

"My tea breaks strictly conform to Tax Office policy," Fred said, standing his ground.

Walter was noticeably agitated. "It's the fact that you walk off and I have no idea where you go." Walter spoke in such a loud voice that other staff members began to look over.

"Walter," Fred stated in a steady and controlled voice, "I religiously go to the same place two times a day. I also tend to go with other members of our team. If you were to lean over and peer out the window when we go off, you'd be able to observe me as I walk to the coffee shop across the road."

"I can't be glued to my desk to observe you. I want you to leave a note on my desk each time you go off," Walter stated, again in a very loud voice.

Fred gazed at Walter for a few seconds trying to gauge whether Walter was serious, but he couldn't tell. "Walter, if that's what you want, that's what I'll do. I shall leave a note on your desk each time I go off."

Fred then wrote a note, placed it on Walter's desk face down and walked away. Walter looked at the note and turned it over. It read: 'I'M OFF!'

Fred was working late, something he was getting in the habit of doing, when Walter approached him in a huff and puff.

"Drive me home," Walter blurted out, but Fred refused.

"Listen, I've booked a government car but I've had too many drinks and shouldn't drive," Walter divulged.

"Why don't you just take the train?" Fred suggested.

"I need to take some stuff home this afternoon," Walter pleaded. He started to get rowdy so Fred eventually gave in.

In the late afternoon of the following day, the team's telephone rang and Fred answered. "Listen, I won't be able to make it back to the office so I want you to clock me off," Walter directed.

"Forget it, Walter, it's never going to happen. I could get the sack!" Fred sternly replied, but this didn't seem to bother Walter.

"Listen, you just clock me off!" Walter ordered.

"Now you listen!" Fred shouted and replaced the receiver with a bang.

Soon after Fred hung up, the phone rang again. He let it ring. An officer from an adjoining team eventually walked across and answered the phone. After a short time, the officer hung up, walked over to the clock card machine, picked out a card and clocked it off.

*　　*　　*

On 1 July 1986, the 270 King Street office was opened as the Victoria North office. It was part of the planned decentralisation of the Tax Office, whereby personnel at King Street would eventually be relocated to the northern inner suburb of Moonee Ponds.

There was also a major restructuring within the Tax Office with the introduction of the new legislation that brought in self-assessing. Up to that point, the Tax Office included the areas of Assessing and Investigations. With the advent of self-assessing, those areas were to be wound up, making way for Audit and Appeals. This also led to a corresponding movement of staff.

Staff who liked field work tended to opt for Audit. Staff who were not keen on public contact or who preferred to do purely technical work tended to opt for Appeals where the main task was to determine taxpayers' objections to their tax assessments.

A rivalry developed between Audit staff and Appeals staff. Some of the auditors were of the view that they would properly raise the taxes, only to have the officers in Appeals negotiate too much away. The Appeals staff dismissed the auditors' view.

Over the ensuing years, the large number of outstanding appeals reduced dramatically.

Chapter 6 – Schemes

Fred received notice that he was to be transferred due to operational requirements. He was pleased with the transfer as it resulted in him being liberated from Walter's clutches.

On 30 January 1987, Fred reported to Matthew Weston on the fourth floor at 365 Little Collins Street, Melbourne, referred to as the CML building.

Fred was placed on a new team with a group of unfamiliar faces. He was introduced to Alice Watts, Ron Hammond, Dennis Pie and Jim Kostas.

Fred settled in well with the team, which topped the audit figures nationally. Notwithstanding the team's success, its members were finding promotions hard to come by. It appeared that the only officers who gained promotion in their area were those who got on well with the director, Sean Duffy. Sean was a pleasant chap who was reasonably approachable, although he had his favourites.

Matthew suggested that Fred should consider seeking promotion to the Victoria North office. Fred was not keen on the prospect of eventually moving to Moonee Ponds, but accepted that it would give him his best chance for advancement. He applied for the next batch of promotions to Victoria North office and, in the blink of an eye, was promoted to Schemes.

On 6 July 1987, Fred reported to Kelvin Brown and was introduced to the longstanding members of the team: Mark Hughes, Keith Casey and Ernie Lyons. Kelvin was in his 60s and his other staff members were in their 40s. Given the generational gap, Fred was happy to learn that both Eva Demetriou and Joe Breton were also promoted to the team.

The team was one of two in a section referred to as Priority Control. Kelvin was the manager of one of the teams and Jack McIvor, also in his 60s, was the manager of the other.

Priority Control had the responsibility of effecting adjustments on tax schemes based on settlements negotiated between taxpayers and the Tax Office. The schemes primarily involved 'trust stripping' and 'bottom of the harbour' cases. Keith took great delight recounting the story of how the legislation on the bottom of the harbour arrangements emerged.

"They called the legislation the Taxation of Unpaid Companies Tax or TUCT," Keith stated with a giggle and, as he continued his explanation, he burst into laughter. "However, the legislation was originally going to be called the Federal Unpaid Companies Tax, which would have made it FUCT!"

Ernie then explained the various other areas on the floor. "You've got the scheme areas that negotiate the settlements. The main manager there is Barry Knight. His nickname is Barracuda due to his never-ending quest of pursuing tax avoiders and tax evaders. Barracuda's nemesis is a member of his team named Doros Day. Doros is a practical joker and they're always at odds."

Ernie turned his head as he continued his explanation. "On the other side we've got the specialist assessors. For example, the guy sitting down over there is the film assessor and his name is Alf Star. Can you believe it? A film assessor with the name Alf Star?"

"When people refer cases to him they write on the movement slip 'FILM STAR'," Mark said and he laughed.

"Don't tell me that the guy named Brian Principal is a teacher assessor," Joe suggested.

"No, he's in the mining area," Ernie responded. "But funnily enough, the manager of the teacher assessors is Adam Student."

"Staff who refer cases to him write on the movement slip 'TEACH STUDENT'," Mark said and they all laughed.

Barracuda was particularly grumpy one morning and he swiftly castigated a woman who had overstayed her welcome in visiting Doros during morning tea break. It was when Barracuda left the floor that there was a spread of chatter as to why he was grumpier than usual.

Barracuda had two framed pictures on his desk, which were strategically placed on either side of his air ioniser. One picture was of the Commissioner of Tax. The other picture was of a Swami who had a bright red dot on his forehead. It was rumoured that Doros altered a picture to make them a closer pairing.

Fred approached Barracuda's desk and looked at the picture of the Swami but there didn't seem to be anything unusual. He then observed the picture of the Commissioner and the change was obvious. The Commissioner had developed a bright red dot in the middle of his forehead.

Chapter 7 – A Working Holiday

Towards the end of 1987, a few officers were discussing an adventurous idea—a working holiday in Europe—and they were canvassing people for travelling companions.

Fred wasn't particularly interested until he learned that one could only work in England if they had a British passport or a working holiday visa and, in order to qualify for the visa, a person had to be less than 28 years of age. In a couple of months, Fred would be 27.

Fred changed his tune and was now eager to tag along, but everyone else pulled out. *It's my trip around Australia that never happened all over again*, Fred thought. However, he then decided to bite the bullet and make the trip on his own.

Fred was finalising his travel plans when positions were advertised so he applied. He was fortunate that the selection process was finalised in good time and he gained promotion.

Fred was to report to Michael Hill at 270 King Street. Michael was a quietly spoken gentleman who was supportive of Fred's working holiday.

"You'll need to include the reason for leave and seek approval for your accounting work overseas," Michael explained. "Also, note that the leave form requires that you specify the dates you'll be on recreation leave and leave without pay. It's office policy that you exhaust all your recreation leave before applying for leave without pay."

Fred had initially completed his leave form by applying for his leave without pay first, followed by his recreation leave; however, on Michael's advice, he changed his leave form to accord with office policy.

Fred was ecstatic as he jetted off on his 14:15 CX100 Singapore Airlines flight to London via Hong Kong; the commencement of his seven-month trip. He had recently been promoted and was now on an adventure of a lifetime.

Arriving in London, Fred found accommodation in a hostel for young professionals. He was then able to score contract work as an accountant. He enjoyed a three-month stint working in London and travelling around Britain.

On 16 June 1988, Fred set off on his organised tour of Europe. It was when the tour reached Austria that he was involved in a traffic accident. He landed himself in hospital while the tour moved on.

Fred spent two weeks in hospital and an extra week in home care. When he had sufficiently recovered, he continued to travel around Europe.

Fred returned to Australia on Thursday 20 October 1988 and was back at work the following Monday. Later that week, he enquired with Personnel about his leave.

"Pity you weren't on annual leave at the time of your accident as you could have got your annual leave reinstated and changed for sick leave," a pleasant-sounding woman said. "However, as you were officially on leave without pay at the time of your accident, there's nothing we can do."

So much for office policy, Fred thought.

Fred re-acquainted himself with his workmates and asked whether anything had happened during his absence.

"They're going to do away with the tea ladies in December," Eva mentioned.

"The Commissioner is commencing a Large Audit program, which is planned to include the audit of Australia's top 100 companies for the first time ever," Joe added.

After further discussion, almost as an afterthought, Fred was also advised that as a result of the appeals against the last promotions he had been rolled.

Fred took the news in his stride, although he felt that it was grossly unfair that the Merit Agency considered it appropriate to roll someone while they were overseas without having a chance to defend their position.

Fred was relocated to the Commonwealth Centre on the corner of Spring and La Trobe Streets—the Green Latrine. It was the same building where he had undergone his medical examination before commencing with the Tax Office back in 1982.

Fred joined a team that was effectively in limbo. They were instructed not to commence any new cases due to the reorganisation of the office as part of the Large Audit program. In lieu of work, the auditors pursued various activities, such as studying, researching, reading, crosswords and playing cards.

The office was also undergoing a revamp of positions. The clerical classes were restructured under 'Administrative Service Officer' (ASO) and 'Senior Officer Grade' (SOG) levels. As part of this process, there were positions advertised for promotion and Fred applied for an ASO Class 6.

The selection process was taking an eternity and word was getting around that there had been a major stuff-up. The applicants were soon advised that there was a problem with the advertised positions and they needed to lodge new applications. Fred lodged another application and a new selection process was underway. It would take another few months before the process was complete, which was considered a fast-track process given the large number of applications and positions.

Fred was notified in a letter: "Congratulations on being promoted and your appeal against Mr Will Power has been upheld". He was fuming.

"What appeal? I didn't appeal, I detest the appeal system. And against Will Power? He's such a great guy!"

Bumping into Will, Fred raised the selection process. "Will, I don't understand why they sent the letter stating that my appeal against you was upheld. I wasn't aware that they were to treat the second application as an appeal. I didn't compare myself to anyone else, I didn't mention any names and I certainly didn't mention your name."

As usual, Will was upbeat. "Don't worry about it, Fred. I know how this place works. They had to cover up the fact that they had stuffed up the process by conducting an appeal process rather than redoing the applications. They just didn't tell anyone. I thought it was just a second application as well. There are no hard feelings."

Fred sensed that Will was genuine in what he said; however, he was still upset. He knew that the official record would stand that Fred's appeal against Will had been upheld.

The Tax Office was allocating auditors to various areas as a result of the restructure under the Large Audit program. Fred was hoping that he would make one of the Large Audit teams; however, he ended up back on a Business Audit team at 270 King Street.

During this period, the appeals system had changed so that appeals were not permitted for positions at the ASO 6 level and above. Fred was relieved as it meant that he didn't have to be concerned with the appeals system and having staff rolled ever again.

Fred reflected on his career and missing out on a place in the Large Audit program. He then thought back to the enjoyable time he had had on his overseas holiday and organised another trip. He was highly excited as he jetted off on Saturday 15 July 1989, destined for the Middle East and North America.

Chapter 8 – Large Audit

Returning to work on 23 October 1989, Fred was ecstatic to learn that he had been transferred to Large Audit after all. He reported to Adam Butcher.

Adam was preoccupied with some administrative matters before he turned his attention to Fred. Adam introduced himself and then the rest of the team: Katie Mills, Pia Talia, Michael Crimmins, Jack Sweeney and Errol Jonaitis.

Fred regained the motivation that had escaped him in the last couple of years. He completed some initial company profiling work before being placed on a company tax audit with Katie and Jack. The team obtained detailed information about the company group before they met with its representatives to make the logistic arrangements. The company accommodated the audit team in a separate room.

When Fred turned up on his first day at the company premises, Jack was seated reading the newspaper. After completing the sports section, he turned to Fred.

"Fred, you're an ASO 6 and I'm a SOG C. The way I see it, I'm at the higher level and I expect that you will aspire to get to my level. I will therefore allow you the opportunity to do most of the work to give you the best chance for promotion." Jack nodded, then recommenced reading his newspaper.

Fred smiled. He had no immediate thoughts of promotion, but he was happy about being given the reins on the audit and the chance to delve into the technical issues.

Katie arrived and Jack's eyes lit up. He folded away his newspaper and commenced chatting with her. Katie was an attractive woman in her early 30s with blue eyes, golden brown hair and a soft complexion. Her attractiveness was complemented by her amiable and sociable character.

Fred was comfortable in the entertaining surroundings where he had the luxury of continuing his work and joining in with the social chit-chat from time to time.

The team conducted the audit from the company premises from

Monday to Thursday and returned to the Tax Office on Fridays to write up the reports and monitor the audit's progress.

Fred desired to improve his technical knowledge and considered undertaking further postgraduate studies. He discussed various study options with Errol Jonaitis.

"I'm going to undertake a Master of Taxation at Melbourne University," Errol said.

"That sounds great," Fred replied. "I was considering the same course, but I've decided to do it in 1992."

"Why 1992 and not now?" Errol asked.

"I'll be undertaking the Accountants professional program."

Fred enrolled in the professional program and was content in his routine of work and study. He progressed with the company tax audit and picked up on a few irregularities in the accounts. The more issues he uncovered, the more animated his team members became.

Positions were advertised for promotion in Large Audit and Fred applied. He was comfortable with the interview; however, he was unsuccessful with his application. Opting for feedback, he was advised that he had insufficient experience in auditing large companies. He wasn't too upset as he was enjoying his work and figured that with further Large Audit experience, he should eventually be rewarded.

In May 1990, the Tax Office commenced a new mobility policy. Fred was flabbergasted when he was advised that he was to be rotated back to Business Audit and immediately sought an explanation from Adam.

"I can't shed any light on this decision," Adam said. "All I know is that it came from management."

"I can't understand it," Fred complained. "I've only been in the area for just over a year and there are many other auditors who have been in Large Audit for much longer. How can they justify moving me and not others as part of this mobility policy?"

"I don't know," said Adam, shrugging his shoulders and shaking his head.

Fred wrote up the technical issues on the company tax audit that proposed substantial adjustments and handed them over to Adam and Jack. Adam thanked Fred for his efforts and wished him well. Jack returned to his desk with a spring in his step as he examined the audit file in greater detail.

It was evening when Fred caught his number 55 tram homeward bound. He glanced out the window as the tram travelled through Royal Park and passed by Melbourne Zoo. It was dark, but the moonlight emitted a strong glow that cast eerie shadows off the trees. He noticed a sorry, forlorn creature looking back at him. The creature was a reflection in the tram window and the reflection in the window was him.

Chapter 9 – Overseas Beneficiaries

The following week, Fred was summoned into an office and was greeted by the director of Business Audit, Mr Brian Peace.

"Pleased to meet you, Fred, and welcome to the area," Brian said.

"Thank you sir, but I must admit that I'm not happy to be sent back to Business Audit after just one year in Large Audit. It was a complete surprise and disappointment to me," Fred stated.

Brian looked Fred straight in the eye. "I think I understand your disappointment; however, management have made their decision. We have a challenging task in Business Audit dealing with scheme cases and your experience with tax schemes would be greatly valued. I can also guarantee that I will give you whatever support you need."

Fred took a moment to reflect on what Brian said, particularly since he sensed the comments to be sincere. *I've never heard a manager be so direct and commit his support. The guy actually seems to be sincere. I could either mope about the situation or do what I've always done and just get stuck in and do the work.*

After the moment of contemplation, Fred replied. "Even though I'm not happy with this move as part of some mobility policy, I'll do the job to the best of my ability and I'm genuinely grateful for your commitment of support."

Ironically, after Fred's move, the mobility policy was not used nor heard of again.

Fred was introduced to his new team members, led by the manager, Edward Dennis.

Edward was passionate about his team's work and, even though the rest of the team seemed indifferent, Edward's enthusiasm rubbed off on Fred.

Fred was quick to get up to speed on the scheme cases and the relevant law. Most of the cases involved the same few tax agents and the team selected those involving the more blatant tax avoidance arrangements. The team worked on a proposal that Edward presented to Brian and he gave them his wholehearted support.

Fred issued Section 264 notices on a couple of cases, demanding the taxpayers to attend an interview. He then sat down with Edward to commence constructing questionnaires, arranging the logistics and preparing the equipment.

The first taxpayer was on time for the meeting, accompanied by his tax agent. Edward escorted them to an interview room of the Tax Office at 270 King Street.

Fred welcomed them and explained the procedure. "Thank you for your attendance under the Section 264 notice. As outlined in that notice, the matter concerns your business arrangements under the trust structure. We have formalised this interview under Section 264 due to the nature of your arrangements and the need for us to obtain full details. It is for this reason that we will be requiring you to take an oath or affirmation that the information you provide here today is the truth and it is also the reason why we will be taping this interview."

"Whoah, whoah, whoah," the taxpayer gasped as he placed both hands in the air and turned to his tax agent. "These are normal family arrangements that have been cleared by my tax agent."

"We accept that these are family arrangements, given the large number of overseas family members who have been allocated distributions from the trust over many years," Fred stated. "Although it appears that none of these beneficiaries have received any of those distributions. I assume that each one of the beneficiaries has been willing to loan back these distributions."

Fred took a breath before he continued. "I appreciate that a commercial rate of interest has been credited for each of the numerous beneficiary loans, for which you are claiming a full tax deduction for the interest while paying the interest withholding tax at the much lower rate. I note that the interest is also being loaned back. These loan accounts are accumulating to such large amounts that the beneficiaries may be keen to know exactly how much they are owed."

Fred took another breath before he wound up his explanation. "Of course, we will also be requiring full details of all the beneficiaries as we will be notifying the respective tax authorities in the relevant countries pursuant to our tax treaty obligations of how much interest income has been allocated to them over the years. I expect that the tax authorities would be eager to ensure that the beneficiaries have included the interest as income in their tax returns. So, are you ready for me to start the tape and commence the interview?"

The taxpayer put both hands in the air again. "Hang on a moment," he said, looking over to his tax agent once more. "I may be willing to settle."

The team issued several more Section 264 notices that prompted more settlements. After giving the tax agents a taste of what they could expect for each and every one of their clients, Edward and Fred were contacted by the tax agents to meet with them. Settlement negotiations ensued and they soon arranged in-principle agreements for all of the clients.

Once the team had made the necessary arrangements, it was issuing amended tax assessments like a production line. During this process, Fred was requested to attend a meeting at one of the tax agent's offices. The secretary escorted Fred into a room. He was seated at the far end of the room, opposite the door, with his back to the wall.

After a little while, a man who was unfamiliar to Fred entered the room. He closed the door, took a seat opposite Fred and introduced himself. "As a senior member of this firm, I've heard that the Tax Office has specifically targeted and singled us out," the man alleged.

"As far as I am aware, that is definitely not the case," Fred responded with a defiant look.

"The arrangements that we have adopted are widespread and the fact that you guys are pursuing us without touching the others would indicate to me that you are targeting us and giving my firm a bad name," the man argued.

"Sir, I have examined many tax returns adopting these schemes and many of them relate to your firm," Fred stated. "However, if you have any information whatsoever about any other tax agents who are involved in these schemes, I would be happy to take those details."

The man gave Fred a hard looking over before he got up and left the room. Fred was a little shaken by the experience and reported it to Edward and then to Brian.

Brian's reaction was swift. "Thanks for advising me of this. I'm prepared to take this matter further if you consider it appropriate that something should be done."

"Nothing more needs to be done," Fred responded. "I thought it was my duty to report the matter and, as usual, I appreciate your support."

It was only two months after Fred had rejoined Business Audit that promotions were advertised. It was indicated that there would only be a couple of positions, with one position virtually guaranteed to someone who had been acting in the position for some time.

Nevertheless, Fred applied and was summoned for an interview. The interviewers were Brian Peace and Angus Warr. Fred was happy with his responses to the technical questions, but felt uncomfortable answering hypothetical case studies.

Fred was keenly welcoming the conclusion of the interview when Angus asked a final question. "Now, imagine I'm a member of your team and I want to know whether I can take a month's annual leave starting next week. What would be your immediate response?"

"I would need to be satisfied that it was acceptable based on operational requirements. I would also confer with Personnel to ensure that you had the required amount of leave credits," Fred responded.

"But I want to know whether I can have the leave now!" Angus stated aggressively, raising his voice. "I don't want to have to wait until you check with Personnel!"

Fred was unsettled by the unexpected tone of Angus's voice and the rough nature of the request. "Well, if you were to be so insistent to have an immediate response, the answer would be no!" Fred responded in an equally raised voice.

At the end of the interview, Fred departed the room disconsolate. He considered the interview to be one of his worst performances and resigned himself to the prospect that he had little hope for promotion.

After a couple of weeks, Brian called Fred into his office. "The selection process has been finalised and I expect that you wouldn't be surprised to know that Tim Tam was rated first in the order of merit and has gained promotion," Brian said and waited a few moments before he continued. "I budgeted for two positions, which had been approved. I therefore have a second position to fill and you were rated second. Congratulations, Fred, you've been promoted."

Fred thanked Brian and took a little time to digest the unexpected, good news. He felt a surge of relief and was truly grateful to Brian. It was the first time in his career that a superior officer had given him such unbridled support and he was determined to ensure that Brian would not regret his decision to promote him.

The significance of the promotion would not be known until many years later as it was to be one of the last prior to a Tax Office promotion freeze that was to last half a decade.

Chapter 10 – Business Audit Manager

On 26 July 1990, Fred assumed his position as Business Audit manager. He was introduced to his new team of Lina Lupino, Soula Pappas, Peter Millstone, Santo Palermo and Orlando Cozza.

Fred took the time to have a chat with each member of the team and went over their current work. He undertook a stocktake and noted that there were a number of delayed cases on hand.

"What are these cases?" Fred asked.

The auditors looked around at each other and were silent. Eventually, Orlando spoke. "They belonged to a former auditor who has since left the office."

"So why haven't they been re-allocated?" Fred queried.

There was a further moment of silence, during which time the team members looked at each other again. It was Orlando who spoke up once more. "The auditor left a real mess and none of us felt that it was our responsibility to deal with it."

Why in the hell didn't the previous manager deal with this? Fred thought, but he expected he knew the answer. "Come on, Orlando, give me a hand to locate these files," he instructed.

"I don't really want to take over this mess," Orlando admitted.

"That's okay," Fred advised. "The team will fix this mess together."

With Fred's encouragement, Orlando seemed to develop an enthusiasm for his work, which was observed by the other members of the team and, after a while, the others began approaching Fred to ask him to be involved in their cases as well.

Santo completed few cases and, when he did, they would usually produce no revenue results and would be signed off with 'No further action' (NFA). Santo seemed proud of his lack of productivity, as he would often be heard declaring his favourite catchcry: "Another day, another NFA!"

Santo attempted to take advantage of Fred's assistance; however, Fred soon tired of having to repeat his advice.

"Santo, it's no use coming up to me all the time and asking me the same questions. I've given you my suggestions and guidance so you may wish to act on them," Fred explained. "I'm happy to assist you, but there is no way I'm going to do your work for you."

Staff members at the Victoria North office were planning for their move to Moonee Ponds. Fred was not keen to move to the suburbs so when the chance came to put in for a swap to the Melbourne office, he was swift to express his interest. Although he wasn't holding out much hope, he managed to gain a swap.

*　*　*

In July of 1991, Fred fronted up at the CML building and reported to Mr Richard Head. Richard didn't mince his words. "You've got big shoes to fill. You're replacing Rick Terra who ran the best performing Business Audit team last year and I expect the team to perform equally well this year with you as manager."

Fred made his way to his new team.

"G'day," he said in an elevated voice.

The team members acknowledged his greeting, but seemed indifferent to his arrival. Fred settled into his desk and noticed that the team members were just looking at him. He finished unpacking, sat down and returned their stares.

"Well, do you think we should get to know each other a little better?" Fred asked.

The responses ranged from shrugs to grunts.

"Well, I'm Fred Campari and apparently I've got big shoes to fill. I've been told that you guys were the best performing team in Business Audit last year and it is expected that the team will perform equally well this year."

"Yeah, right," a guy from the back row called out. "Rick made sure he put through all the good cases. We've got no chance to be the best team this year."

"What's your name?" Fred asked.

"I'm Bart Peeters."

Fred looked around to the others on the team. "So, what do the rest of you think?"

They looked at one another before another voice was heard.

"My name's Peter Williams and Bart's right. All the good cases have been finalised and we don't have many on hand. We've got no chance of performing well this year."

"So none of you have any good cases on hand?" Fred queried.

"I'm Andrew McInnes and I've still got a couple of good cases. I held them off."

"Are you from Scotland?" Fred pried, detecting a gruff, Scottish accent.

"Yes, I am," Andrew responded in a slightly uplifted tone.

"Anyone else have any good cases?" Fred asked.

"I'm Sam D'Angelo and I've got a couple of cases, but they aren't much. They're just your standard Case Selection cases."

"You say the Case Selection cases aren't much, but aren't they supposed to be the most appropriate cases for audit?" Fred asked, knowing full well that this was often not the case.

"You've got to be joking," a woman sneered.

"What's your name and what do you mean?" Fred quickly countered.

"I'm Maria Grande and Case Selection cases are rubbish."

"You think we could select better cases?" Fred asked.

"Of course we could," said Maria as she proudly raised her head.

Fred looked at the last team member, a delicate creature with a soft complexion, bright blue eyes and blonde hair. "What's your name and what do you think?" he asked her.

"My name is Anna Door and I think we can perform well because I have faith in this team."

The response struck a chord with Fred as it did with the others.

A brash young man wearing a designer suit suddenly barged in.

"Who are you?" Fred immediately asked.

"I'm Goran Popov," was the swift reply. "Why, who are you?"

"My name is Fred Campari, I'm your new manager and you're just in time to attend our first team meeting."

"Team meeting?" Goran asked. "Why are we having a team meeting?"

"We are going to discuss how we are going to be the best performing team for the year ending 30 June 1992. So let's go to the meeting room."

Once the team assembled, Fred continued. "So how do you guys want this team to operate?" he asked.

"You're the team manager," Goran stated. "You're the one who's supposed to run the team."

"I guess that's normally the case, but you are the ones who have to do the work," Fred said. "I see my role as supporting you to do the work."

The team members agreed on how they wished to operate from a procedural perspective and then got down to the casework.

"You mentioned that Case Selection cases stink, so how do you propose we select our cases?" Fred asked.

"There are loads of taxpayers who live well above what is indicated by what they declare as income in their tax returns," Andrew said.

"That's true," Fred agreed. "So how do you suggest we go about selecting these types of cases for audit?"

The team members spent most of the day working on a strategy to the point where they thought they had developed a methodology to select and audit their own cases.

"So what do we call this project?" Maria asked.

There was much deliberation before Andrew made a suggestion. "What about the Wealthy Individuals Project?"

The team members scratched their heads and shrugged their shoulders before the project name was adopted. They then arranged a meeting with Richard to seek his approval. Richard was supportive of the project, although it came with a stern warning.

"You are given approval on the expectation that you achieve your quotas for the year and the team strive to be the number one team in Business Audit."

The team members were excited that they had been given approval to undertake the project, as it was stated to be the first of its kind. They were quick to fine-tune their strategy before they obtained the source information upon which they would commence their case selection.

The team requisitioned tax returns for those taxpayers who could be identified. For those taxpayers that could not be identified, the team sent the data to the Non-lodgement area.

The team worked out a case selection rating system, ranking the cases from 1 to 10, with 10 being the most appropriate cases to audit. They then requisitioned the previous year's tax returns for the high-risk cases and waited for them to come through.

The team members worked hard to get to the stage where they had a good stock of cases to audit, although the tax returns were taking time to arrive. As a result, by halfway through the financial year, the team had only commenced a few audits. Fred encouraged them to start further audits while he took over the case selection processes himself.

In addition to the team's project work, there were requests for other assignments and public speaking engagements at various external forums and discussion groups. The experienced team managers were quick to decline the requests, so Richard would look to Fred. As Fred didn't know how to say no, he was invariably lumbered with the additional tasks.

Fred was so overwhelmed with the work that he hardly ever took a break and was exhausted by the end of each day. Early one evening, he sat back in his chair and looked over to the corner of his desk to observe his newspaper, still folded. He hadn't taken the time to read it, something all too common of late.

As the 1991 calendar year drew to a close, Richard called the team to a meeting. They took the opportunity to update Richard on the status of the project. They advised that they had referred 100 cases to the Non-lodgement area and had a stock of 100 high-risk cases for audit.

"This is all well and good," Richard stated, "but what about your quotas?"

Fred was expecting that the inevitable question would come up. "We have completed about 20 per cent of the case turnover and collected about 30 per cent of our projected revenue; however, I'm sure we will do much better in the second half."

"This really isn't good enough and there will be no excuses if you don't get your quotas at the end of the year," Richard threatened.

*   *   *

Fred was relieved to have completed his Accountants professional program and was keen to undertake a Master of Taxation at Melbourne University. However, that was until the new Tax Office study leave policy was published. He was stunned to learn that the only course the Tax Office would support was a new Tax Office program.

Errol Jonaitis rang Fred and showed little sympathy. "You should have done your Masters at Melbourne University when I did it," Errol stated.

"Yeah, thanks Errol, that's easy to say after the event," Fred said. "Who would have known that the Tax Office would have spent big bucks to enter into an exclusive contract?"

Fred was not happy, but enrolled in the only course the Tax Office sponsored.

*   *   *

The team members continued with their project and they were now progressing through their audits at a cracking pace. Fred provided Richard with a project update, but Richard was unimpressed and expressed his view that the project would be a flop. Fred was determined to be upbeat and, as he was keen to return to Large Audit, he made a proposal to Richard.

"If you consider our task to be so insurmountable, do you agree to transfer me to Large Audit if our team is successful with the project and we achieve our quota?"

"You're on," Richard stated spontaneously.

The team members continued with their work and, soon after the close of the financial year, the results were tallied. It was revealed that the team had, in fact, achieved its quotas for cases completed and for revenue raised.

Richard was amazed, but it was no surprise to Fred. However, what did surprise Fred was that the team had also topped the results for the year. The team was the best performing Business Audit team for the second year running.

"I'd like to thank you all for your good work," Fred proudly stated during the celebrations. "I don't think you should ever underestimate your achievements; it was a great effort and it more than justified the faith that people had placed in you."

The team members had hardly completed their rejoicing when they were notified that a number of changes were to occur: Peter and Bart had gained transfers to Moonee Ponds office, Goran was bound for Geelong office, and Anna, Sam and Andrew were all destined for Box Hill office. Furthermore, Richard Head was bound for Moonee Ponds and was to be replaced by Michael Hunt.

Given that the team was to disband, Fred organised a final team meeting and luncheon. The meeting was a pleasant gathering where Fred again thanked them all for their achievements. As the group was about to head off for lunch, Fred interrupted.

"Hang on, you have to wait for the award ceremony."

Fred called out each award, the nominees and the winner. As the winner came up, they were handed a certificate and a small gift. The honour roll with the award, the winner and the prize read as follows:

55

Congeniality award – Anna Door – tiara
Hard nut award – Maria Grande – packet of walnuts
Worry wart award – Sam D'Angelo – set of worry beads
Attendance award – Peter Williams – diary
Best dressed award – Goran Popov – long johns with middle leg
Politically incorrect award – Bart Peeters – adult playing cards
Blow you own horn award – Andrew McInnes – small bugle

The team members then set off in high spirits to enjoy their final team lunch.

Days later, Fred contacted Richard concerning the deal they had made about his promised transfer to Large Audit.

Richard shook his head. "Due to my move to Moonee Ponds, I am no longer in a position to act on the deal. You will need to take up the matter with your new manager."

Appalled by the way Richard had washed his hands of their agreement, Fred approached Michael.

"The deal predates my tenure so I don't see how I have any obligation to honour it," said Michael. "However, I am willing to consider a transfer to Large Audit if I can arrange the conditions."

In a matter of hours, Michael recalled Fred with a proposal. "I have discussed the matter with management and they would be agreeable to a transfer, but on one condition," Michael advised.

"What's that?" Fred asked.

"That you first work in Illegal Audit for a year."

Chapter 11 – Illegals

After Fred's previous experiences, he was dubious whether any agreement with management would be honoured; however, he was keen to move to Large Audit and Michael's offer seemed to be his only chance. He agreed to the one-year transfer to Illegal Audit, although he insisted that the agreement be put in writing and signed by a senior executive.

On 22 July 1992, Fred found his way to the secure area contained in the CML building. He was allowed entry by a formal-speaking officer named Ken Doll.

"G'day, I'm supposed to report to the manager, Dan Druff," Fred advised.

"Dan's not in at the moment," said Ken, "but I can show you around."

Ken showed Fred his workstation and then guided him around the area, while providing a running commentary.

"There are a dozen personnel in Illegal Audit, making up the two teams. There have been a few movements of staff over the last few months, with further changes anticipated when the teams are re-constituted as part of the move to the new building later this year at Casselden Place," Ken advised.

They approached Ken's team and he introduced Fred to Ned Mackie, Robert O'Brien, Paul Wild and Brian Ralph. Fred was then introduced to the final member of the team—the familiar face of Joe Breton.

Ken proceeded to the other team and introduced the team manager, Steve Aniston. Steve then introduced his team members: Graham Tuff, Vince Viaggio, Jason Malouf, Jerry Spacey and Sunny Chopra.

Fred was to assume an unusual position whereby he was not part of either of the two teams. His official title was technical advisor, being responsible for providing technical assistance to the teams, as well as undertaking his own cases.

The teams were working on various projects as well as one-off cases involving illegal activities. They also undertook contact roles with various law enforcement agencies.

One of the audits was on a brothel, which for some reason was requiring a significant amount of research. Ned was closely examining some of the records associated with the brothel audit and his eyebrows raised so many times they almost became a flutter.

"Some of these prostitutes are racist!" Ned exclaimed.

"Why do you think they're racist?" asked Ken.

"Look here, it's in black and white," Ned declared. "Some of the women don't do Greek!"

*　　*　　*

Fred had been in Illegal Audit for a few weeks when he fell ill. He collapsed at home and was admitted to the casualty department of the hospital. His condition was described as pericarditis—a build-up of fluid around the heart. A tube was inserted into his chest to drain the fluid. His condition was stabilised and he was transferred to a ward. He was exceptionally relieved when they removed the tube from his chest and his fever subsided.

Fred's family visited him and assembled around his hospital bed. There was Rosa, Michael, Gina, Fred's brother-in-law, Matthew, his six-year-old nephew, Joseph, and his three-year-old niece, Portia.

Fred looked at them and reflected on what he was doing with his life. He had spent so much of his time on his work and studies that he wondered whether he had neglected the most important thing in his life: his family.

Fred's poor health caused him to struggle through his semester's studies. He was fortunate to have completed his research papers prior to his hospitalisation, but he only had a couple of weeks before his exams and was grossly underprepared. He botched his second exam and was sure he would fail. However, to his surprise, he was awarded credits for both of his subjects.

Fred returned to work after a few weeks and there was much activity concerning industrial action.

"The unions are planning to strike," informed Joe Breton, a union representative.

Fred had never experienced a strike and he was caught up in the excitement of what they dubbed the 'National Day of Industrial Action'. Management warned staff that any union member who partook in the strike would be docked.

On 30 November 1992, union representatives and members were amassing for their march around the city centre. Fred was assembled with a number of his union comrades behind large banners. The crowds became mobile and chanted for workers' rights.

Fred was initially subdued, but became buoyed by the presence of many office workers who made themselves visible out of various buildings around the city with waving and shouts of support.

The next day, managers were roving the Tax Office to confirm whether staff had joined the strike. Fred was stirred by the protest march and was content to have played his part in the act of defiance against management.

"Did you take part in the strike?" a manager asked Fred.

"I sure did," Fred proudly responded.

Chapter 12 – Casselden Place

There was some movement in Illegal Audit when Dan Druff was replaced with a new manager, Billy Banks, and Ken was to be replaced with a new team manager named Pat Potts. Further, in the beginning of 1993, the last batch of Melbourne office staff was moved to their new building at Casselden Place.

Fred considered it appropriate that the new Melbourne office, situated at 2 Lonsdale Street, was the same location the brothel of Madam Brussels had thrived years before and was adjacent to the site where the Commonwealth Centre—the Green Latrine—used to be.

Illegal Audit personnel moved into their high security area, to much excitement. The guys settled in with the two teams positioned in two distinct groups, while Fred was sidelined to a workstation along the windows. Billy had his own office, although he was spending less and less time there as a case he was previously managing was dragging on and he was continually being called away.

Billy's increased periods of absence led him to make an announcement. "Guys, if I could have your attention. My ongoing commitment to a case has meant that I am not in a position to continue my managerial responsibilities at this stage. The decision has therefore been made to rotate the higher duties of my position between the two team managers, Steve and Pat."

Billy's departure from the Illegal Audit area resulted in a dramatic change in the work dynamic: it was mayhem. Steve brought a telescope into work and set it up in front of the window adjacent to Fred's workstation.

"How can you justify bringing in a telescope to work?" asked Ned.

"It's called surveillance," Steve responded.

Fred was continually being disturbed by the passing parade of telescope observers.

"Hey, if you look towards the bay, you can actually see the ships come in," Sunny said with a smile.

"Fellas, over there at the hotel rooftop swimming pool, models are doing a swimwear photo shoot!" Jerry exclaimed.

The guys began coming from everywhere with Jerry giving updates. "Wow, now they're taking off their tops!" he shouted with excitement.

It then developed into a fracas.

"Give me a look!" Sunny shouted.

"Hey, it's my telescope, give me a look," Steve said.

"Okay, you've seen enough, it's my turn!" Ned yelled.

In the mornings, the guys developed a ritual whereby they would lock Graham into an empty full height steel cabinet. Led by Jerry and ably assisted by Sunny and Vince, they would physically force Graham kicking and screaming into the cabinet and lock him in. As if this wasn't enough, he was always installed upside down. Graham would bang away on the door and sides for several minutes before he would be released from his cabinet incarceration.

Sunny and Jerry were the worst of the practical jokers and they got into the habit of going to the pub for lunch and drinks. On occasion, when they were too far gone, they would ring Steve—the acting manager at the time.

"We're taking the rest of the day off," Jerry would declare.

It was apparent that Steve couldn't handle the duo; however, he refuted any suggestions that he was soft. "No manager could handle Sunny and Jerry," he would say.

When Steve's time as manager ended, Pat had his turn. Sunny and Jerry repeated their stunt of not coming back to work after a decent lunch session at the pub, but Pat didn't seem too concerned. The next day, he ambled over to Jerry's and Sunny's workstations.

"By the way, boys, I've docked your pay for yesterday afternoon," Pat informed them.

"What did you do that for?" asked Jerry.

"You need prior approval to take leave and you didn't have prior approval," Pat replied.

Sunny and Jerry argued their case for some time, but it fell on deaf ears and they didn't seem to take too many long lunches from that time on.

Jerry's curtailment in his lunches resulted in him being more of a nuisance at work. Fred was usually able to bypass Jerry's behaviour; however, one day Jerry was unrelenting. Fred continued with his work and was heading to the photocopier when Jerry came from behind and grabbed him in a headlock. It came as a surprise to Fred, who just stood his ground.

Jerry held on to Fred as he boasted to the others of his fighting prowess. Fred stood firm and then flipped Jerry over the top of him, sending him crashing onto the photocopier. Jerry was in shock as photocopying parts flew around the room. Fred nonchalantly strolled back to his workstation. He was not troubled again.

Fred was in the last semester of his studies when a professional development workshop was offered to staff. Fred obtained approval from Pat, his manager at the time, to attend the course along with other staff. Days after the course, Fred was contacted by the professional development manager, Silva Beat.

"Hi, Fred, it's Silva Beat and I've noted that you went on the training session but you did not lodge a leave form."

"There's no need for me to lodge a leave form," Fred said. "The course was offered to all staff, I gained approval from my manager and the time was correctly taken as normal work time as per standard Tax Office practice."

"No, that's not the case in your situation," Silva stated. "You are an approved student who is granted three hours a week study time and, as you had already taken your three hours, you should have taken other leave to attend the course."

"That's ridiculous," Fred argued. "Study leave is granted to approved students, which is over and above the normal professional development training allowed. The suggestion that once an officer becomes an approved student they are somehow denied the opportunities of other staff is incorrect and clearly discriminatory."

"Fred, I don't know why you are making such a fuss over this," Silva countered. "I'm giving you the opportunity to put in a leave form, otherwise I'm going to be forced to arrange that you be docked."

"I have no intention of putting in a leave form," Fred stated.

The next day, Silva visited Fred and she continued discussion about the leave. "Fred, I can't understand why you won't take the opportunity to put in a leave form," Silva repeated. "Otherwise, I'm going to have to dock you."

"Well, I can't understand how you don't see that what you are attempting to do is discriminatory," Fred argued. "I have no intention of putting in a leave form as this would result in action that

I consider to be clearly unnecessary and inappropriate."

"Fred, if you don't agree to put in a leave form, I'm going to dock you!" Silva insisted.

"Silva, I have absolutely no intention of putting in a leave form," Fred declared as he folded his arms. "So instead of attempting to force me to do what you want, I suggest that you do what you think you should do and I will do what I think I should do."

Silva proceeded to follow through with her threat and Fred was docked one day's pay for being absent without leave—AWOL.

Fred immediately sought advice from the union and was contacted by a union representative named Percy Grinder. Percy obtained details of the incident and arranged a meeting with management. In attendance was the management team of Ronald Ray and Donald Hay, two managers from Large Audit, and Silva Beat.

Percy went over the facts, which were not in dispute. He then made representations on behalf of Fred. "This situation is absurd. Management had no basis to deny Fred work time to attend a work training session where he had been granted prior approval from his manager," Percy stated.

The management team was unmoved as they all supported each other and the action Silva had taken.

"I would also like to add that as the professional development manager at the same level as my manager, Silva had no line of authority to direct that I be docked," Fred suggested. "My manager approved my attendance at the training course and Silva's action to effectively overturn this decision was completely out of order."

Donald and Ronald looked over to Silva before there was a response. "Silva had the authority to dock you," Donald stated.

Fred was left wondering where they could go from there.

"Well, then," Percy said. "Given the broad ramifications that this action may have for all staff seeking study leave in the future, the union will be seeking an official Tax Office policy position from national office."

The management team members were twitching and turning as they squirmed around in their seats. They then looked around at each other before Ronald confirmed management's stance.

"Do as you wish, we are comfortable with our position," Ronald stated, although his response lacked any conviction whatsoever.

Percy contacted Fred when national office came down with their decision. "Hi, Fred. National office has confirmed the Tax Office policy. Members of staff are given equal opportunity to attend work training sessions during work time regardless of whether they are approved students on study leave."

"You wonder how the management team didn't get it. It seemed to be a no-brainer," Fred said.

"I agree," Percy replied. "It should have been a no-brainer, but the management team still didn't get it."

Fred was paid back his salary and received a number of calls of support from students and staff when they learned of the outcome.

Joe Breton congratulated Fred on his win, although he qualified his congratulations. "With management, you might win the battle, but you never win the war. Once you're blacklisted in this place, they will always get you back."

*　*　*

Fred completed his studies at the end of 1993 and decided to move out of the family home. He looked around for a few months before he found a small house in the northern suburbs, which he managed to secure with the aid of a fairly substantial mortgage.

It was an emotional time leading up to Fred's move as Gina had left home at the age of 20, some 18 years earlier, and Fred's departure would mean that Rosa and Michael would no longer have any of their children in the household.

Not long after Fred's move, positions were advertised to join a highly publicised Tax Law Improvement Project. Fred was looking for a challenge and considered that the project had the potential to be an important initiative, so he applied and was granted an interview.

The interviewers were two senior executives, Neil Bag and Garry Sack. Fred approached the interview with some excitement.

"I believe the project has the potential to fundamentally improve the tax laws," Fred commented towards the end of the meeting.

"The project brief is to rewrite and simplify the existing laws. There is no scope to make improvements to the laws," Garry clarified. "What do you think of this and would you still be interested in being part of the team?"

"It sort of makes nonsense of the project name," Fred said with a smile, although the joke obviously fell flat with the interviewers as they gave him a serious staring down. "I feel that merely re-writing the existing tax laws without attempting to improve them may be a lost opportunity," Fred replied. "However, if this is not in the scope of the brief, I would still be interested in being part of the team and I would work to the best of my ability."

Fred felt deflated as he left the interview and his expectations were low. Even so, he waited in anticipation for some form of advice, but it never came.

During 1994, enterprise bargaining and union amalgamations were gaining pace. The Federated Clerk Union (FCU) had folded into the Public Sector Union (PSU) in 1992 and, from 1 July 1994, the PSU amalgamated into the Community and Public Sector Union (CPSU). The amalgamations were part of the ACTUs grand plan of converting some 300 unions into 20 super unions.

Many of the union members were not impressed with the drive for the unions to amalgamate, as the moment the unions merged into larger ones there was an immediate and noticeable reduction in union representation. Whereas the union representatives were previously highly visible and approachable, they soon became rare species.

These events encouraged many officers not to renew their union dues, with Fred being one of them.

It was approaching Fred's one-year anniversary in Illegal Audit and, based on his written agreement, he had the opportunity to be transferred to Large Audit. He was still completing a number of his Illegal Audit cases and wasn't scheduled to complete his Masters course until the end of the year. Further, he learned that the Large Audit teams were required to travel frequently. He reflected on these facts before he approached Billy.

"I wish to refer you to a written agreement that states that after a year in Illegal Audit I will be transferred to Large Audit," Fred advised. "I've considered my situation and I'm prepared to extend my time in Illegal Audit by another year."

"That's fine with me," Billy said. "However, I'll have to check with management."

It took Billy little time to get back to Fred and confirm that another year in Illegal Audit was approved.

After Fred completed his second year in Illegal Audit, being the end of his agreed extended stay, he was very much looking forward to his transfer to Large Audit. He was upset to hear the gossip that he had simply used his time in Illegal Audit as a stepping stone to Large Audit. It was true in a sense, but it was also suggested that he had just bided his time and was unproductive. When Fred heard the allegations first hand, he became riled sufficiently to draw a response.

"So you guys say I just twiddled my thumbs in Illegal Audit. On the contrary, in my two years in Illegal Audit I completed more cases and brought in more revenue than either of the two teams. If I'm considered to have been slack, what does that say about all of you?"

Chapter 13 – Banking

On 16 August 1994, Fred was to report to Maxwell Adams, the manager of one of the audit teams. Petro Kafes, an Executive Level 1 on the team, welcomed Fred. They were talking in the vicinity of Maxwell's unoccupied workstation when a diminutive man with beady eyes came buzzing around the room, eventually landing among them.

Petro introduced Fred to Maxwell.

"Hi Maxwell," Fred said.

Maxwell was looking every which way. "Hi, Fred. Call me Max, everyone calls me Max."

Before Fred had a chance to say anything else, Max was off.

"Max seems to be fairly busy," said Fred.

"He's busy all right," Petro replied with a snigger. "Busy with his gambling and womanising, I suspect, but not so much with his work."

Petro then introduced Fred to the other members of the team: Jenny Fan, Laura Murr, Pas Napoli, Paul Macello, Con Cosmatos and Alex Pavlidis. "Our team is currently conducting initial profiling work ahead of undertaking a tax review of a company in Sydney," Petro advised.

Fred spoke to each of the team members and they provided him with a snapshot of the team dynamics. Max was a token manager, being preoccupied with his own pursuits. Laura was another token member of the team, being Max's favourite. Petro had found his niche of doing most of the administration work for Max, which left the rest of the team to do the work.

Max was only seen at work intermittently; however, he seemed to miraculously pop up whenever his presence was required by management.

There had been a number of changes since Fred had left the Large Audit area back in 1990. The lobbying by big business and tax advisers seemed to have succeeded in making significant changes in the way audits were conducted.

The success of the Large Audit program was considered by many staff to be largely due to the fact that the auditors could access documents that revealed critical details concerning the compliance attitude of the taxpayers and their tax planning schemes. The Commissioner had a legal right to obtain documents that were not subject to legal professional privilege. However, the Commissioner came under great industry, business and political pressure to heed the demands of the powerful lobbyists.

The Tax Office released guidelines for *Conduct of Taxpayers and ATO Auditors for Complex Audits* as well as guidelines for *Access to Lawyers' Premises*. The effect of these guidelines was that auditors were restricted in gaining access to documents and hamstrung in the manner they conducted audits.

The large companies had apparently also wised up from the initial onslaught of the Large Audit program. Where they had previously recorded their tax planning strategies, there was now a tendency to minimise the amount of detail they would put down on paper. Tax planning appeared to have gone undercover, which made conducting Large Audit cases that much harder.

The team members completed the profiling and preliminary examination of the company and prepared for the initial interview.

They flew up to Sydney and stopped by their accommodation to drop off their baggage before they made their way to the company. They assembled in the meeting room and were seated at one side of the table. The company representatives, comprising the chief financial officer, the senior tax manager, the tax manager and three support staff, were seated at the other side of the table.

The meeting covered the purpose of the tax review, the accommodation arrangements and the logistics.

As the meeting was coming to a close, Max asked about access to the company's cafeteria.

"The cafeteria is on the third floor and you are free to make use of it," the senior tax manager advised.

Max turned around. "There you go, Jenny," he stated. "You can save some more money by making use of the cafeteria."

The company representatives eked out a wry smile, but were not amused.

The team made their way to their hotel accommodation. Jenny had booked cheaper accommodation so Petro, Pas, Paul, Alex and

Fred escorted her there, with Fred carrying her bag. When they arrived at Jenny's hotel, she thanked them and bid them goodbye.

The rest of the group made their way down Darlinghurst Road and found a place to eat. They had a few drinks at a bar before heading back to their hotel along Oxford Street.

"Gee, that woman's pretty good looking," Fred commented.

The woman then walked up to a person who appeared to be a female friend. "How's it going, Bob?" the woman asked in a husky, male voice.

Max met the team the next morning and Petro couldn't resist telling him of Fred's attraction to a transvestite. When the audit team met with the company representatives, Max could not hold his tongue.

"You know the guys went for a walk along Oxford Street yesterday evening," Max advised, "and Fred fell in love with a trannie!"

The company representatives eked out a wry smile, but were not amused.

The following night, Max made a point to engage the team in a dinner, although Jenny declined as she preferred a takeaway meal in her hotel room. Max led the guys to a pub and it was no coincidence that the venue had poker machines.

After dinner, Max was quick to pressure the boys into trying their luck. "Come on guys, contribute some funds and we'll share in the winnings," Max proposed.

Max took 20 dollars each from Pas, Paul, Petro, Alex and Fred. It was notable that Max didn't put in any money himself. He then proceeded to lose the money in a flash.

"Do you want to try again?" Max asked.

It was at this point that the guys stated they had had enough and headed off.

The team wrapped up the week in Sydney and reassembled back in Melbourne where they got together to discuss the plan for the tax review. As Max was unavailable, he appointed Petro to facilitate the meeting.

It was conspicuously quiet until Fred spoke. "We've got the high risk areas identified in the Tax Office Compliance Plan. We've also profiled the industry information that has highlighted further risks. Why don't we start with this information so at least we have some confidence that we've covered the main known risks?" he suggested. His proposal was met with silence.

"We can also examine the company's file structure to organise a system to select documents to identify additional risks," Fred added.

"What Fred has outlined is pretty much what I was thinking," Petro stated. "Unless anyone else has other ideas, I suggest that we use this as our basic strategy."

The team members made preparations for their second trip to Sydney and the commencement of the tax review. Max was unavailable to travel, so he appointed Petro to act as the manager.

The first stage of the review was to examine the company file structure and then commence requisitioning files. It was only a couple of days into the week when the senior tax manager made an unannounced visit.

"You guys were supposed to be doing a targeted risk review but you seem to be fishing," he said.

There was silence until Fred spoke up. "Sir, I wouldn't use the term 'fishing'. Our review is a strategy formulated to identify the highest tax risks. This entails a process of covering risks identified through the Tax Office Compliance Plan and other sources. In addition, we are also responsible for identifying strategic risks peculiar to specific corporations and industries. Part of this process will require the requisitioning of files, some of which will be undertaken on a random basis; however, I can assure you that every file requisitioned forms part of our overall targeted strategy."

The senior tax manager took a moment to consider the response before he left the room.

"He seems to have accepted your explanation," Alex said. "But what in the hell were you on about?"

"I'm not entirely sure," Fred replied. "However, in a sense, I guess you could say that I conceded, at least in part, that we *were* fishing."

The team continued examining the files and each time Alex went up to collect another file and passed by Fred, he gave Fred a tap on the back of the head.

"What is with you, Alex?" Fred asked, glaring at him. "Could you please stop hitting me?"

Alex passed by Fred once more and again gave him a tap on the back of the head. Fred cracked it, immediately looked around, found a hole punch and threw it at Alex, which hit him square in the back.

Alex whirled around. "I get the message," he said. "You didn't have to start throwing things."

Fred was not touched again.

*   *   *

A Large Audit conference was to be held in Sydney and, as Max's team was involved in one of the first tax reviews, its members were asked to make a presentation. Max was unavailable for the meeting, so Petro was asked to facilitate the session.

"Who's interested in doing the presentation?" Petro asked. No-one expressed any interest. "What about you, Fred?" he suggested.

"I don't know, Petro," Fred replied. "What's wrong with you?"

Petro procrastinated for a while before he replied. "Well, I suppose I could, but I thought I'd give you the opportunity."

"Well, that's very kind of you, but I don't want this opportunity," Fred advised.

There was dead silence for an extended period, which Fred considered to be a ridiculous situation. "If no-one else wants to do the presentation," Fred eventually said, "then I'm prepared to do it."

At the Large Audit conference, Petro opened the team's presentation by providing an introduction where he noted the make-up of the team and gave a chronology of the tax review. He had only spoken for a short time when he called Fred to the dais.

Fred stepped up on the platform and delivered a detailed presentation on the topic: "Tax Review—Best Practice". The presentation went over well, with Fred receiving a number of compliments from senior staff.

*   *   *

The team was getting to the end of its review and out of 120 potential audit risks it had narrowed them down to 20 audit issues. Based on the selection criteria for audit, there were three risk areas that remained. Pas identified one risk concerning derivative trading and Fred identified two risks concerning swap trading and international transfer pricing. A team meeting was called, which Petro chaired as Max was unavailable.

"There are three specific issue audits to be conducted: transfer pricing, swaps and derivative trading," Petro said. "Pas identified the derivatives trading so he can work with Laura on that issue. Jenny, Paul and Con expressed an interest in transfer pricing so they can

71

have that issue, which leaves Fred and Alex to take on the swaps issue."

Petro brought the meeting to a close and approached Fred. "I went to special lengths to ensure that people were allocated the issues they had identified," Petro explained.

"Well, I am working on one of the issues I identified," Fred stated, "although I would have preferred to have been working on the transfer pricing issue."

Fred's comment seemed to be lost on Petro.

"You know, I asked the company's tax manager whether he was happy with my performance," Petro advised. "He said he was very happy."

"Given that you didn't identify any tax risks, I'm not surprised that he was very happy with your performance," Fred said. "In fact, I would have thought that he would have been absolutely ecstatic."

Fred briefed the team members who were assigned the transfer pricing issue and handed over the file that included a detailed draft questionnaire. Paul took the file and handed it over to Jenny.

"No worries, Fred," Con stated reassuringly. "We'll take over the transfer pricing issue from here."

Alex and Fred commenced examining their swaps issue. They reviewed the files and the relevant rulings before drawing out a broad strategy that they submitted to Max. He spent little time before he approved the plan.

After a few weeks, Fred learned that both of the other issues had been written off. The derivatives trading issue was finalised after Pas was satisfied that the company was following industry practice. The transfer pricing issue was finalised after the team members considered the reply to a questionnaire.

Fred was surprised that the transfer pricing issue had come to a speedy end and he sought to find out why.

"We considered that it would be easier to concentrate on the specific aspect identified rather than expand the issue to other areas," Paul advised. "So we issued a specific enquiry rather than your extensive questionnaire."

"We also sent the information we had to the Internationals area," Jenny said. "They didn't suggest anything and they doubted whether there was much in it."

"I must say, though, once we got the responses to our query we kind of thought that maybe we should have used your more detailed questions," Con added. "Ah well, we'll know better next time."

Fred was unimpressed with the handling of the transfer pricing issue and turned his attention to the swaps audit.

Alex and Fred travelled to Sydney on three occasions until they got to the point where they could home in on specific areas to confirm whether there were any audit adjustments. They put a business case to Max for one final trip to Sydney. Max said he'd check with management before he came back with a response.

"Your business case for a further trip to Sydney has been declined," Max advised.

Alex and Fred were puzzled.

"Max, we've spent weeks conducting this audit and we've got to the stage where one more trip should provide the information we need to establish whether there are any adjustments and to finalise the case," Fred explained.

Max showed little interest in the reasoning and instructed them to finalise the case based on the information they had. He then quickly trotted off.

"Gee, I just don't get it," Alex commented. "We had a chance to get an audit result and they choose to let it go."

"I don't get it either," said Fred. "Maybe they want to keep our team's record intact by not getting an audit result."

Not long after, an advertisement was calling for expressions of interest for higher duties in Complex Advisings. No-one appeared interested, as it was rumoured that the position involved dealing with some of the more difficult private ruling requests. However, Fred saw it as an opportunity to undertake more challenging work, so he applied and was successful.

Fred reported to the manager of Complex Advisings, Ray Becker. Ray was a friendly chap, although he didn't provide Fred with much guidance about the job.

"As a Senior Advisings Officer, you have full responsibility to deal with the more complex private binding rulings," Ray explained.

Fred examined the private binding ruling applications that were allocated to him and organised the cases into degrees of difficulty. He commenced with the cases requiring further information and issued questionnaires to get them moving while he dealt with the more straightforward cases.

Fred completed his quota ahead of schedule; however, there seemed to be an influx of complex cases and Ray was quick to extend Fred's acting duties.

*   *   *

Tax Office management arranged a time-out in Sydney, which was promoted as an opportunity for management and staff to discuss Tax Office directions and strategies, as well as to network and get to know each other.

The days were packed with sessions and activities that took full advantage of butcher's paper and whiteboards. The evenings involved further activities over dinner, although on the last evening, the activities were dispensed with and the participants were encouraged to enjoy a dinner out.

The various industry segments tended to gravitate to their own areas, with the senior executives being spread among the groupings as they set off to dinner in taxis.

It was a pleasant evening where they enjoyed views over Sydney Harbour. The senior executive who joined the Banking crew was Hugh Pugh. Hugh did not endear himself to the group, as he was intoxicated and mouthing off about how he had progressed through the ranks of the Tax Office with minimal effort.

Discussion then turned to the topic of professional qualifications and various officers at the table described their postgraduate studies.

"It's good for you guys to gain postgraduate qualifications," Hugh interjected. "Of course, I managed to gain a senior executive position through the management stream so I didn't have to worry about studies."

Dinner came to an end and the groups were jumping into cabs to head back to their hotel. Hugh jumped into the front passenger seat of a cab as Alex, Pas and Fred squeezed in the back seat. The guys in the back were all smiling as they were thinking the same thing. *At least we'll have a senior executive pay for the ride.*

As the cab pulled up outside their hotel, Hugh quickly unbuckled his seatbelt and jumped out. "Thanks, driver," he said. "Someone in the back will get it."

*   *   *

A senior executive named Bruce Bull was rumoured to have a bugbear for tea breaks so it didn't come as a surprise to staff when he was assigned a project to deal with absenteeism. It was reported as a serious Tax Office-wide problem, although in reality the problem was confined to a small pocket of staff in one office. However, now that Bruce was put on the case, he appeared hell-bent on blowing the issue out of proportion.

After Bruce had finalised his report, he went on a travelling roadshow to present it to staff around the country. He made it to Melbourne office, where he explained the policy.

"The absenteeism policy came about due to the problem concerning absenteeism from the Tax Office that had developed into a serious nationwide issue. The policy has been signed off by the Tax Office executive and sets out the expectations of staff. Generally, officers are allowed to leave the workplace when they are on official duty, in which case their managers should be aware of and be able to account for their staff's whereabouts. Exceptions to this main rule are absences for lunch and tea breaks."

Bruce seemed to blossom as he came to those parts of the policy that were dearest to his heart. "While lunch breaks are a right, whereby officers use their own time, tea breaks are on office time and are therefore a privilege. It has therefore been decided that officers are to restrict their tea breaks to two 15-minute tea breaks per day."

The officers in attendance were amazed that after a year of investigation, a design process, Tax Office executive approval and a travelling roadshow, Bruce had managed to come up with a policy that was the existing, longstanding Tax Office policy.

Bruce then asked if there were any questions.

One of the attendees, sporting a grin, put up his hand. "Bruce, your policy seems all well and good in that you have comprehensively dealt with physical absences, but what about mental absences?"

Bruce looked hard at the man as he twitched and turned in his struggle to find some words to reply, but he failed to provide an answer.

Staff resumed their work practices as if nothing had changed and the pre-existing problem apparently continued unabated. The absenteeism policy was effectively mothballed, never to be heard of again.

*　　*　　*

Fred's team had a few changes when he returned from his acting stint in Complex Advisings. Pas had been transferred to another industry segment and Con ended up on another Banking team. They were replaced by two new people, Robert Romano and Ray Tweed, who came from other Banking teams.

After a short time, Fabio Zappa also joined the team. Fabio was in his early 50s and a true gentleman. Fred was comfortable talking with Fabio, who had excelled at university, but due to a series of diabolical and convoluted bad luck, ended up at the Tax Office.

"In the days when I joined the Tax Office, there weren't too many people from non-English speaking backgrounds," Fabio explained. "Even though I'm third generation Australian, my Italian name saw me subjected to a lot of racism and discrimination. I'd be seated on my own and given the most mundane duties. There wasn't a day that went by that I didn't hear slurs about my ethnicity. Things seem to be a little better nowadays. I guess there are a lot more ethnics coming through so the racism doesn't seem to be as bad."

Fred was saddened to hear the hollow story of a man whose spirit had been broken. The only thing that seemed to keep Fabio going was the goal of obtaining his government pension.

The team was assigned its next audit case in Melbourne. Max attended the initial meetings with the company and then left the team to do its job. As usual, Petro assumed the role of filling in for Max as manager.

The team was provided spacious accommodation at the taxpayer's office. For some reason, it was considered appropriate to bring in a set of carpet bowls to the company premises. Petro was up to play, and Ray, being the most animated in all things social, was keen to join in. With a little encouragement, Paul joined in too. As they went through their bowling routines, Fred eventually piped up.

"Guys, this is ridiculous; what if the company staff or tax manager walks in?"

"Don't be such a party-pooper," Ray responded.

"Yeah, in any case, they usually ring before they come in," Petro said.

Max was keen to have regular team lunches in what he described as his effort to maintain team morale. They attended a Christmas lunch where Max spent most the time bragging about his gambling expertise. At the end of the meal, Max insisted on collecting the money and quickly counted it.

"That's fine," Max stated. "We can leave now."

Max left, as did Laura, while the other team members remained looking at each other.

"Did anyone see Max actually put in any money?" Robert asked. The others had to consult each other before they agreed that they thought he hadn't.

"If we ever go out for lunch with that guy again, we'll each wanna bring along a conductor's coin dispenser and thumb out just enough to cover what we had," Robert joked.

"Not that there's ever likely to be a next time," Fred added.

*　　*　　*

Just over a year after Fred had left the family home, his mother began to show some worrying medical signs. Michael went to great lengths to arrange various appointments to ascertain the nature of Rosa's condition. It was when a neurologist organised for her to be kept in hospital to undergo a series of tests that there was some indication of the problem.

The neurologist explained that Rosa had progressive neurological deterioration and confirmed her condition in a letter dated 3 January 1996. It also noted that he believed she required nursing home care.

Michael refused to place Rosa in a nursing home and dedicated himself to his wife. He cared for her up to the point when he could no longer physically manage.

In 1997, Michael relented and placed Rosa into a nursing home where he visited her every day. Gina and Fred visited her whenever they could. Above all, the family members supported each other and tried to maintain a positive attitude under difficult circumstances.

Settling into a routine, Fred felt disillusioned with work and depressed about his mother's condition. He hadn't gone away for a holiday in eight years and felt he needed a break so he organised a holiday to South America for February and March of 1998.

Fred had already booked and paid for his holiday when promotions were advertised for Senior Officer Grade (SOG) B and SOG C positions. He rang the contact person on the selection committee to enquire about lodging an application.

"The selection process is scheduled for the period you will be on leave," the contact person said. "But, by all means lodge an application. You never know, you might be that good that you get a position without having to sit an interview."

Fred was not impressed with the contact person's flippant

attitude, but he lodged an application as he thought he had nothing to lose.

Chapter 14 – Internationals

The selection process was still in progress when Fred returned from his holiday; however, he had not been shortlisted for an interview. It was a first for Fred and he was fuming as he tried to rationalise the situation.

How could I not be shortlisted? Everyone else on my team who applied was. They don't have the same level of qualifications, they don't do as much work, nor have they achieved as much. I just don't get it.

Fred was upset with the way things had turned out and he was even more demoralised when everyone else on his team who applied for a SOG B position gained promotion.

"I'm at a complete loss to understand how this could have happened," Fred told Alex.

"I expect that as you were on holidays and couldn't attend an interview, the selection committee decided not to shortlist you to avoid any inconvenience," Alex suggested. "With the recent promotions, the teams in Banking are undergoing a reorganisation and the prospect for those who remain doesn't look good. On the other hand, there are opportunities for transfers to Internationals and I'm applying. Perhaps you should too."

"I understand that Internationals isn't heavily involved in tax audits," Fred said. "I'm more interested in practically applying the law through active compliance work."

Alex gained his transfer to Internationals and ascertained that the area was embarking on increased compliance work on multinational enterprises. This was enough to sway Fred, who quickly lodged an expression of interest as well.

While awaiting his fate, Fred continued to feel disillusioned with the Tax Office. He considered that one of the few pleasures he had in his life was going away on holidays so he organised another trip for Europe and Africa from July to October 1998.

Soon after Fred had arranged his holiday, he received a telephone call from a new senior executive in Banking named Shaun Lamb.

"I understand you have put in for a transfer to Internationals,"

Shaun said. "However, I have new plans for Banking and I'd very much like for you to be part of it."

"Thank you for requesting me to stay," Fred replied. "However, I've spent four years in Banking and I feel as though I've made a reasonable contribution so I am now looking to seek out further challenges."

After Fred had put down the receiver, the telephone rang again.

"My name is Luke Roll and I'm a member of the selection committee for positions in Internationals. The committee has reviewed your expression of interest and you are precisely the type of person we are looking for. We would be pleased to meet with you to discuss a position with us," Luke advised.

Fred met with the selection committee and was encouraged with the planned direction of Internationals. He explained his leave situation and the committee was happy to work around this.

As Fred departed Australia for his overseas holiday on 5 July 1998, he reflected on his mixed feelings. He was greatly disappointed at missing out on a SOG B promotion in Banking, but was hopeful that there would be new opportunities in Internationals.

*　　*　　*

Returning to work, Fred was greeted with the news that the Tax Office had implemented a performance management system and that Executive Level 2 (formerly SOG B) officers were to be in line for performance pay, with the first payment due in October 1998.

On 13 October 1998, Fred fronted up at Internationals. He was met by Alex who showed him around and introduced him to the staff present. Fred was unfamiliar with most of the people, although he was pleased to be reacquainted with Dennis Pie.

Dennis was talking to Fred when they heard a squeaky voice approaching from a distance. The voice belonged to Donna Dolittle, a middle-aged, roly-poly woman who was a senior executive in Internationals.

"Hi, Donna. This is Fred Campari and he's new to the area," Dennis said.

"Yes, I've heard about Fred joining our area," Donna said as she waddled towards them. She was wearing a long, flowing dress that appeared to have a cage crinoline, as it swayed from side to side. "It might be an idea if we had a chat."

Donna escorted Fred into her office and commenced describing various aspects of her ongoing work in Internationals and her overseas delegations.

"We like to encourage staff to be knowledgeable across all aspects of international issues rather than specialising and developing a narrow focus," Donna emphasised.

"That's fine," Fred advised, "I prefer to learn as much as I can and to deal with the full spectrum of issues."

"We're organising international contacts for each Victorian office and I was thinking of allocating one of them to you," Donna further advised. "I want you to take on Moonee Ponds. While the other Victorian offices seem to be operating well, Moonee Ponds has proved to be a real challenge. It has a number of outstanding international tax cases, some of which have been in progress for years, and the compliance teams seem intent to do their own thing. Even though we've dedicated our most senior and experienced staff members to it, it's got to the stage where they're not even talking to us."

"I'm happy to take on the task," Fred immediately responded.

Donna seemed surprised by the positive reaction. "You'll also be expected to take on all the international tax cases," she clarified.

"That's good to hear," Fred stated confidently. "I'm happy to work on the cases. I'm also glad to hear that you are up-front about what's in store, as it provides me with greater certainty about my responsibilities."

Exiting Donna's office, Fred was keen to meet the rest of his new co-workers. Most of the Internationals personnel were located in Melbourne office, as was the Economist area, which was undergoing expansion to assist with the compliance work in transfer pricing.

Fred was introduced to the people in Melbourne one after the other. He was surprised to learn that, contrary to Donna's information, most of the staff members tended to specialise, restricting their work to specific areas of international tax.

Transfer pricing appeared to be the most popular work undertaken. A number of voluminous transfer pricing public rulings had been drafted during the 1990s and Internationals was now starting to ramp up its work with risk assessments, audits and Advance Pricing Arrangements (APAs).

APAs provided taxpayers the opportunity to agree on transfer prices with the Tax Office based on the 'arm's length principle' via agreements that usually spanned three to five years.

While the audits and risk assessment work were generally conducted by officers up to Executive Level 2.1, the APAs were primarily run by the more senior officers. This was little wonder as the APAs involved frequent international travel. The senior executives also sought to market APAs around the globe.

Fred found this initiative most unusual as APAs were conducted at the request of the taxpayer and other leading tax administrations tended to have strict criteria before they would accept an APA onto their program. On the other hand, the Tax Office senior executives seemed to enjoy their international travelling roadshows to market APAs.

The senior executives would sometimes assemble in Melbourne office for meetings. It was like being in an airport terminal, as they came in from around the world. Their main topic of conversation was comparing their respective travel itineraries.

"I'll be in Paris and London next week," boasted one senior executive.

"I went to Europe last month and next I'll be going to Washington DC and New York!" another senior executive bragged.

*　　*　　*

Robert Wordsworth was one of the Executive Level 2.2 technical leaders in Melbourne Internationals and he allocated Fred a couple of technical cases to get him started. Fred completed his technical analysis after a couple of weeks and presented the cases to Robert.

"I'm surprised by the rapid turnaround and the high quality technical papers," Robert commented as he read through the analysis. "I'd like you to present one of the issues at the next Internationals technical forum scheduled for December."

Fred was feeling a buzz as he became more familiar with the staff and the work. He presented at the technical forum and received favourable reports. However, Ted Bear, an Executive Level 1 officer in Internationals, was quick to track Fred down.

"You really should know what you're talking about before you start mouthing off at a technical forum," Ted commented. "People have been looking at that issue for some time and you just come into the area and think you know it all."

"Did you detect any technical flaws in my analysis?" Fred queried.

"No, but I think you should pass your work through more

knowledgeable, senior officers before you present things at a technical forum," Ted said.

"Would you say that Robert is one such officer?" Fred asked.

"Oh yeah, he's probably the best," Ted replied.

"Well, he actually reviewed the paper before I made the presentation," Fred said, smiling. "In fact, he was the one who suggested I make the presentation."

Ted had a dazed expression. "Oh well, that's all right then," he grumbled, and walked off.

Dennis overheard the conversation and approached Fred. "Don't worry about Ted," he remarked. "The best comment I've heard about him was that the only thing they hadn't done with him was bury him."

Fred was relishing his time in Internationals. He was getting involved in the more complex technical work as well as chairing committees and presenting at training courses. It was work that no other officer at his level was taking on.

There were soon positions advertised at Executive Level 2.1 in Internationals and Fred was weighing up whether he was worthy of applying. It was the encouraging comments from officers at all levels that swayed his decision.

The committee members were Kevin Jansen from Sydney office and Cindy Wee from Melbourne office. Both were Executive Level 2.2 technical officers in Internationals.

During the job interview, the committee members took turns asking technical questions where they probed the applicant's knowledge of international tax legislation, examples of how they would apply the law and the policy objective of the legislation. Notwithstanding Fred's limited time in Internationals, he drew on all his background knowledge, qualifications and experience.

Fred rounded off his presentation in response to the final topic. "I invite you to raise any remaining issues you may have so that I may seek to address them."

Cindy and Kevin gave each other a fleeting glance with a hint of a smile.

"No, I don't think that is necessary," Kevin stated.

Fred left the interview room glowing. *You know, even if I don't get a position, I'm glad I applied as I think that was the best interview I've ever had or possibly will ever have.*

The selection committee didn't need much time for their deliberations and to notify the results. The two successful applicants were Ryan Wills and Fred Campari.

Greta Perry, one of the applicants, was enraged by the outcome. She grudgingly congratulated Fred. "I couldn't believe how they just asked technical questions," she complained.

"Well, they were for technical positions," Fred suggested.

Greta pouted. "If I knew they were going to ask technical questions, I would have been better prepared."

Chapter 15 – International Risk

The promotions were effective on 26 April 1999. Fred was uplifted as he felt that his work had been rewarded, and showed his gratitude through even greater efforts. His responsibilities were growing, including the takeover of a number of high profile cases previously dealt with by Executive Level 2.2 officers.

One of the cases was a transfer pricing case where the team manager was one of Fred's previous managers, Adam Butcher. Fred arranged a meeting with the audit team and asked Robert Wordsworth to attend the meeting at Moonee Ponds office.

The attendees had a friendly introductory discussion, although the meeting became a bit heated when Fred moved on to the topic of the transfer pricing audit.

"We've had Internationals people come over here espousing theoretical concepts, but they had little idea about how to put the theory into practice with the audit," Adam stated.

"Transfer pricing is not an easy area to tackle," Fred commented. "It involves an understanding of the industry, how the corporate group fits within the industry and an examination of the company's operations and transactions on a global scale."

"We've been working on this case for years and we've accumulated volumes of information, but it's been of little use," stated Fleur Amari, a woman on the audit team. "We've had you people from Internationals come over here and try to tell us about transfer pricing, but they've been useless. We've also had the most experienced auditor, Damian Bath, who worked on this case for years. He produced a position paper, which has since been discounted and Damian has since retired. What makes you think you can make a difference?"

Fred's response was immediate. "I've read through the audit file that your team has compiled over the years and I think you guys have done some remarkable work. You're right, you do have a great deal of information; in fact, you may already have most of the information required. We just need to make sense of it. As for the position paper,

I think it is one of the strongest transfer pricing cases I've seen so I wouldn't be discounting it at all."

There was a noticeable change in the mood. Robert appeared to sense it as he added to the conversation. "That's right, don't concern yourself too much about what you don't know. Start off by putting down what you do know and gaps will start appearing if there is information that we don't have."

There was a growing curiosity as Adam countered. "But how do we structure the information in a useful way?"

"Adam, I noted that you and a couple of others on the team had undertaken the transfer pricing training school. Remember the importance of detailing the functions, assets and risks of the company in the context of their industry," Fred posed enthusiastically.

"Yeah, I remember that," another member of the team called out.

Fred continued. "I would strongly recommend the others on the team undertake the training as soon as possible. I am also looking to contract two retired tax officers, Damian Bath and Tony Milano, in order to draw on their expert advice in specific areas where we can make use of their extensive knowledge and experience. I think this team can really make inroads into these transfer pricing issues and I'd like to assist you to do this."

The team members looked at each other and then to Adam.

"Fred, I remember you from when you used to be on my team," Adam stated. "I've got a pretty good idea of how hardworking and dedicated you are so I'm willing to give you a go."

*   *   *

Fred considered that he had enough on his plate when Donna called upon him to chair a selection committee for Executive Level 1 positions, with Helen Glaxos of Internationals assisting.

Fred wasted no time with the selection process and engaged one of the listed consultants as the scribe. The consultant's name was Liam Nelson.

There were only 10 applicants and all were given an interview. Liam produced his report and presented it to the selection committee. Helen and Fred reviewed the report and both considered that it failed to reflect their thoughts in many respects.

"I just write the report as I see it and when I hand it over, you are free to make whatever changes you consider appropriate," Liam advised.

Fred got to work and rewrote the report to the stage where Helen agreed that it appropriately reflected their views. Out of 10 applicants, there were only two who stood out as having satisfied the selection criteria. One was Alex Pavlidis and the other was a person from outside Internationals named Terry Jeffrey. Both were promoted.

*　　*　　*

Towards the end of 1997, a high profile lawyer was appointed to the Tax Office in a specialist position as a senior executive. The appointment was one of many senior executive promotions, with a large number coming from outside the Tax Office. These promotions seemed to be the commencement of numerous dubious appointments at senior levels over the ensuing years, with the number of senior executives in the Tax Office exploding.

The lawyer came across as a go-getter, a trait not common to the Tax Office. It was only a year into his tenure that the rumour mill started up and there was much gossiping among the staff until the lawyer's employment was officially terminated.

*　　*　　*

During the course of 1999, Fred was not only dealing with his matters at work but also with a tragedy that was unfolding at home. In the early morning of 28 July 1999, Fred received a telephone call.

"Rosa has passed away in her sleep," said a woman from the nursing home.

After Fred put down the receiver, he fell to his knees and broke down. He spent some time crying before he pulled himself together and rang Michael. "Dad, I've just had a call from the nursing home and they advised that Mum has passed away."

"I'd like to visit my wife," Michael immediately stated, without any sign of emotion.

"I'll call Gina and then come to your house," Fred suggested. "I can drive us from there."

As soon as Fred put down the receiver, he broke down again. He spent more time crying and had difficulty composing himself. He took a couple of deep breaths before he rang Gina. "I've just had a call from the nursing home and they advised that Mum has passed away."

87

There was silence.

"Gina, are you there?" Fred asked. Then he heard the sound of crying. "Gina, I've told Dad and we are going to visit Mum. I can pick you up along the way."

"Fred, I can't go now," Gina wailed as her crying became louder. "I feel faint and my legs are paralysed."

"That's all right," said Fred. "You rest now and you can visit when you feel up to it."

Fred gathered some things together and drove to Michael's house. "Dad, I've brought some of my stuff so I can stay with you for a few days," Fred said.

Michael's expression was solemn and he was momentarily silent before he spoke. "That's good, son, now let's go."

Fred spent a couple of weeks with his father, trying to come to terms with his mother's passing.

Chapter 16 – International Tax Strategy

When Fred returned work, a number of the Moonee Ponds cases had progressed well, although other cases were at a standstill as the audit teams lacked specialist tax and industry knowledge.

Fred was racking his brain with thoughts of how to tackle the situation when he was handed a letter. It was an invitation for Tax Office staff to attend an international tax conference in the US.

Fred examined the letter for several minutes before he got a light bulb moment and telephoned Adam. "Hi, Adam. I wish to discuss an invitation from the US to attend an international tax conference."

"Moonee Ponds also received a copy of the letter," Adam advised. "The executive considered the invitation and decided not to attend the conference."

Fred's workstation was located adjacent to that of Mario Guerra, an Executive Level 2.2 officer in Internationals. Mario picked up on Fred's disappointed mood.

"What's up?" Mario asked.

"It's a pity that the Moonee Ponds guys didn't see the value in attending the conference," Fred said. "It would have been an ideal opportunity to network with our counterparts in the US and around the world as well as being able to meet up with industry experts."

"So what if they didn't think it was worth going? There's nothing stopping you putting up a business case if you think it's worth it," Mario nonchalantly suggested.

Fred looked at Mario. "You're right," Fred replied, "What is stopping me putting forward a business case?"

"You can include my name to accompany you," Mario added. "I wouldn't mind a trip to the US."

Fred drafted a business case to attend the conference as well as to meet up with industry and transfer pricing experts. The objective was to address the blockers and make headway into resolving longstanding audits and APAs. The proposal was for three Tax Office staff to travel: Martin Harris (Economist), Mario Guerra (Internationals) and Fred Campari (Internationals).

The business case was drawn up and sent to senior executive John Kennedy.

"So, you are sending it to the one and only senior executive John F. Kennedy," Mario commented.

"Does John Kennedy have exactly the same name as the former president of the United States, John Fitzgerald Kennedy?" Fred enquired.

Mario looked at Fred with half a smile. "No, not exactly. In the case of the senior executive, the 'F' stands for an obvious expletive."

After a week, Fred received a telephone call from a team manager in Moonee Ponds named Paul Bundey. "We received an email from senior management," Paul advised. "They queried why Moonee Ponds didn't consider it worth attending the international tax conference when Internationals put up a business case to attend."

Fred was about to explain when Paul continued. "I'm aware that you touched base with Adam Butcher and that he advised you of the decision that we wouldn't be attending the conference, but we are now going to lodge a business case to attend as well."

"That's great," Fred stated. "I can provide you with a copy of the Internationals business case if you wish."

"That would be helpful," Paul said.

Internationals and Moonee Ponds were informed that the business case was approved, with the officers to travel being Paul Bundey, Martin Harris and Fred Campari. Mario Guerra missed out and he was not impressed.

The Tax Office representatives jetted off to the US where they attended the conference, networked with tax officers from various jurisdictions and met with industry and transfer pricing experts.

On Fred's first day back at work, he started writing a report to summarise what they had learned. Once completed, he distributed a copy to the Internationals executive and the Moonee Ponds executive. He was then asked to present the report at the Internationals technical forum where there would be two special guests—senior executives Debra Farmer and Chad Stone.

Debra was first on the agenda with a talk about her latest overseas delegation to France. She gave a passing reference to the technical topics discussed at the meeting followed by a detailed explanation of the comfortable villa style accommodation and a visit to the wine region.

After Debra wound up her talk, Fred was invited to make his presentation.

Fred thought he'd commence with a light-hearted comment. "Thank you for the opportunity to report back on the US trip where, unlike some of the overseas trips that are not much more than a jaunt, we had a productive trip that was directly relevant to our work."

Fred's opening remark dropped like a lead balloon and gained an immediate, negative reaction of a chorus of grumblings from the senior executives present.

"I'm only joking," Fred sought to clarify; however, the element of truth in the statement could not be dismissed.

Fred proceeded with his presentation, which he delivered with confidence, eloquence and professionalism. He then wrapped up his presentation. "The trip was of tremendous value as we learned critical information and made crucial contacts, which I am confident we can use to resolve a number of longstanding international tax audits and APAs."

There was a moment of silence before Chad spoke. "Regardless of the fact that you may resolve certain cases, I hardly think this is good enough. I would expect that you should be in a position to develop an overarching international tax compliance strategy."

Fred reflected on Chad's statement as he turned over the page on his pad to reveal a clean page and made a note: "Need to develop an overarching international tax compliance strategy!"

After the meeting, Mario approached Fred. "You seem to be fed a lot of shit lately," Mario commented. "I've found over the years that the more shit one is fed, the more one gets used to the taste."

Fred got to work to develop a strategy. He concluded his analysis and made recommendations that formed the basis of a project initiation brief for an international tax compliance strategy to be driven by the Moonee Ponds office. He then arranged to present the brief at the next Moonee Ponds executive meeting.

"Good morning, ladies and gentlemen," Fred began his opening speech. "Thank you for this opportunity to speak to you. I've been fortunate to be working with members of Moonee Ponds, including Adam Butcher, Paul Bundey and their respective teams. They are tackling some of the most difficult international issues and I am encouraged by the work they are undertaking. I'm also encouraged by the involvement of the Economist area and I note the attendance of Martin Harris here today."

"The positive direction of the international tax work is indicated by the approval of the business case to attend an international tax conference and to meet consultants in the United States," Fred continued. "Following this trip, I spoke to the Internationals technical forum where Chad Stone was in attendance. As I explained at that forum, and I reiterate here today, with the current work being undertaken by the Moonee Ponds teams, the intelligence from the trip to the US as well as the potential benefits to be drawn through the engagement of specialist consultants and meetings with international tax jurisdiction contacts, I am confident Moonee Ponds can progress and complete some longstanding cases."

Fred took a breath before he continued. "Chad indicated his support for these approaches when he encouraged the possibility of not only resolving existing casework, but to take the initiative to develop an overarching international tax compliance strategy."

Fred waited a moment for his audience to absorb the significance of the comment before he concluded his address. "I recognise that the proposal is a tall order and that such an initiative may not have been attempted before; however, the opportunities in developing such a strategy are great. I appreciate that this initiative will require significant resources but I am confident that the resources applied to this project will be far outweighed by the benefits. We can't be disadvantaged by better understanding the industry, including the players and drivers within the industry. This strategy has the potential to not only focus on addressing transfer pricing and international tax risks that have been noted in consecutive Tax Office compliance strategies, but may well assist in addressing other tax issues and risks across the industry. I ask the Moonee Ponds executive to consider and hopefully approve the strategy. Thank you."

Fred waited for a response and, after a few moments, Nick Johnson, a senior executive in Moonee Ponds, spoke.

"Paul, what are your views?" he asked.

"I echo Fred's sentiments and support the proposal," Paul readily stated.

"What about you, Adam?" Nick queried.

"We've come some way with our cases and it's been partly due to Fred's contribution. However, if we are to make real inroads into the industry, we need to take decisive action. I support both Fred and the proposal," Adam said.

Nick appeared to be contemplating a decision when another officer spoke out. "Fred, my name's Ima Fuller and I'm a technical leader in Moonee Ponds. I have to question such a use of our resources. We've got a lot of immediate demands on a number of issues that pose a far greater risk than international. I would vote against the proposal."

Nick reflected for a few moments before he expressed his views. "I'd like to thank Fred for his address and everyone for their thoughts. I'm conscious that such a strategy would involve a significant amount of time and resources. I also appreciate that there now seems to be some headway being made in resolving some longstanding cases. After these cases are completed, I question what we would have learned and what situation we will be in going forward. I suspect not much and not great. However, Fred's proposal gives us an alternative. It is an opportunity to learn about the industry and the taxpayers within the industry that may place us in a much stronger position to deal with the risks and issues going forward. I think we should seize this opportunity. Gino Cursio, you will be the Moonee Ponds representative on the project and you can select another officer to be the project leader. Congratulations Fred, I approve your proposal."

Martin Harris, Gino Cursio and Fred set out a high level plan for the strategy, which included agreed positions concerning the main objectives, staffing issues and a time plan. It took a while to formalise the name for the project as the International Tax Strategy, with the acronym ITS. They then agreed to reconvene in earnest once staff returned to work early in the year 2000.

Chapter 17 – Higher Duties

The millennium bug did not cause any noticeable problems so Tax Office management concluded that the significant expenditure applied to safeguard the computer systems was justified.

The first official meeting for ITS was chaired by Gino and he introduced the officer who was nominated to be the project leader, Frank Nero. Martin was the Economist representative and Fred was the Internationals representative. Other Moonee Ponds staff would be assigned to the project, as required.

Frank gave a background of his experience and boasted how he had dealt with pricing issues and had previously engaged consultants. Fred was encouraged until he heard Frank's next comment.

"So with my previous experience, I really can't see the need for ITS."

Notwithstanding Frank's misgivings, the team proceeded with the project and commenced to draw up a business case to engage consultants.

Days later, Donna called Fred into her office. "I'd like to give you higher duties," she said.

"Why?" Fred queried.

Donna seemed surprised that Fred had questioned the offer. "I need someone to take on the responsibility of chairperson of the Transfer Pricing Committee as the senior officers have been redeployed and I couldn't think of anyone more suitable," Donna explained.

Fred readily accepted the higher duties and Donna then mentioned one other thing. "Oh, and by the way, I also need you to be the chairperson of a selection committee for Executive Level 2.1 positions in Internationals."

Fred was now overwhelmed with work and considered that the best way to deal with it all was to complete it as expeditiously as he could. To assist him with the selection committee was one of the more experienced officers in Internationals, Rory Rogers.

"I'm keen to progress the selection process as soon as possible and I've decided not to engage a scribe," Fred advised.

"I don't mind," Rory responded. "Provided you write up the report."

There were only a few positions to be filled and four of the Internationals staff indicated that they would be applying. However, Fred found it odd that the officer he considered the most likely candidate, Joe Gauci, was not one of them. Fred checked with Joe and he confirmed that he did not plan to apply.

"I find this strange, Joe," Fred said. "You seem to be undertaking the most complex cases and the most difficult technical work that would easily fit within the responsibilities of an Executive Level 2.1 officer so I would have expected if anyone was to apply from Internationals it would be you."

"I've not really been that highly thought of by some of the senior people in Internationals," Joe said. "I wouldn't expect that I'd have much of a chance."

"I don't know on what basis these people hold these views, but I don't expect it could be based on your work," Fred said. "I can't make any promises; however, I can assure you that as far as I'm concerned, you will be judged purely on merit."

When the deadline for lodging applications expired, there were 20 applications. Fred scanned through them and was pleased to see an application from Joe.

Rory and Fred were quick to set down their rating system, whereby applicants who failed at least one of the two most important criteria or any two criteria would not be shortlisted. They agreed to go through their own personal ratings and then come together to discuss them.

When they met, they were consistent in their ratings with 19 out of the 20 applicants. The one applicant where they differed was Lou Marcou. Rory had rated Lou marginally suitable, while Fred rated him unsuitable.

Fred was most uncomfortable to allow Lou to go through as he had rated Lou marginally unsuitable on two criteria, with one being one of the most important.

"Lou's been in Internationals a long time and I think that he should be given the benefit of the doubt," Rory stated.

Fred deliberated over the situation for some time and was still uncomfortable, but he eventually relented to Rory's suggestion of shortlisting Lou.

The selection committee finalised their shortlist, with eight of the 20 applicants to proceed to an interview. Fred presented the list and supporting documentation to Donna as the delegate. Donna examined the list and her reaction was immediate.

"Joe Gauci is rated first but some senior officers don't think too much of him."

"You know very well that Joe is taking on some of the most highly technical work in Internationals and the reason for that is because he's good," Fred responded. "It shouldn't be a surprise to anyone that he would be rated so highly."

In the end, Donna reluctantly approved the shortlist and the applicants were notified.

The selection committee proceeded with the interviews, which largely confirmed the rankings as per the written applications. After the interviews, Rory and Fred worked out their own individual rankings before meeting to discuss them.

Rory didn't have any major issues with any of the applicants. However, there was one applicant who was causing Fred concern, being the usual suspect of Lou Marcou.

Fred was of the view that Lou had failed to establish that he was suitable on more than one of the criteria.

Rory agreed that Lou had interviewed poorly and was borderline on a couple of the criteria, but he held firm. "I've worked with Lou and he's all right. I also know that Lou is rated highly by senior executives. This should be enough to tip him over the line."

Reflecting on the information, Fred tried hard to reconcile their differing views; however, he was still uncomfortable.

Rory could see that Fred was unsettled with the situation and he made one final attempt to sway his opinion. "In any case, it shouldn't make any difference as there are only expected to be a couple of positions, so it's not as if he's going to get a promotion."

Rory's last statement was enough to persuade Fred to finalise the list. He presented the final order of merit to Donna, who gasped before she uttered her reaction.

"You've rated three applicants as highly suitable, three as suitable and two as borderline suitable. How in the hell did you end up with Joe on top?"

"Joe approached the interview with confidence and answered

every question appropriately. He gave us well-reasoned, technical arguments that covered most of the possible issues from various perspectives. He gave us more in 40 minutes than we could extract from any of the others in an hour. Not only did we rate him number one, he was head and shoulders above any other applicant," Fred responded assertively.

Donna continued down the list until she reached the end. "You rated Lou last."

Fred observed a moment of silence before responding. "Unfortunately Lou didn't do himself any favours with a substandard application and performing poorly on the day of the interview. It was, in fact, glowing referee reports and senior executive recommendations upon which we gave him the benefit of the doubt for an interview and in rating him as borderline suitable."

Donna grudgingly handed the order of merit back to Fred and instructed that he could promote the top two people on the list.

Donna was soon called away for another one of her overseas delegation tours of duty and Drew Looney, another senior executive in Internationals, took her place. This meant that Drew would also take over as delegate to complete the selection process for the Executive Level 2.1 positions in Internationals.

"Fred, if you've got the order of merit for the selection process, I'd like to have it," Drew demanded.

"Yes, I have the list. We've already promoted Joe Gauci and Dennis Pie who were the top two applicants, so why do you need the list?" Fred asked.

"You don't have to worry about that," Drew stated, although Fred was very worried.

"Henry Baker ... we don't have to worry about him anymore; he got a promotion elsewhere," Drew muttered. "There are four people left on the order of merit. I shall promote them all."

Fred's jaw dropped as Drew rushed off to make good his edict. Sophie Savvas, an Executive Level 2.2 in Internationals, was at her workstation when Drew stopped and had a few words to her before he moved on again. Fred did not know what Sophie had been told; however, her wry smile made him suspect that she had been told that Lou, a long-time friend of hers, was to be promoted.

*　　*　　*

Voula Vrakas, an Executive Level 1 officer in Internationals, returned from long-term leave. Voula was reasonably quiet, although she came to life at lunchtime and tea breaks. She was particularly sprightly one day when several of the Internationals officers went for their regular morning tea.

"You know that Drew doesn't like how most of the staff tend to go on their tea breaks at the same time," said Voula.

"Drew should know when we go to tea break," Fred responded. "And what's so urgent that can't wait 15 minutes?"

"Well, he just finds it annoying that he can't get hold of people during this time," Voula advised.

"If the matter is truly urgent, my mobile phone is listed so he could easily call me," Fred stated sarcastically.

Voula did not respond, but Fred suspected that his comment would find its way to Drew.

When the group returned from tea break, Fred continued a conversation with Andre Szabo, an Executive Level 2.1 officer in Internationals.

"I find it strange that Drew raised the issue about tea breaks with Voula and not with the rest of us," Fred commented.

"It's not strange at all," Andre said. "Voula and Drew are good friends. Voula unofficially operates as Drew's ear to the ground and reports back to him. That's part of the reason why Voula gets away with doing such a small amount of work."

"So what do you think will happen about the tea breaks?" Fred queried.

"Oh, nothing," Andre stated with confidence. "Drew's always had an issue with tea breaks but he doesn't have the guts to personally confront anyone about it."

Chapter 18 – Office Restructures

In the late 1990s, the Economist area was quickly expanding to more effectively tackle transfer pricing and was to be restructured as the Economists. With this development, it was apparent that they were exerting more influence on the transfer pricing agenda.

Fred sensed that there was a growing tendency by the economists to more readily reject the 'comparable uncontrolled price' (CUP) methodology when it suited them. He was dismayed with this shift as the OECD guidelines specified the CUP as the preferred methodology.

The Economists seem to be doing their own thing, Fred thought, *and one day this may come back to bite us.*

Fred was enthusiastic about the high priority work he was undertaking in transfer pricing and was toying with the idea of undertaking a thesis on the subject, so he put the idea to Donna.

"What would you base your thesis on?" Donna queried.

"I've been working on a number of transfer pricing cases that apply the accepted OECD approach, which is exclusively based on the arm's length principle; however, this approach appears to have its limitations," Fred stated. "This is particularly evident with highly vertically and horizontally integrated multinational corporations. Given the globalisation of industry and developments in the technological, accounting and regulatory environments, it may be the time to consider the development of more up-to-date and modern approaches."

Donna stared at Fred with a look of consternation.

"I also consider that the arguments the OECD consistently puts forward against the Global Profit Apportionment approach to be rather unconvincing," Fred opined. "I was planning to undertake an extensive study on various approaches to more effectively tackle transfer pricing and to try to formulate more appropriate approaches or combination of approaches."

"I've been heavily involved in transfer pricing," Donna boasted. "The arm's length principle has been widely accepted as the most appropriate approach so I wouldn't waste my time if I were you."

*　　*　　*

Both Ryan Wills and Fred had been promoted to Executive Level 2.1 positions at the same time. It was now over a year that they had been in their positions and they were overdue for their annual reviews, which included a base pay review. They were both on the bottom of the pay range and were likely to stay there unless Donna or Drew did something about it.

"I was thinking about approaching Donna and Drew about my review. Were you going to chase it up as well?" Fred asked Ryan.

"I'm well aware that we should have had a pay review. In fact, it's compulsory to have one and they are usually conducted in August, so I should chase it up," Ryan said. "However, since you are going to ask anyway, could you also bring up my situation?"

Fred managed to catch up with Donna in her office as Drew was away on another overseas delegation.

"As you're probably aware, staff members must have an annual review at the end of each year," Fred advised. "The reviews are usually conducted in August; however, Ryan and I haven't had ours yet."

"Is that right?" Donna stated with a grin. "Yeah, I suppose I should do them."

Donna then got sidetracked and, as she often did, started talking about when she was an auditor, her work on overseas delegations and so on. Fred managed to get Donna back on the topic of the pay review and she eventually indicated that she'd get onto it.

Fred had to bring up the topic of the pay review another couple of times before Donna finally came around to do them. Fred was further annoyed when he learned that Donna conducted Ryan's review before his.

A week later, Fred was called in for his review. During the meeting, Donna spoke on just about every topic other than Fred's work. Fred tried to guide Donna to his documentation detailing his achievements.

"Fred, I'm well aware of your work and you've progressed quite well so I will approve an increase in your pay to a level that I consider reasonable," Donna said.

Donna completed Fred's rating and gave him 9 out of 12. Donna came to the new rate of pay, but left it blank and picked up another

100

form. She went back to the new pay rate and deliberated further before she inserted '$77 000'.

"What do you think about that?" Donna asked.

"I think that's reasonable," Fred replied.

Donna was filing her papers when Fred alerted her to the fact that the form needed to be signed and dated. Donna pulled it out and got Fred to sign. Donna then signed and inserted the date of 19 December 2000.

"I guess I can have a happy Christmas now," Fred remarked.

Chapter 19 – New Design

In early 2001, Donna called Fred into her office. "I was considering giving you more higher duties," she advised.

"I appreciate the offer but it might be better if you selected someone else," Fred stated.

"Why?" Donna asked with dismay.

"I've got quite a large workload and I want to ensure that I complete the work effectively. I think that if I took on more work, I might be spreading myself too thin," said Fred.

"The opportunity is partially in recognition of the work you have been doing," Donna explained. "The truth is that our Executive Level 2.2 officers have been redeployed, which has resulted in a lack of expertise to undertake the higher level transfer pricing work. You're really the only one with the capability to undertake this work, which includes being delegated the role of Competent Authority."

The moment Fred heard about the opportunity to assume the Competent Authority role, he raised his eyebrows and accepted.

Fred thrived on undertaking the Competent Authority role, which allowed him to provide guidance and set strategies on the highest profile transfer pricing cases on a national basis. He was also keen to re-engage in his casework and compliance strategies.

There was a restructure of the Moonee Ponds office, which resulted in a shake-up of all senior executive positions.

Fred was disappointed with this decision as it meant that Nick Johnson was to be relieved of this duty. What incensed Fred even more was that Ima Fuller, the only person who voted against the ITS initiative, was to be given a specialist senior executive case leader role.

Ima was quick to get involved in a number of the high profile cases, including a transfer pricing case that Fred considered to be one of the strongest transfer pricing cases he'd seen.

Ima reviewed the case and invited herself to the next taxpayer meeting. Fred recommended that the taxpayer be given the ultimatum to settle on reasonable grounds or the Tax Office would raise amended assessments; however, Ima had other ideas.

"I'm confident that I can get a settlement at the next meeting," Ima boasted. "The case has been going on for some time and it seems that the stage is right to close a deal."

Fred thought Ima was kidding herself. "Ima, this taxpayer has never settled a case and I'm sure they have no intention of settling this case unless we virtually give it away," Fred asserted.

Ima was unperturbed. "Fred, I'll take over the meeting and I'll show you how it's done. I'm confident that we will get an in principle settlement by the end of the meeting."

The team attended the meeting, which was also attended by Adam Butcher, Martin Harris, Ima and Fred.

"This case has been going on for some time and I think we should be working to bring it to an end," Ima stated. "I have reviewed the file and we seem to have exhausted all avenues. Today is the day that I think we should come to a financial settlement."

The tax manager and staff of the company appeared complacent.

The tax manager then calmly replied. "Ima, we are certainly encouraged by your personal involvement. We see this as an opportunity to have this case properly considered. We agree that we have come a long way but we didn't see this settlement meeting as actually involving any dollar amounts."

Fred was almost going to laugh as he saw Ima sink into her seat. The meeting continued without gaining any advancement whatsoever and the Tax Office staff left with their tails between their legs.

"I think that was useful," Ima said. "We obviously have a bit more work to do before we will be in a position to settle this case."

* * *

The ITS project was being stymied as Frank Nero was doing little to progress it. Frank was always giving excuses; however, Fred was of the view that he didn't understand the strategic direction and didn't appreciate the opportunities that the project provided.

When Frank complained about not having much time to spend on the ITS project due to other higher priority work, Fred suggested that maybe they would need to consider someone else to do the job. Frank was pleased to step aside.

Gino conceded that Frank's other priority work was restricting progress on the project; however, he was at a loss to think of anyone else to take over.

Fred was quick to mention the name of Gavin Black.

"That's a possibility," Gino said, "but I'll have to give it some further thought."

Within a couple of days, Gavin was appointed project leader. The moment Gavin was appointed, the project gained momentum. Gavin was able to organise a team, collate the various information and commence to draft a report, with Fred invited to draft the international content.

*   *   *

With the passing of the financial year ending 30 June 2001, Fred managed to arrange an appraisal meeting with Donna.

Donna commenced with one of her elongated monologues and was chatting away for a while before she finally got around to discussing Fred's work.

"Fred, all reports I've heard about you have been good. I have to admit that you have undertaken the most difficult cases and you seem to be making good progress on all fronts. After much thought, I've decided to increase your base salary from $78 500 to $81 500."

Fred blinked. "I'm extremely grateful for the gesture. I was only expecting a salary increase to the top of the Executive Level 2.1 range; however, you have placed me within the Executive Level 2.2 range," he said. "Even though I'm aware that this is likely to be moderated down, I'm still very grateful."

"Don't worry," Donna reassured, "it won't be moderated."

Fred received approval to go on annual leave and jetted off to Mexico.

Upon his return, Donna had gone on another overseas delegation with Drew replacing her as Fred's manager. Drew called Fred to a meeting.

"Could you explain your understanding of your pay review with Donna?" he asked.

Fred was uncertain why Drew was raising the matter but he explained his understanding. "It was a standard annual review where we discussed my base pay and performance pay. As part of my base pay review, Donna rated me 10 out of 12 and, in recognition of the high level work I'd been undertaking, she recommended my base pay be increased to $81 500."

"Donna has placed you on higher duties on occasion; are you sure she hadn't meant to place you on higher duties on this occasion as well?" Drew queried.

104

Fred was totally nonplussed as to what Drew was on about. "Drew, higher duties and the annual pay reviews are completely different and separate processes. Donna and I discussed the matter during my annual review and she confirmed her intention to place me into the Executive Level 2.2 range. I am absolutely clear about this."

"I'm uncertain whether Donna intended for this increase in pay to be a permanent increase as part of the annual review or whether it was for higher duties. What I'm prepared to do for you is to increase your salary level to $81 500 for six months," Drew suggested.

Fred thought Drew was a dill and he moderated his thoughts before he responded. "Drew, that doesn't seem right. The result of what you are proposing is that, after the period of higher duties, I will revert back to my original salary, in which case, I would be deprived of any base salary advancement at all."

Drew reflected for a moment before he came up with another brainwave. "Yes, I must admit this doesn't seem to be fair. What I'm prepared to do is give you the higher duties for six months and then direct Personnel to give you a permanent pay increase to $79 500 thereafter. I will also take up this matter with Donna when she returns."

Fred was incensed, but did not make any further comment on what he considered to be a ridiculous proposal. He never knew whether or to what extent Drew took up the issue with Donna when she returned from overseas. He expected that it wouldn't have made any difference as he was convinced that Drew's intention was to follow through with his own agenda and Donna's intention was never really of concern to him.

*　　*　　*

In early 2002, Internationals was called upon to adopt a New Design model. A report had been completed and it was now required to follow through with its implementation. Drew appointed Julia Jessop to head the implementation team. Drew then selected a number of staff from around the country to make up the team. Fred was surprised when Drew asked him to be one of them, given how Drew shafted him with his pay and that he had a heavy workload.

"The implementation of the New Design is a real opportunity for you to make your mark, which is of vital importance to the operations of the International area going forward," Drew told Fred.

Fred relished a challenge and he thought that he may as well try to put his best foot forward in an effort to prove himself to Drew. The New Design Implementation team included Julia as project leader, Jenny Angel and Tom Christian.

During the first meeting held in Canberra, Jenny Angel was keen to ascertain what the implications were for her area. Tom Christian was quick to add that he was also keen to confirm the likely impact for his area.

Julia was adamant in her response. "The job of the implementation is just that. It is to implement the report that has been drawn up by the New Design team. To that end, and as part of this process, we will be implementing practices to align with the current specialisations. Therefore, I expect that the work your respective areas are currently undertaking will be continuing. It is also important to point out that the process was not, of itself, to result in any promotions."

Once Jenny and Tom received the response they were seeking, they pulled away from the New Design Implementation team. It was apparent that they were there to protect their vested interests and, once their fears had been allayed, their attendance ceased and their positions were replaced.

The meetings of the New Design Implementation team weren't coming up with much so Fred took some initiative.

"I've taken the liberty of drawing a spreadsheet with these headings: Recommendations, Proposed Plan, Responsibility, Deadline Date and Completion Date," he advised. "I've also populated the spreadsheet based on the issues raised in the New Design report."

Fred handed copies around the table and the other team members' eyes lit up, although their responses were muted.

"That's good, Fred," Julia eventually remarked. "I'm sure we can make some use of this."

In subsequent meetings, it was apparent that the spreadsheet set the agenda for the implementation.

The New Design Implementation team was progressing well and had reached the end of the first stage of a two-stage process. Fred was determined to take his holidays and was granted approval to take annual leave. He attended his last meeting before his departure and briefed the team on his work.

"The spreadsheet is up to date, as is the template that sets out details for the various action items. I have commenced drafting the roles and responsibilities for one of the new positions, which can be used as a guide for the other positions. I've also started a template for staff preferences."

Fred handed over the various pieces of his work as he explained it to them. The team members seemed like vultures as they took hold of the information.

Julia thanked Fred for the work and wished him a happy holiday.

Fred enjoyed his holiday in South-East Asia and arrived back at work on 23 October 2002. The New Design Implementation team had continued from where Fred left off and had progressed to the stage where all the roles and responsibilities had been drafted and the staff preference form had been issued.

By the end of 2002, the New Design model for the International area had been completed, with a number of staff relocated into different teams. Fred found it curious that, contrary to Julia's initial statement that the New Design implementation for Internationals was not to result in any promotions, a number of staff had in fact been upgraded.

Fred remained in his previous role, although his position was renamed Internationals Manager and he would be managing a small team of staff: Christine Suresh, Kitty Kat and Lou Marcou.

As an Internationals Manager, Fred was now allocated all international issues. Although he had a team, he was finding the need to play an active role in almost every case.

Kitty was reputed to be the most knowledgeable on the new legislative measures, so Fred specifically selected her for a particular case. They attended a workshop where a number of technical issues were discussed.

The audit team proposed to put together a technical paper to apply the general anti-avoidance provisions on the grounds that the taxpayer structured arrangements to gain a tax benefit by means of tax deductions on debt to finance investments.

Fred couldn't identify any problems with their line of argument and asked Kitty whether she had any views in the light of new legislation.

"I don't see any problems with the position proposed by the audit team," Kitty stated reassuringly.

Subsequent to the workshop, Fred discussed the case with others who had worked on the new legislation and their immediate reaction was that the deductions sought to be struck down would be allowable in any case under new legislative provisions.

Fred consulted Kitty about the new provisions with Kitty boasting how she knew all about them.

"So, given the new legislation, is it correct that there would not be a case to apply the anti-avoidance provisions?" Fred queried.

Kitty took a few moments before she responded. "Well, of course not."

"So why didn't you mention this at the workshop?" Fred asked.

"Oh, I don't know," Kitty replied. "I guess it didn't connect."

As time progressed, Fred was finding that a lot didn't seem to connect with Kitty.

Kitty was soon granted the position of personal assistant to Donna. She was only a couple of weeks into the job when Donna was heard growling.

"What in the hell is going on here?" Donna cursed.

Apparently, Kitty was filing emails in folders without actioning them, although some required urgent attention. Staff expressed surprise that Kitty had stuffed up the job, but Fred considered it to be true to form. Kitty was promptly relieved of duty and replaced by Terry Jeffrey.

Terry soon had everything well-managed and under control. More importantly, Terry ensured that Donna's workload was reduced to a minimum. Terry's remarkable success in the role was easily measured by the blissful sighs of relief that emerged from Donna's office.

Chapter 20 – Canadian Meetings

A letter of invitation was sent from Canada to the Tax Office to attend meetings during March 2003. The meetings had been mooted in the trip to the United States during the international tax conference and this was to be the first.

The ITS report had been completed and presented to the Tax Office executive in late 2002. The success of ITS was reflected in the broader adoption of the initiative in the Tax Office, and the Canadian meetings was an opportune event to present ITS internationally.

At the Canadian meetings, Gavin Black made a presentation on the ITS report, Gino Cursio presented high-risk industry issues, and Fred made a presentation on the international tax technical aspects of ITS. The feedback from the meetings was highly positive and provided critical information in the Tax Office's efforts to conclude the last few ongoing international tax cases.

There was only one of the long-standing transfer pricing cases remaining. It was the case in which Ima had involved herself and was adamant she could settle. It had been running for several years with Adam Butcher as the team manager, although he had since retired. Gerry McDermott had now taken over the team manager role.

Martin Harris and Fred accompanied Gerry to a couple of meetings with the taxpayer; however, Fred's insistence that the case should not be settled, but amended assessments raised and the case litigated if necessary, saw him being sidelined. Ima's main contribution to the case was to allow the audit to drag on.

After a few months, Fred contacted Gerry to seek an update.

"We're looking into settling the case and Ima has got me to run various figures based on different scenarios," Gerry said.

"Scenarios?" Fred queried. "What do you mean by that?"

"We are reviewing the case in the light of the settlement guidelines and the various risks, such as the uncertainty in the law and the risk of losing the case through litigation," Gerry explained.

Fred didn't like what he was hearing, as he was aware that the settlement guidelines could be interpreted in any way to give a desired result. "So what sort of figures are you looking at?" he pried.

Gerry was a little downbeat when he initially spoke. "The original assessment with tax and penalties was around $200 million but the current range is $25 million to $50 million and we're probably looking at the lower end." Gerry seemed a bit perkier when he continued. "The company stated that a settlement of around $25 million would be the biggest financial settlement they would have ever made and Ima's rapt with such an outcome."

Fred couldn't believe his ears. "Gerry, to my knowledge the company has *never* made a financial settlement with the Tax Office so a one dollar settlement would be the largest settlement the company would have ever made!"

Gerry hesitated before he made one final admission. "Well, we don't know for sure whether they'll actually be making a payment, as the company indicated that a review of its books may uncover a couple of credit adjustments in the same years that would reduce this amount."

"So what you're telling me is that we may not actually get any money out of the company?" Fred queried.

"That's possible," Gerry confirmed.

Chapter 21 – Applications & Appraisals

In late 2002, promotions were advertised for Executive Level 2.1 and 2.2 positions in Law and Compliance. The positions were to be appointed nationally, although separate selection committees were established for the different states. The selection committee for Melbourne was made up of Gerard Clement, as chairperson, and Robert Hulls.

Fred applied, was shortlisted and was requested to provide referee reports. He asked three people to be his referees: Donna, Drew and his current manager, Elvis Priestley. Elvis was the only one who provided a written referee's report and Fred was surprised to find that the ratings weren't as high as he had expected, so he thought he'd better give Elvis a call.

"Hi, Elvis. I was wanting to query your ratings for my referee report, as the ratings are only average," Fred stated. "I have consistently gained superior ratings in my performance appraisals, including from you, so I find this to be inconsistent."

"That's fine, Fred. Your appraisal is an assessment of the work you are currently doing. This is different to the referee report that requires ratings on how the referee expects the applicant would perform at the higher level of the position applied for," Elvis explained.

Elvis's approach seemed odd to Fred. He had never heard of such an approach being taken before.

"Elvis, I'm sure that other referees aren't taking this approach," Fred said. "In which case, I'm likely to be handicapped."

Elvis was unmoved. "If other referees are taking a different approach then they're doing it wrong and I can't help this."

After the job interview, the selection process was delayed and Gerard took the opportunity to update Fred.

"Fred, I thought your application and interview were outstanding. The selection committee rated you very highly. In fact, you were rated number two in Melbourne. However, there seems to be a problem."

There always seems to be a problem, Fred thought as Gerard continued.

"None of the managers who requested positions in Melbourne are prepared to select the person who was rated first and they have been directed that they have to select the candidates in order of merit. The only way a manager can deviate from the order of merit is if they make a business case to justify selecting someone lower on the order of merit based on their suitability for a particular job. Unless a manager selects the first person on the order of merit or makes a business case to select someone else, the Melbourne order of merit list will not be used to fill any of the positions." Gerard paused. "I would have thought the Internationals position was one such position where Donna could write up a business case for you."

"I wouldn't hold out on Donna going out of her way for me," Fred stated. "Based on what you are saying, it appears likely that numerous promotions will be handed out in all offices around the country, except for Melbourne. It seems ridiculous to me that national positions are awarded by separate selection committees and it's likely that people will be disadvantaged simply because they happen to be in Melbourne."

"I agree with your view," Gerard sympathised. "However, there's little I can do."

Once alerted about the situation, Donna approached Fred.

"You know I've got a position to fill in Internationals and I've had a number of officers who have asked me about filling it. I would have been keen to give one of them the job; however, I was instructed that I had to go on the order of merit. I understand that you are rated second on the list."

Donna was silent, as if she was waiting for Fred to react. He finally did.

"Yes, I was rated second. I guess that gives you something to think about and might even help you make a decision," Fred stated sarcastically.

Fred was ultimately unsuccessful with his application and Donna failed to fill the vacant position in Internationals.

The decision of the selection committee was confirmed in a letter to Fred, which read:

> The selection process is completed and we are unable to offer you a position on this occasion. You were found suitable; however, there are no vacancies in the current climate. You have been placed on a merit list for future consideration.

Fred considered the letter to be phony and that the real reason positions were not granted in Melbourne had nothing to do with the current climate. The reality was that the Melbourne order of merit was not used, as no-one was promoted from the Melbourne list. On the other hand, there were numerous promotions handed out in other offices around the country.

So much for the Tax Office being an equal opportunity employer, Fred thought.

Soon after, Drew approached Fred.

"I was really fortunate to be able to fill an Executive Level 2.2 position," Drew boasted. "In fact, I had to rush and fight to get it through before the selection committee's order of merit list was established."

Fred was motionless and quiet as Drew felt the need to rub in the fact that he had simply handed out a promotion, yet had denied one to Fred who had been rated superior for promotion through a formal process. Fred's only respite was to take a six-week holiday in South America.

Upon Fred's return to work, he learned that Mario Guerra managed to gain promotion to a senior executive position. Fred was congratulating him when Mario's phone rang. Fred overheard Mario over the phone as he confirmed his promotion and said thanks.

"Who was that?" Fred asked as Mario hung up the phone.

"That was John Kennedy," said Mario.

"So I take it that he congratulated you on your promotion?" asked Fred.

"In his own way, I guess he did," Mario responded. "Good old JFK said that I didn't deserve it."

*　　*　　*

Errol Jonaitis rang Fred. "An Executive Level 2.2 technical position is to be advertised," Errol advised. "I think the position would be ideal for you."

"You know very well how unsuccessful I've been with career advancement and you expect me to apply again?" Fred asked.

"Yes, I know you've been unlucky; however, you can't deny yourself future opportunities based on past failures and I think this job's right up your alley," Errol said.

Fred's interest was growing slightly, although he still held out.

"Fred, if you really want a challenge, then this job is definitely for you. The guy who was doing the role as an Executive Level 2.1 couldn't handle it as he thought it was too demanding. They have now upgraded the position to an Executive Level 2.2, but I understand that he still won't be applying."

"I guess the job may be worth considering," Fred said as he thought about it a little more. "Maybe I'll give the contact person a call."

Fred rang the contact woman, who strongly recommended that he apply.

The timeframe was short so Fred quickly drafted his expression of interest and lodged it on the day of the deadline.

A short time after, the contact woman gave Fred a call. "Hi, Fred. I've gone over your expression of interest and I thought it was of a very high standard; however, you were unsuccessful. In fact, you were extremely unfortunate as you were a bee's dick away from getting the position. The position went to Randy Rider."

"Randy Rider? Isn't he the person who was working in that area in the role as an Executive Level 2.1?" Fred queried.

"Yes, that's right, and funny you should mention an Executive Level 2.1 in the area as there's actually an Executive Level 2.1 that I can offer you."

"That's all right. I'm not interested in the Executive Level 2.1 position," Fred replied.

As soon as Fred replaced the receiver, he rang Errol.

"You wouldn't believe it," Fred said. "I received a call about the promotion and was advised the outcome of the Executive Level 2.2 position. It went to Randy Rider."

"Randy Rider?" Errol repeated. "I didn't think he was going to apply."

"But wait, it gets better," Fred continued. "I was then offered an Executive Level 2.1 position in the same area."

"So, did you accept it?" Errol asked.

"You've got to be kidding!" Fred cried out. "It's obvious what's happening here. Randy couldn't handle the job so they reward him by giving him a promotion and then create another position under him for someone to actually do the work that he couldn't do in the first place! Don't you just love this joint?"

Soon after, Executive Level 2.1 and 2.2 Compliance positions were advertised. Fred had just about given up on ever being promoted, but this didn't stop him from applying. He lodged his application for an Executive Level 2.2 position before he went off on his annual holiday, this time bound for Cuba.

When Fred returned to work, he received advice that the compliance selection committee had been formed and was to be made up of two people: Simon Bell, and Barry Sykes as the chairperson.

Alex Pavlidis applied for an Executive Level 2.1 position and discussed the selection process with Fred.

"With all the high profile work you've done in the last few years, you'd have to have a good chance for promotion," Alex commented.

"I wouldn't be too sure about that," Fred replied.

Shortlisted for an interview, Fred was asked to provide a referee report. He was not looking forward to the referee report from Elvis Priestley and his concern was justified. As usual, Elvis's ratings were average, adopting his unique approach that would no doubt handicap Fred once more.

Fred was called up for the interview and, in Fred's estimation, the interview proceeded reasonably well, until Barry raised the issue of the ITS initiative. "Fred, you mentioned here in your application that you initiated the International Tax Strategy. Could you explain how?"

"Sure. Following a trip to the US that was also attended by Paul Bundey from Moonee Ponds and Martin Harris from the Economists, I drew up a Project Initiation Brief that was to be the catalyst and forerunner of the International Tax Strategy or ITS," Fred explained.

"Hang on a moment!" Barry responded abruptly. "I'm aware that ITS is a project actually run by the Moonee Ponds office."

Fred was stunned with Barry's outburst and tried to clarify his answer. "Yes, it is a project run out of the Moonee Ponds office. However, I was the one who initiated it."

"As far as I know, the Moonee Ponds office has been responsible for the ITS project."

Fred couldn't believe what he was hearing and made another attempt to reconcile their contradictory positions. "I presented a strategy to the Moonee Ponds executive, where I initially recommended the project and which Nick Johnson, as senior executive, approved. From that time on, Moonee Ponds most certainly then took up the running; however, I did initiate the project."

Barry seemed irritated that his view was being challenged. "Fred, let's just accept that the Moonee Ponds office has been running ITS and that you may have had some involvement in it. We should now move on."

Fred was subdued for the rest of the interview, which was mostly due to the fact that Barry kept cutting him off as he attempted to elaborate on his responses. Barry thanked Fred for his time before he was allowed to leave.

Fred was not surprised to learn that he had failed to gain promotion. Although he was rated suitable, this was never going to be a good enough rating to be successful. He felt more disillusioned than ever and his dispirited mood was not lost on his father.

"Son, you seem upset. What's the matter?" Michael asked.

"Nothing much, although work can be a bit frustrating at times," Fred replied.

"So what's the problem at work?" Michael persisted.

"I've applied for a number of promotions over the last few years, but I've been unsuccessful every time," Fred advised.

"I thought they were happy with your work and that you were consistently achieving excellent performance appraisals," Michael said.

"Yes, they always seem happy with my work and they do give me excellent performance appraisals," Fred replied. "However, I still can't seem to manage to get a promotion and I can't understand why."

"Fred, do you think that it might be because of racism or discrimination?" Michael suggested.

"No, I don't think so," Fred responded with a doubtful tone. "Although I've never really thought about it."

"Son, you've reached a reasonable level and you receive a reasonable pay," Michael said. "Sometimes a person may have to accept their place in life and be content with what they have."

Chapter 22 – Father's Care

Michael had a poor heart condition that was being managed by medication but after Rosa passed away, his condition started to deteriorate. It was suspected that the strain of taking care of Rosa over so many years may have taken its toll.

Fred's phone rang in the early morning of 24 March 2004. He had a premonition it would be his father, so he rushed to the phone.

"I'm not feeling well," Michael said under heavy breathing.

Fred headed straight over.

Michael was white, perspiring and shaking, so Fred immediately called an ambulance.

The ambulance arrived, the paramedics went to work and it didn't take them long to make an assessment. "Michael's heart is very weak and we need to take him to hospital."

Fred followed the ambulance to the hospital and the cardiologist who was treating Michael greeted him.

"Michael's heart is functioning very weakly and, even if we are able to stabilise his condition, we cannot guarantee that his heart would be able to function normally. We recommend that a pacemaker be fitted. As next of kin, do you give your permission for this procedure?"

Fred readily gave his approval. He then contacted Gina and advised her of the situation. Gina made her way to the hospital and she arrived as the cardiologist re-emerged.

"The operation has been performed and Michael is doing well," the cardiologist advised.

The pacemaker gave Michael a new lease on life, although he was finding that living home alone was becoming a burden. Fred considered moving in with his father; however, it was evident that Michael would need 24-hour care. Michael was the first to suggest that he should trial some of the low level nursing homes and, over the course of the year, he tried three nursing homes and was particularly pleased with the last.

"A free space is available, so you can move into a permanent place straight away if you wish," the nursing home administrator advised.

Although Michael was keen, he didn't want to rush his decision so he declined. But the moment Michael returned home he was regretting that he hadn't taken up the offer.

"Don't worry, Dad, all you need to do is to express your interest in a permanent placement and you should get one soon enough," Fred stated reassuringly. "In any case, it may be a blessing not going in a rush as you have a number of administrative matters to attend to."

Michael looked around the family home and reflected. "All the work that I put into this home … what's going to become of it? All my work, what a waste," he said softly.

"You raised our family in this home and we have a lot of happy memories. It hasn't been a waste," Fred commented, although Michael was still looking upset. Fred went on. "You don't have to sell the property. You could always rent it out."

Michael's response was immediate. "No. I don't want to rent it out and I don't want any more trouble."

Michael walked outside and made his way into the shed. Fred followed Michael and, the moment he entered the shed, Michael spoke.

"I did a lot of work in this shed, too. Many long hours, making and fixing things."

Fred was touched and he then got an idea. "Dad, I don't know whether I ever mentioned it to you, but I've been thinking about buying an investment property. What better property to buy than the family home?"

The moment Fred uttered those words, Michael's eyes lit up with hope.

"You don't have to worry, Dad," Fred said as he placed his hand on Michael's shoulder. "I'll buy the home and keep it in the family."

Michael, Gina and Fred visited the family solicitor, Joe Stasio. Joe stated that he could arrange the sale of the property and provide associated services.

The Campari family agreed on a sale price of $300 000, which was supported by a market appraisal from a real estate agent and which they considered represented market value. However, Joe noted the council valuation of $350 000.

"Council valuations are usually conservative," Joe stated. "You may have difficulty in establishing a market value of the property for less than that."

Joe then wrote down a few figures. "Michael, you might want to spend some money as you will be close to losing your old age part-pension," he advised.

"What could I spend the money on?" Michael asked.

"You could buy a new car or go on a holiday," Joe suggested.

"How am I going to go on a holiday in my condition? And I don't believe in wasting money," Michael responded.

"That's okay," Joe stated. "I will attend to everything."

Michael gained a place in the low level nursing home and Fred assisted him to move in. A few days later, Fred visited his father to see how he was settling in.

"I'm really happy with my decision and I like the place very much," Michael advised. "You know, I've had a couple of walks after dinner with a woman and last night she asked me to give her a kiss."

Fred arrived back at his place and rang Gina. Portia answered the phone, said hello and called out for her mother.

"Mum! It's Uncle Fred!"

"Hi, Fred, have you visited Dad?" Gina asked.

"Yes, I have and I think he's found a girlfriend," said Fred, smiling.

"What, after only a few days? What do you think about that?" Gina asked, her voice reaching a higher pitch.

"Good luck to him," Fred said. "He's always done the right thing, fulfilled all his commitments and he's been alone for a number of years. I think he deserves a bit of happiness."

Chapter 23 – German Meetings

A letter was sent from Germany inviting the Tax Office to attend meetings. It was another invitation emanating from the ITS initiative. A business case was drafted, listing Gino Cursio and Gavin Black as the Moonee Ponds nominees and Fred as the Internationals nominee.

The international work in Moonee Ponds had progressed to a stage where they had implemented what they had learned from ITS and had completed all of the longstanding international tax cases. The multi-lateral meetings in Germany were an opportunity to present the completed ITS report and broader Tax Office international strategies.

The German meetings were held in May 2005 and were considered by all participants to be a success. Upon their return, Gino, Gavin and Fred drafted a detailed travel report.

"I've heard that you've been on another junket," Donna told Fred with a smirk.

"Well, I guess you could call them junkets," Fred commented. "However, at least the junkets have been instrumental in addressing some of the longstanding international tax cases in Moonee Ponds."

"The cases would have come to a conclusion at some stage and they weren't such a big deal," Donna suggested.

Fred was unimpressed by the comment and felt compelled to respond. "I find it strange that you suggest the cases were not such a big deal as I distinctly remember that you gave me the job with Moonee Ponds because they were a major challenge and that they had longstanding cases that weren't going anywhere."

Now that Fred had started giving Donna a piece of his mind, he found he couldn't stop.

"Further, you should be well aware that the Tax Office Compliance Plan had transfer pricing as one of its highest risk priorities year after year. If you also recall, after I gave the presentation of my initial US trip, Chad Stone instructed me to develop an overarching international tax compliance strategy. I think

I can safely say that I met every one of these challenges."

"Yes, I do recall Chad's instruction," Donna said smugly. "However, I wouldn't have thought you would have taken him seriously. Senior executives often make overwhelming demands but most of us know that they don't really expect staff to follow through and, even if they do, they're just doing their job."

Fred expected that Donna would have the last word, but he did not anticipate the degree of vitriol and sarcasm in her voice, particularly given all the work he had undertaken for her.

Fred returned a wry smile and walked away.

Chapter 24 – Ageing Care Less

A few months after Michael had been in the nursing home, Social Security reassessed his financial situation and determined that he was no longer eligible for the old age pension.

"It seems unfair to me that a person who works hard their whole life ends up without any support from the government," Michael complained.

Soon after, Michael was notified by the nursing home that, due to the fact that he was no longer a part-pensioner, his fees were to increase. The result of having lost a minor pension resulted in his fees increasing to over $100 per fortnight.

Michael was upset by the situation but Fred attempted to reassure him.

"You shouldn't worry about it, Dad. You have enough superannuation pension to get by. In any case, I will look into your financial situation with Social Security and assess things. I'm sure you will be eligible to get the aged pension soon."

Even though Fred had a general power of attorney and medical power of attorney for Michael, he was having trouble getting information out of Social Security. After making numerous enquiries, he resorted to request the information under the freedom of information legislation. He drafted a letter, which Michael reviewed and signed.

Social Security responded to the letter with detailed information concerning the basis for the calculation of Michael's annual income. Fred examined the information and was eager to pass on the findings.

"Dad, I've reviewed your financial situation based on Social Security's information and, if my calculations are correct, you should be eligible for an old age part-pension in the near future."

Michael seemed to acknowledge Fred's report, but his response was muted. "That's all right, son."

Michael had developed a relationship with a female resident named Marguerite. They enjoyed each other's company and arranged to be accommodated in adjoining rooms with interconnecting doors. One day, Fred was visiting Michael when Eva Spearman, the head nurse, passed by Michael's room and called Fred aside.

"After giving the matter some considerable thought, I've decided to separate Marguerite from Michael," informed Eva.

Fred wrinkled his brow. "They're so happy together; why would you want to do that?"

"Michael is starting to show some worrying behaviours and this is causing Marguerite great concern," Eva advised.

Fred was surprised by Eva's statement. "I've spoken to Marguerite and Michael and they both indicated to me that they enjoy each other's company," Fred said.

Eva seemed irritated. "Marguerite is hardly going to open up to you. There is also the fact that Marguerite and Michael are both demanding and they feed off each other, which is causing unnecessary trouble to staff."

When Fred got home, he examined the nursing home's residential care agreement and noted the clauses that covered the resident's rights and responsibilities.

Fred rang Eva the following day. "Hi, Eva. I've got a copy of the nursing home's residential care agreement here and it sets out the circumstances whereby the provider can move residents. It's clear to me that you do not have the authority to move Michael unless he agrees with the move—and he doesn't agree."

Eva was obviously frustrated by the discovery. "Well, if you are going to apply those requirements, I might not be able to move Michael so I'll just have to move Marguerite," Eva threatened.

"If you seek to move Marguerite, you will still need to ensure that she agrees with the move and, based on what she has told me, she doesn't want to move either," Fred stated.

Eva did not respond and hung up the phone.

Neither Michael nor Marguerite were moved.

Chapter 25 – Changing of the Guard

During 2005, a review of the International area determined that the Internationals managers would no longer be managing staff and would be required to undertake administrative and risk assessment work.

Fred was most upset that he could no longer undertake compliance work and discussed the latest changes with Joe Gauci.

"I don't know why the Tax Office seems to be limiting the number of audits they do and focussing on undertaking risk assessments and giving risk ratings," Fred stated.

"There seem to be a lot of worrying changes in the Tax Office," Joe said. He lowered his voice as he continued. "I just want you to know that I'll be resigning soon."

"Why would you want to leave a well-paid job before you are eligible for your superannuation pension?" Fred queried with surprise and disappointment.

"I've been employed by this organisation for nearly 30 years and I've had enough. I really can't stand management. I've worked out my finances and have got to the point where I should be able to manage. I'd prefer to be doing something I enjoy rather than endure any more of this place," Joe revealed.

Fred could understand Joe's feelings towards management; however, he thought that Joe should stick it out and not let management win. After further discussion, Joe's desire to leave was communicated as much through the sad tone of his voice and the forlorn look in his eyes as it was by the words he articulated.

"I respect you and your decision," Fred eventually told Joe. "I wish you all the best."

On 10 October 2005, Fred embarked on a holiday to Chile and Argentina. When he returned, there had been a selection process and the Internationals area gained the services of two new Executive Level 2.2 officers: Duke Box in Melbourne and Jimmy Dick in Brisbane. Neither of the two officers had previous international tax experience.

Duke made heads turn when he appeared in Internationals for the first time. Onlookers witnessed a frameless body draped in a black, two-piece suit—visually, a two-piece bag. He wore a black knitted vest that appeared to function as a bib as it displayed healthy pieces of food crumbs and dried-up sauces, sprinkled with flakes of dandruff. As he slowly shuffled along clenching his briefcase in front of him, he looked like the Grim Reaper.

An Executive Level 2.2 team leader position in Internationals had been vacated and it was granted to an Executive Level 1 officer, Marleen Swift, on higher duties as an Executive Level 2.1. Marleen had wiry hair that matched her wiry physique. She was an obsessive fitness fanatic who was always keen to take it up to the guys with any form of physical competition.

There was much disquiet in Internationals as people tried to rationalise how an Executive Level 2.2 position that was suitably job sized under the New Design could be filled by an Executive Level 1 officer in the capacity of an Executive Level 2.1.

"Who came up with that kooky decision?" Fred enquired.

"It was Drew Looney, of course," said Andre.

"Well, that explains how the dumb decision came about," Fred joked. "It was a decision made by a Looney tune."

Marleen had only been in the job for a short time when she sent an email to staff on the issue of tea breaks. She wrote:

> The current practice where officers go off for morning and afternoon tea is unacceptable. Staff members in Melbourne office should have a long tea break in the morning and a short, takeaway tea break in the afternoon.

People were incensed by Marleen's email, particularly as she had never previously raised the matter with them. Gossip began to flourish that Marleen had raised the tea break issue as it was a perennial bug bear of Drew's and she wanted to impress him.

Fred wasn't going to let Marleen get away with the stunt and he replied in an email, which he copied to the relevant staff as well as the other Executive Level 2.2 officers in Melbourne. Fred raised a number of points ranging from Tax Office policy to flexible working arrangements. He suggested that there be a meeting to discuss the matter before he considered whether it should be escalated.

It was rumoured that Drew didn't want the matter escalated and had a discreet word in Marleen's ear. Marleen then addressed the team in Melbourne.

"Maybe I should have raised the matter informally before sending the email and I will reconsider the issue," Marleen stated.

The matter was not raised nor heard of again.

Marleen spent much of her time on the telephone when she would speak very loudly.

"I don't know why she speaks over the phone so loudly," Andre commented.

"Yeah, I know," Fred responded. "If she's going to speak that loudly, she doesn't really need the phone, she could just stick her head out the window."

Staff would overhear telephone conversations between Marleen and her friends where they listened in bewilderment as she tried to talk and laugh at the same time.

"I have no idea how the person on the other end of the phone could understand her," Andre commented.

"The answer's simple," Fred responded. "She's obviously talking to a kookaburra."

Chapter 26 – Troubles of the Heart

Towards the latter part of 2005, Michael's health had taken a turn for the worse. He was having episodes where his behaviour was becoming erratic, which usually resulted in being admitted to hospital. The main symptoms were described as lack of oxygen, build-up of fluid in the lungs, chest infections and kidney infections. On each occasion, the hospital was able to stabilise Michael's condition and he would then be sent back to the nursing home.

On 3 April 2006, Michael had his next appointment with his electrophysiologist where Fred had to provide Michael with a great deal of assistance to make it to the specialist's suite. Dr Flint conducted his examination and indicated that all seemed in order with his device.

"Dad's had shortness of breath and his ankles are noticeably swollen. I'm concerned about his health. Is there anything you can suggest?" Fred asked with a gravely concerned look.

Dr Flint appeared a little put out. "To date, I've only been involved in managing Michael's defibrillator. I haven't been involved in his general heart functioning and medication as this was being handled by his cardiologist."

"I'm aware of this; however, since Dad moved to the nursing home he hasn't seen a cardiologist. I've arranged an appointment with a new cardiologist who works at the hospital where he is usually admitted, but that appointment is not until 28 April. Is there anything you can suggest before then?" Fred asked.

"You'd best refer the matter to the cardiologist," Dr Flint said.

Fred escorted Michael back to the nursing home and, two days later, Michael was admitted to hospital where they managed to stabilise his condition.

Fred saw Dr Battaglia, the resident GP at the nursing home, and asked him for a referral to the cardiologist; however, Dr Battaglia seemed resistant to doing so.

"I've been attending to your father's general wellbeing and there are a number of factors that need to be managed," the doctor explained. "Your father has been making some irrational statements that he has never been happy living at the nursing home and something about losing his pension."

Fred was upset by the doctor's comments and attitude. "Excuse me, but when Dad arrived he actually told us that he was very happy to be at the nursing home. Further, he did, in fact, lose his pension. This wasn't an irrational statement, it was the truth."

"Oh well, in any case, Michael has been exhibiting some abnormal and inappropriate behaviour," Dr Battaglia stated. "I fear that he is presenting some mental issues and I have recommended that he see a psychiatrist. If his behaviour cannot be addressed, we may have to see whether he should be admitted to a psychiatric facility."

Fred was astonished by the course that Dr Battaglia was planning. "What you are proposing is surprising to me and it only strengthens my resolve to ensure that all aspects of Dad's health are appropriately addressed. I would therefore ask you once more to provide a referral for the cardiologist."

Fred used an insistent tone, causing Dr Battaglia to hesitantly draft a referral for Dr Day.

Fred then rang Dr Day's office. "My father has an appointment on 28 April; however, he has been admitted to hospital. Would it be possible to arrange for Dr Day to see him in hospital before his outpatient's appointment?" Fred requested.

"That shouldn't be a problem," the secretary advised. "Just ask the nursing staff at the hospital and they should be able to arrange it."

Fred saw the nursing staff at the hospital and made the request for Dr Day to visit Michael, leaving a copy of the referral letter.

The following day, Fred checked with the staff, who advised that the request had been recorded, but not followed through. He pleaded that the request be made again and this time followed through.

The next time Fred visited the hospital, he learned that Michael had developed some complications with his kidneys and was referred to the specialist unit. The request to have the cardiologist visit Michael had still not been followed through.

Fred visited Michael and then saw the registrar. He explained the situation, handed the registrar a copy of the referral for the cardiologist and made yet another request for Dr Day to visit Michael.

"Michael has complications that are a priority, but we will look into your request," the registrar responded.

Once again when Fred visited the hospital, he was frustrated to discover that they had still not acted on his request for a visit by the cardiologist.

"Michael has improved and if he keeps on improving, he should be able to go back to the nursing home," the hospital staff reassured him.

Later that week, Fred received a telephone call from Michael.

"Son, they've taken me out of hospital to a strange place. I don't know where I am," Michael said. The state of his confusion was evident in his voice.

"Dad, they indicated that you might return to the nursing home," Fred said gently.

"No, it's not the nursing home, it's a strange place," Michael insisted.

"Dad, see if you can get a nurse or a carer on the phone." Fred waited until he heard a voice. "Where is my father?" Fred demanded.

"Oh, he's at the rehabilitation hospital and he seems very distressed," a woman advised.

"Could you put my father back on the phone, please?" Fred asked. When he heard Michael's voice, he said, "I'm coming straight over."

Fred left work and went directly to the rehabilitation hospital. Michael had been given a bed but his belongings were all over the place.

"Dad, do you know where your toiletries bag is?" Fred enquired.

"No, I don't," Michael replied, looking shaken. "They just threw everything in a garbage bag. They made a real mess."

"Don't worry, Dad, we'll put your things away and then I'll get whatever you need."

Fred arranged Michael's possessions, obtained additional clothes and purchased a new bag of toiletries. When Fred returned, he confronted the nursing staff.

"Excuse me, it was indicated to me that my father was likely to be returned to the nursing home, but he's ended up here and no-one had the decency to advise his family."

A nurse responded in an even tone. "I understand your dissatisfaction. Michael was transferred at short notice via ambulance. But the family should have been advised. I don't know what happened.”

Michael was still in the rehabilitation hospital when he had his appointment with Dr Day. Fred escorted Michael to the cardiologist's suite. His immediate impression of the doctor was that he was a straight shooter and Fred was encouraged by this.

Dr Day reviewed the referral and examined Michael's records. “I don't see any record of Michael having an ultrasound of his heart.”

Fred was unsure what Dr Day was talking about. “I'm not aware of him ever having had an ultrasound,” Fred stated.

While Dr Day was further examining the documentation, Fred raised the concerns about Michael's abnormal behaviour and how they seemed to occur prior to hospitalisation and then ameliorated once he was stabilised.

“It's not uncommon for people with cardiac problems to exhibit abnormal behaviour. When the heart is functioning below capacity, which is pronounced when there is a build-up of fluid, there is likely to be less oxygen going to the brain,” Dr Day nonchalantly responded.

Dr Day ceased reviewing the documentation and turned to Michael and Fred. “There is no doubt that Michael's heart function is weak, but I think I can take some action to improve his health situation. The first thing that we really need to do as a matter of urgency is to have an ultrasound. I can then look to optimising the device and reviewing Michael's medication. How does that sound?”

Fred looked to Michael. He was silent.

“I think that sounds promising,” Fred responded. “What do you think, Dad?”

“Yeah,” Michael replied in a soft voice. “That sounds all right.”

Fred and Gina visited Michael regularly and they were consistently advised that Michael was gradually improving and should be able to return to the nursing home soon.

On one of Fred's visits to the rehabilitation hospital, Michael appeared downtrodden.

“Fred, you don't have to visit me; you look after the rest of the family,” Michael stated.

Fred was surprised and saddened by the statement. “But Dad, you are the most important part of the family. I really want to visit you.”

One evening, Fred noted that Michael was in bed wearing his underwear but without his pyjamas. All of Michael's pyjamas were placed in the laundry basket.

"I'm very cold," Michael said.

Fred looked for a carer and eventually found one watching television. "Excuse me, sir, my father doesn't have any pyjamas and he is cold. Could you provide him with a pair?"

"Okay," the carer said. "I'll get them in a minute."

Returning to his father, Fred applied some moisturising cream to his feet and cracked elbows. He then applied some heat rub to his arthritic back. The carer still hadn't brought the pyjamas so Fred went in search of him. The carer was still watching television, even though commercials were showing.

"Excuse me, when exactly do you think you'll be able to get up and get those pyjamas?" Fred firmly asked.

The carer seemed most put out, but got up, trudged no more than 20 metres, opened a cupboard and handed over a pair of pyjamas. Fred gave the man a serious stare before he took them and returned to his father.

The next time Fred visited Michael, it was in the early afternoon and Michael was in bed.

"Oh, he's being very lazy today," a carer stated. Fred approached Michael and the moment he sensed Fred's presence, he tried to get up. Fred was about to assist Michael when the carer intervened.

"Oh, don't try to lift him. I'll get the lifting machine."

Fred continued to assist Michael to a sitting position. "It's okay, I've helped my father to get up many times," Fred advised.

The carer was insistent. "No, no, wait till I get the lifting equipment!"

Fred held off until the carer returned. "I couldn't find the lifting equipment, but never mind, I'll help him up." The carer proceeded to drag Michael off the bed by his arms.

"What do you think you're doing?" Fred cried out. "You're going to make him slide off the bed!"

Fred stood in front of Michael and placed his arms around his waist. He then lifted him up until his legs straightened and swivelled him onto the chair.

The carer was looking on. "Well, there you go, he can do it if he wants to," she commented.

Fred was outraged. "What are you saying? Are you suggesting that he's doing it on purpose? He is a very sick man!"

A nurse who was looking on quickly approached and waved the carer away. "No, no, no, I'm sure she wasn't suggesting that."

On 29 May when Fred arrived to take Michael for the ultrasound, he was confronted by the nursing staff.

"Why is Michael having an ultrasound?" they queried.

Fred considered the question to be most odd. "Michael was referred for the ultrasound by his cardiologist," he advised.

"This is most unusual," a nurse stated. "We usually don't have inpatients being referred for an ultrasound."

Fred shook his head as he sensed that the situation was becoming bizarre. "Michael had an outpatient's appointment where the cardiologist recommended the ultrasound. I fail to see how the fact that he happens to be in hospital at the time makes any difference."

The nurses were still resistant. "We doubt whether the ultrasound can be allowed but we will contact the cardiologist."

After a few moments one of the nurses returned. "We've contacted Dr Day and he confirmed that he had recommended the ultrasound as being necessary."

Fred didn't say a word but escorted Michael for the ultrasound.

On 31 May, the secretary from Dr Day's office rang Fred.

"The results from Michael's ultrasound were not good and Dr Day wishes to bring forward Michael's next appointment to 2 June."

"Just how bad were the results?" Fred queried.

"Michael's heart function is estimated at 11 per cent."

The information stunned Fred and he immediately rang Gina. "Those bastards at the hospital, they totally stuffed up the management of Dad's health. The results of the ultrasound have come through. Dad's heart is functioning at only 11 per cent!"

"Oh my God!" Gina cried out. "So the poor man is a lot worse than the hospital have ever let on?"

"That's what I suspect," Fred continued, in a voice diminishing to one of resignation. "Dad presented a lot better than his true condition and they thought he'd be fine when, in fact, he's seriously ill."

On 1 June, Gina visited Michael and then rang Fred. "Fred, Dad's not very well and they're suggesting that he may not be able to make his appointment tomorrow."

"Don't you worry," Fred asserted. "I'll be taking Dad to that appointment."

Fred arrived at the rehabilitation hospital on the morning of 2 June. He said hello to Michael, who was responsive but noticeably weak. The nursing staff were expecting Fred and they suggested that Michael may not be well enough to travel.

"It's a very important appointment and I intend to take him," Fred stated.

Fred was surrounded by a number of medical staff. He was unaware who they were but one by one they gave him advice.

"Michael is not well. He's not in a fit state to travel. In fact, the strain of taking him in a car could kill him."

Fred did not have any faith in any of the medical staff. "I need to have Dr Day see my father and I want to take him," he reiterated.

The medical staff conferred. "We'll ring Dr Day," one of them said.

As the medical staff trod off, a priest arrived and introduced himself. He then commenced to give Michael the last rites. Fred was trying to comprehend what was happening. *Is this precautionary or is Dad about to die?* Fred then found himself joining the priest in prayer. As the priest finalised the prayers, the medical staff returned.

"We have spoken to Dr Day. He stated that we couldn't stop you if you were insistent in taking your father; however, we don't recommend this. Alternatively, we can take him to the main hospital via ambulance and Dr Day can visit him there."

Fred thought about it for a moment before he spoke, as if he was in a daze. "Yes, take Michael in an ambulance to the hospital and Dr Day can visit him there."

Fred followed the ambulance to hospital and accompanied Michael to a hospital bed. As soon as the nursing staff were briefed of Michael's condition, they immediately got to work.

Gina rang Fred on the Saturday morning of 3 June. "Fred, I got a call from the hospital and Dad's been categorised as code blue!"

Fred hung up the phone and went straight to the hospital. By the time he got there, Michael was in bed and Gina was at his bedside.

"Apparently Dad was seated for breakfast and collapsed. A nurse rushed to his aid and he has since recovered," Gina explained, stress marking her face.

Gina and Fred stayed at the hospital the entire day. Fred had a break and, when he returned, Gina had a break. When she returned, Fred was looking out the window. She approached him.

"Fred, are you all right? You're crying; what's happened?"

Fred took a breath before he spoke. "Michael was faintly calling out something and I thought I could make out 'Gina' so I thought he was calling out for you. I then heard him calling out for 'Gina, mia mamma'. His mum died when he was a baby, he never really knew her, but after 80 years, he was calling out to her. He was calling out to be reunited with her."

Gina stayed until mid-evening when she left the hospital. Fred felt compelled to stay and it was late evening when he said goodnight to Michael. He left the room and then re-entered to give his father another kiss on the forehead.

The next day, on Sunday 4 June, the family was notified that Michael had passed away.

Gina and Fred gave each other support as they tried to come to terms with the series of events that led to Michael's demise.

"It's not fair the way it all had to end for him," Gina commented.

"It has come to an end for Dad," Fred stated, "but the matter hasn't come to an end as far as I'm concerned."

Chapter 27 – Medical Complaints

After some investigation into various organisations, Fred sent a letter of formal complaint to the Health Commissioner. The letter detailed complaints against Dr Battaglia and the hospital.

Fred received a reply, which required him to complete the official complaint forms and authorisations. He put together the authorities, separate complaint forms for Dr Battaglia and the hospital, a copy of the referral from Dr Battaglia to Dr Day and a copy of Michael's death certificate, which he enclosed with a letter.

After a few days, the Health Commissioner sent Fred notice that the complaints had been referred to Dr Battaglia and the hospital.

Within a month, Fred received a letter from the Health Commissioner that included a response from Dr Battaglia. Fred read the document and was incensed by the arrogant, condescending and dismissive tone. He tried to be as objective as he could; however, as many times as he read it, the letter remained offensive to him.

> Losing a dear parent is always a cause for deep emotional distress and can leave us feeling that more could have been done. I empathise with the family for the long ordeal over the period their father's medical condition deteriorated, eventually resulting in his death. Nevertheless, in my 29 years of practice I have never had an official complaint lodged against me. I have always conducted my practice with great care, competence and deep empathy for my patients. The complainant is under the false misconception that cardiac failure can only be managed by cardiologists.

Fred gave a copy of the response to Gina and, as she read it, Fred made comments. "Dr Battaglia only seems concerned about protecting his reputation and his business, which I expect really do need protecting. He highlights that he has never had an official complaint. Well, he won't be able to honestly make that statement again."

As Gina read the response, she developed a maddened expression of disgust. "So, what do we do now?" she asked.

They considered what to do next and resigned themselves to the fact that they lacked evidence to make a proper case against Dr Battaglia. They decided to await the response from the hospital and seek further evidence before deciding their next step.

Fred considered that it was important to obtain records from Dr Day, as it was Michael's appointment and the test prescribed by Dr Day that he believed highlighted the mismanagement of Michael's health. He sent a letter to the doctor requesting all documentation from the appointment.

After a couple of weeks, Dr Day responded: "As Michael was an inpatient at the time of my involvement, all requests should be directed via the hospital".

Fred then received a letter from the Health Commissioner that noted an option for conciliation and attached the response from the hospital, which read:

> Following a review of Mr Campari's medical history and discussion with clinicians responsible for his care, it seems that his medical management was not compromised in any way and his standard of care was appropriate throughout his various admissions. However, as the family were disappointed with aspects of his care, this is regretted.

Fred felt he was getting standard responses from the various bodies that appeared to have one primary objective, which was to deflect any blame. He drafted another letter to the Health Commissioner, replying to the responses from Dr Battaglia and the hospital. He tried to make it brief and limited the response to six pages. He then gave the letter to Gina for review.

Gina read the letter and advised that she thought it was fine.

Fred was about to seal the envelope when Gina said that she would also like to include a separate letter from her and she handed it over.

Fred read the letter, thanked her, took a copy for his records and enclosed it in the envelope.

Gina had made a heartfelt description of her experiences, which was emotional and revealing. Even though Fred was taking the initiative with the complaints, Gina's letter made him aware that she had been shouldering her own personal pain.

Fred enquired about seeking information from the hospital and, from what he could ascertain, he needed to make a request under the Victorian freedom of information legislation. He did so in another letter.

Within a week, the hospital contacted Fred and stated that they could provide him with Michael's complete medical records, which he could either have access to read or have the documentation copied at a cost. Fred said that he would appreciate a copy.

The hospital provided the documentation and included a note: There is no correspondence in respect to the appointment with Dr Day on 28 April 2006.

Fred was getting frustrated as he felt he was getting the run-around. He then decided to send another request to Dr Day. On this occasion, he sent a formal request.

After a month, Dr Day responded. The doctor wrote: As Mr Campari was an inpatient at the hospital at the time of my involvement, I do not have any information. I have no results, nor a referral letter as these would have been filed in the hospital notes.

Now infuriated, Fred was convinced that he was being fobbed off. *I'm sure there's a legal obligation for Dr Day to have maintained the documentation and I don't buy his excuse that the documentation would have been filed in another location. In any case, this would not have relieved him of his legal obligation to keep a copy.*

Fred did some research as to what he needed to enforce his rights to the information and was deflated to learn that he needed to make yet another complaint to the Health Commissioner. He drafted a letter, where he provided a detailed background and enclosed copies of previous correspondence.

A man from the Health Commissioner soon telephoned Fred.

"I've read your correspondence and it seems odd that the documentation could not be located. It is documentation that they have a legal requirement to maintain. I will make some enquiries and get back to you," he advised.

The man from the Health Commissioner soon contacted Fred again and Fred detected a change in the tone of the man's voice. "I've reviewed your complaint and I must ask what sort of information you are seeking?"

Fred was stunned. "If I have a legal right to the documentation, then I shouldn't need to outline the sort of information and should simply be provided with it," he said.

"Well, yes, you do have that right; however, there seems to be a problem with the documentation going missing. So what information do you expect to obtain that you don't have?" the man persisted.

Fred was incensed. "I've already detailed what I expect should have been in the doctor's file; however, I want everything that was in there. If this information has not been kept, as it legally should have been, shouldn't there be some follow-up?"

The man replied with a statement. "As the information is not available and you appear to have everything that is available, there doesn't seem to be anything else we can do to address your complaint."

Fred felt that he had exhausted all avenues and had exhausted himself in the process. He sensed that he had hit brick walls at every turn and the only prospect of getting any answers seemed to be through conciliation.

Gina and Fred prepared for the conciliation meeting with the hospital. They had endeavoured to have staff involved in Michael's care present; however, all the people they nominated had either moved on or were unavailable. The meeting was at the hospital premises with the participants listed as: Mr Fred Campari, Mrs Gina Poilin, Dr Gavin Thames (Hospital Representative), Leanne Robson (Hospital Representative) and Linda George (Conciliator).

During the first 45 minutes, Linda met with Gina and Fred to detail the process and what the complainants could hope to get out of the meeting. The hospital representatives then entered and Dr Thames was soon explaining the hospital's position.

"Yes, I was heavily involved in Michael's care and we knew for some time that he was dying. The hospital took all reasonable steps. We were even preparing contingencies just in case he improved to have him admitted to high level nursing care. Unfortunately, Michael was in the later stages of cardiac failure and there was nothing anyone could do."

Gina and Fred looked at each other in bewilderment.

"How is it possible that the hospital always knew my father was dying when the members of staff were telling us all along that he should be all right and should be able to return to his low level nursing care?" Fred asked, frowning and shaking his head.

"It must have been a breakdown in communication," the doctor suggested.

"How is it possible that it was a breakdown in communication?" Gina queried, placing her elbows on the table, leaning forward with a serious expression. "When I specifically asked the question in the presence of a social worker and a doctor whether my father was dying, I was assured that he would be going back to his low level care nursing home."

Dr Thames just repeated his previous verse. "I can only explain it as a breakdown in communication among staff."

"How do you explain the fact that my father was placed on his own in a cold room on the basis that he was disturbing other patients, even though he was seriously ill?" Gina then argued. "How could this have been a breakdown in communication?"

Dr Thames seemed unmoved. "I can assure you that I was heavily involved in Michael's care and the level of care he had was appropriate."

Once the parties had gone over their points, Linda asked whether there were any more issues that they wished to raise. Gina and Fred looked at each other, both with an expression of resignation.

"I don't see that there's much point in going any further," Fred commented.

Gina and Fred left the meeting feeling gutted.

"That doctor reckons he was involved in Dad's health management. I've never seen his name on any of the medical records and I have never come across him before. Have you ever heard of him?" Fred asked.

"Never heard of him," Gina responded. "The whole thing was a load of crap."

"All these government bodies seem to be in cahoots and these conciliation processes are just a form of damage control. The only chance anyone really has to get any form of justice is to sue them in court!" Fred said.

"They produce all these policies, principles and mission statements, but it's all rubbish," Gina added. "What's the point of all that when they don't provide a sick old man with the care he needs and they don't treat him with basic dignity?"

Weeks later, Gina contacted Fred to see how he was going.

"Are you all right?" she asked. "You seem upset."

"I'm okay," Fred replied. "It's just that I received the latest council market valuation on the family home and the value decreased from $350 000 as at 1 July 2004 to $300 000 as at 1 July 2006. I understand that property prices may decline, but nowhere near that much over just a couple of years and how often do council valuations decline? You know, if we had sold the property based on what we originally agreed, which I suspect would have been closer to the market value at the time, Dad would never have lost his pension. Nothing really worked in favour of the poor old man."

Chapter 28 – Tax Law

At the time when Fred was dealing with his father's issues during early 2006, there had been a number of changes in the organisational structure at work. Internationals was to be split in two with the legal area joining Tax Law and the remaining area to form the new International Compliance.

Officers were invited to place their preferences. Fred saw it as an opportunity for a change and opted for Tax Law. The results were notified and, even though everyone else was granted their preference, Fred was disappointed to have been placed in International Compliance. What upset him even more was that he would be the Executive Level 2.1 officer on a team reporting to two Executive Level 2.2 officers, neither of whom he considered to be good technicians. He expected that he would not only have to do most of the technical work, but would also have to go through the burden of having to explain every detail of the technical issues to them.

Drew Looney contacted Fred to gauge his reaction. "Fred, I know you put in a preference for Tax Law but the job you will have is very challenging and will allow you to work on the most difficult and demanding cases and issues."

Fred could sense sarcasm in his voice. "Drew, this is exactly the type of work I've been doing for the last six years. I've worked pretty hard over those years and I think I should have earned the opportunity to do something different. I acknowledge that you can place me wherever you want and I'm sure you know that wherever I'm placed I will do the work to the best of my ability, but if I am to work in this compliance area, I will not be happy."

Drew did not say much more and hung up the telephone.

Soon after, Drew contacted Fred once again. "Fred, I have an offer for you. Someone was earmarked for Tax Law, but I am willing to swap them with you."

Fred was content with the swap and readily accepted the offer.

Tax Law was established, with one of the senior executive leaders named Jessie Messenger. Along with Fred, the Executive Level 2.1

technical leaders were Kim Weasel, Ivan Dali and Anton Georgiou. The Executive Level 2.1 team leader was to be Marleen Swift who, to everyone's dismay, continued to act on higher duties.

Kim was an obese, butch-looking female with a pixie haircut. She was unhappy with the work arrangements as she wished to be the team leader and she complained to Jessie.

Jessie arranged a telephone hook-up with Kim, Ivan, Anton and Fred.

"I am a substantive Executive Level 2.1 and Marleen is a substantive Executive Level 1 officer acting on long term higher duties," Kim argued. "I believe that I should be given first option for the team leader position."

"The reasons for having Marleen as Melbourne team leader are to free the rest of you to concentrate on technical issues and to enable Marleen's continued development," Jessie explained. "It should not be seen as an adverse reflection on any of you."

Once the hook-up ended, Kim and Marleen were absent from the workplace when the others engaged in humorous conversation.

"What a strange bird this Jessie woman is," Ivan said.

"Free us up to do technical issues?" Anton added. "Why can't Marleen do any technical work?"

Fred couldn't resist being drawn into the discussions. "Marleen's continued development; how much development can a person get? Why does Marleen keep on getting this preferential treatment of ongoing acting and how is this fair to the other Executive Level 1 officers?"

It wasn't long before Jessie followed up with another hook-up, this time attended by all the relevant officers, including Marleen. Jessie explained her plan. "I'm going to introduce an ongoing 12-month rotation policy for the team leader role. I've had an expression of interest from Kim. Therefore, Marleen will assume the position for the first year, then Kim for the next year, then X ... etc."

The hook-up ended and, once Kim and Marleen were absent from the workplace, Ivan, Anton and Fred engaged in further humorous conversation.

"What sort of drugs are these senior executives on?" Ivan asked.

"Who's this 'X' person who is to follow Kim?" Fred queried.

"I might go last, which would make it 2010 to 2011," Anton suggested.

"You'd be retired by then, wouldn't you, Anton?" Fred asked.

Anton did not reply, but sported a cheeky smile.

Soon after Marleen was installed as team leader, there was a focus on physical activity and she mooted the idea for a social game of soccer.

Marleen instigated discussion about a soccer match and the word soon got around to other areas. Marleen generated sufficient interest from the other Tax Law areas that had an overabundance of participants for a side. The International staff had just enough players to place on the field; however, they didn't have any reserves.

Marleen noted that Fred was a non-starter.

"Fred, we need you. Why don't you want to play?" she asked.

"I've got better things to do during my lunchtime than play a social game of soccer," Fred replied. "I'm really not interested."

Marleen was not one to give in and, after a few days of ceaseless badgering, Fred eventually relented.

It was a warm, sunny day when the two Tax Law soccer teams—International and Other—assembled at Carlton Gardens. The interest in the game was evident by the large number of fans and onlookers who turned up. There was much discussion about the rules and an office worker was put up as the referee due to his experience in umpiring some games of Australian Rules Football.

The game kicked off with much screaming and cheering. The play started with a basic kick to kick when Fred managed to move the ball forward. After a bit of skirmish, the International team managed to squeeze in a goal and the crowd erupted.

It was nearing the end of the first half when Fred started to feel unwell. He waved to be substituted. While he was off the ground, the Other team moved the ball forward and one of their players kicked the ball over the goalie. As there were no goal posts, the rule was that anything over the goalie's extended arm length was no goal. Fred was directly behind the goalie and witnessed the ball go over the goalie's outreached arm, even though he had jumped up for the ball. However, the referee saw it differently and gave the all clear for a goal.

There were excited protests and disputation; however, the referee was unmoved and the goal stood. The half-time whistle blew with the score at one all.

The International players huddled and there was much discussion about the tactics going into the second half. Fred thought the strategy they had adopted in the first half was sound; however, the consensus was to push players forward in an effort to score more goals.

The second half commenced and most of the International players went forward so Fred considered that he'd better fall back. The game was played in the International team's defensive half, but most of the players still stayed forward.

Early in the second half, Fred turned and felt a twinge in his left knee. He attempted to run for the ball a few times, but he sensed that something was amiss. In the meantime, the Other team was able to push the ball forward and the ball went out of bounds. Fred positioned himself for the throw-in when the opposition player threw the ball single-handedly in a roundhouse fashion over the top to a teammate who slotted in a goal. Fred looked to the umpire and yelled in protest for the obvious foul throw, but the referee once again gave the all clear for a goal. Again, there were protests and disputation from the International players; however, the referee was unmoved and the goal stood.

The game continued with the Other team pushing the ball forward but the bulk of the International players staying in the other half of the ground. Fred could show little resistance to the oncoming blitz and, even though their goalie saved many strikes, the International team's defence crumbled.

The whistle heralded the end of the game to the joy of the Other players and to the relief of the International players. The final score was five goals to one.

The moment Fred cooled down, he felt great pain in his left knee, which had swollen up considerably. Fred approached Colin Sharp, who was a first aid officer and present at the game.

"You should attend the first aid room and I'll arrange to place a cold pack on the swelling," Colin said.

Fred showered before he made his way to the first aid room. Colin arrived and gave Fred a cold pack and a First Aid Incident Report.

"You should complete the incident report and I can be a witness to the injury," Colin said.

Fred struggled to make his way home and spent the weekend in much pain. Returning to work, he completed the incident report and was encouraged by Colin to complete a claim for worker's compensation under Commonwealth Care.

Fred had an MRI that revealed a lateral meniscus tear and an arthroscopy was performed. The damage to his knee was worse than expected as there had been internal bleeding, and he was off work for a few weeks. He was doubtful that his claim for worker's compensation would be approved. However, to his surprise, it was.

*　*　*

When Fred returned to work, he was allocated a high profile case that Simon Bravey, an officer with a reputation as an outstanding technician, had previously dealt with. The case concerned matters raised by external parties in response to a Tax Office Interpretative View.

The taxpayer's advisors considered that the Interpretative View was incorrect and they objected to a private ruling that adopted the view. Fred was required to work with two Executive Level 2.2 officers—Jimmy Dick and Duke Box.

Fred drafted a preliminary view and emailed it to Jimmy and Duke. The preliminary view agreed with the decision in the Interpretative View; however, it queried whether the reasons for the decision were technically accurate. Due to the sensitive nature of the case, Fred was finding that Jimmy, Duke and other senior officers were reluctant to make a decision.

Once Simon heard that Fred was dealing with the issue, he hounded Fred about its progress, as well as expressing concern about the preliminary view. Fred sensed that Simon was placing pressure on him to minimise any changes that might reflect badly on him.

Fred endeavoured to reassure him. "I've agreed with your original view and I am not seeking to change this view, but I consider that the reasons for the decision need to be corrected."

The explanation did not appear to allay Simon's concerns, as he continued to hound Fred.

The participants to the case finally accepted Fred's position and he sent around the proposed new Interpretative View for comments.

Simon took some time before he provided his comments. He highlighted the fact that there was no change to the original decision, expressed concern about the new direction by trivialising the changes and suggested that they should be making a minor amendment rather than withdrawing the original Interpretative View and issuing a new one.

"I'll give your comments due consideration," Fred told Simon.

Fred read Simon's comments and dismissed them. *So you're reputedly one of the best technicians*, Fred thought. *So much for reputations in the Tax Office.*

The new Interpretative View eventually issued, but more importantly to Fred, when the court's judgement on the objection was handed down, it confirmed Fred's analysis. However, for reasons unbeknown to him, he was overlooked for any praise, with Jimmy and Duke bathing in all the glory.

Chapter 29 – A Simple Interpretative View

The structure of Tax Law was to be changed whereby the team leader role was to be upgraded to an Executive Level 2.2 position. As a result, Kim became the beneficiary of the role she sought, as well as being given higher duties on an ongoing basis without any selection process.

Kim was allocated a case that she described as a simple issue requiring a straightforward Interpretative View. Shane Simmons from Perth was assigned the case officer role, Fred was to be the technical clearance officer and, as usual, Kim took the approving officer role. As Kim and Shane were taking leave early in the new year, Fred was happy to draft an initial analysis paper.

When Kim and Shane returned from leave, they held a telephone hook-up with Fred where they discussed his analysis paper and readily agreed on his preliminary view. Shane was unsure how to commence the Interpretative View, so Fred volunteered to draft it for him.

Within a week, Fred sent through his initial draft.

Kim quizzed Fred about his draft before she went off to consider it. She then sent through an email response, where she wrote:

I've read the Interpretative View and resisted the urge to write my own version. I've tracked some changes to Fred's version. Feel free to make suggestions. I will then send a clean version to Clark Kane for his comments, followed by a wider distribution to key stakeholders.

As Fred read the email and the attached document, he had to laugh. *You've resisted the urge to write your own version? If you were to write your own Interpretative View, that'd be a first. Instead, you opted to adopt my version and just delete a couple of paragraphs. Jolly good show!*

Kim forwarded the draft Interpretative View to Clark Kane and rumours were soon flying that the view was taking some heat at senior levels. This was confirmed in an email from the senior ranks that noted:

Given the apparent controversy about the issue, rather than producing an Interpretative View, a public ruling should be produced for consideration by the Rulings Panel.

The moment the issue was elevated to a public ruling, Kim positioned herself to play a more prominent, although selective, role. She sent an email where she wrote:

> Fred Campari of Tax Law will be taking over the ownership and authoring of the public ruling; however, I will continue to have a role, perhaps as co-author.

The elevation of the issue to a public ruling increased the technical and administrative work that a public ruling entailed. Together with Fred's other duties, it meant he was now under the pump. Further, the high profile nature of the public ruling attracted a cast of thousands of staff becoming involved.

It took more than two months before Fred had developed the public ruling to a stage where all the stakeholders were comfortable.

After escalating the draft ruling, Fred soon received an email that requested various documents to be prepared for the Rulings Panel.

The deadline for the information was 6 July 2007 and Fred was about to go on leave so he got cracking. By the end of his last week, he had done as much as he could and sent an email to Kim, where he noted:

> I've attached the latest draft of the public ruling, the Approval Form and Briefing Note. As I am on leave from today and not due back until 3 July, I'd appreciate it if you could prepare the Executive Summary in my absence.

Fred arrived back in Australia from his overseas holiday and managed to catch a nasty cold. He visited his doctor, who readily gave him the rest of the week off. Fred fronted back at work on Monday 9 July and started ploughing through his emails.

There was a series of emails concerning the scheduled meeting for the Rulings Panel. As Fred proceeded through the emails, he noted that the deadline for the documentation was 3 July, although they then allowed an extra week to submit it.

Fred checked with Kim. "Did you send off the Executive Summary as I requested before I went on holidays?" Fred asked.

"I was going to do it last week," Kim replied. "However, they gave an extra week to submit it so I left it for you."

"But I was on sick leave over that week," Fred reminded her.

"You've still got a day to do it," Kim stated, unsympathetically.

Fred got to work at 7.05 am the next day and started putting together the documentation for the Rulings Panel. He continued to work on the documentation and sent an email at 6.00 pm that attached the documentation, including an Executive Summary. After 11 hours in front of the computer, he left the office with discomfort in his lower back and feeling completely pissed off.

The moment that the documentation was sent through to the various stakeholders, there were urgent comments bouncing around from all quarters.

"This issue had been previously decided contrary to the view in the proposed public ruling and this needs to be resolved," one party stated.

"We really must have examples," another party suggested.

The moment the communications were passed down the line, this triggered a hive of activity. Separate initiatives were taken to come up with specific examples and develop a chronology of previous Tax Office views that were relevant to the issue.

The examples were developed with the assistance of the audit teams. A chronology was pulled together on all previous Tax Office views that related to the issue, but none revealed any views contradictory to the view in the proposed public ruling. A team of Tax Office staff scoured the Tax Office minutes and found that, indeed, the issue had been discussed over a number of years.

Clark Kane, who had meticulously examined the history of the issue, touched base with Fred.

"You know, everyone in the Tax Office seems to agree with us, although there was one, high-ranking tax officer who took a contradictory view," Clark revealed.

"I guess this explains why the issue is so sensitive at the highest levels," Fred responded.

The issue was presented at two separate meetings of the Rulings Panel. There was resistance from one party, although his objections were not supported by anyone else and his suggestion that the most extreme examples may be attacked under the general anti-avoidance provisions was readily dismissed.

Fred coordinated the drafting of the minutes to the Rulings Panel meetings and amended the public ruling in line with the suggestions made.

"I think you've knocked it out of the park," Clark commented to Fred before he emailed it on to all the relevant stakeholders.

The authoring team was expecting that the next step would be for the public ruling to be publicly issued for comment. However, the next thing that happened was for the background papers to be sent to a senior executive by the name of Aaron Lincoln. Aaron expressed the desire to become more deeply involved and, soon after, he advised that the public ruling would be put on hold.

Fred went on leave for his annual overseas holiday. When he arrived back at work, he ploughed through his emails and was astounded with what he read. He immediately got on the phone to Clark.

"Clark, what in the hell happened while I was away?" Fred asked. "I thought the Tax Office was to put the public ruling on hold; however, it looks like it's about to issue!"

"The plan took an about-face the moment Aaron Lincoln became involved," Clark advised. "The public ruling has been rewritten and it's now set to issue as a draft."

"Yeah, it's been rewritten," Fred exclaimed, "but I'm still down as the author!"

"If you have any questions, you could always contact Aaron," Clark suggested.

"No way," Fred stated. "That's one place I don't want to go."

"Well, you've got a week before it issues," Clark advised.

"That's right," Fred acknowledged. "I just don't know what I'm going to do with all that time."

The public ruling issued as a draft and Fred fielded numerous queries and concluded with a standard statement. "I encourage you to provide a written submission and highlight all the matters that cause you concern."

When the time for submissions expired, Fred worked with Clark to produce a detailed report on the written responses and a draft compendium. Fred also wrote a proposed final public ruling.

After a couple of months, Aaron sent an email where he noted:

> I consider that the Tax Office lacks the requisite knowledge to progress the public ruling to a final ruling. We will engage an expert to assist in this regard.

Clark and Fred spent much of their time fielding queries about the public ruling and continually requesting extensions of time for its finalisation.

Weeks later, a series of emails came through from a line of senior executives who decided to defer the finalisation of the public ruling indefinitely.

On receiving this news, Fred gathered all his files and placed them in storage.

Chapter 30 – Comical Care

Fred had been experiencing increased pain in his lower back since the day he had worked 11 hours in order to have the documentation ready for the Rulings Panel. After a few weeks, he had reached the point where his back pain was chronic.

Fred lodged an incident report and requested a workstation assessment, which was undertaken the following week. The assessment officer suggested that Fred should seek medical advice.

Fred visited his doctor and was sent for a CT scan. He had his follow-up appointment with his GP, who then sent him to an orthopaedic surgeon, Dr Bones.

"Your back condition does not warrant an operation," Dr Bones advised. "However, I do recommend that you consult a physiotherapist."

The physiotherapist recommended a routine of stretches, which Fred adopted and, over the next couple of weeks, he experienced a dramatic improvement in his condition. He was allocated a consultant within the Tax Office named Filomena Fila, who was responsible for dealing with Fred's claim for worker's compensation. He was instructed to fill out the relevant Commonwealth Care form and to include all supporting documentation.

Fred lodged his application and the next thing he received was a request for him to attend a consultation with a neurosurgeon arranged by Commonwealth Care.

Commonwealth Care followed up with a letter to Fred advising of the decision to reject his claim. He was surprised, as it was clear to him that the injury was caused by prolonged sitting at his workstation. He then read the report from the neurosurgeon, which concluded that Fred suffered lower back pain due to degenerative disease of the lumbosacral spine.

Fred was incensed by the finding. *This report is rubbish. I had no prior history of back problems, the injury can be directly associated to a particular incident at work and I haven't had a re-occurrence since. How can it possibly be concluded that I've got a degenerative disease?*

Fred was so upset by the decision that he lodged a request for a review.

Commonwealth Care responded with the determination to affirm the original decision. The statement of reasons repeated the original conclusion and highlighted that Fred had an underlying degenerative back condition which was, on the evidence of the neurosurgeon, prone to episodes of pain.

Fred was convinced that this was false and his frustration was growing. He then escalated the matter by lodging an application for review of the determination.

Fred then received a letter from the lawyers representing Commonwealth Care, which enclosed T-Documents.

Fred was contacted by the Review Tribunal and a telephone conference was organised. He hooked into the telephone conference that was also attended by the Conference Registrar as well as the lawyers representing Commonwealth Care. They discussed the process and canvassed the idea for Fred to revisit his specialist for another opinion.

Fred made a follow-up appointment with Dr Bones and sought his professional advice.

"I have a number of requests concerning lower back conditions and the probability that work contributed to the injury," said Dr Bones. "There is no doubt that there would be a connection; however, it is impossible to prove exactly to what degree. Commonwealth Care routinely refers these cases to a specialist who could quite easily run off a generic report that attributes the condition to a degenerative ageing disease. Everyone has a degree of degeneration; however, most people wouldn't even know they had it. In your case, I suspect that you've had a degree of degeneration and that it's highly likely that work tipped you over the edge. I could write a report to this effect and recommend a degree of significance to which your work contributed to the injury. But I would have to charge you for it and, since I have a backlog of such requests, it would take a few months."

"How much would the report cost?" Fred asked.

"I charge a standard fee of $800," Dr Bones quoted.

"My claim is for less than $400 and I have to pay $800 for a specialist report?" Fred queried, raising his eyebrows. "I'll have to think about it."

Over the next few months, Fred received letters from the Review Tribunal concerning summonses to produce documents from his doctor, his physiotherapist and his specialist. It virtually covered his full medical history. Fred also received word from Filomena that Commonwealth Care's lawyers had requested his personnel file.

"My personnel file!" Fred exclaimed. "On what basis would they seek and be permitted to obtain my personnel file?"

"Commonwealth Care has a legal right to the file," Filomena advised.

"I would like a copy of the documentation from my personnel file provided to Commonwealth Care," Fred requested.

Fred read through his personnel file and wondered what relevance it had to his Commonwealth Care claim, although he did find some of the information intriguing.

The file included a reference from the Tax Office to his employment agency in London dating back to 1988. The reference noted: "Mr Campari has proven himself to be a capable and conscientious officer and his conduct and attendance have been quite satisfactory". It also included details of when he was docked for attending the training course and he homed in on the explanatory note: "Fred is to be repaid as he should never have been docked".

In October 2008, Fred received a letter from the Review Tribunal advising the hearing date of 22 January 2009. Commonwealth Care's lawyers sent a copy of the respondent's statement of facts, issues and contentions. The information included a number of court cases to support the position taken by Commonwealth Care.

The supporting court cases highlighted the heavy burden of proof on applicants to establish that their injuries were significantly caused by their work. Regardless of the fact that Fred was convinced that his work was the significant factor that inflicted his injury, he was developing an appreciation that the nature of his injury was such that it could not be easily proven.

In November 2008, Commonwealth Care's lawyers sent Fred a copy of a follow-up medical report from their consultant neurosurgeon. Not surprisingly, the consultant found no reason to change the opinion he expressed in his original report.

Fred then gave the matter further consideration. *Seems odd that Commonwealth Care pays out on an injury sustained in a social game of soccer but doesn't pay out on an injury that was sustained at work. It shouldn't be called Commonwealth Care; maybe it should be called Comical Care!*

On 1 December 2008, Fred sent a letter formally withdrawing his application for a review of the determination.

Chapter 31 – New Entrants

During 2007, an officer named Bee Hive was promoted to an Executive Level 2.2 in Tax Law. She was an unusual character who seemed to have a social phobia, preferring to go off on extended tea breaks on her own. She often slipped out of the office wearing dark sunglasses and a dark, floppy hat.

The only social interaction Bee involved herself in was for the team to conduct the quiz from the daily newspapers. Bee simply would not relent until the team undertook 'the quiz'. It was therefore ironic that when complaints were made about the quiz, it was Ivan Dali who was the person targeted for blame.

Bee also hassled Alex Pavlidis with her incessant Con jokes.

"What do you call a Greek artist? A Con artist. What do you call a place where Greek cavemen once lived? A Concave. What do you call a Greek exam? A Contest. What do you call a Greek falling out of a plane? Condescending."

Bee did her own thing during her first year in Tax Law, claiming that she was finishing off work from her previous area. In her second year, she gradually became involved in some of the international work.

Bee had a unique approach to her work, which was typified by her attitude. "I refuse to sign off on anything until I'm comfortable with every aspect of the case," she stated.

Fred took this to mean that Bee would not be signing off on anything.

It was a mystery how Bee could have gained rapid promotion to an Executive Level 2.2, although she gave people some sense with her boast. "I worked on a case with a senior executive and when promotions were advertised, I asked her if she'd be prepared to write up a referee report for me. She not only agreed, but stated that I could write my own report and she'd be prepared to just sign it!"

Bee was allocated an audit case involving an interpretative international tax issue. Alex referred a technical paper to her and, after several weeks and pressure from the audit team for advice, Bee finally made a determination.

"I really don't have the time to deal with this issue so I think my role should be reassigned," Bee said.

The case was reallocated to Fred. He read through the technical paper and within a day reported back to Alex. Alex then relayed the outcome to the audit team. The following day, the team thanked Alex for the advice and the case was closed.

Tax Law also gained the services of two senior executives, Ly Low and Benny Heel. Ly was to assume the position of Tax Law Manager. Benny would be working on Special Projects and was to commence on his pet project—Private Rulings. Ly and Benny were good friends and worked very closely together.

Ly had only been in Tax Law for a short time when there were rumblings about his novel ideas. He was due to visit Melbourne to have one-on-one chats with staff. As Fred was due to be on holidays, he missed out on the exercise.

Upon his return, Fred asked a number of the staff about their one-on-one meetings with Ly. None of them came up with anything of significance. Ivan was the most descriptive. "Ly seems to like the sound of his own voice. He just went on and on, rambling away. I didn't say much. I just let him talk."

Fred felt the need to confirm whether there was anything of importance that came out of the one-on-one meetings so he checked with Kim.

"No," Kim replied nonchalantly, gazing at her computer monitor.

"Based on what I've heard, I understand that it's business as usual," Fred said, but there was no reply. "Is that right?" he then asked.

"That's right," Kim eventually replied in a humdrum tone. "It's just business as usual."

Nevertheless, there was a distinctly different feel in the area, with officers running around undertaking work that was strictly outside the scope of the responsibilities of Tax Law. The result was that the "business as usual" work fell on fewer officers who were soon found to be very busy.

Chapter 32 – A Last Application

Executive Level 2.2 positions were advertised and Fred was being hassled by members of his team to apply.

"I don't think so," Fred responded. "What's the point?"

However, the cries for him to apply were growing.

"Fred, you're the most experienced and knowledgeable person in Tax Law; you really should apply," Chloe Callas urged.

"The other Executive Level 2.2 officers don't have anywhere near as much international tax background as you and they don't contribute to the degree that you do," Theo Onassis said.

Such comments were starting to resonate with Fred and he contemplated applying. He then considered whom he could nominate as referees. The obvious contenders were his existing manager, Kim Weasel, and his previous manager, Duke Box.

Fred got on the phone to Duke. "Hi Duke. I was planning to apply for promotion. If I did apply, is it okay if I put you down as a referee?" he asked.

"I'm glad to hear that you're applying. I would most definitely support your application," Duke stated emphatically.

Fred then checked with Kim. "I was about to apply for promotion and, as you are currently acting in the position as my manager, I was wondering whether it was okay to place you down as referee. However, if you will also be applying, due to the obvious conflict of interest, I'd have to nominate someone else."

"It's good that you're applying," Kim said. "I won't be applying, as I'm currently acting in the team leader position as an Executive Level 2.2 so you can put me down as referee."

Fred was about to lodge his application when he thought he'd better double-check with Kim.

"Are you sure you won't be applying?" Fred asked.

"Yes, Fred," Kim replied. "I can confirm that I won't be applying."

Fred lodged his application via email in the morning and, after lunch, Kim approached him.

"I've been on the phone with Bill Pecker who's acting as a team leader in Perth and he strongly recommended that I should apply to protect my interests so I will, in fact, be applying," Kim advised in a blasé fashion.

Fred shook his head as he rang the selection committee contact person, who advised that he should select another person as referee and to submit an amended application. He thought about it for a little while before he concluded that the only viable person would be Helen Glaxos, who had acted as his manager prior to Duke.

Helen was in International Compliance, which had been restructured once again as International Risk. Fred contacted her and she was happy to be nominated as his referee. They then had a chat.

"So what does your area now do, exactly?" Fred asked.

"We are taking on more strategic and risk assessment roles," Helen replied.

Fred was used to vague responses from Helen and he couldn't resist following up to clarify what she meant. "So when high-risk international issues are identified, what does your area actually do?" he asked.

"We report the issues to the various intelligence areas and they form part of the overarching Tax Office risk strategy," Helen replied.

"What about international audits?" Fred queried. "Does anyone do them anymore?"

"Well, of course they do," Helen snapped back. "The Business Lines do them."

"It's unbelievable, isn't it? We have so-called international specialists in International Risk and Tax Law, but none of these international specialists now seem to be involved in any audits," Fred commented. "That's going to have to come back to bite us one day, don't you think?"

Helen just shrugged her shoulders.

Following the conversation, Fred sent a follow-up email to the recruitment area with his amended application showing Helen as his replacement referee.

The selection process was dragging on and it had come to the time when Fred was about to go on holidays so he sent an email to the selection committee. He wrote:

> Please be advised that I am going on annual leave. If I need to be contacted during the period of my absence from 9 May to 20 June 2008, I should be contactable at my personal email address (certainly

difficult when on the Trans-Siberian Railway, I suspect).

Fred enjoyed his holiday and arrived back to the news that he had an interview on the day of his return. He spent the morning reading his two referee reports from Helen and Duke, as well as preparing as best he could for his interview.

Fred met the two selection members, John Carr (Chairperson) and Mary Bran. The interview went smoothly and Fred was reasonably happy with his performance.

It took a few weeks before Kim received a telephone call from the selection committee, although she was her usual discreet self. "I can't disclose any information at this stage."

Soon after, Fred received a telephone call from John Carr.

"Fred, I've got some good news and some bad news," John advised. "The bad news is that there has only been one successful applicant and you have not been successful in being promoted at this stage. The good news is that you have been rated number six in the order of merit and, once we iron out a particular issue, we are confident that further positions will be made available."

The problem that needed to be ironed out was in respect of the person who was rated second on the order of merit. None of the managers wished to select them for promotion and, until they did, the other positions on the order of merit could not be selected.

Déjà vu, Fred thought.

It later emerged that the expected temporary problem could not be ironed out. This confirmed the worst fears—that the selection process in Melbourne only produced the one promotion. As usual, there were numerous promotions in other offices around the country.

Anton was uncharacteristically eager to discuss the promotions with Fred.

"Did you hear that Gerry McDermott gained a promotion to a senior executive?" Anton asked.

"Yes, I did," Fred confirmed. "I'm sure he deserved it as he always just did what he was told."

"It's a pity you didn't perform well with your application for promotion," Anton commented.

"I rated sixth in the order of merit, with every applicant rated above me—and some even below me—all acting on higher duties as Executive Level 2.2 officers and who had the support of senior

conversation, spoke. "Gee, I could hear him having a go at you. Even though you were the approving officer, I was the technical clearance officer who is supposed to check the technical aspects of the Interpretative View at two separate stages of the approval process."

"Well, I guess you're lucky," Fred commented. "By the way, the typo in the Interpretative View was from quoting the legislative provision. I recall you saying that Irene Chong, as case owner, had cut and pasted those quotes directly from the legislation?"

"That's what I thought," Ivan responded. "But obviously I was wrong."

Allen sent an email to various staff, including Irene, Ivan and Fred. Allen advised that he decided to withdraw the Interpretative View, with the reason that the Tax Office was reconsidering its position.

Kim, who had overheard Fred's telephone exchange with Allen, subsequently sent an email authorising the withdrawal of the Interpretative View, with the reason that it was incorrect.

Allen then sent an email advising Kim to change the reason for the withdrawal, as the reason was that the Tax Office was reconsidering its position and not that the Interpretative View was incorrect, as it had not yet been determined that it was wrong.

Fred read the emails and turned to Ivan. "What a huge klutz that Kim is. She obviously overheard my squabble with Allen and just used the reason that the Interpretative View was incorrect. She completely overlooked the fact that Allen instructed her in the email to use the wording for the reason to withdraw being that the Tax Office was reconsidering its position."

Soon after, Irene Chong rang Ivan and he put his phone on speaker so that Fred could listen in. "Allen was looking for someone but as they weren't around, he took the opportunity to talk to me," Irene said. "Allen stated that even if the Interpretative View was technically correct it was substandard—there was a typo—and it needed to be written in such a way that the explanation was much clearer and not subject to misinterpretation."

"What do you think about that?" Ivan asked Fred.

"Allen said that he would be keeping me in the loop," Fred replied. "But I guess there is an exception to this where the information indicates that *he* may be wrong."

*　　*　　*

The gatekeeper of Tax Law sent an email to Fred allocating a case concerning a request for a private ruling. Fred read through the referral before he contacted the Business Line representative, Gary Serpico. They discussed the case and agreed that International Risk should also be involved.

Fred contacted International Risk and they suggested that the case was one that should be referred using the referral template. Gary completed the template and referred it to International Risk.

Within days, Greg Costas from International Risk responded. He wrote: "As Tax Law had already agreed to examine the private ruling on the basis that there is a precedential issue, International Risk will not be involved".

Fred was perplexed by Greg's statement because no-one had identified any precedential issues and Tax Law had not agreed to examine the private ruling on this basis.

Fred examined the case in greater detail and satisfied himself that, in fact, there were no precedential issues. However, he did identify that the case involved transfer pricing and, in accordance to Tax Office guidance, it was mandatory to refer the case to Transfer Pricing.

Fred communicated his views to the Business Line contact officer, Emma Parker, who agreed with the proposed course of action, but advised that she was unaware how to draft the referral. Fred offered to do it for her.

Fred sent the email referral to Emma, who on-sent it. As it so happened, the referral needed to be sent to Greg Costas. Greg was unhappy to be sent the referral and was reluctant to act on it; however, the Tax Office guidance gave him no option and he grudgingly complied. Greg forwarded the email to Gene Pool of Transfer Pricing and Gene accepted the matter as being properly referred.

As further documentation was being lodged by the applicant, Fred was relieved that he had been instrumental in referring the case, as the information was directly relevant to transfer pricing.

The moment the matter reached Transfer Pricing, they set up a team to handle the case and engaged the Economists.

Prior to going on holidays, Fred raised the private ruling case with Kim.

"Fred, if there are no precedential issues identified, I can't see the point in keeping the file open," Kim stated. "You can close the file and leave my name as a contact person just in case any issues were to crop up."

Kim and Fred agreed on the course of action and Fred sent an email to Emma and Gary. As usual, Fred copied Kim into the email. It read:

> I will be on leave from Friday. I've discussed the case with my team leader, Kim Weasel. Kim recommended that as there have been no precedential issues identified it would be more appropriate to direct the international matters to International Risk and Transfer Pricing. If you have any queries or concerns, please contact me up to Friday and Kim thereafter.

Chapter 34 – A Christmas Break-Up

During the time Fred was on holidays in late October 2008, the Melbourne office of Tax Law gained the services of an Executive Level 1 officer named Cas Boer. Cas was in his late thirties with excellent qualifications and experience in the private sector in Australia as well as overseas. He was also highly productive with a natural enthusiasm for his work, which resulted in him being allocated some of the more challenging cases.

After Fred arrived back from holidays, he received a telephone call from the gatekeeper of Tax Law.

"Another referral has been sent with similar issues to a previous private ruling you were recently involved in so I suspect you are best placed to receive this latest referral," the gatekeeper said.

The referral was sent via an email and it included a statement: "Please consult Barbara Butt on this case".

After reviewing the case, Fred rang Barbara. "Hi, Barbara. I've been referred a private ruling case. I do not consider that there are any precedential issues; however, the Business Line has drafted a report concluding that none of the income is attributable to Australia; however, I consider that part of the income may be attributable to Australia and that the Transfer Pricing area should be involved."

"It doesn't sound like there would be any precedential issues," Barbara said. "So you can proceed to advise the Business Line as you have outlined."

"Do you wish to see the email with the report from the Business Line before I send the response?" Fred asked.

"No, that won't be necessary," Barbara replied. "You can just send the email raising the concerns of Tax Law."

The following day, Fred was in the course of drafting the advice when he picked up a voicemail message from Benny Heel, the senior executive responsible for the special project on private rulings. His call concerned the private ruling case and he instructed Fred to provide a report on it immediately.

Kim overheard Fred muttering about Benny's request.

"What's up?" Kim asked.

"I was discussing a case with Barbara yesterday and we agreed on a way forward. Benny has now become involved and has directed me to write a report on the case. I have no idea how he heard about the case or what his problem is," Fred explained.

"Barbara was scheduled to meet with Benny this morning," Kim advised. "I suspect she's probably advised him of the case."

I wonder what Barbara told him, Fred thought.

Fred sent Benny an email response and attached the report from the Business Line. Benny then sent an email where he wrote: "Please send me the reasons for the Business Line's decision and, if you have anything in writing indicating your own view, I want that too".

Fred sent an email response, where he wrote: "The reasons for the Business Line's decision are reflected in their report. There is nothing currently in writing reflecting my views".

The Tax Law team in Melbourne office had a meeting on the morning of Friday 19 December. When Fred returned to his workstation, he picked up a voicemail message from Benny where he asked Fred for a written response to a series of questions concerning the current private ruling case as well as the similar private ruling case he had previously been involved in.

Kim noticed that Fred was flustered. "What's the problem?" she asked.

"Benny's flying off the handle about these cases," Fred advised.

"What cases are these?" Kim queried.

"The current private ruling case and the previous private ruling case that I referred to Transfer Pricing for which you were the contact person when I went on leave," Fred advised.

Kim gave a look of concern. "So did they contact me?" she queried.

You're asking me whether you had been contacted? Fred thought.

"Not that I was copied into or that I am aware," Fred replied, trying to keep the incredulous look off his face.

"Well, that's all right then," Kim remarked.

Fred replied to Benny's email, where he wrote:

> I was referred the first private ruling case and arranged for it to be referred to Transfer Pricing. The officers from Transfer Pricing and the Economists dealt with it in conjunction with International Risk and the Business Line. The second private ruling case is currently under consideration.

After sending the email, Fred set off to join his team for their Christmas lunch. When he arrived at the restaurant, he was very upset.

"That Benny is unbelievable. He sends out email after email with all these demands and I have no idea what he's on about. Sometimes I think that he's NQR," Fred stated.

"What do you mean by NQR?" Ivan asked.

"You know … not quite right in the head," Fred responded.

"Why don't you just say it as it is?" Ivan suggested. "He's a psycho!"

The team had their Christmas lunch, with the main topic of conversation being Benny. Most of the team agreed that he was an oddball, although Kim was conspicuously non-committal and Bee thought he was great.

When Fred returned from lunch, he received another email from Benny, copied to numerous officers. Benny wrote:

> Fred, I tried to ring you on your mobile, but could not speak to you. This forced me to contact Emma Parker of the Business Line. Apparently, on the first private ruling, you prepared a referral to Transfer Pricing and had no further involvement in the case. I also spoke to Gene Pool of Transfer Pricing, who agreed that there was no reason why you could not have been involved. Accordingly, I am concerned Fred that you did not consider it necessary for Tax Law to have been closely involved, let alone that it was the sole responsibility of Transfer Pricing. I now want you to ensure that the Business Line has obtained all the documentation relevant to deciding the second private ruling and for you to prepare a detailed technical report for review by Barbara Butt and Jimmy Dick.

Fred could not believe what he was reading. Benny had contacted people and made statements about him that he considered to be untrue. He thought about it over the weekend and the first thing Monday morning he sent an email to Benny. Fred wrote:

> For the record, the case was referred to Transfer Pricing to address the transfer pricing aspects of the ruling request. I did not consider the matter to be the sole responsibility of Transfer Pricing. They in fact dealt with it in conjunction with the Economists, International Risk and the Business Line. I acknowledge your instructions and I am acting on those immediately.

Benny was quick with a curt reply: "Okay, why did you not determine the private ruling?"

The latest email threw Fred. *Why does he think that I should have determined the ruling?* he thought. *It's never been the practice for Tax Law to determine private rulings.*

Fred tried to contact Benny on the telephone and he left a message on his voicemail. "Hi Benny. There have been quite a few emails going back and forth; maybe it would be better if we were to discuss the matter."

Soon after, Kim approached Fred. "I spoke to Benny and he told me to pass on the message that he wouldn't be speaking to you," Kim advised. "He wants you to follow the directions outlined in his email and to copy Ly Low and him into any email you send of your action."

Immediately acting on Benny's email, Fred contacted Emma Parker of the Business Line and advised of the instructions under which he was operating. Fred then sought to confirm that he had all the documentation obtained by the Tax Office. Emma checked and was sure that Fred should have them all. Fred then started to amass all the documentation ahead of the Christmas break in preparation for him to review when he returned to work in the new year.

The Tax Office closed down at midday on 24 December 2008 and Fred's first port of call was the Elm's Family Hotel.

Gene Pool came over to Fred and raised the private ruling case. "Benny rang me and he was off his rocker. He tried to put words in my mouth," Gene advised. "I told him straight. The case was properly referred to Transfer Pricing and we dealt with it appropriately."

Over the Christmas break, Fred had time to reflect on the past couple of years with his father's issues, the medical complaints and his work at the Tax Office. He was once a believer in institutions and arms of government but his recent experiences had left him disillusioned. He had now lost faith in and respect for all forms of bureaucracy.

Fred didn't have much of a festive season, as his mind was preoccupied with the job that lay ahead of him when he got back to work.

On New Year's Eve, Fred made a resolution. *I'm going to do my best to do my work. I won't stick my neck out and I won't make any complaints. I don't want any more trouble. I just want to live life with some peace of mind.*

Chapter 35 – Problem Cases

Fred got back to work on Monday 5 January 2009. He examined the documentation on the private ruling case and rang Emma Parker from the Business Line.

"I need to ensure that I have all the relevant documentation. Can you confirm that I have all of the documents obtained by the Tax Office?" Fred asked.

"I can confirm that you have all the documents obtained, which were the documents considered sufficient in order to rule," Emma explained.

"I'm also of the view that we have the necessary information in order to rule, but if I come across any additional information I consider necessary, I'll let you know," Fred stated.

Fred aimed to have a preliminary view ready by mid-January, enough time for Barbara and Jimmy to review the case by the end of the month.

While the Business Line concluded that none of the income was attributable to Australia, Fred's findings were that part of the income was attributable to Australia.

Fred sent his report to Barbara and Jimmy, copied to Kim, his manager, as well as to Ly and Benny, as directed.

Jimmy touched base with Fred and quizzed him about his preliminary view. Jimmy took regular pauses, seemingly to absorb what he was being told before he asked his next question.

At the end of the discussion, Jimmy was conspicuously silent in providing any meaningful responses, which made Fred dubious as to just how much Jimmy understood.

"I'll spend some more time to consider the preliminary view," Jimmy advised after some deliberation. "It may also be worth awaiting the return of Barbara Butt," he added, as his voice took on an eager tone.

When Barbara returned to work, she had a telephone hook-up with Fred and Jimmy. Fred was quizzed again about his preliminary view and he went through a similar exercise to the one he had previously undertaken with Jimmy.

Barbara and Jimmy took a moment to reflect before Barbara spoke. "There are a number of ways in which one could write a report; however, I think that you could draft the report differently."

Fred took down notes as Barbara outlined how she wished to have the report restructured, although there were no comments in respect of the technical analysis. Barbara directed Fred to produce the updated report while she was away on further leave.

During Barbara's absence, Jimmy contacted Fred.

"I've checked the documentation and noted that there are a number of documents under the contract that you do not appear to have," Jimmy observed.

"Not all the documentation had been requested as it was considered that they were not required in order to rule," Fred explained.

"I think we should be getting every single document before we rule," Jimmy advised.

Fred considered the approach to be most unusual. "Under the law, we are only obliged to request additional information if it is required in order to rule," he stated.

Jimmy became agitated. "If we are requested to rule then we have the right to request every single document!" he snapped back.

Fred had never heard of such an approach and knew that it wasn't technically correct; however, he resigned to the fact that Jimmy was the senior officer and the one to make the decision.

"If this is the way you want to go," Fred responded. "Then so be it."

The Business Line advised that the case was due to be reviewed. Fred sent through the latest version of the report, which was consistent with the findings in his initial report, as approved by both Barbara and Jimmy.

Barbara, Jimmy and Fred attended a hook-up with the Business Line, with Jimmy commencing the discussion.

"Tax Law's position is that all the documents are needed. If the taxpayer wants a ruling then they must provide all the documents referred to in the contract," Jimmy stated.

"Tax Law does not agree with the taxpayer's treatment of income under the contract," Barbara continued. "We are of the view that at least part of the income is attributable to Australia."

The private ruling case was then subject to senior management's review process, with Barbara, Jimmy and Fred attending the meeting. Fred was finding the hook-up boring and his mind was drifting. When he tuned back in, he heard the voice of Benny Heel.

"If only the correct amount of assistance had been provided with the first private ruling case, maybe many of the current problems would have been averted."

Benny didn't mention any names, but given the comments Fred was reading in emails and a sense of what he was getting from various quarters, he knew the criticism was targeted directly at him.

Barbara, Jimmy and Fred then attended a hook-up with the applicants of the private ruling where Barbara took the initiative and launched into expressing her views in a very aggressive and brash manner. "We don't agree with the company's treatment of income and we will require all the documentation. At this stage we consider that at least some of the income is attributable to Australia."

After the hook-up, the applicant contacted Gary Serpico from the Business Line and he then telephoned Tax Law to advise them of his discussion. "The applicant queried the need for all the documents as part of a private ruling request. I stated that they may wish to consider an Advance Pricing Arrangement rather than a ruling; however, the applicant insisted on a ruling."

Fred was becoming increasingly frustrated. *You idiots*, he thought. *It's not the applicant's call to decide whether the Tax Office should rule or not. The Tax Office should have refused to rule in the first private ruling request as it is inappropriate to deal with a transfer pricing matter as a private ruling.*

Chapter 36 – A Mid-Year Review

Kim sent an email to Ivan, Anton and Fred, where she noted:
> As part of the mid-year reviews, we need to discuss performance ratings, which need to be sent off by the end of March.

Fred was the first to have a mid-year review meeting with Kim.

"Ly Low has the view that you don't even satisfy a fully effective rating of 3 and 3; however, I think that you are at least a 3 and 3," Kim commented during the meeting.

"On what basis would Ly be of the view that I wasn't fully effective?" Fred asked.

"I don't know," Kim replied. "The only adverse thing I ever told him about you was that you tended to just do your job and nothing more."

Fred was astounded by the revelation. "I help out and render assistance more than anyone else in Tax Law. Why would you ever tell him something like that?" he asked, with a slight quiver in his voice.

Kim just shrugged her shoulders without offering any explanation.

Kim and Fred went through Fred's casework and Kim acknowledged the heavy workload as well as the wide variety and complexity of cases that Fred had undertaken. She assessed a rating of 4—Superior—for what he had done and a rating of 3—Fully Effective—for how he had gone about his work. The documentation showing these ratings was signed off by both Kim and Fred.

Kim advised Fred that Ly wished to have a discussion with him, as he did not have a one-on-one discussion with Ly as he had been away on holiday.

Fred soon received an email from Ly, copied to Kim:
> In order to maximise what can be achieved in our discussion, please provide me and Kim with correspondence in relation to the first private ruling case, why you thought it should be referred to Transfer Pricing, and a chronology of your involvement in the case.

Fred responded with the following email:
> As requested, I attach correspondence concerning the private ruling

case and a chronology of my involvement. The private ruling case involved transfer pricing issues and it was therefore mandatory to refer the case to Transfer Pricing.

During morning tea break, Kim received a telephone call. She left the coffee shop and was seen pacing up and down outside with her mobile phone to her ear.

Fred was in the library when Kim approached him. "Ly wants to cancel the telephone hook-up scheduled for this morning. He wants me to go through the documentation you emailed to us for the purposes of the hook-up and to go through all the guidance material relevant to the role of staff in Tax Law. He also stated that I should micro-manage you and repeated his view that you wouldn't even rate a 3 and 3," Kim said.

Fred was shocked. "Did you advise Ly that we've already had my mid-year review discussion and that you rated me a 4 and 3?"

"No, I didn't," Kim responded.

Confused, Fred asked, "Why not?"

"Ly was wound up," Kim meekly replied, "and I didn't want to upset him any further."

Fred jumped up from his seat. "This is bullshit!" he exclaimed and walked off.

Fred felt he was being bullied so he contacted the Harassment Officer, Colin Deeks. He briefed Colin on what had transpired and Colin reflected on what he was told.

"Based on what you have said, it sounds like you are being harassed and it is of concern and a surprise to me that your manager doesn't appear to be giving you any support whatsoever," Colin said.

The moment that Colin uttered the words, "you are being harassed," the gravity of the situation immediately weighed on Fred.

"You can register the matter with Tax Office Complaints or complete an Incident Report," Colin continued. "I can also attend any meeting for moral support."

"Thanks, Colin," Fred replied, his voice choked up with emotion. "I'll think about it."

Colin sent Fred an email that included a hyperlink to the Tax Office counselling service.

Fred then stumbled across an old workmate, Morris Levy.

Morris looked at him in concern. "Are you all right?" Morris asked.

Fred filled him in with the day's events.

"You should consult with the union," Morris immediately suggested.

"I haven't been a member of a union for years," Fred advised. "In any case, the matter has already commenced so I can't expect the union to take me on."

"Fred, you are being pursued by senior executives. You can't expect the Harassment Officer to counter them. Your only chance is to join the union," Morris stated authoritatively. "I'll give you the details of John Lazarus. Why don't you contact him, tell him the situation and see if he's willing to help. What have you got to lose?"

Later, Morris sent Fred an email that contained John's contact details. Fred was reflecting on the matter when he was copied into an email from Kim to Ly, which read:

> Please confirm when you will be available to reschedule the discussion with me and Fred. Will you wish us to fly to Canberra or will you be flying down to meet with us? Also, given I'm likely to need to take time off next week, can we meet in the week beginning 6 March?

Fred suggested that Kim check her dates. Kim followed up with another email, where she wrote: "Sorry, obviously meant 6 April".

Fred didn't need too much more convincing that Kim was a nincompoop and that the union was his only hope of support, so he sent off an email to John Lazarus. He wrote:

> I discussed my situation with a work colleague (a union member) and he suggested that I should contact you. I'd be interested in joining the union if it could assist me. An issue was first raised by a senior executive before Christmas and it has been raised again in the context of performance management. I am not a union member but I wish to enquire whether the union could assist if I were to join the union now.

Fred was on tenterhooks as he waited for a reply to come through. It soon did via email. John wrote:

> We would need to have a discussion about the situation, what you may want us to do, what is involved and your commitment to supporting our union in turn. We can chat tomorrow if you like.

Fred could hardly wait until 10.00 am the next day, when he rang John. He briefed John on the situation and John reflected for a short time before he commented.

"These senior executives really seem to have it in for you. Are you sure the matter isn't more serious? I mean, you haven't embezzled a heap of money and got it hidden somewhere?"

Fred was not really in the mood for jokes. "Of course not. If I had embezzled a heap of money, I'd hardly be here talking with you."

John then made a series of statements, as if he was thinking out loud. "I don't know these senior executives, but if they are as aggressive as you make out, they may be liable to do anything. If they are looking to sack you, the unfair dismissal laws may be more restrictive as you are an Executive Level 2 officer with a salary over $100 000. The fact that they are senior executives would mean that the other senior executives would automatically side with them."

The bleak picture that John was painting was not very encouraging to Fred and he was starting to despair. John continued. "It may be tough, but I think we can assist you. However, you must be prepared to pay one back-year union dues, commit to stay a union member and, most importantly, be prepared to fight this thing. What do you say?"

Fred was unequivocal with his response. "I accept these terms and I'm prepared to do whatever it takes to fight this thing!"

At 12.05 pm on Thursday 26 March, John sent an email inviting Fred to become a member of the union with the agreed terms and a concluding statement: "Just complete the form, send it to the union office with your payment and keep in touch".

By the end of the day, Fred was a member of the union.

Chapter 37 – Another Mid-Year Review

Kim approached Fred to involve him in a case. "I'd like you to supervise Ralph Flynn on a public ruling. I'd do it myself, but you have current experience working on public rulings," she explained.

Kim, you would never have done it yourself, Fred thought, *and it's because you're a lazy heifer.*

Fred discussed the case with Ralph, who indicated that he should have the latest version of the public ruling within a week.

On 1 April, Kim approached Fred. "Could you provide me with a summary of your work on hand and the work you have completed in the year to date upon which your mid-year discussion was based?" Kim asked.

Fred had previously provided this information for his mid-year review meeting with Kim so he thought it unusual that she was asking for it again.

"Is this an April fool's joke?" asked Fred.

"No, it's not a joke," Kim replied.

"What's the purpose of this request?" Fred then asked.

"Ly has requested this information."

Fred was wondering what was going on.

"Is this request being made just of me or is it also being asked of others?" Fred queried.

Kim seemed hesitant. "It would be for everyone," she replied, although she didn't sound sure, which made Fred suspicious.

Fred sent off an email with his list of cases to Kim.

Soon after, Ralph sent Fred an email, which attached a draft public ruling. Ralph noted: "I'm keen to have the ruling forwarded to Rick Hudson, the approving officer, before Rick goes on leave".

The question in the public ruling had been approved by the senior executives and Fred considered the decision to be correct. He then emailed Ralph, where he wrote: "I've reviewed your draft public ruling and I think that it's taking shape. It should be okay to send it on to Rick for an initial look".

The following morning, Fred overheard Kim on the phone with

Ly. Fred knew it was Ly as his voice emitted to such a high volume that it was audible to him a metre away. Fred then went off for a tea break. When he returned, he noted that Kim had left.

Fred saw Zoran Varga, who sat across from Kim. "Has Kim left?" he asked Zoran.

"Oh boy, has she left," Zoran replied. "It's one of the rare occasions that I've heard Kim raise her voice. She stated something to the effect 'if you want something to be said to Fred, why don't you tell him yourself?' She then slammed down the phone and stormed out!"

Fred didn't like the sound of that and it made him wonder what Kim wasn't prepared to tell him and, as she refused to follow Ly's instruction, what Ly was going to do now.

*　*　*

Ralph sent an email to Rick, copied to Fred, where he wrote: "Please find attached my public ruling, which has already been reviewed by Fred for your consideration and approval".

Later that day, Rick sent an email to Ralph and Fred that stated: "I've had a quick read and it is right. I'll look at it properly on my return from leave".

Fred then received an email from Ly, copied to Benny and Kim. It read:

> I've discussed your mid-year review with Kim Weasel and Benny Heel. We have decided that Benny will conduct your mid-year review. Kim and I will participate. Organise travel to Canberra next Wednesday and provide the following information by COB Friday:
> - a listing of matters you have worked on this year to date;
> - an example of your contribution to each matter;
> - an explanation of why you concluded that all the documents were not relevant for the current private ruling case;
> - an explanation of why you concluded there were no precedential issues in the previous private ruling case;
> - your performance agreement; and
> - your officer feedback report.

Fred read Ly's email and was amazed. What Ly was instructing him to do required at least a week to pull together. Plus Ly wanted him to arrange flights to Canberra. If Fred had any doubt about Ly, this email put it beyond doubt in his mind. *This guy is crazy.*

Fred sent a copy of the email to John and they arranged a meeting for later that day.

Fred was the first to speak. "This is ridiculous! Nobody could amass all the information he has requested in a couple of days. He also wants me to organise flights and go to Canberra. I've already had my mid-year review and Benny isn't even my manager!"

John was pensive before he replied. "He may not be your immediate manager; however, he is a senior executive in the line of authority so he can do your mid-year review on that basis. The issue I have is this: if you have already had your mid-year review, I don't think there is any scope to do another one. In which case, he would not have any authority to do so."

John took another moment before he continued. "I find it strange that these senior executives are going to these lengths just because they have taken exception with the way you dealt with a case, particularly where your immediate manager was kept abreast of it. I think that you are entitled to know exactly what the problem is. I would draft two emails. The first being a freedom of information request for any emails Ly has concerning you that you do not already have and the second challenging his authority for undertaking a second performance review."

Fred was about to head off to act on John's instructions when John made another comment. "Fred, we don't know how this matter is going to develop so I would recommend that you commence to have regular check-ups with your GP."

Fred didn't think too much about the comment but he agreed. He then drafted the two emails, one for the freedom of information request and the other challenging the authority for undertaking a second performance review. He passed them by John before he sent them off.

Fred was awaiting the next bombshell to hit when Kim stated that she wished to have a word with him in private. They went to an interview room.

"Ly mentioned how he was in Benny's office when Benny received copies of the emails you sent them. Ly wants me to pass on the following messages," Kim advised. "Benny and Ly acknowledge that you have involved the union and they accept this as your right. They will deal with the freedom of information request. They both noted the view that they did not have authority to conduct another mid-year review and they would look into this."

Fred attended a doctor's appointment with his family doctor, Dr Papas, and explained his situation at work.

"So how is this situation affecting your health?" the doctor asked.

"I can't say whether it's directly affecting my health but I've experienced upset stomachs, loss of weight, trouble sleeping and I actually fear going to work as I don't know what might happen next," Fred explained.

Dr Papas took a moment in reflection. "That's interesting," he eventually stated.

Fred was offended by the comment and his reaction was spontaneous. "Interesting? It's more than interesting—it's hell!"

"Of course, it would be; however, I think that your situation can only be alleviated by addressing the matter at work," Dr Papas stated.

"My union representative mentioned that it would be important to have my health condition monitored," Fred advised.

"I'll give you the names of a couple of psychologists who may assist you in dealing with the matter at work," Dr Papas suggested.

Fred left the doctor's office unimpressed with the treatment he had been given. He was even less impressed when he followed up with the psychologists the doctor had listed for him. He couldn't find one of them and the other specialised in family break-ups.

Ly sent an email to Kim, copied to Benny and Fred, which noted: "I would like you to submit the documentation of Fred's mid-year review and a copy of the record of mid-year review discussion".

Fred met with John over lunch.

"Have you visited your GP and is he monitoring your health?" John enquired.

"Yes, I did visit him," Fred advised, "but he didn't monitor my health; he suggested that I needed to address the matter at work."

John was uncompromising in his response. "This is not good enough. You need to have your health monitored. You need to find another doctor."

Later in the day, Kim sent an email to Ly and Fred. The subject was Fred's mid-year review and it attached the documentation requested by Ly, being the summary of Fred's work, the officer feedback form and the record of mid-year review template. Fred noted that Kim's comments and rating of 4 and 3 was per their mid-year review discussion.

In the midst of all Fred's calamities, Kim assigned a case to

Gordon Hirsch, an Executive Level 2.2 in Adelaide, which Fred was working on with Lauren Stamis and Dianne Fallon, two Tax Law officers in Perth. As Dianne was going on long-term leave, Gordon would be replacing her. Dianne had completed a detailed report on the case at the direction of Allen Lion, the senior executive responsible for Interpretative views. Gordon reviewed the case and organised a telephone hook-up with Lauren and Fred.

"I think I can justify an alternative view," Gordon suggested.

Lauren was first to respond. "Dianne has written a detailed report, with which Fred and I assisted. It considered an alternative view, but concluded that the law didn't support it."

Fred was quick to support Lauren's statement. "That's right. Dianne, Lauren and I agreed that the legislation does not appear to support the alternative view."

Gordon was unmoved. "I've read Dianne's report and, while I agree with the bulk of it, I consider that we can rely on two rulings that provide a precedent for an alternative view."

This time, Fred was first to react. "We also considered these rulings. In fact, I understand Dianne was heavily involved in them. However, those cases are clearly distinguishable from ours."

Gordon was adamant that he could support an alternative view. "I will draft an Interpretative View for your consideration," he said.

"What if we don't agree with it?" Lauren queried.

"Well, Allen will have the last word," Gordon replied.

Gordon soon produced his draft Interpretative View and sent it to Lauren and Fred via email.

You've got to be joking; this is ridiculous! Fred thought. *Gordon has just cut and pasted slabs from the other rulings and jumped to his desired conclusion without any justification whatsoever.*

Fred sent a detailed response in an email to Gordon, with a copy to Lauren, explaining the rationale for debunking Gordon's alternative view. Gordon subsequently sent off an email to Allen, copied to Lauren and Fred. Fred was not impressed with how Gordon had worded his email. Gordon had noted that Dianne and Lauren had produced the report, with no mention that Fred was also involved. Gordon also noted: "Fred is of the view that a constructive basis for an alternative view is not possible given how the legislation is drafted".

Fred was most upset that Gordon had misrepresented his

comments and was tempted to clarify the situation, but thought he would leave well alone. However, Allen sent an email to Fred asking him to explain himself.

Fred immediately responded in an email, where he wrote:

> I wouldn't go so far as to say that the alternative view is not possible given how the legislation is drafted, although I note that I am ascribed these words in Gordon's email. My comments actually referred to my view that there is no legislative basis that supports the position in the Interpretative View. I have attached the email where I provided my thoughts to Gordon, which I hope assists with your query.

Allen sent an email that simply stated: "This is helpful".

Ly then sent an email with attached documents in response to Fred's freedom of information request. Fred examined the documents and they did not reveal anything untoward, which left him mystified of the catalyst for the crusade by the senior executives.

Chapter 38 – A Mid-Year Appraisal

Fred soon received yet another email from Ly, copied to Benny and Kim. Ly wrote:

> I was surprised to receive your email refusing to meet with Benny, Kim and me in Canberra. Benny and I must meet with you and Kim in person as soon as possible. We need to relay our concerns about what you have done on the first private ruling case. We also need to achieve mutual expectations. Further, you need to show us how you perform your duties. I want you and Kim to travel to Canberra next Wednesday and I want you to provide the information I previously requested by COB next Monday.

Kim promptly replied to confirm her attendance at the meeting.

Fred reviewed the email and thought how deceitful Ly was. *You initially communicated through Kim that you were to review the question concerning the authority to conduct another mid-year review and then come back to accuse me of refusing to meet with you.*

Fred conferred with John before he sent an email to Ly, copied to Benny, Kim and John. Fred wrote:

> In my email I did not to refuse to meet with you. In terms of relaying your concerns about what I have done on the private ruling case, I believe that I have a right to know your concerns. I therefore request that you put your concerns in writing. In order for your expectations to be mutually agreed upon, I request that you explain in writing what your expectations are. In respect of how I perform my duties, I have advice from my union that you do not have the authority to conduct another review. Based on what I have outlined above, it is inappropriate to provide you with the information you have requested. I propose that a date for a meeting not be set until the matters I have raised have been addressed.

Fred's health was deteriorating and this was not lost on Carlo Giro, a union representative.

"You don't look very well," Carlo commented. "You really should take some time off."

"You may be right," Fred responded. "I just need to find a supportive doctor."

"You should visit my doctor," Carlo suggested. "He's a decent guy with a military background so he's had solid experience and I'm sure he'd give you sound treatment."

Fred didn't need too much convincing and visited Dr Wells after work.

"I've had a few problems at work and a patient of yours, Carlo Giro, suggested that it might be worth visiting you," Fred stated.

"Yes, I know Carlo, he's been coming to see me for some time," Dr Wells advised.

Fred proceeded to give an explanation of his predicament and, as he spoke, Dr Wells asked selective questions.

"What about your parents?" he asked.

"Both of my parents have passed away," Fred replied.

"Do you live with anyone?"

"No, I live alone."

"Do you have any family and, if so, do you see them much?"

"I have a sister and I hear from her on a weekly basis. She's really good in that she keeps in touch with me, but she's got her own family."

Dr Wells took a long stare at Fred as if he could tell as much from Fred's eyes as he could tell from what Fred said. Then he began giving some advice. "I'm sure you've got good friends at work; make sure you keep on talking with them. Your sister may have a family of her own, but you're her family too so don't just rely on her contacting you; you ring her. I'm sure she'd appreciate it and you could do with the support."

"I've seen my regular doctor and he suggested that I needed to deal with the situation at work," Fred advised. "Although he did suggest that I could see a psychologist."

"I understand you have a free counselling service provided by your employer," Dr Wells replied. "You should make use of it. What about your manager?"

"My manager?" Fred repeated. "She hasn't provided any support and has basically just stepped aside to allow senior executives to take over."

"That doesn't sound right," Dr Wells said. "Where's the chain of command?"

Fred shrugged.

Dr Wells didn't have to hear that the union representative

recommended that Fred should have his doctor monitor his health; he did it automatically.

"Your blood pressure reading is 120 over 80, which is perfect. However, I want to see you next week. Have you got much sick leave?"

"I've got almost a year's accumulated sick leave," Fred advised, rolling down his sleeve. "I would appreciate an attendance certificate for this visit, but I don't want any further time off. I need to continue to go to work to fight this thing."

"You would think that employers would support guys like you," the doctor commented.

"Thanks, Doctor," Fred responded. "I really do appreciate the support."

Fred left the doctor's clinic and, for the first time in a long while, he felt a little reassured.

The moment Fred got to work the next day, he arranged an appointment with the Tax Office counselling service.

Later that morning, Fred received an email from Ly, copied to Benny and Kim. Ly wrote:

> You refused to meet with us in Canberra by not organising to travel, stating that you had advice that we did not have authority to conduct an appraisal, and not providing the information requested ...

[Ly's email went on in a form of writing rant, running into pages.]

> ...You must meet with us in person. Kim has already confirmed her attendance. Please confirm by COB tomorrow that you will meet with us next Wednesday and provide the information requested by COB next Monday.

Fred referred the email to John and contacted him by telephone.

"Ly's email is very convoluted and difficult to understand," John said.

Fred explained his understanding of the email and what he thought may have been the concerns with the private ruling cases. They then worked together in an effort to determine the most appropriate wording in reply.

During the course of drafting a reply, Fred felt compelled to make an admission. "John, this is all becoming a bit overwhelming."

"Regardless of how overwhelming it may seem, you need to treat this whole process as a game," John suggested.

Fred understood that John was trying to help but he felt exasperated. "I find it hard to treat my career as a game. I wish this matter could go away so I could just concentrate on doing my job."

Fred subsequently sent an email to Ly, copied to Benny, Kim and John. He wrote:

> My email was not intended to be a refusal to meet with you; rather, I wanted to resolve certain issues prior to a date for a meeting being set. I agree to meet with you in Canberra next Wednesday and will provide the information requested by next Monday.

Fred was taking a breather when an email was sent by Rick Hudson to Ralph Flynn and Fred concerning Ralph's public ruling. Rick noted: "I have used tracked changes to highlight some suggestions for your consideration".

Fred looked at the latest version and was astonished by the extent of the tracked changes. He then realised that the version Ralph used was based on a different question to that approved by senior management.

Rick could have simply advised us that the wrong question had been used and let Ralph make the changes. Instead, he went out of his way to highlight the changes himself. Fred thought. *I wonder what he's up to.*

Fred immediately contacted Ralph.

"The question that you based the public ruling on isn't what was approved by senior management. Why didn't you use the approved question?" Fred asked.

"I used the question along the lines of earlier discussions," Ralph responded.

"But Ralph, that question had been superseded by the version approved by senior management. I can't understand why you didn't just use the approved question."

"Oh well," Ralph responded in a blasé fashion.

Soon after, Fred was in the library when Rick appeared.

"Thanks for picking up on the fact that the wrong question was used in Ralph's public ruling," Fred told Rick.

"That's okay," Rick said. "However, should we be copying Benny Heel into these emails?"

Fred considered Rick's question to be most odd. "Benny will be required to sign off on the public ruling in due course and at the appropriate time; why would you want to include him in the emails in the ruling's early development?" Fred queried.

"Oh, I was just wondering," Rick said with a wry smile.

The following Monday evening, Fred was experiencing some chest discomfort that quickly got worse. He was having trouble breathing and it got to the point where he thought he may be experiencing a heart episode.

Dialling the triple zero emergency telephone number, Fred described his symptoms as tingling and numbness in his fingers, numbness in his left arm, breathlessness and discomfort in his chest.

"We will send an ambulance; please leave the front light on and the front door open," the operator instructed.

The ambulance soon arrived and the officers examined Fred. "Your blood pressure is a little high at 140 over 90; however, the tests have come up normal. We don't think you're having a heart attack. Would you happen to be experiencing any stress in your life?" one of the ambulance officers asked.

"Well, things at work are a little difficult at the moment," Fred softly admitted.

"If you could get rid of that stress at work, it may remedy your condition," the ambulance officer suggested.

After Fred's experience of the evening before and the fact that the ambulance officers were of the view that he may be experiencing stress at work, he wondered whether he should be completing an incident report. He enquired at work and they confirmed that he should. He was still unsure and decided to raise the matter with John.

"You are most definitely obliged to complete an incident report," John said. "However, I don't think this will necessarily help you. Completing the report may be useful if you wish to claim your sick leave on Commonwealth Care, but it will result in additional red tape with Personnel and it will also raise suspicions by management that you are faking it to detract from the performance issues."

"I have heaps of accumulated sick leave," Fred reasoned, "and I certainly don't need any added red tape to worry about. Maybe I'll leave it for now."

Fred attended his appointment with counsellor Sarah Lane from the Tax Office counselling service.

"So, what's the problem?" she enquired.

Fred gave Sarah the background. She seemed surprised that his manager provided no support and that senior executives were pursuing him so aggressively.

"You should seek assistance from your GP and have them consider a referral to a psychologist," Sarah suggested.

Fred was astonished by Sarah's comment. "But aren't you a

psychologist?" he asked.

"Yes, I am," Sarah confirmed. "However, as we are sponsored by the Tax Office, there is a limit to the extent of assistance we can provide."

Later that day, Fred visited Dr Wells. "I'm struggling at the moment and my condition seems to be getting worse. Yesterday evening, I experienced some chest discomfort and called an ambulance. They checked my blood pressure, which they indicated was a little high and suggested that it may be due to stress," Fred advised.

"I'm not surprised to hear about your symptoms," Dr Wells stated. He checked Fred's blood pressure. "Your blood pressure is indeed high at 150 over 90. Given your current health condition, I'd suggest that you take the rest of the week off."

Fred considered the recommendation for a moment. "I need to complete some work this week and I have to fly interstate, so I'd prefer to struggle through," he said. "However, I appreciate that I have your support if I need it."

"Okay, but you make sure that you come back next week so I can check on you," Dr Wells stated.

Fred sent off his documentation to Ly, copied to Benny and Kim. He also arranged the flights to Canberra for Kim and himself.

Fred discussed the impending meeting with John, who recommended that he should have union representation and made himself available to attend via telephone.

"Don't be concerned if initially I don't say too much," John said. "I want to listen to how the senior executives play things out."

Fred advised Ly via email that he had invited his union representative to attend the meeting and he was hit with another special delivery email from Ly, copied to Benny, Kim and a person named Alison Moore. Ly wrote:

> The meeting is expected to involve the discussion of the affairs of taxpayers. Accordingly, I am prevented under the secrecy provisions from agreeing to John Lazarus participating in the meeting. Alison Moore will be taking notes of the meeting and a draft record will be made available to ensure that it comprises a correct record of what was discussed. You will be provided with a copy of the final record.

Fred forwarded the email to John, who was quickly on the phone. "The secrecy provisions cannot be used as a reason to deny an officer union representation," John automatically stated. He recommended a response, which Fred used as the basis for the email he sent to Ly, copied to Benny, Alison, Kim and John. Fred wrote:

> I appreciate that the meeting may involve the discussion of taxpayer affairs; however, I understand that this does not restrict my rights to union representation and that I am entitled to union representation where the meeting concerns my performance.

Fred attended his next appointment with the Tax Office counselling service. By this time, the pressure of the situation was starting to show on him.

"It may help if you try to place what's happening into some sort of perspective," Sarah suggested. "What do you think would be the worst thing that can happen to you at this meeting?"

"I don't really know as I don't know what the problem is. I couldn't imagine anyone going to these extreme lengths unless it was something serious. If it is serious, maybe I could be demoted or even sacked," Fred said.

"Would life be that bad if you were to be demoted?" Sarah asked.

Fred tried to come to terms with the prospect, but it seemed too preposterous. "Of course it would be bad. I've always been considered to be a hard worker and a high achiever. To be demoted when I know I don't deserve it would be unbearable."

"Well, I expect it wouldn't be that bad, but if it were, it still wouldn't be the end of the world," Sarah stated, although this didn't assist in allaying Fred's grave concerns.

The day before the Canberra meeting Fred thought it might be advisable to have a chat with Kim as she had been conspicuously silent throughout the whole affair.

"Kim, this situation has been particularly difficult for me as I do not know what Ly's problem is and he has not been willing to provide me with any details whatsoever." Fred came to a pause. Kim did not exhibit any reaction and did not respond.

"Can you shed any light on what I can expect from Ly in Canberra?" Fred asked.

"This situation has been difficult for me as well," Kim replied. "But I honestly don't know what he has planned for the meeting."

"Well, whatever happens, I hope that I can count on your support," Fred said.

Kim reflected before she eventually spoke. "Yeah, I'll give you my support."

Fred returned to the workplace, while Kim went elsewhere. As soon as Fred was visible, Theo Onassis approached him.

"I told Kim that you were one of the best performers and that she should support you. She said that she would," Theo said.

Christine Suresh overheard Theo's statements. "I hope she does support you," Christine commented. "However, I've worked with Kim before and based on everything I've seen and heard of her, she has shown that she does little to support anyone else; she's only interested in looking after herself."

Chloe Callas was also present and expressed her sympathies. "This whole thing is so unfair. They've picked on the wrong guy as you are one of the best performers I've worked with. Women in power can be real bitches, men in power can be absolute bastards, but people who suck up to them can be the worst."

Martin Chang was an officer who had joined the team in Tax Law in recent times. He seemed disturbed by the situation and also spoke to Fred. "Ly is the boss so you should obey him," Martin said.

"Normally, I would agree with you," Fred replied. "However, what if I believe that I have done nothing wrong and that what he is doing is wrong?"

Martin did not reply to Fred's question, but he did whisper some advice. "In Chinese culture, wearing red underwear is considered to give you luck."

Fred left the office and went home by tram. He got off at Bell Street in Coburg and, as he was passing Dimmeys department store, he noticed that there were underpants on special. He walked in and saw red underpants for $1 a pair. He purchased the remaining stock and, from that day on, he wore red underwear to work every day.

John made contact with a senior tax officer who specialised in industrial relations. The gossip going around was that Ly resisted Fred having union representation until higher level senior executives put him in his place and he eventually, although reluctantly, caved in.

Word of Fred's calamity with Ly was getting around the Tax Office nationally.

"Your matter has reached Brisbane office and the gossip going around is that there is this Cappuccino guy who is standing up to the bastard!" a visiting officer from interstate said, smiling.

"Well, I guess the gossip is not completely wrong," Fred said with a grin. "My surname is that of an Italian drink; they just got the wrong drink."

Chapter 39 – A Private Ruling Rolls On

The applicant's representatives of the private ruling made arrangements for some documents to be sent to the Tax Office; however, other documents could only be made available to be accessed on site.

Barbara confirmed that all documents were required but she would not be available to examine them. It was therefore left for Jimmy and Fred to attend on behalf of Tax Law, with Gary Serpico representing the Business Line. The available tax officers proceeded to the applicant's office to examine the documents.

There was a general discussion before various applicant representatives explained the documentation. Some of the documents were in folders that were easy to photocopy. The Tax Office representatives were then presented with volumes of documents that took up the whole boardroom table. Fred looked over at Jimmy, who seemed at a total loss as to how to approach the situation.

Fred didn't feel inclined to assist Jimmy, but Jimmy had been mulling over what to do for some time.

"We can photocopy the contents pages, peruse the documentation and then write up a description," Fred eventually proposed.

Jimmy appeared to be buoyed by the suggestion and that was what they did. As they proceeded, a representative of the company began a conversation.

"I don't understand what all this information has to do with the ruling request," the representative said. "Why did you want to examine all this documentation?"

Jimmy was at a loss for words and Fred felt no compulsion to make any comment; however, Gary came to Jimmy's aid.

"If we are to rule then we need to examine all the documents referred to in the private ruling request," Gary said.

The representative did not seem convinced and Fred could understand why.

Returning to work, Fred reviewed the documents and considered that they had no bearing on the interpretative issue concerning the private ruling. He updated his report for the documents examined and sent the latest version of the report in an email. There was then a lull in activity.

Fred sent an email to Barbara and Jimmy, where he noted:

> I will be on leave from 29 May to 26 June. I expect that we should be able to finalise the Tax Law position prior to 29 May. Could Barbara, yourself and I discuss the best way forward?

Shortly after, Barbara sent an email to Jimmy and Fred. She noted:

> We need to finalise our position before Fred goes on leave. Our current view is that some of the profits are attributable to Australia but we don't know how much. Maybe a private ruling isn't the appropriate product.

As Fred read Barbara's email, it got him thinking. *Well done, Einstein. It took you four months to work out something that someone with a basic knowledge should have worked out from the outset!*

Jimmy then sent an email to Barbara and Fred. He wrote:

> I agree with your comments, Barbara. An Advance Pricing Arrangement would have been the best product. However, I had a chat with Benny and he's keen on finding some way to say that all the profits are attributable to Australia.

Fred considered the two emails from Barbara and Jimmy to be most telling. They confirmed his previous suspicions as to what was going on. It was now clear to him that Benny was calling the shots and he would only settle with an outcome where all income was attributable to Australia. This would avoid the need to apportion the attributable income, sidestep the transfer pricing issues and circumvent the need for an Advance Pricing Arrangement.

Fred thought about the emails as he left the office late Friday afternoon.

Barbara, Jimmy and Fred had a hook-up on Monday afternoon of the following week. Barbara and Jimmy seemed most unhappy that they couldn't come up with a credible argument to make all the profits attributable to Australia. They then stated that they may seek further information.

Chapter 40 – An Ambush

Kim and Fred flew to Canberra and presented themselves for the meeting. As they entered the room, there was a fat man with coke-bottle glasses and frizzy hair that sprouted from the sides of an otherwise bald head. The man was wearing drab, grey slacks and a cream coloured, open-necked shirt that appeared as if it had never come in contact with an iron—it was very crinkly.

Fred was about to ask if he could help the man when Kim spoke.

"Hello, Ly," she said.

Ly? Fred wondered. *He's a senior executive? I thought he may have been a cleaner.*

A woman and a man then entered the room and everyone introduced themselves. The woman was Alison Moore and the man was Benny Heel. When Fred laid eyes on Benny, he was taken aback by his appearance.

Benny had thinning, jet black hair with a greasy comb-over. He was lanky and bony with his torso and limbs all crooked and twisted. His clothes draped his body, appearing many sizes too large. He wore a white shirt with sleeve garters and black slacks with suspenders. Fred considered it appropriate that Benny completed his ensemble with a black bow tie, which was crooked. However, Benny's most striking feature was his beady, dark brown eyes that seemed to be locked on Fred.

Benny ensured that people sat in his desired seating positions. Kim was to sit to his right, Alison to his left, Ly was to sit by his side and Fred was to be seated directly opposite him.

"So I guess I get the hot seat," Fred quipped.

Benny was completely expressionless and his focus on Fred was unrelenting until he was momentarily distracted when John dialled into the meeting.

Ly gave some preliminary introductions. "The purpose of this meeting is as set out in my email and to fulfil my responsibilities as a senior executive. Further, Benny needs to be across high-risk private ruling cases, being one of the highest priority special projects," Ly said. "As we will now proceed to discuss the private rulings, I will hand over to Benny."

Benny's beady eyes widened instantaneously at his cue and he wasted no time. He handed out pre-prepared folders that contained tagged documents. He was very deliberate as he gave his initial explanation. "Fred, I wish to more clearly understand the decisions you made in the private rulings, to discuss the obligations and duties to progressing a private ruling, and to go through the relevant corporate guidelines in the folders that are relevant to understanding your responsibilities."

Benny hardly took a breath before continuing. "We need to have a shared, clear understanding of the aspects of the corporate guidelines that are relevant to the decisions you made in the private ruling cases."

Benny then embarked on a barrage of questions that Fred had difficulty keeping up with. He hardly had any chance to reply as Benny intervened and expressed his own views of what Fred should have done. Fred felt he was subject to an interrogation.

Benny then honed his attack. "My first major concern is that you concluded that something as significant and complicated as this arrangement was not a precedential matter. It was obviously a significant issue. Why didn't you feel the need as the responsible Tax Law officer to find out more?"

Fred tried to pick up on the most important points. "There were clearly no precedential issues identified in the case. Furthermore, as there was a transfer pricing issue and based on the relevant Tax Office guidance, it was mandatory for the case to be referred to Transfer Pricing."

Benny was quick to counter. "Fred, the transfer pricing matter is secondary to having first determined the ruling."

Benny's being ridiculous, Fred thought. *He doesn't understand—maybe he's just not listening or maybe he just doesn't care.*

Benny went on and on in a tirade, pressing the same points over and over; however, his regurgitations did not make his statements any more rational to Fred. He then reiterated his view once more. "Fred, you should have determined that the case was precedential or, as a senior officer, you should have been interested in becoming involved."

Fred's mind was going into overdrive as he considered most of

Benny's statements to be absurd. "There were no precedential issues identified in the case, everyone was of this view and the basis of involving oneself because it is a significant case or a case of interest is not supported by any Tax Office guidelines whatsoever."

Benny quoted particular paragraphs from a number of Tax Office guidance to press the point that Fred should have done more to assist with the case. Fred's response, that he believed he gave the appropriate level of assistance up to the time he went on leave, was routinely dismissed.

Fred noted that Ly had a constant smirk. Kim was silent and looking into space, which prompted Fred to try to involve her. "Kim had been briefed on all my decisions and was copied into all my emails. She never raised any concerns at all."

"Well, that would have depended on what you told her," Benny quickly replied.

Fred was confused as to what he meant by this statement and he looked over to Kim. However, Kim seemed to have found an attractive spot on the ceiling. Her eyes were fixated on it and she stayed silent.

"You did not obtain all the relevant documents in the private ruling case as I had instructed," Benny stated, and then went through a number of paragraphs in various Tax Office guidance and court case decisions. "All documents under a contract must be obtained in order to rule," he concluded.

Fred had heard a number of ridiculous statements by Benny during the meeting, but he felt his anger boiling over upon hearing his last statement. "Excuse me, I have never heard of the suggestion that all documents referred to in a contract were required in order to rule. Where is this written?" he asked.

"Oh Fred, it should be obvious to a senior officer that all documents under a contract must be obtained before one can rule. It's obvious and implicit," Benny stated in a most sarcastic, demeaning and supercilious manner.

To Fred's amazement, Kim finally uttered some words. "We've been going for almost three hours now. Don't you think it's an appropriate time to have a break?"

Ly agreed, but before they broke for lunch, he made a final statement. "I've recently decided that I will change the reporting requirements so Fred reports to Benny for this reporting period.

Fred, as for all this information you have provided about the cases you have worked on this year, it will be useful for Benny in going forward."

Fred was astonished by Ly's decision that he report to Benny and could not believe how Ly had made him produce all the information in time for the meeting and now he wasn't even going to refer to any of it. *What a bastard,* he thought. *How vindictive can a person get?*

Just before they went for lunch, John asked Fred to give him a call during the break. Fred exited the room with Kim. "Gee, I'm surprised that Ly made the decision that I am to report to Benny," Fred said.

"Yeah, it's a surprise to me too," Kim responded.

"I have never heard nor been aware of a view that all documents referred to in contracts were required before the Commissioner could rule," Fred stated.

"No, neither have I," Kim revealed.

Fred stopped dead in his tracks and looked at Kim as she strode off. *You bitch,* he thought. *Why didn't you say that during the meeting? So much for your support!*

Fred contacted John during the break and John spoke off the bat.

"The overwhelming reaction I have is that these senior executives are bullying you. I have to know at this point whether you are willing for them to have their way or whether you wish to fight this."

Fred's reply was automatic and emphatic. "As far as I'm concerned, I've done nothing wrong so I feel I should fight this."

Alison, Kim and Fred were the first to return. Ly and Benny arrived soon after and then John was telephoned.

Benny continued from where he left off. "So, having led Fred through the various corporate guidelines that state that officers must request all relevant information in order to rule, it is obvious that this requires all documents referred to in a contract."

"Just because you are of this view does not mean that it is right," John stated.

Benny's eyes and mouth opened wide concurrently—like a blowfish. Ly reacted by puffing up his cheeks with his eyes bulging. Fred thought they looked like two children who had been caught out or hadn't got everything their own way.

"It's important that all material facts are obtained by an officer in order to rule," Ly stated.

"I wish to have a word with Fred alone," John requested. "Could everyone else please leave the room?" The others looked at each other and murmured as they left.

As soon as Fred gave the all clear, John spoke.

"Well, if you are going to fight, I'll request for Ly to put in writing the reasons for you to have to report to Benny," John said. "You'll need to write a report to counter the accusations and you'll also need to address all the legal points that have been raised, including the point that Ly made about the materiality of the information."

"I'm prepared to write a report to counter their arguments," Fred responded. "But as for the materiality point that Ly made, it's wrong. The obligation for requesting additional information is based on whether it is required in order to rule, not its materiality."

"Are you suggesting that a senior executive doesn't know what he's talking about?" John asked.

"Exactly," Fred replied. He got up and summoned the others back to the room.

"Fred is concerned about the decision to change reporting arrangements. He will request that Ly puts in writing the reasons for this decision. We can put this request in writing," John stated. "Fred will then write submissions on the issues that have been raised in the meeting and these will be escalated to whomever is appropriate."

No-one had anything more to say and the meeting was called to a close.

When Fred returned to work on the morning of the next day, members of his team were quick to quiz him.

"How did the meeting go?"

"I wouldn't call it a meeting," Fred responded. "It was more like an ambush."

Chapter 41 – Back to the Private Ruling

Fred noted an email from Barbara, copied to Jimmy. Barbara wrote:

> I've been working on another version of our report. I'll hand it to you now to work on. There's not a right or wrong way to write a report but the attached will give you an idea of how I'd approach it.

Barbara's version of the report made changes to the format and the contents, while the legal analysis appeared the same. Fred read the report with some curiosity.

Barbara's been instructing me on what to do with my report and now she has taken it upon herself to work on a separate report, Fred thought. *What's she playing at?*

Benny sent an email to Barbara, Jimmy and Fred, with the attachment of an email from the Business Line with the case plan that included a deadline for the final decision. Benny noted: "Let me know if there is any reason why you think we can't make the deadline".

Barbara, Jimmy and Fred discussed the matter prior to Barbara responding to Benny's email, which she copied to Jimmy and Fred. She wrote:

> I've discussed the case with Jimmy and we have concerns about meeting the deadline. Once we see what Fred has completed by Friday, Jimmy and I will be better placed to evaluate whether the deadline is realistic.

Fred was now convinced that Barbara was setting him up for a fall, most likely with Benny's support, if not by his direction. Fred sent off the latest version of the draft report to Barbara and Jimmy in an email, ahead of their hook-up the following morning.

In the meantime, Fred went to another counsellor appointment and described what had occurred at the Canberra meeting.

"So your worst case scenario didn't eventuate," Sarah said.

"No," Fred replied. "However, the way things are going, I feel anything could happen."

When Fred returned to the office, he noticed an email from

Barbara, copied to Jimmy, noting: "I've regained confidence in attributing all the profits to Australia".

Fred read the statement and he was gobsmacked.

Barbara arranged a three way hook-up with Jimmy and Fred, where she seemed very upbeat.

"Guys, I think we have been approaching this case all wrong. I got staff to do some searches and we have come across some useful cases. We should amend the report to reflect this approach. Fred, I want you to chase up the court cases and rewrite the report."

Fred had drawn up a submission in response to the allegations Benny had made against him at the meeting in Canberra, as well as his own minutes from the meeting, and emailed them to John for his views. He then obtained the court cases Barbara had instructed him to get and forwarded them on before he attempted to rewrite the report.

John sent Ly an email requesting the reasons in writing for his decision requiring Fred to report to Benny rather than his team leader. Days later, Ly responded in an email where he wrote:

> I cannot agree with the contention that I am required to put in writing the reasons for changing the reporting arrangements; however, I invite you to provide authority for the contention.

John reviewed Ly's letter and contacted Fred. "I'll have to consider whether we pursue the request," John said. "Ly stated that he was going to produce minutes of the meeting, but we haven't received them yet. I think we should hold off sending him your submission and minutes until we get something from him. However, it has been useful that you have drafted a submission and contemporaneous minutes to the meeting prior to you going away. Go and have a good holiday."

Fred had not progressed the report very much, as he considered that the court cases Barbara had identified had little relevance to their case. He was starting to feel unwell with the sniffles and a headache. He did as much as he could on the report and sent it to Barbara and Jimmy in an email. They were scheduled to have a final hook-up the following morning, being Fred's last day at work before he went on holidays.

After work, Fred went to the gym; however, he started feeling worse. He decided against having a work-out and, as he was leaving the gym, he experienced a dizzy spell. He then set off to visit his doctor.

"You look unwell," Dr Wells immediately commented and he didn't look surprised when Fred confirmed the fact.

"I'm supposed to be leaving for an overseas holiday over the weekend," Fred advised.

"I want you to take precautions against the influenza virus and I'll write you out a prescription so that you can take the pills with you overseas," Dr Wells said. "I also suggest that you take it easy before your departure so I'll give you a sick leave certificate for tomorrow."

Fred dropped into the Tax Office later that day to leave details that he would be on sick leave the next day and organised his "out of office" voicemail and email. He then took the doctor's advice by taking it easy over the next couple of days.

On Sunday 31 May 2009, Fred jetted off on holidays, where he could leave his troubles behind, at least for a few weeks.

Chapter 42 – A Performance Appraisal

Fred arrived back at work and started going through his emails. While he was away, the Business Line had sent an email to the applicant of the private ruling seeking further information.

Fred contacted Barbara Butt to gain an update of the private ruling and to re-engage himself.

"You don't have to worry about the case anymore. I'll be taking responsibility for it, but I'll keep you in the loop," Barbara curtly advised.

Based on what Fred knew of Barbara, when she said not to worry about the case, he expected that he should be very worried and when she said that she would keep Fred in the loop, he expected that she would keep him in the dark.

Fred touched base with Emma Parker from the Business Line.

"Oh, it looks like we'll be declining to rule," Emma advised.

The news came as a surprise to Fred, but it didn't surprise him that Barbara had failed to advise him of that critical fact. *So much for Barbara keeping me in the loop*, he thought.

The next email that caught Fred's eye was one from Ly to the Establishments area, copied to Benny and Kim, which concerned a request to change Fred's requirements to report to Benny.

Fred was expecting an email from Ly containing the minutes of the Canberra meeting; however, they were not forthcoming. He contacted John to advise him of this and they arranged a meeting. Also in attendance were Carlo Giro and Roy McFly, another union representative.

Fred provided a background of his industrial dispute for the benefit of Carlo and Roy. "Benny reportedly contacted Gene Pool from Transfer Pricing and asked him if there was any reason why Tax Law shouldn't have had an ongoing involvement in the case. Gene's reply was that there was no reason," Fred advised.

"I'm sure if Benny had asked Gene if there was any reason why a drover's dog shouldn't have had an ongoing involvement in the case he would have also replied that there was no reason," Roy quipped.

"This case is ridiculous!" Carlo commented. "The senior executives seem to have contravened every requirement in the Agency Agreement dealing with performance management. They shouldn't be allowed to get away with this!"

"The Agency Agreement sets out guidelines," John advised.

"If they are only guidelines, what's the point of them then?" Carlo queried. "Does this mean that the only real avenue to get any form of justice is through civil action?"

"No, the union is helping to seek justice," John replied as he turned to Fred.

"You know, this experience has been the worst of my career," Fred confessed. "The whole affair is outrageous and I hate it. I just wish the ordeal would go away and I could concentrate on doing my work."

*   *   *

Ly sent an email to Kim and Fred, copied to Benny and Alison Moore. It attached a record of the meeting held in Canberra. Ly noted: "If you think the attached record is not accurate, please send me an email with words you think reflect a more accurate record".

Fred forwarded the email to John and wrote:

> Ly has finally come up with the minutes for the meeting. I suspect Benny and Ly produced the wording ascribed to them and the wording ascribed to others are those of the minutes taker. The result is that the wording ascribed to Benny and Ly is detailed and complete, while the wording ascribed to others is incomplete and, in parts, incomprehensible. I propose to go through the minutes and make changes I consider appropriate.

Fred sent his reply to Ly's email with his changes to the minutes of the Canberra meeting, which he copied to Benny, Kim and John.

Ly soon sent an email reply. He wrote:

> I am not able to accept your changes to the record of our meeting. I require you to identify all deletions and additions you have made to the record. I have identified a number of places where you seek to record that you said something that you did not say. I warn you not to make any statement that is not an accurate record.

Fred read the email with dismay. Ly was accusing Fred of doing what Fred thought that Ly had done himself. *What a hypocrite you are*, he thought. He then phoned John.

"Ly appears to apply different rules to me than he does to himself," Fred said. "I'm not sure how to respond, as his words have a threatening tone."

"You are quite within your rights to use wording in the minutes that better reflect the messages conveyed at the meeting," John advised and assisted Fred to draft his reply.

Fred then received an email from Benny, copied to Karen Whitby. Benny wrote:

> I confirm that I will be conducting your annual appraisal in Melbourne at 10.00 am on Monday 10 August 2009. I will be accompanied by Karen Whitby. Please let me know if you will be accompanied by a support person by COB Monday 3 August 2009. I do not consider that you will meet at least the fully effective rating based on my current knowledge. I want your annual appraisal meeting to be recorded. Please let me know if you consent to the meeting being recorded. I want the information set out below by COB Monday 3 August 2009.
>
> * A list of the matters you have worked on for the 2008-2009 year.
> * At least one example of your contribution to each matter.
> * A copy of your performance agreement.

Fred spent little time considering Benny's email before he forwarded the email with his thoughts to John. He wrote:

> I've quickly read through the email but I will need to take a closer look before I formalise my thoughts. This is the first time I've been formally advised that I was not on track to get a 3 and 3 rating. My mid-year review was 4 and 3 but it appears that Benny is not concerned with due process. I'm going for a walk to get a bit of fresh air now and will touch base with you later.

Fred couldn't stop thinking about the latest emails from Ly and Benny. There seemed to be no end to what they were prepared to do to get their way. He proceeded to painstakingly go through his original draft of the minutes for the Canberra meeting and tracked the changes he had made as per Ly's instructions.

After consulting with John, Fred sent Ly a reply email, copied to Benny, Kim, Alison and John. Fred wrote:

> I changed the draft minutes in a genuine attempt to provide information that I considered better reflected the discussions, placed the comments in clearer context and provided a more complete picture. Advice I received from the union was that this was an appropriate approach. As you instructed, I have tracked my changes with the additions and deletions I made.

Fred attended a meeting with John Lazarus, Carlo Giro and Roy McFly. They discussed arrangements for Fred's annual appraisal and it was agreed that Roy would attend as his support person. Fred also agreed to give consent for the meeting to be recorded.

Fred sent an email to Benny, copied to Ly and Karen Whitby, which attached the documentation for the annual review. Two days later, Fred sent another email that attached the record of annual appraisal. In the self-assessment section of the form, Fred included a rating of 4 and 3 as per his mid-year review by Kim.

Fred then received an email from Benny, copied to Ly and Karen Whitby. Benny wrote:

> In preparation for your annual appraisal meeting, please ensure that Roy McFly is provided with the guidelines on the role of support persons. To ensure that we comply with our obligations under the secrecy provisions, I will be using codes at the meeting to refer to the cases. The example you provided of your contribution to Ralph Flynn's public ruling is after Rick Hudson had redrafted it. I want you to forward to me your earlier email to Ralph by COB today.

Fred was not so surprised to receive correspondence from Benny that he considered strange; he had now become used to it. As he read the email, a number of thoughts popped into his head. *Why devise codes for the cases where they already have identifiable item numbers? It's completely unnecessary. More pieces of the jigsaw now appear to be falling into place. Benny has relied on conniving informers to get his information and, in the case of Ralph's public ruling, his informer was Rick Hudson.*

Fred was having a discussion with John when he mentioned a professional business course he was undertaking.

"I'm not going to bother to apply for study assistance for my final semester of study as I'm sure Benny wouldn't approve it," Fred said.

"The Tax Office promotes continuing professional development so you should apply," John insisted. "The Tax Office is not a concentration camp."

"It may not be a concentration camp," Fred replied, "but sometimes it seems like one."

Fred took John's advice and applied for study leave.

In response, Benny sent an email, where he wrote:

> To enable me to consider your study leave application, provide me with general information provided to students by the Institute about the course, a hard copy of the course materials for which you are enrolled, and your study application.

The moment Fred received the email response from Benny, he had an overwhelming thought. *Why in the hell did I ever bother applying? This man is completely nuts!*

Fred deliberated for a while before he sent what he considered to be an appropriate reply. He wrote:

Please find attached a brochure that provides general information for the course and my study application. As the course material is provided to students and subject to copyright, I cannot provide you with a hard or electronic copy of the material, but as you will be in Melbourne next week, you are welcome to view the material.

Later that day, Fred managed to send off one final email. It was to Ly and Benny, copied to Alison, Kim and John. Fred wrote: "Please find attached my submission in response to the statements you made at our meeting in Canberra".

Chapter 43 – Another Ambush

Benny made an appearance on 10 August at around 9.00 am. He busily rushed over to Fred and instructed him to print out a copy of the submission Fred had emailed the previous Friday. Benny seemed highly agitated, even more than usual.

Standing over Fred as he was seated at his workstation, Benny was turning pages from the copy of the submission document. "You mention that you received information that they were proceeding on the basis of undertaking an Advance Pricing Arrangement rather than a private ruling. Did you receive an email in respect to this?" Benny asked as he pointed to a paragraph in the submission.

Fred couldn't recall ever having received any specific email. "I don't believe so," he responded. "I would have been referring to all the information I received through a series of emails, comments made by the Business Line staff, as well as the fact that a team was formed, including staff from Transfer Pricing and the Economists, to deal with the case."

"I have all the information on this; are you sure?" Benny questioned.

Fred thought hard before he replied. "I'd have to go through all my emails to be certain but I'm pretty sure that I didn't receive a specific email."

Benny sped off.

Fred perused his documentation in preparation for his annual appraisal. *This year has not been one of my better years,* he reflected. *However, I still would have produced more work and dealt with more complex cases than most of the staff in Tax Law. Under normal circumstances I'd get a 4 and 3; however, Benny has already indicated that I won't even be getting a 3 and 3. I therefore expect that he'll give me a 3 and 2 or, if he's feeling particularly mean, a worst case scenario would be a 2 and 2.*

As Fred's mind was filled with thoughts, Bee Hive spoke to him.

"Fred, I'd like to give you a word of advice. Try not to disagree with everything that Benny says. It may be in your interest to concede to him on some matters."

"I'd be prepared to agree with Benny if I considered that what he said had some merit," Fred stated. "However, I'm hardly going to concede to him if I believe he is clearly wrong."

As Bee gave an expression of disapproval, Fred received a telephone call. It was the concierge, who advised that Mr Roy McFly had arrived. Fred fetched Roy and, as the time for the meeting arrived, Fred collected his documentation and headed off to find out his fate.

Benny welcomed Roy and Fred, confirming that the meeting would be taped. Karen Whitby set up the recording device.

"I've brought along the course materials for this semester's subject for which I had applied for study assistance for your review," Fred mentioned.

"You can just leave it," Benny snapped back at him. "You can now go through your self-assessment and present your case to justify your rating of 4 and 3."

Fred was unprepared by the request, as his previous annual appraisals involved a two-way discussion of the work undertaken in an effort to reach an agreed rating; however, the process that Benny was adopting was obviously to be different. He commenced to go through what he had done.

Once Fred completed the section he looked up at Benny. Benny was fixated on his copy of the document and was silent so Fred continued. He moved on to the section on how he had undertaken his work.

Fred was proceeding through his paper, reciting the examples listed under each heading. He got to the stage where he was practically reading from the paper so he paused. "The rest is as outlined in the paper; did you want me to continue?" Fred asked.

"Go on," Benny replied.

Fred continued and eventually got to the end of the document.

"Right," Benny stated in an elevated voice before he began to give his appraisal. He commenced with the work that Fred had done and proceeded to go through the spreadsheet that Fred had prepared. He then subjected Fred to an onslaught of the most vicious criticism on each and every one of Fred's cases. His conclusions had a common theme—Fred's contribution to each case was either negative or insignificant. What was most concerning to Fred was that his reasons for his findings were based on statements that Fred considered to be misleading, misrepresentative or blatantly untrue.

"There is one case where you were criticised by the staff in the Business Line," Benny alleged. It happened to be the case Fred had taken over from Bee.

"I worked with Theo Onassis on that case and he specifically mentioned that the Business Line team was happy with the advice," Fred immediately commented.

"No, they weren't!" Benny barked back. "You had a real opportunity to provide assistance and you failed."

Benny presented Fred with a document and pointed to some wording. "Do you confirm that you wrote this and that this was the only contribution you made on the case?" Benny asked.

"I can confirm that I wrote what is in the email," Fred said. "However, I would have to examine the case in its entirety to gauge the extent of my contribution."

Fred was about to refer to the email history where he had made other written contributions, but Benny pulled the document away. Benny wasn't interested in explanations; he obviously had his own agenda and he was running with it.

At one stage, Karen intervened. "Fred, do you wish to respond to any of these statements?"

"I would have wanted to respond to each and every one of these statements," Fred said, opening his hands in sheer exasperation. "However, I do not see that I'll have a fair opportunity to do so at this forum."

Fred sensed that Benny was his executioner and there would be two casualties: Fred and the truth.

Benny wound up his feedback on what Fred had done and he then came to the rating. "Fred, I had utmost difficulty in rating your work; however, I thought I'd be generous to you. I'm rating you a 2."

Fred could not believe his ears. *You say you're being generous by giving me a 2? That's just borderline. Good God, what in the hell are you doing? That means I'm looking at my imagined worst case scenario—it couldn't possibly be any worse, could it?*

Benny then moved on to the section of how Fred performed his duties and he took on an even sterner persona. He proceeded with a new round of criticism, but this time the contempt in his voice was more evident.

However, Karen interrupted. "The recording has come to a stop; I will need to load another CD," she advised.

"I estimate that we have about 15 minutes to go," Benny said. "Do you wish to have this recorded as well?"

Fred looked over to Roy for the first time. Roy was looking down, motionless and seemingly dumbfounded.

"Roy, should we get the last part recorded as well?" Fred asked.

"Yeah," Roy managed to eke out, nodding slightly.

"We've been going for almost three hours,' said Karen. 'Why don't we have a 15-minute leg stretch?"

Roy and Fred went for a walk around the block.

"He's criticised just about everything you've done," Roy commented in disbelief.

"Yes, he most certainly has," Fred responded, "but he's misrepresented the facts on every one of my cases. All of my contributions were adopted in the final products and yet there have never been any issue with them. He's full of crap!"

"He's had absolutely nothing positive to say. It's incredible!" Roy said, the anguish evident in his voice.

The meeting resumed and Benny made a couple of general, but nonetheless scathing, comments. "Fred, I have noted a couple of points that you made in your appraisal. In respect of your good officer feedback, I must say that I have personally spoken to senior officers in Tax Law and they do not have a high opinion of you. In respect of your high level of qualifications, I can only say that these raise my concerns about you even more."

Benny pursed his lips and then continued. "Fred, you've been very high maintenance. Your failure to meet with Ly and me caused an unnecessarily heavy burden on us. However, what I find the most frustrating of all is that you simply cannot accept all your failings." Benny sat back. He seemed to become more and more comfortable as he expelled his venom. Although he savoured his next words most of all. "So, after considerable deliberation—and yes, I have given this much thought—I cannot justify any rating other than a 1."

Fred was stunned. He had just got hit with the worst possible rating. A rating of 1 was unsatisfactory, requiring an inefficiency process to be put in place.

Fred felt like a zombie as he walked back to his workstation with Roy. He took his seat as Roy phoned John.

"Hi, John. Fred's just had his annual appraisal and he ended up with 2 and 1 … no, not two to them and one to him. A rating of 2 for what he did and a 1 for how he did it.”

Fred could hear John yell out from the other end of the phone. “Shit!”

After a little time coming to terms with the magnitude of the situation, John, Roy and Fred met to discuss the matter. The agreed outcome of the meeting was for John to lodge a dispute notice.

Fred then received the following email from Benny:

> Would you please confirm in writing your spoken advice to me at approximately 9.00 am on Monday 10 August 2009 at your workstation in Casselden Place that the information you refer to in your submission was not received by you in an email but was instead received by you as spoken advice? I want you to provide this in writing by COB today.

Fred had to compose himself before he forwarded the email to John. As he waited for John to reply, he re-read the email and tried to think back to his discussion with Benny. In the process of drafting an email reply, Fred was contacted by John.

“There’s something funny going on about his request; I smell a set-up,” John said. “Perhaps you should check with the Business Line people. I bet he’s spoken to them.”

Fred contacted Gary Serpico. “Hi, Gary. I’m trying to clarify details concerning the first private ruling case. As I understood the situation, the team was proceeding on the basis of undertaking an Advance Pricing Arrangement; however, somewhere along the line a decision was made to provide the private ruling.”

“No. We were always going to rule,” Gary replied. “An Advance Pricing Arrangement was to be considered after the ruling.”

Fred noted the strength of his voice and the definitiveness of his reply. “But I never received anything that conveyed this,” Fred stated.

“Oh yes,” Gary insisted. “There would have been something that went around.”

Fred was confused and he called John. “I contacted Gary from the Business Line and his recollection is completely different to what was my understanding,” he advised.

“Well, it’s obvious that there are people who are saying things that are casting doubt on your honesty,” John stated. “Benny seems to be having another crack at you. If he can show that you may be lying, he might try to do anything, even sack you! I would send him an email and throw this issue back in his face."

After consulting with John, Fred replied to Benny, copied to John. Fred wrote:

> After I received your email request, I contacted Gary Serpico from the Business Line. Gary's recollection of the matter was contrary to mine. Gary was of the view that they were always going to rule. I advised Gary that I did not recall ever receiving anything to this effect. Gary was sure that there was something that went around communicating this. If you have any such email, I would appreciate a copy.

The following week, Fred received an email from Benny, where he wrote: "The emails I have in my possession on the private ruling are the emails you have".

Fred searched through his emails, but he could not find anything concerning a decision on the private ruling case. He then thought he'd check the Cases computer system. After checking numerous postings, he stumbled across a couple of critical ones.

Fred quickly drafted an email to John, copied to Roy McFly and Carlo Giro. Fred wrote:

> I can now confirm that there were, in fact, emails that went around; however, they were not sent nor copied to me. One email was from Jerome Byron in the Business Line that essentially advised of the decision to revert back to a private ruling as an Advance Pricing Arrangement was to be considered after. Another email was from Sidney Sigley in Tax Law who suggested that it should be clarified whether the taxpayer still wanted a private ruling given that it wouldn't provide them the certainty they were seeking. Sidney also queried the need for his ongoing involvement, as the Business Line already had all the required experts engaged, which did not include me. These emails contradict what the Business Line has been saying and confirm what I've been saying all along.

*   *   *

Fred was copied into a series of emails concerning the resurrection of the public ruling that he had previously worked on that senior executive Aaron Lincoln had put on hold. The first email was from Adrian Britain with the note:

> Tax Law can recommence working on this case. Clark Kane was involved before his retirement. Fred Campari was the Tax Law officer originally involved but I am not sure whether he is still involved. Perhaps Ly Low can advise who can work on this from Tax Law.

Ly soon responded in an email that was copied to Fred: "I advise that the Tax Law officer who will be responsible for the public ruling is Craig Miller".

Ly followed this with another email to Kim, copied to Craig and Fred: "I would appreciate you making sure that Craig has everything he might need".

Fred touched base with Craig, briefed him on the case and sent through all the relevant information. He then sent an email to Ly, copied to Kim and Craig, where he wrote:

> I have noted your emails communicating your decision that Craig Miller will be the Tax Law officer who will be responsible for the public ruling. I have updated the systems and attach a summary of the case.

After two and a half years of having worked on the issue, it took an instant for Fred to be stripped of the case and have it handed over to another officer.

Fred then sent an email to Benny, where he wrote:

> I have completed my 2009 Annual Appraisal confirming that the annual appraisal discussion has occurred. I do not agree with your assessment and I do not agree with your comments. I confirm that I wish to have the decision referred on for review.

Benny forwarded an email to Fred that showed he had sent off Fred's 2009 annual appraisal documentation for review.

Benny then sent an email to Ly, the gatekeeper and all the managers in Tax Law, copied to Fred, where he wrote:

> Until further notice, when allocating work to Fred Campari every matter requires assignment of at least two officers of Tax Law. Fred must assume full responsibility for managing the case, researching the matter and authoring the decision. Further, one of the Executive Level 2.2 officers must be assigned as overseer on every case.

Chapter 44 – Health & Wellbeing

During the course of 2009, Fred was experiencing a number of health issues. He visited his doctor, complaining about stomach pain, chest pain and bleeding from his rear end.

Fred was sent for an ultrasound, where the report concluded that his liver, spleen, kidneys and gall bladder were normal. He considered this unusual as his spleen was supposed to have been removed as a result of the traffic accident during his overseas working holiday back in 1988, some 20 years earlier.

Fred saw his doctor and was referred to a colorectal surgeon who recommended that a colonoscopy be conducted. He underwent the colonoscopy where he received the all-clear. The bleeding was advised to have been caused by external haemorrhoids.

While his haemorrhoids, upset stomach and chest pains persisted, he was also developing pain in his left shoulder and lower neck. His condition was worsening to the point that he was experiencing numbness and a tingling sensation down his left arm and in the fingertips of his left hand.

Fred visited his doctor and was referred for a CT scan. The scan revealed the prior scapula trauma and fracture, which was also caused by the traffic accident during his overseas working holiday back in 1988. While his scapula appeared to have healed, his cervical spine revealed intervertebral disc degeneration and disc bulging at multiple levels.

Undergoing physiotherapy on a weekly basis, Fred was subjected to upper body traction and mobilisation. He was also guided through various exercises and stretches, which he was required to perform repetitions of throughout the week. But although he followed this routine of exercises and stretches, the pain persisted. He was then referred to a rheumatologist.

An MRI scan was conducted, which revealed that Fred was suffering from a condition known as cervical spondylitis. The rheumatologist gave him literature about neck care, showed him neck exercises and discussed local heat application and partial neck immobilisation.

While all this was going on, Dr Wells was also monitoring Fred's general health and gave ongoing advice and support. It proved to be of tremendous value, especially during the time of Fred's performance issues and his annual appraisal.

It was on 10 September 2009 when Fred went to afternoon tea with members of his team that he felt physically and emotionally drained. He could hardly lift himself from his seat. His co-workers observed his state.

"You look terrible," Theo commented.

"Yeah," Ivan added. "You really should see a doctor."

Fred visited Dr Wells and, by the time he made it to the clinic, he felt exhausted. When Dr Wells called his name, he entered his room and dropped into the patient's chair. The doctor didn't have to ask any questions. He automatically took Fred's blood pressure.

The doctor took a few moments before he spoke. "Fred, your blood pressure has shot up to the high 160s over the high 90s. Given that your blood pressure is usually in the normal range, you are likely to be experiencing hypertension. In the past, I've asked whether you wished to have some sick leave, but you haven't availed to it. Now, as your doctor, I strongly recommend that you take some time off."

Fred didn't even try to speak, he simply nodded.

Dr Wells then perked up. "Good, now I'm going to give you a week off. When you come back next week, I want to do some blood tests and we'll take it from there. In the meantime, take it easy, but don't be lazy. Get out, be active and get yourself better."

Fred lifted himself from the chair and had commenced making his way out of the doctor's office when he turned around. "Thank you, Doctor," he said.

Making it back to the Tax Office, Fred rang John. "I've visited my doctor and he's given me some time off."

"You'd better make sure that you have a medical certificate for all the time that you take off," John was quick to advise.

"Don't worry, John," Fred reassured him. "I only take sick leave when I have a certificate."

Fred took the doctor's advice and kept active. After a week, he returned to Dr Wells' clinic. The doctor was able to report that Fred's blood pressure had markedly improved.

"It's amazing how dramatically one's health can improve without stress," the doctor commented. "We'll take the blood tests and I think you should take one more week off, then come for another visit and we'll ascertain whether you're right to go back to work."

Fred took the time off to go for walks, go to the gym and visit his sister and friends. One evening, he dined with some of his friends, where he updated them on his work situation.

"Yep, there's no doubt that all your health issues stem from stress," Brian commented.

"I can understand how high blood pressure is associated with stress; however, I can't see how my other health issues would be," Fred commented.

"I was going through a stressful period when I experienced shoulder and arm pain," Brian advised. "When the stress went away, so did the pain. A person's body reacts in the most unpredictable ways under stress."

Fred doubted his ailments were all as a result of stress so he did some research on the internet. As he delved into his health conditions, he was surprised to ascertain that there were possible links with stress for every one of them. *Good Lord. The high blood pressure, the haemorrhoids, the upset stomach, the chest pain and the neck pain may all have been caused through stress.* As the discovery came to his full realisation, one more thought popped into his head. *Those despots!*

*   *   *

When Fred returned to work, he was greeted by a number of emails. One had been forwarded by Benny that contained advice from the Commissioner concerning a review of delayed private rulings—the Rulings Review. Meetings were arranged between the delegate of the Rulings Review and the responsible officers. Of the six cases listed for Tax Law, Fred was the responsible officer for three of them.

"Benny was enquiring about you in relation to the Rulings Review meetings," Theo advised. "I told him that you were on sick leave and he asked what your problem was. I suggested that it may be the problems you've had with a pain in the neck." He grinned.

"I didn't think Benny cared," Fred joked.

"Gee, Fred, you seem to have quite a few cases that are to be looked at by the Rulings Review, while I don't have any," Anton remarked with a snigger.

"I expect the more cases one does, the greater chance one has to have their cases reviewed and that may be the reason why you don't have any," Fred replied sarcastically.

"Benny seems to be taking an active interest in the Rulings Review visits, which are reported to be reviews into private rulings and the reasons why some of them are taking so long," Ivan said.

"There should be no mystery why the cases are taking so long—it's all because of Benny," Fred stated. "He approaches requests for private rulings like an audit. He keeps on asking unnecessary questions or requesting more information, which is why most of the cases he's involved in are over a year old. In the end, usually either the applicant withdraws their ruling request or the Tax Office declines to rule."

Fred had also received an email from Benny while he was away. It read:

> I've decided not to approve your study leave application. I would have preferred to make my decision when you were not on leave so that I could discuss my decision with you; however, I did not want to delay my decision any further.

Fred read through the attached document that set out the reasons for rejecting his leave. He noted that for every reason he gave in support of his study leave, Benny repeated the same points and converted them to a negative statement by simply inserting the word "not". Even though Fred had handed over his course materials for Benny's perusal, Benny stated that he did not have the time to read them and highlighted the fact that Fred had failed to provide him with a copy of the materials as he had instructed.

You could have arranged to get a copy of the study materials yourself, Fred thought. *But no. Instead, you give directions and expect people to just blindly follow them, even if your instructions would have resulted in someone breaching copyright and acting in a way that was improper or even illegal.*

The Rulings Review meetings were arranged with Tammy Walker as the delegate. Fred attended the meetings for his cases, along with Colleen Coolidge, as the business manager, and Kyle Stevens, as technical leader.

Tammy asked a series of questions about each case. She did not identify any problems with the technical aspects or the system processes; however, she did pursue questions concerning the Tax Law involvement in the cases.

"The practices of Tax Law do not appear to have followed the processes outlined in Tax Office guidance material," Tammy suggested. "Why is Tax Law involving itself in cases that do not involve precedential issues and why is a senior executive involved in each one of these cases?"

Fred's eyes lit up, as Tammy had hit the nail on the head as to why the cases were overdue.

"The other areas don't have the capability with technical international issues so Tax Law really needs to assist them," Colleen advised.

"Yes, that's right," Kyle was quick to agree. "Benny appreciates that he has a broader responsibility on technical issues, including a compliance responsibility."

Tammy looked confused but she did not follow up. Fred was disappointed, as Tammy had the answer but she chose not to pursue it so Benny was let off the hook.

Chapter 45 – Dealing with Crises

Fred was exposed to the share market on two fronts: through his superannuation and his personal share portfolio. The weight of information indicated that the global markets were heading downward so he decided to transfer his superannuation to the cash investment option in November 2008.

Fred reviewed his share portfolio. It cost a total of $200 000, which was financed through a bank loan. His portfolio had grown to over $400 000 at the height of the market, although it had been pegged back by the end of 2008. He gave some thought to liquidating his portfolio; however, his problems at work were all consuming so he ended up holding on to his shares to weather the financial storm.

As the financial markets deteriorated during 2009, Fred saw his share portfolio dwindle to around $100 000, which left him exposed to an outstanding debt of over $100 000. What concerned Fred even more was the fact that the family home was mortgaged as security.

Fred's concerns at work reached their heights towards the end of 2009 when the fear of losing his job became more than just a remote possibility. His fear escalated with the prospect that he could also lose the family home. His mind cast back to the comment he had made to his father: *"You don't have to worry, Dad, I'll buy the home and keep it in the family."*

During the period when Fred was on sick leave for a couple of weeks in September 2009, he thought hard about his situation. He agonised over making a decision and eventually called Gina.

"Hi, Gina. I've been doing a bit of thinking about my problems at work and my financial situation. I've decided to sell my house and move into the family home."

"You're selling your house?" Gina said. "I thought you liked living there. Why don't you sell the family home instead?"

"Oh no," Fred reacted instinctively. "I'd prefer to live in the family home and I couldn't sell it."

Fred quickly arranged to sell his house and moved into the family home. This eased his mind of his dominant financial fear and allowed him to refocus his mind on his work problems.

Fred was under pressure to do his usual work, as well as dealing with the performance issues. It was pressure that he had to endure during 2009 and 2010. He tried to follow the advice of his doctor and friends; however, he found that it wasn't easy. As much as he concentrated on every decision and task he had to carry out each day, his preoccupation with the work performance issues was taking a toll.

Gina and Fred kept in contact and they often caught up on weekends. He stayed in touch with his closest friends outside work and made it a regular event to meet up with them every week for dinner. At work, he kept in contact with a close group of friends and met up with them for lunch every Friday. Fred also caught up with his university friends whenever they arranged drinks. While all the other groups Fred associated with were aware of his work problems, his university friends were not. He was grateful for this as it allowed him to socialise and forget about his problems for a short time.

On the other hand, Fred was paranoid about many of the people in the Tax Office. *Do they know that I'm being pursued on performance issues?* he wondered. *If so, I hope they realise that all the accusations against me are unfounded and unfair. It appears true that it's during the hardest times that one finds out who their real friends are.*

Fred produced his documentation for his annual appraisal review. After having it proofread by John and Roy, he sent it off. It comprised two attachments: the first was a report in response to comments made by Benny from the Canberra meeting and the second was a response to the comments made by Benny during the course of his annual appraisal meeting.

Fred was confident that the responses and evidence he submitted would establish that the comments Benny made were misleading, misrepresentative or blatantly untrue. He waited for an outcome with anticipation.

In December 2009, Fred received an email from the review panel. They wrote: "Due to the technical nature of the work you have undertaken, we have appointed Vincent Carr to review your work".

Attached to the email was a copy of the report from Vincent and the request to respond within 14 days before the panel met to make its final decision. Fred read through the report, which was restricted to three issues involving two cases out of a total of 28 cases he had worked on during the year.

The first issue was the first private ruling case where Vincent concluded: "Although it was not unreasonable for Fred to have formed the view that the ruling application did not raise any precedential issues, I nevertheless do not accept that Fred dealt with the matter in the proper and appropriate manner. Fred had not discharged his obligations in accordance with corporate requirements".

The second issue considered the second private ruling case. Vincent noted: "Fred was reported to be in the process of sending an email and referring the case back to the Business Line. Benny was made aware of what Fred was proposing and he intervened".

Fred was now seeing another dimension to how the situation had come about. It centred on Barbara Butt and what she had obviously reported to Benny. The fact that Barbara supported what Fred was proposing to do was a point that she had conveniently withheld. Fred felt the whole situation was a frame up. Barbara had given Benny the ammunition and he went out to hunt him down.

Vincent further concluded: "Although the question of whether further information or documents should be requested before the Commissioner can rule is a question of judgement, an Executive Level 2.1 officer exercising sound judgment would have requested the documentation".

Fred was amazed how Vincent could have made such an unfounded conclusion. Vincent had not identified what the information was nor how it was relevant. Vincent also failed to reconcile how there were numerous senior officers involved at the time and none of them considered that the information should have been requested. *What of them?* Fred queried.

The third issue that Vincent selected for review was Ralph's public ruling, where Fred was specifically requested by Kim to assist. Vincent concluded: "Fred approved a public ruling and allowed it to be escalated to a senior Tax Law officer where it was loosely drafted".

Fred accepted this point. Even though he did not create the mistake, he had failed to pick up on it. Even though he did not have a formal role on the case and was doing the job that his manager should have been doing, he was the one to be brought to account.

Vincent then made his final conclusion: "I can see no reason to doubt Benny's appraisal, although I recommend adjusting the ratings from 2 and 1 to 2 and 2".

Fred reflected on the report and the findings. *Vincent found that it was reasonable for me to have concluded that the issue was not precedential whereas Benny was of the view that it was precedential. I was right, Benny was wrong. Vincent considered that the documents requested in a private ruling are only those that are required in order to rule, whereas Benny considered that all documents to contracts must always be requested. I was right, Benny was wrong. Even though requesting additional documents is a matter of judgement and all the other senior officers at the time were of the view that further information was not necessary, nevertheless I was expected to have requested the information.* Fred then reflected on the words that John had said: *Senior executives are always going to side with their own.*

Fred rang John and advised him of the email. "I've received word from the review panel and they have provided a report that largely confirms the findings by Benny, although they have marginally changed my rating from 2 and 1 to 2 and 2," Fred advised. "I will be making further representations on a number of points."

"By all means, make the points that you consider appropriate," John said. "However, once you've completed your response, whatever the outcome, maybe this should be the end of the matter."

The last words John uttered surprised Fred. *John was so supportive to fight this thing and now he's suggesting that I let it go,* he thought. "I'll have to think about that," Fred replied.

After drafting his response, Fred sent it to John and Roy to review. Roy provided some feedback in an email response: "I would not use the word discriminatory in the two instances where you used it; you may wish to use the word inconsistent".

Fred heeded Roy's advice, sent off his comments and again waited with anticipation.

Chapter 46 – Who Can You Trust?

Fred continued with his cases and reported to Bee on a few of them.

"Make sure you get all the relevant source documents, as you have a tendency not to get them," Bee mentioned.

"Bee, that's not correct," Fred stated, frowning. "I always ask for the documents that I consider necessary in order to rule."

"I distinctly remember warning you before Christmas last year about that case where you had so much trouble with Benny that you needed to get all the relevant documents," Bee stated. "You didn't and see what happened."

Fred was now most disturbed by Bee's comments. "Bee, what you are saying is simply not correct. The case concerning documentation to which you refer was not raised as a problem before Christmas, but early this year. Further, it wasn't that I hadn't requested the relevant documents. Benny expected me to request all the documents."

"Well, obviously all the documents would have been relevant," Bee said, with a smirk.

Fred had had enough of Bee's smart alec remarks. "Okay, Bee. I know you prefer not to get involved in my cases until I have produced my best effort and had it approved by the technical clearance officer; however, I wish to draw something to your attention now so that we don't have trouble down the track."

Fred carried documents over to Bee's workstation and sat down next to her. He commenced going through the documents as he explained.

"In addition to the information provided in the private ruling request, Adrian Castle and I requested and have received documents that were considered necessary in order to rule. However, there are other associated documents that I consider unnecessary. Going on Benny's view, we should be asking for them. So I ask you, do you want me to ask for these other documents?"

Bee examined the documentation and thought about it for some time before she started talking to herself out loud. "I think the documents you have identified are the only ones we need to rule. The other source documents just aren't relevant." She then fell silent before she blurted out questions. "Have you checked with Adrian? What does he think?"

"Yes, I spoke to Adrian over the phone and he agrees with me," Fred advised.

Bee seemed mildly excited as she spoke. "Okay, send Adrian an email and advise him that we are of the view that we have the information necessary in order to rule and ask him to confirm whether he agrees." She paused and shook her head. "No, no, no. Better still. Send him an email outlining your preliminary technical analysis and how *you* think we have the information necessary in order to rule and ask him to confirm whether he agrees."

Fred looked at Bee in her excited state and couldn't get over the juvenile way in which she wanted the case handled.

Angela Farina from International Risk was visiting Melbourne office and spoke to Fred. "I'll be resigning in early 2010 and International Risk is looking for an Executive Level 2.1 officer to replace me. Why don't you talk to Helen Glaxos or Drew Looney about it?" Angela suggested.

Fred thought he'd never want to work for Drew again; however, his situation in Tax Law and reporting to Benny was so dire that he found himself contacting Helen.

"Hi, Helen. Angela mentioned that International Risk may be looking for an Executive Level 2.1. If this is correct, I'd be interested," Fred said.

"Yes, we are looking for an Executive Level 2.1; I'll mention it to Drew and let you know," Helen suggested.

Helen then visited Fred at his workstation. "I've spoken to Drew and he's happy to have a chat with you," Helen stated. "Just give him a call if you wish to speak to him."

As they continued their conversation, Bee entered the area after a lunch where she had obviously had a bit to drink. She took her seat and started speaking loudly. "You don't have to quieten down just because I've arrived," she said.

Helen and Fred looked at each other and were both lost for words.

"I didn't say anything bad about you, Fred," Bee stated out of the blue. Helen and Fred again looked at each other, both feeling uncomfortable.

Bee continued making statements. "I really didn't. I didn't say anything bad about you, Fred."

The more Bee made her statements, the less convincing she sounded. Fred already suspected that Bee had badmouthed him and he now thought his suspicions were confirmed. *That bitch!* Fred thought. *I wonder what bad things she said about me.*

Drew and Fred arranged to have a discussion and they met in Drew's office.

"I hear that you're having a bit of a problem at the moment," Drew commented.

Fred expected that Drew would have known about his woes; however, he didn't expect that he would raise the matter up-front.

"Yes," Fred confirmed. "I have been having a bit of a hard time."

Drew looked at Fred and he appeared rather smug as he spoke. "Well, I'm not concerned about that. What's relevant to me is that we are looking for someone to undertake a risk identification role. I expect that you would be ideal for the position and I would be happy to have you on board."

Drew seemed highly positive and Fred was encouraged. However, Drew then changed his tone. "But we do have some budgetary restrictions and we need to consider our overall staff profile so I would need to wait to see if I can get approval," he added, rather sombrely.

As Drew continued, Fred realised that the speech was similar to those he had heard a number of times before. He suddenly realised that Drew's words sounded hollow, just like the previous times when Drew had ultimately denied him positions and he resigned to the fact that Drew had absolutely no intention of throwing him a lifeline.

Returning to his workstation in Tax Law, Fred took a moment to observe the usual goings on. Kim was undertaking two of her favourite activities: social club events and footy tipping.

Bee was agitated, which usually meant that it was one of the rare occasions when she was required to initiate some work. However, a subsequent telephone call and her punching of the air indicated that she had most probably managed to palm off the case to someone else.

Anton was busy grazing on his food. It wasn't so much that he ate a lot, as he was in reasonable shape for a man his age, but that most of his time was spent in opening and closing his drawer every time he withdrew a morsel of food. He made noises as he split his crackers to the point that he appeared to be splitting the atom. However, his big production number came when he introduced his nutcracker and commenced cracking his walnuts.

The sounds emanating from Anton's workstation seemed to harmonise beautifully with the guy in an adjoining workstation who regularly bounced his tennis ball.

As Fred turned to complete the circle, he witnessed Ivan studiously examining his computer monitor. *At least someone seems to be doing some work around here*, Fred thought, but as he headed towards the printer to collect some documents, he noticed that Ivan wasn't actually doing any tax work at all. He had his completed Sudoku proudly displayed on his desk while he was checking the share market prices on the internet.

And I'm the one who was plucked out of this cesspool to be crucified, Fred thought.

*   *   *

Fred was suffering ongoing pain from his cervical spondylitis so he was referred to a neurosurgeon who recommended that his condition was best managed through physiotherapy. He persisted with the treatment until the end of 2009 when official news came through that Ly Low and Benny Heel were both to move from Tax Law. Fred's health condition then miraculously improved, which made him think. *I guess it should be no surprise that with Ly and Benny leaving, so did the pains in the neck.*

Chapter 47 – Performance Management

The departure of both Ly and Benny was met with almost unanimous sighs of relief. One exception was Bee, who took the time to phone them to wish them both well. Fred was silent during both telephone conversations; however, when Bee commented that they should clone the likes of them, Fred gave out a yelp.

When Fred reported the departure of Ly and Benny to John, John's reaction was instantaneous. "This has to be a good development."

Fred's abysmal annual appraisal meant that he was denied performance pay for the year. *How ironic. I'm being denied performance pay in the very last year that it is to be paid*, Fred thought. *Where's the luck?*

The performance management of Fred left a legacy for the senior executive destined for Tax Law, so he waited nervously to learn who the new senior executive was to be. An email was sent around that attached a Senior Executive Update advising that the new senior executive was Lisa Lovelace.

Kim managed to arrange to be transferred out of Tax Law to a newly created position where her higher duties at the Executive Level 2.2 would continue. This resulted in Tax Law being short a team leader.

Lisa advertised for expressions of interest for the team leader position. Soon after, Lisa sent out an email that noted: "I can now confirm that Chris Alexakos will be starting in the team leader position. Please give him every assistance in his new role".

Nearing the time for the next round of mid-year reviews, Fred telephoned Lisa.

"Have you received a final decision about last year's annual appraisal?" Lisa asked Fred.

"No, I haven't," Fred advised.

"I suggest you send the review panel a reminder," she said.

Fred was preparing an email enquiry to the review panel when he received an email from Barbara Butt, copied to Lisa and Jimmy Dick. Barbara wrote:

You may remember back to when you were working on a private ruling that Jimmy and I gave you feedback on a report you had prepared. If my memory serves me correctly, I think we pointed out where we thought the report was deficient in the legal analysis. Attached is the final version of our report that you may use as a guide.

Fred was astonished that after a year of Barbara working on the case that she had completed a private ruling report. He also couldn't believe how much nerve Barbara had in sending such a misleading email.

You turd, Fred thought. *You say that from memory you think you gave me feedback that my report was deficient in the legal analysis. You should be well aware that you didn't give me any feedback whatsoever on the legal analysis of my initial report. I wrote my report in a few weeks on my own, while you spent over a year with the aid of a team to produce a report and I expect you still got it wrong.*

Reading the report, Fred had to contain his laughter. Barbara had simply cut and pasted slabs of information from public rulings and court cases to support her line of argument, one which Fred considered to be fundamentally flawed.

Having printed out the report, Fred's only pleasure was in filing it away—in the security waste bin. His only regret was that he couldn't place the report in the location where he considered it truly belonged, which was straight down the toilet.

Fred sent his email to the review panel enquiring about his performance appraisal. Later that day, he received an email response:

Dear Mr Campari, the panel is of the view that, having considered all of the information, it has decided to accept the report of Vincent Carr. The panel supports your overall assessment as an Executive Level 1 by Benny Heel. Although, the panel has decided to adjust your rating to 2 and 2. If you are dissatisfied with this decision, you may choose to lodge a dispute.

Fred produced a wry smile when he saw that they had mistakenly noted "Executive Level 1" instead of "Executive Level 2.1". However, the smile was wiped from his face when he thought back to the allegations against him that had now been confirmed by a panel of senior executives and, as many times as he re-ran the allegations in his mind, he simply could not believe them.

It was always going to be the case that the senior executives would stick together, Fred thought. *Even though they couldn't agree with Benny's technical views—and how could they? —nevertheless they supported his allegations.*

In considering whether to lodge a dispute, Fred knew that it would involve a referral to a senior executive in the Tax Office who was not technical and who was sure to simply support the other senior executives. Fred felt that the whole affair was an extreme injustice and that he should fight on. On the other hand, although John was initially gung-ho about fighting the matter, he was now signalling a different message. Fred sensed that he would be fighting against the odds and he was also acutely aware that he had to contend with his ongoing performance management and health issues.

Fred sent Lisa an email that attached a spreadsheet with a list of cases he had worked on during the 2009-2010 year and a draft performance agreement.

Fred was scheduled to have his mid-year review with Lisa, which was also to be attended by Chris Alexakos. At the meeting, it didn't take long before Lisa put a question to Fred.

"So what are your intentions regarding your previous year's annual appraisal? Do you think you will be lodging a dispute?"

Fred took a deep breath before he responded. "I'm really not happy with this whole affair." He took another breath before he continued. "However, I guess I have to accept the fact that senior management are of the view that I haven't been doing my job properly and I think I should concentrate my efforts on improving my performance so that I am considered to be at least fully effective in their eyes."

Lisa seemed comfortable with his response and she outlined her position. "I do not see the practicality of you reporting directly to me. I will therefore arrange that you report directly to Chris and that your performance is judged based on your work going forward."

Fred was still apprehensive about his situation, but he realised that Lisa had been placed in a difficult position; a position whereby he was considered a problem and she was obligated to deal with him.

"That sounds fair," he replied.

Fred met with Roy and John to advise them of his decision. "I feel like I'm taking a big risk here, because if I'm adjudged to be falling short of being fully effective for a second year in a row, I am likely to be in big trouble," Fred said.

There was a moment of silence before Roy responded. "Yes, I think if this did occur, it would be a problem for you."

Lisa sent around an email where she wrote: "Congratulations Barbara". Fred looked to the email history, where it noted: "We are pleased to announce that Paul Woolley has recommended Barbara Butt as senior executive".

Theo, Ivan and Anton all waited until Fred finished reading the email.

"I see your friend is now a senior executive," Anton commented.

"She's hardly my friend," Fred responded. "I expect she earned the position."

"Earned the position?" Ivan questioned. "Paul Woolley is friends with Benny and the only way Barbara would have earned the position would have been because she's a dirty, lying scoundrel!"

"I agree," Fred said. "Those qualities seem to be the prerequisites to getting a senior executive position in this establishment. But I don't care. As long as I don't have to put up with the bitch any more, I'm happy."

Shortly after, word got around that Kim Weasel was permanently promoted to the position of Executive Level 2.2. It was a discrete position that was selectively advertised.

"That Kim is a skank who never deserved a promotion," Anton complained.

"I agree, but you've got to hand it to Kim, she always seems to be in the right place at the right time," Ivan commented.

Fred was contemplative for a little while before he spoke. "Yes, I agree that you have to hand it to Kim. She appears to have stuffed up just about every job she's ever had and yet she still keeps on getting promoted."

*   *   *

An invitation was distributed from Edward Bean, a senior executive who was interested in meeting staff. A number of staff accepted the invitation, more so out of curiosity than anything else. At the meeting, Edward mentioned that he'd be starting a transition to retirement.

"I'll be scaling back my work days from five days a week to four days a week," Edward explained. "However, I don't expect that this will impact on my productivity."

Fred contained his laughter as he thought, *I suspect you could scale back your days from five days a week to zero days a week and this still wouldn't impact on your productivity!*

*   *   *

Fred received an email that he was to coordinate an Interpretative View project. Attached was a spreadsheet listing hundreds of Interpretative Views to be reviewed in order to determine whether they needed to be updated, withdrawn or replaced.

Fred set up a system of recording the cases that included who they were to be allocated to and the provision for tracking their progress. The project was classified as low priority and the cases were to be undertaken over time as business as usual. Fred was permitted to draw on a dedicated team to undertake the work.

Fred was also allocated a number of cases progressively over the performance period in accordance with the instructions handed down by Benny Heel. With every case, Fred was the case owner, which meant that he had the responsibility of undertaking all the technical work as well as all the system and administrative functions.

Fred enjoyed doing the technical work but disliked the time consumed completing the system and administrative tasks. No-one else in Tax Law was required to undertake all these duties. He felt that these working arrangements had nothing to do with performance management and everything to do with punishment.

As Fred was seated one day, he overheard Chris Alexakos speaking on the telephone and he knew he was talking to Lisa Lovelace.

"I'm surprised. He's doing exceptionally well," Chris stated. "In fact, his work is among the best I've seen."

Fred didn't know who Chris was talking about, but he was hoping that it was him.

Chris scheduled annual reviews and Fred's was the first. In line with previous years, Fred produced a list of the cases he had worked on during the year. He had not completed as many cases as he had averaged in prior years but, given his added responsibilities, he considered that it was reasonable.

Chris went through Fred's cases and took a moment before he shared his views. "Fred, I really can't fault your work. It's obvious that you are a competent and experienced officer and, as you have probably noticed, I tend to approach you above all others if I have a technical question. I have no qualms in rating you as fully effective."

Fred thanked Chris for his comments before he joked. "Chris, you've performed a miracle. In a matter of less than a year you have transformed an officer who was completely incompetent and useless to an officer who is now fully effective."

Chris shook his head. "I must admit, based on your experience, capability and work ethic, I really can't see how anyone could have given you such a poor appraisal as the one you received last year. What happened?" Chris asked.

Fred then took the next hour to explain.

Fred felt relieved as he returned to his workstation.

After Anton completed his performance review, he was loitering around Fred's workstation. He stayed for a lengthy period with a smirk on his face.

"How did you go with your performance appraisal?" Anton eventually asked Fred.

Fred sensed that Anton was in one of his smart-arse moods. "I did okay," he replied.

"So did you improve on last year?" Anton queried. His tone was sarcastic.

Fred was rarely impressed with what Anton had to say and this latest statement infused him with pure disdain, but he kept silent.

"You know Chris stated that he was very happy with what I've been doing," Anton boasted.

It was at this point that Fred exploded. "He's happy with what you've been doing? What have you been doing? Cracking walnuts!"

Anton's smirk was wiped off his face and it was replaced with his usual stunned mullet expression. He then returned to his workstation with his tail between his legs.

Anton, Ivan and Fred were at their workstations when Lisa visited one morning and advised that she may have a chat with them later in the day. It was around 5.00 pm when she made a brief appearance.

"My apologies," Lisa said. "I've been called away for most of the day and I've got to go to catch my flight soon, but how are things going?"

Anton was uncharacteristically quick to speak up and he went on and on about a case he was working on until Lisa cut him short.

"That's interesting," she remarked. "How is it going with you, Fred?"

"Things have improved markedly," Fred replied. "However, there is a loose end that I would like to have reviewed."

"Okay, why don't you contact me?" Lisa suggested.

Fred drafted an email to Lisa and attached the email that Benny had sent him, setting out the instructions on the allocation of work. Fred wrote:

> Further to our brief talk last Wednesday when I mentioned a loose end, I draw your attention to Benny's email. As far as I am aware, this instruction is still in force. My view is, since I have been assessed as fully effective in my 2010 annual appraisal, that this would be grounds for me to return to normal duties.

Lisa sent an email to Fred, copied to Chris, where she wrote: "I have spoken to Chris about this matter and we agreed that Chris can advise the leadership team that you are to resume work as usual".

Receiving the email from Lisa prompted Fred to forward it with an email to John Lazarus, Ron McFly and Carlo Giro. Fred wrote:

> Gentlemen, I'm forwarding this email FYI. Based on my 2010 performance appraisal and the attached email reply from Lisa, my performance issues appear to have been resolved. If I were to have pursued my civic duty, had the intestinal fortitude and a lazy $100 000, I should have taken this matter further. Though obviously not through any Mickey Mouse internal Tax Office process. This is a thought that has pervaded my mind and I expect it will do so for some time to come. However, I have decided to take the easy option and get on with my life. Thanks again for all your assistance and support, it proved invaluable, especially during my darkest hours.

Chapter 48 – Back to Abnormal

Fred was perusing the latest taxation rulings issued by the Tax Office when he noted one on the same topic as the public ruling he had worked on for over two years—the public ruling that senior executive Aaron Lincoln had put on hold.

Fred couldn't help but chuckle as he read the ruling, as it had a similar legal analysis to the initial version drafted years before. Although, his chuckle soon subsided and he became solemn as different thoughts entered his mind. *The intervention by senior management was so obstructive and time wasting. The legal interpretation was so clear from the very beginning. Well done, senior management!*

Fred attempted to approach his work with new vigour and a positive attitude. However, he found that cases were still being allocated to him as the case officer to do all the managing, research and authorship. He mentioned this to Chris, who promised to raise the matter at the next work allocation meeting.

Chris came off the phone and Fred heard him whisper in exasperation. "That bloody Barbara!"

"What's up?" Fred asked.

"I mentioned that you were seeking to have work allocated as approving officer and Barbara Butt responded that you should just do the cases you are given," Chris advised. "I've noted that there are a few people under performance review and it appears that Barbara is involved in each one of those cases."

"How ironic," Fred commented. "Barbara seems to go out of her way to get involved in the performance management of staff when maybe she is the person who truly deserves to be performance managed."

Advertisements were soon published for Executive Level 2.1 and 2.2 positions.

"Are you going to apply?" Anton sarcastically asked Fred.

Fred had to contain himself before he replied. "Very funny, Anton. You know very well that I've been struggling to regain my reputation in my current position."

A number of officers applying were the same ones who had applied when Fred last had. When the successful applicants were notified, those same officers were all promoted. Chris was also promoted, with his acting position as an Executive Level 2.2 team leader position being made permanent. Fred absorbed the information, contemplating what could have been if the senior executives had not ruined his career.

At the same time that Chris was promoted, two women also gained promotion: Dorothy Nasser and Sally Rhimes.

Sally was in her early thirties. She was a career public servant who had advanced through the ranks at a rapid pace. She boasted that her success was largely due to a senior executive who had acted as her mentor since she was a graduate.

Dorothy was in her late twenties, with external experience. She had been in the Tax Office for only a couple of years. She was an exceptionally confident young woman, which was often manifested with an air of arrogance.

There seemed to be a competitive air between Dorothy and a lady from Recruitment who sat across from her named Vera Yates.

"So, are we going to have the opportunity to witness a decent cat fight today?" Fred queried as the pair became a bit feisty with one another.

The women simply rolled their eyes.

Dorothy would often criticise the messy state of Vera's workstation, which was justifiable as Vera did indeed have items littered on and around her desk, including food that had been left to fester for days.

One day, Dorothy was engaged in a prolonged monologue, criticising Vera in her absence, when Fred couldn't resist blurting out a comment. "Well, at least Vera's got a decent rack."

"So she's well endowed, so what?" Dorothy snapped back.

"I was referring to Vera's rack of herbs and spices on her desk, not her well-rounded, voluptuous breasts," Fred joked. "Not that I've been looking."

"No, not that we've all been looking," Theo added. "And not that there's anything wrong with that."

Another move was that of Tom Knuckles, who was in Tax Law and who was successful in gaining a promotion to Tax Counsel. People were congratulating Tom when Ivan, Theo and Fred joined in.

"Well done," Fred told Tom. "Although you'll have to park your effervescent personality somewhere as there's no place for personality in Tax Counsel."

Tom mentioned that he would be undertaking the Victorian Bar's readers' course. "I hope to be admitted to the Bar," Tom advised and the moment the comment was made, the jokes started flying.

"Is this readers' course followed by a writers' course and an arithmetic course?" Fred quipped.

"He's doing a course just to be admitted to the bar," Theo commented.

"We're already being admitted to the bar," Ivan waded in. "The pub bar!"

*　*　*

Zoran Varga sent Fred an email that noted: "Just FYI—Dianne Fallon, Charles Milne and I have finalised the review as instructed by senior executive Allen Lion of the 2008 Interpretative View where you were the approving officer. The new Interpretative View will issue and is attached. Same outcome, just more detailed reasoning".

Fred read the Interpretative View and sat back. *So after almost three years with numerous staff on various teams reviewing the Interpretative View, the outcome was that the view was, in fact, correct and Allen was the one who was wrong. Bravo, Allen, and thanks for keeping me in the loop.*

*　*　*

Fred went on holidays in June 2011 and, when he returned in July, he asked Theo whether there had been any developments while he had been away.

"None that should concern you," Theo reassured him. "Although Ivan decided to retire on a whim and just left."

Fred was pleased to send an email to the team members who were part of the Interpretative Views project. He wrote:

> FYI, if my records are correct, we have completed 163 review cases. Seems like a lifetime ago since we commenced the project, with team members coming, going and even retiring during that time. I appreciate that you were required to complete these low priority cases while you were doing your higher priority workload, but this didn't stop you getting the job done. Congratulations to all!

As Fred sent off the email, a manager was heard cursing. "Come and take a look at this!"

Chris and Theo walked across to the manager's workstation and read off his monitor.

Theo yelled, "Oh, what?"

Dorothy scurried across, read off the manager's monitor and shouted, "This is bullshit!"

"What in the hell's going on?" Fred asked and was allowed to read the following email sent to various managers:

> It has been brought to the attention of senior executives that there have been excessive tea breaks being taken (Fred Campari and his mates?). This should not be allowed to continue. It may require that their swipe cards are monitored so that their wayward work patterns can be properly dealt with. You will need to take appropriate action to deal with this problem.

The sentiment of the Executive Level 2.2 officers was unambiguous.

"I'm going to reply to this email to challenge the basis for it!" Chris asserted.

"This is ridiculous!" Dorothy declared. "There's nothing wrong with what you guys are doing and people in other areas are much worse with their tea breaks!"

Fred tried to place the email into some sort of perspective. "I suspect someone has made a complaint. I also suspect that the complainant must be someone who has the ear of the senior executives, in which case the validity of the complaint would not be queried, but expected to be acted upon."

Dorothy would not be silenced. "I don't care what people report. I'm not going to put up with false claims and I'm not going to have my actions restricted for fear of rumours. I think we should recommence the team quiz and continue our tea break privileges."

"You may well be in a position to do as you wish and get away with it; however, others may not have this luxury and may be the ones who are blamed. A prime example is when Bee used to insist on doing the quiz, it was Ivan whom they blamed," Fred reasoned.

Dorothy eventually became more subdued about the situation, during which time one of the managers sent an email response noting that the managers had already dealt with the issue of tea breaks and that it was no longer an issue.

The matter died down. Even so, it left many people bitter.

"There are spies among us," Theo warned.

*   *   *

Tax Office staff were sent an email advising that there would be public attention concerning a staff member who was to speak out about alleged Tax Office behaviours following their whistleblower complaint.

The Tax Office's response was the standard "No comment".

The Tax Office can always draw on its trump cards of privacy concerns and the secrecy provisions to keep information hidden, Fred thought.

Whistleblower complaints were made under public service legislation where the employees were to be protected and for the alleged breaches to be properly investigated.

During 2011, there had been much gossip within the Tax Office about employees who made whistleblower complaints and that one of them who pursued the matter was handed special treatment. Subsequent to the complaint, it was rumoured that management alleged the employee's leadership behaviours were unsatisfactory, stripped the employee of leadership responsibilities, bullied and harassed the employee, directed the employee to undergo a psychiatric medical examination, and refused to allow the employee to be transferred to another area. The end result was that the employee suffered a breakdown.

Hearing the rumours was one thing, but evidencing the case first-hand alleging Tax Office behaviours that breached code of conduct hit home for Fred. It was later reported that the staff member had left the Tax Office with gossip of a confidential payout.

How bizarre that the Whistleblower legislation, the very legislation that was meant to protect an employee, seems to have been used to crucify them, Fred thought.

Chapter 49 – Law Restructure

The Tax Office had mooted a restructure of the Law area in an effort to provide better technical decision-making at the coalface. The restructuring had been in train for some time and there now seemed to be some movement. In preparation for the restructure, there was a stocktake of cases on hand across all of the Tax Law areas.

It had long been reported that the other Tax Law areas had much more work than the International area; however, it came as a surprise when the figures showed that out of all the cases on hand, International accounted for almost half of them.

An email was sent to Tax Law staff providing instructions to act on outstanding Interpretative Views as part of the transition to the new structure.

The email embedded an attachment with the Interpretative Views on hand. Fred opened the attachment and was astonished with what he saw. The older cases were around two years old and Fred was aware that Allen had a hand in every one of them. One of the outstanding cases in particular caught his eye. It was the very case about which Gordon Hirsch boasted that he could come up with an alternative view.

The next stage of the Law area restructure allowed staff to place expressions of interest. Fred elected Big Business and, once he had made his decision, others began querying his choice.

"Big Business is the only area that has committed to maintain and value people's specialisations and I'd also prefer to have some say in my destiny," Fred explained.

The movements were advised in short time, with Chloe Callas being the first to be advised that she was destined for Small Business. Sally Rhimes was off to Medium Business. Dorothy Nasser, Chris Alexakos and Anton Georgiou were to be part of the new Law area. Duke Box, Theo Onassis, Cas Boer and Fred were destined for a new Techo Group in Big Business.

Fred received an email with the subject "A sincere thanks". The email contained a letter from representatives of the Law area. The letter expressed their personal thanks for his contribution, continued dedication and professionalism. Everyone else who was leaving the Law area apparently received the same letter.

Fred was to be bestowed another honour. He received an email entitled "Years of Service Celebration". He was congratulated for reaching an employment milestone of 30 years in the public service. He was invited to a presentation ceremony to be held in the amenities area. The email noted that the direct manager and senior executive would also be invited. Confirmation of attendance or non-attendance was requested. Fred did not reply to the invitation and did not attend the ceremony.

The site manager visited Fred's workstation and handed him his "Certificate of Recognition" for 30 years of service. The site manager then shook Fred's hand, congratulated him and walked away.

Fred looked around the floor at staff who were occupied doing whatever they were doing. He stood up and made an announcement. "I've just been presented my 30 years of service certificate and I'd like to thank everyone who has assisted me over those years."

He noticed that the staff were all still going about their business and his words fell on deaf ears. *How appropriate,* he thought as he sat down to continue his work.

Chapter 50 – Destination 735

Fred enjoyed a relaxing overseas holiday until his return to work on Monday 2 July 2012. The Melbourne office had relocated during his absence so he made his way to the new office. He found it curious that the project to relocate was named "Destination 735", as the office ended up at 747 Collins Street, Docklands.

There was no-one around when Fred arrived on his floor at 8.40 am. He found his workstation, identifiable by the boxes bearing his name. He tried to settle in, although he was having trouble with his telephone and computer.

Anton arrived on the scene, but he proved to be useless, rendering zero assistance. Roman Cox, Fred's new manager, was next to arrive and proved to be just as useless. It wasn't until Chris arrived that Fred received some useful aid.

Fred spent the whole day on the telephone with the Help people and had a couple of visits from Systems people before his problems were resolved. He then settled into his workstation, pleased with the 270 degree views of Port Phillip Bay and surrounds.

Staff welcomed Fred back to work as they arrived. He perused his emails and discovered that many of them focused on a review being conducted on Big Business. Looking at his other emails, Fred noted one from Penny Farthing, an Executive Level 2.2 who had been transferred into Internationals. The email set out work required for new international tax legislation. The main task was to review all the existing Tax Office international products.

Fred contacted Penny to gain further information, but Penny seemed to have little idea as to how to proceed. Fred asked a number of probing questions, which prompted Penny to delegate full responsibility over to him.

Fred would be a member of the Techo Group's International Tax team with the other five members: Denise Chew, Lauren Stamis, Hoa Lu, Theo Onassis and Adrian Castle.

After gaining approval from Penny, Fred sent an email to the International team. In the email, Fred explained the new legislation, attached a copy of the instructions for the review and explained a master spreadsheet set up to facilitate the recording of the review, detailing the various products and, for each product, the allocated case officer and reviewing officer.

The International team made a fine working unit and, in a matter of weeks, they had completed the review and the master spreadsheet. Fred was proud to send out an email, noting: "FYI, the review of the international tax documents has been completed. Thanks to everyone for their fine efforts".

Expecting some feedback from Penny, Fred didn't hear a peep. Instead, he was contacted by staff from International Risk.

"A national phone hook-up is to be organised and we'd appreciate it if you could attend," the contact said. "Oh, we'd also appreciate it if you could send through your master spreadsheet."

Fred met up with Morris Levy for afternoon tea.

Morris appeared unsettled. "International Risk has been undergoing a review, with management stating that we were top heavy with too many Executive Level 2 officers and that the area was underperforming," Morris revealed.

"Well, it's no secret that a number of people have been asking what the staff in International Risk actually did. However, the criticism was aimed at management who had stripped the area of many of its functions and created the current structure," Fred said.

"Well, management are stating that the area is unproductive and are pointing the finger at staff. They are indicating that the performance appraisals of staff will be marked down," Morris divulged.

"I don't expect that you will be marked down," Fred said, although Morris's expression told a different story.

"My mid-year appraisal was to be just with my manager, Voula Vrakas; however, Daryl Sandwich, as our senior executive, was invited to attend so I invited my union representative. A woman from Personnel was then invited to attend," Morris explained.

"It sounds like a cast of thousands," Fred commented, not really knowing what to say to hide his concern. "So how did it go?"

Morris appeared slightly upset as he explained. "The meeting got out of hand with both sides arguing about the process. Daryl actually left the meeting at one stage. The upshot was that they argued that I should be marked down in line with the area."

Fred was silent for a while, not wanting to say anything negative, but he finally spoke his mind. "I can understand management acting in such an improper manner, but I'm very disappointed with Voula. She had the choice of making a stand to support you or just doing what management told her to do and we now know what sort of person she really is; she's a management stooge."

Morris was stoic in his fight against Tax Office management and his pursuers backed off. Voula was soon replaced as his manager and his new manager left well alone. The outcome was that Morris was found fully effective and there was no performance issue.

Chapter 51 – Big Business

The Techo Group was relocated within the Docklands building to be closer to the staff they would be servicing in Big Business. Fred's workstation was nestled in between those of Cas Boer, Theo Onassis and three other Techo Group staff members, Sarah Boo, Kasin Cutlett and Philip Latio. Fred found Sarah and Kasin to be two pleasant neighbours and Philip to be rather strange.

Fred joined his old mates from Big Business for lunch, which had developed into a Friday tradition. Robert Romano and Paul Macello were both concerned with the Big Business restructure and the prospect of losing their jobs. Carlo Giro was planning to work on, although he was not overly concerned about being made redundant. George Hayek, on the other hand, was euphoric about the possibility of a golden handshake.

The union sent an email to union members regarding a review of the Big Business team structures. It highlighted the primary recommendation to recruit Administrative Service Level 4 to 6 officers to replace Executive Level 1 and 2 officers. The union noted that the proposed staffing restructure would dramatically reduce the business area's capability to deal with compliance issues in the big business market and that the revenue from this market was in jeopardy. The union called the proposal irresponsible.

Officers in Big Business were invited to attend a meeting by Tax Office senior executives to discuss the proposed workforce changes.

Buster Basham was the senior executive to facilitate the meeting and Anita Root fronted up as a senior executive to assist.

"The purpose of this meeting is to communicate management's messages, answer any questions and relay any comments back up the line," Buster stated at the outset. "I've been in the office for almost 30 years and these restructures happen from time to time. The main message is that Big Business teams in Melbourne office are too top heavy and we're to move toward more defensible team structures. This would comprise lower level officers taking on more of the operative responsibilities. It is planned that any positions found excess will be handled through redeployments or voluntary redundancies. There will be no involuntary redundancies." Buster looked around the room. "This is the commencement of a consultation process where staff can provide feedback that will be passed back up the line. So are there any questions?"

Buster fielded questions and, in response, he recited the rehearsed management spiel. It was obvious that there was much he did not know. Anita proved to be even less informed as she hardly said a word. Attendees were then invited to make comments.

One person put up his hand. "It has been most upsetting how management's messages have changed over time. At one stage, staff members were being told that there could be involuntary redundancies and this caused people tremendous concern."

"Well, I can now confirm that there will be no involuntary redundancies," Buster replied.

Another participant put up his hand. "You know, this whole process has taken a heavy toll on many people, so much so that some people have joined the union and others have taken out mortgage insurance in the fear that they could lose their job."

"It has been deplorable how management initially put fear into staff by stating that they could be sacked," another participant said.

There was a moment of silence before Buster commented. "Well, this was unfortunate."

"It is not good enough to say that it was unfortunate," a participant called out. "It should be passed up the line that staff considered this to have been inappropriate and unacceptable!"

"We will pass your comments up the line," Buster promised.

*　　*　　*

Paul Peters, from the Techo Group in Melbourne office, and Fred were assigned to assist on a case involving a major multinational audit. They were invited to attend a telephone hook-up with numerous officers from across the country, including staff from International Risk and the audit team.

The audit case had already been in process for over a year before they had engaged the Techo Group. Ahead of the hook-up, Paul and Fred were provided with a mountain of documentation. In all the documentation comprising the audit files, they saw little evidence of any audit work having been conducted.

"We don't really see any major risks in the audit; however, we just wanted the Techo Group to tick off on the high-risk technical issues," said Jenny, the team leader.

"I agree that the case shouldn't involve too much. After all, even if the dividends being repatriated to Australia are being claimed as exempt income to the company, they'll be taxable when they are distributed to the individual shareholders," stated James Casey from International Risk.

"Yes, I agree," Phil Pickles, also from International Risk, was quick to say.

Paul and Fred looked at each other in sheer amazement as they absorbed the naive comments.

The meeting concluded on an agreed plan whereby Paul and Fred would look over the multinational group to examine the technical issues and to tick off on the high-risk areas.

After the meeting, the case officer, Susan East, spoke to Paul and Fred. "I was only recently promoted to an Administrative Service Officer Class 6 position when I was handed over this case. In fact, it is the first audit that I've ever worked on," Susan advised.

"So who's been working with you on the case?" Paul queried.

"No-one really; I've been doing the audit on my own," Susan revealed.

"You've got to be joking!" Fred reacted. "Don't you have a team leader and technical leader to assist you on the audit?"

"Not really," Susan responded. "Jenny is the team leader but she only deals with administrative matters and the technical leader only deals with discrete technical issues as they crop up. That's why I really appreciate your assistance, it being my first audit."

"There were so many people in attendance at the hook-up. Aren't any of them involved in the case?" Paul queried.

"No, they just seem to become involved when the senior executives start asking questions," Susan advised.

Fred couldn't believe his ears. *Is this what Tax Office management considers to be a more defensible team structure? What a joke!*

"The managers don't seem to like me and they bully me," Susan disclosed. "Simon Sez is the worst. He blames me for so many things and yells at me to the point where I cry."

This information maddened Fred. "Did you put in an incident report?" he immediately asked.

"No, I didn't," Susan conceded. "Maybe I should have, but I am afraid.”

“Don’t let them get to you,” Fred stated, even though he knew that this was easier said than done. “If you do your job as well as you can, that’s all that anyone can ask of you and we’ll help you as much as we can.”

Chapter 52 – Getting on with Big Business

An increased number of cases were being referred to the Techo Group from Big Business teams by staff who had little, if any, support from their team leaders, technical leaders or senior executives. Bruno Venus was one such staff member. He was involved in a complex transfer pricing case, which was assigned to Fred to assist.

Bruno was flustered as he spoke to Fred. "I recently had my performance appraisal. You know, my manager stated that I'm just jogging on the spot. I can't believe it! I do my job and they always want more, although they don't seem to know what more they want. And have you ever got a straight answer out of an economist?"

"Well, you know what they say about economists. If you asked two economists for an opinion, you'd get at least three opinions," Fred joked. "You really shouldn't worry about them."

"Don't worry?" Bruno exclaimed. "I'm sick of it all and I feel that I should go on my holidays and not bother coming back!"

"Certainly go on holidays and have a great time," Fred said. "Because when you come back to the Tax Office, the circus will still be in town."

*　*　*

There was much discussion about the annual appraisals, given the changes to the Tax Law areas. The transitional arrangement for the Techo Group was that the annual appraisals would be conducted by the managers they had had during the year. This meant that Cas, Theo and Fred would have their appraisals conducted by Sally.

Fred sent Sally a document capturing his work for the year, his performance agreement, his professional development record and his officer feedback report. He rang Sally just ahead of the scheduled time to confirm the meeting before he made his way to the room. He arrived on time and Sally appeared soon after. It was a cordial meeting, being the first time they had talked since the restructure.

"So how do you think you went this year, Fred?" Sally asked.

Fred referred to the summary of his work. "I feel I didn't achieve anything outstanding; however, I'm comfortable that I completed the full scope of work and the requirements as set out in my performance agreement. I was particularly pleased with the Interpretative View project that I coordinated and which produced a good team effort."

Sally was quick to provide her assessment. "I think that you were professional and a fine role model for the team, especially the graduates, who found you most approachable. From my personal experience, I consider you to be a reliable officer who was a pleasure to work with. I have no trouble in finding you fully effective."

Fred left the meeting in good spirits, not so much for gaining a rating that just about everyone else would get, but because of the uncertain times being experienced in the Tax Office.

Sally took her time to send through Fred's record of annual appraisal. In fact, she had to be reminded and eventually left it until the day before she was due to go on leave.

Fred was quick to confirm his rating as fully effective. He then read the comments that largely accorded to the verbal comments made during the meeting and noticed that an adverse comment had been tacked on at the end.

These management types always feel they have to come up with some critical comment to justify their existence, Fred thought. He then forwarded the email on to his new manager, Roman Cox.

Paul and Fred continued working on the multinational audit case with Susan. It was apparent that there was little auditing work conducted prior to their engagement, so they virtually had to start the audit from scratch. They both assisted Susan to undertake the audit and, just as Susan had described, the team leader and technical leader from the audit team were unheard of unless there were planning or governance issues to deal with.

Paul and Fred drafted requests for further information and the initial enquiries led to further enquiries. During this time, Matt Atkinson, who had been assigned as the senior executive case leader, returned from leave. Paul and Fred briefed him on the case and explained the strategy they had developed to complete the audit.

"When we were assigned this case, we attended a hook-up with a number of officers; however, we learned that Susan was the only staff member on the whole audit team who is working on the case," Paul advised.

"Susan had just been promoted to an Administrative Service Officer Class 6 position and had to deal with the case on her own before we started helping her out, even though it was her first audit," Fred added.

"I know," Matt said. "I had a similar experience when I attended a meeting with a cast of thousands and I thought there was a whole team on this case. It's a good thing you guys are helping her out."

"We are supposed to be providing technical assistance," Paul complained. "We shouldn't be undertaking the whole audit."

"The bottom line is that there's a job to be done and someone has to do it," Matt said. "If there is no-one on the team who can do the job or who isn't prepared to do it, then we really have no option but to do it ourselves."

"What about the team leader and the technical leader? How do they get away without helping the case officer at all on the case?" Paul questioned.

Matt shook his head. "I know, but there's little I can do."

Paul and Fred came out of the meeting room.

"This is unbelievable," said Paul. "You have all these senior officers who are earning a good salary and yet they get away with doing nothing on the case!"

"I know how you feel but this is the Tax Office. I see it happen all the time," Fred said.

"So you think these officers will get away without doing anything?" Paul asked.

"I expect that this is precisely what will happen," Fred suggested. "They can always rationalise it by arguing that the Techo Group had been assigned to do the work so there was no reason for them to be involved. The luxury for them is that if we find nothing they can blame us and if we find something they'll take the glory."

"So you think they won't be held to account for doing nothing?" Paul persisted in asking.

"Held to account?" Fred repeated. "I expect that as senior officers and the fact that they're getting away without doing anything they'll have senior executives supporting them and they'll never be held to account. In fact, they're more likely to be promoted!"

Paul started laughing until he realised that Fred wasn't joking.

*　　*　　*

Fred attended an International discussion group meeting where Sissy Mayfair gave a presentation on international tax. After the session, Fred had afternoon coffee with Sissy and they discussed the latest developments in Big Business.

Sissy, who was usually philosophical about life, seemed disillusioned. "No-one knows how it's all going to end up," she commented. "It all seems to be a huge shemozzle."

"You should be all right," Fred suggested. "Voula Vrakas is your manager and you seem to be doing her a lot of favours by taking on work I thought was part of her responsibilities."

"Yeah, I know," Sissy said. "I'm also conducting most of the international tax training around the country."

"So what in the hell does Voula do?" Fred queried.

Sissy did not reply, but showed her opened hands, shrugged her shoulders and gave a wry smile.

Fred was busily trying to complete his work on hand ahead of his next holiday. Friday 26 October 2012 came around and he ticked off his tasks from his flip top calendar as he completed them. He was pleased to have finished his work before he packed up and wished everyone goodbye. He heard a number of people echoing words of farewell as he walked out and headed off.

Chapter 53 – International Tax Capers

Fred returned to work in early December 2012. As the festive season neared, the season's greetings commenced with an email from Susan East to Paul Peters and Fred. She wrote:

> Thank you very much for your support. Bob Markovski is now my team leader and Firas Kuri is my new technical leader. I really enjoy working with you guys. It's a really supportive team. Merry Christmas!

Nathan Witt, a Tax Law officer, was visiting his friends in the Techo Group when Fred overheard him cursing.

"What's up?" Fred asked.

"I was allocated an international tax matter, which had been passed around from one senior executive to another," Nathan advised.

"So what's the problem?" asked Fred.

"The case stems back to a private ruling request on the question of whether profits were attributable to Australia," Nathan informed Fred.

The moment Fred heard about the nature of the case, he stared at Nathan and gave him his full attention. Nathan noted Fred's reaction.

"Why? What's wrong?" Nathan asked.

"The case you describe is similar to private ruling cases I was involved in that caused me no end of trouble," Fred revealed. "I submitted that some of the income was attributable to Australia and some was not. However, Barbara Butt concocted some ridiculous approach whereby all the income was attributable to Australia."

As Fred finished his explanation, he noticed Nathan's expression turn serious. "What's the matter?" Fred asked.

"Barbara happened to be involved in this case as well and she also came up with the view that all the income was attributable to Australia," Nathan divulged.

"Well, what do you know?" Fred commented. "It seems that Barbara has developed an effective way to deal with attributable income cases."

"Actually, no," Nathan added. "The applicant objected to the private ruling and they were prepared to litigate the matter."

"So what happened?" Fred asked in an elevated voice as he edged closer to Nathan.

"The Tax Office obtained legal advice that concluded that it would be difficult to establish that all the income was attributable to Australia and subsequently settled the case on the basis that only part of the income was attributable. I now have to deal with the settlement going forward," said Nathan.

Fred fell back on his chair and reflected. "So there you go," he remarked. "The bitch was finally properly challenged on her view and she was proven to be wrong."

There was a quiet moment before Nathan spoke. "People like her usually get found out."

"Get found out?" Fred repeated. "Not in the Tax Office. Barbara wasn't found out; she actually got promoted to a senior executive!"

*   *   *

Fred was settling in well with his new working arrangements, although Philip Latio was starting to annoy him. Philip's workstation was close to Fred's, so every noise that Philip made was noticeable to him.

Philip was loud when he talked over the phone, with the strength of his voice and laughter seeming to ascend in line with the seniority of the officer on the other end of the phone. This meant that when Philip had a telephone conversation with a senior executive, his voice and laughter was like being at the opera.

Philip also had the habit of eating his food at his workstation and, like Anton, he would tend to eat throughout the day. This meant that Fred had to put up with an array of noises such as Philip scraping the bottom of every plastic tub to ensure that he lapped up every remaining microscopic particle of food. Also like Anton, Philip fancied his nuts, but whereas Anton liked walnuts, Philip's nuts of choice were pistachios. Philip would spend an eternity circling his empty pistachio nut shells with his index finger to ensure that he had captured all the edible bits. It sounded like he was playing marbles.

*   *   *

Roman Cox procrastinated about holding the mid-year review meetings, but Fred was eventually scheduled. Ahead of the meeting,

Fred provided Roman with a summary of his work for the year as well as the standard forms.

At the meeting, Roman proceeded to embark on his rehearsed management speech. Fred was put off by the fact that Roman did not engage in any eye contact nor in any conversation about his work. He preferred to go through the standard forms and make a series of notes in line with the latest Tax Office buzzwords. Fred's only contribution to the exercise was to agree when he was prompted. It then came to the performance rating.

"Well, as everyone knows, you only need a heartbeat to get a rating of fully effective," Roman commented.

"Is that so?" Fred replied. "I would have thought that there would have needed to be some actual work involved."

"I was thinking of giving you a rating of fully effective," Roman stated. "You know that's what most people get and it's not worth going through all the extra paperwork to give anything more."

"That's fine," Fred stated.

After Fred had his meeting, Paul Peters was next. When Paul emerged, they had a chat about their respective meetings.

"It's a joke," Paul commented.

"As long as I get a rating of fully effective, I'm happy," Fred responded.

"So the fact that you do the more complex cases and a greater number of cases than the others as well as managing staff without getting any acknowledgement whatsoever doesn't bother you?" Paul asked.

"Based on what I've been subjected to in this joint," Fred said, "I count myself lucky."

Chapter 54 – Withdrawing Interpretative Views

One day, Paul began pacing around Fred's desk.

"What's up?" Fred asked.

"I don't believe these Business Line people!" Paul said.

"What's wrong now?" Fred enquired.

"They've been conducting an audit and I was engaged to provide technical advice, which I did," Paul explained. "An Interpretative View was even created based on this position."

"That seems fairly uncontroversial," Fred said. "So what's the problem?"

"The Business Line guys don't want to raise the tax," Paul advised. "They now seem intent on getting the Interpretative View overturned."

"The responsibility for Interpretative Views rests with the Law area," Fred suggested.

"The Business Line officers put together some absurd alternative view and is insisting that the Law area change the position, but the Law area aren't comfortable with their view," Paul said. "The Business Line is now putting pressure to have the Interpretative View pulled."

Fred's response was immediate. "If the Law area caves in to the Business Line, then the Interpretative View will be pulled. Once pulled, the Business Line won't have an obligation to raise the tax and can give the case away."

"But that's ridiculous!" Paul exclaimed. "If they withdraw the Interpretative View then they'll have to replace it with another public view!"

"No, they won't," said Fred.

As it transpired, the Interpretative View was withdrawn with the reason that the position was being reviewed.

Paul wandered over to Fred's workstation and sat on the window ledge. "Do you know they withdrew the Interpretative View?" he asked.

"Yeah, I know," Fred replied.

"They state that they're reviewing the position," said Paul, frowning.

"Yeah, I know that too," Fred responded.

"I really wouldn't have a problem if they issued a replacement Interpretative View, but they're not going to do that, are they?" Paul asked with resignation.

"No, I don't expect they will. They don't need to. The Business Line has obtained what they want and they don't have to worry about raising the tax as it is no longer mandated under an Interpretative View," Fred opined.

"I wonder why we bother studying complex tax laws and coming up with technical decisions when others are just prepared to give everything away," Paul commented, sounding exasperated. "We may as well throw out the tax legislation and just negotiate a tax outcome over a cup of coffee."

"What do you expect when the Tax Office deals with big business taxpayers by adopting the three Cs and big business effectively counters the Tax Office by adopting the three Ds?" asked Fred.

"What do you mean by the three Cs?" Paul queried.

"The three Cs come under the Tax Office's engagement initiative where we bend over backwards for big business through consultation, collaboration and co-design," Fred advised.

"I'm afraid to ask," Paul said. "But what are the three Ds?"

"The three Ds comprise big business's foolproof way to combat the Tax Office," Fred stated and announced his next words with voice projection. "Defer, delay and defeat!"

*　　*　　*

Cas, Theo and Fred were allocated a case and agreed that an Interpretative View needed to be created. They prepared the decision that was adverse to the applicant.

The applicant was advised of the impending adverse decision and that an Interpretative View expressing this position was to be published. The applicant immediately requested that the publication be put on hold as they would seek legal advice from legal counsel. The Tax Office granted the request.

Counsel opinion was duly provided, but the tax officers considered the arguments to be flimsy. However, as the legal counsel advice increased the significance of the issue, the case then required the involvement of Tax Law.

Nathan Witt was assigned the case and he was quick to come to the conclusion that the position set out in the Interpretative View was correct and it subsequently issued.

Two weeks later, Cas, Theo and Fred received an email from Duke Box. Duke wrote: "Gentlemen, below is some feedback on an Interpretative View, which I understand you developed. Please consider the matters raised and determine what needs to be done".

Nathan visited Cas, Theo and Fred to discuss the case. "I am of the firm view that the Interpretative View is correct; however, my boss, Jake Timberlake, asked me to review the case," Nathan explained. "I conferred with a number of highly regarded technical officers and they all agreed that there was nothing wrong with the Interpretative View. However, Jake wasn't satisfied and he instructed me that we should take an alternative view."

"Well, if you could send us the direction from Jake Timberlake in writing, we'll seek the approval from our senior executive to have the Interpretative View pulled," Fred suggested.

Nathan sent through the instruction and Fred forwarded it on to his senior executive who promptly approved the withdrawal.

When the Interpretative View was subsequently withdrawn, Fred walked over to Paul's workstation and sat on the window ledge.

"You know our Interpretative View has been withdrawn?" Fred said.

"Yeah, I know," Paul replied.

"The reason was that a public ruling on the issue is to be created," Fred advised.

"Yeah, I know that too," Paul said. "At least with your Interpretative View they'll be issuing a replacement view."

Fred nodded. "It'll be interesting to see what sort of view they come up with."

*　*　*

Paul and Fred were still engaged on the multinational audit with Susan. The team leader, Bob, and technical leader, Firas, proved to be as useless as their predecessors. They were both replaced with yet another pair: Damian Paddle as team leader and Peter Law as technical leader. To add insult to injury, Bob was promoted to an Executive Level 2.2 position.

Damian and Peter predictably took an arm's length approach to the case, although they seemed to show more interest when it was revealed that the case may actually result in an audit adjustment of around $50 million.

"It was a good pick up, Paul," Fred commented. "Based on the recorded evidence, it looks like the company has slipped up."

"That's true," Paul responded. "However, this multinational had the best technical advice and they've taken advantage of every conceivable legislative concession. I find it hard to believe that they would have made such a mistake. They've already made a number of corrections to the information they've supplied the Tax Office so I'm starting to feel that something's not right."

"The tax advisers have certainly led us down the garden path a number of times on this case," Fred said. "It probably would be a good idea to confirm the facts."

Paul drafted a query, which was approved by Matt Atkinson and issued by Susan. When the reply came in, it left them dumbfounded. The tax advisers had apologised for yet another error and corrected the facts. The audit adjustment had been wiped out.

Paul assisted Susan to complete the case and Fred felt compelled to communicate his gratitude in an email:

> Thank you Susan and Paul for all your good work on this case. Special thanks to Paul who took on the greatest burden from the Techo Group perspective. We completed an audit on a multinational in just over a year on some of the most complex international tax technical issues. The fact that we didn't end up with an audit adjustment in no way diminishes this great achievement. I wish you both all the best.

Paul was approaching Fred's workstation as Fred received an email from him. Paul sat on the window ledge and looked up to the ceiling with a disconsolate expression. Fred then read the email, which was sent by Paul to Matt Atkinson, copied to Fred. It read:

> I had a conversation with Peter Law over the telephone. Peter said that a number of officers on his team had decided a long time ago that there was nothing in the audit and that they had been sidelined. This was not the case. I have not seen any evidence that officers on his team made any decision on the case, much less that there was nothing in the case. Further, they had not been sidelined. The truth is that there was a complete lack of input from officers on his team (other than from Susan). Peter then said I shouldn't have done the work I did. Fred and I were engaged on the case and we did the best we could in trying circumstances. To the extent that I provided more assistance than I would normally is reflective of his team's lack of input. I was very disappointed with the conversation and I told him so.

Chapter 55 – International Tax Rulings

A project was set up to review Tax Office international tax products, which involved the huge task of reviewing and, where necessary, replacing international public rulings and guidance.

Mark Higgins was the project sponsor and Hans Hoff was the project leader. Penny Farthing was to play a central role, but without having any actual responsibilities. She seemed to have found the ideal sinecure.

Penny sent an email invitation for a meeting to consider the rewrite of taxation rulings. The numerous attendees were assembled in the meeting room when they observed Penny for the first time through the opened door. As Penny approached, their eyes widened as they looked around at each other.

Penny had red hair in ponytails plaited on each side and a blunt cut fringe. She had steel grey eyes that were magnified by large, rounded spectacles. She wore a floral dress and a light grey cardigan. Her attire was out of alignment, which made her look unkempt and gave her the overall appearance of a rag doll.

Penny entered the room, placed her satchel on the floor and rested her jacket around the back of a vacant chair. She then stood tall and raised her hands high into the air as if she was about to preach a sermon.

"I'll be asking you all to do some work," Penny announced. She lowered her hands and rubbed them together. "Of course, I wouldn't be asking unless it was of the utmost importance."

Penny took a seat and explained the broad objective of the project, which was to rewrite selected taxation rulings as a matter of priority. After all her theatrics, she allocated only one topic for a public ruling and it went to Fred.

The senior executives who were to sign off on Fred's ruling were advised to be Betty Mason and Perry White, both from Tax Law. Fred wasn't impressed to learn of the two names as, even though they were in Tax Law, by some reports they were not technical. It was therefore no surprise that they were to be assisted by Miles Long.

Miles was also in Tax Law, although he was quick to admit that he had no previous experience in international tax. Fred was becoming most uncomfortable that no-one he was working with on his ruling seemed to have experience in international tax.

The project team was sent the project plan. Fred had a number of concerns with the plan, although his greatest concern was that associated products were to be completed by the same time as his public ruling, but there were no details of what these associated products were. He sought clarification in an email to Mark Higgins, copied to the team members.

Later that day, Mark responded in an email: "I see any associated products that are required to be within your responsibilities".

Fred was seething over the fact that he was not made aware of the breadth of his responsibilities. He sent an email response, where he wrote: "I'll get back to you with a proposal".

Fred submitted a proposal, which he presented at a meeting with the project team. At the end of the meeting, the proposal was approved. There were now to be three related products: Fred's public ruling and two additional public rulings to be developed by Milton Hustler and Theo Onassis. Also in train was another public ruling to be authored by Ferris Wheal.

Within a couple of weeks, Fred sent around an initial version of his public ruling. A workshop was held over a few days where Fred presented his document and was provided with a number of suggestions. As Fred updated his public ruling, Milton and Theo proceeded to develop theirs.

Fred was due to go on holidays. Just before he departed, he sent off an email with the latest version of his public ruling attached.

A month later, Fred returned to work and went through his emails; however, it wasn't until the next day that he read the most telling one from Hans Hoff, copied to the project team. It read:

> Welcome back, Fred. A few of us took the time to brainstorm your public ruling. We almost got halfway so obviously more work needs to be done. We found the process most productive, which is why I'm pushing for a workshop. Both senior executives, Betty Mason and Perry White, were keen for the workshop as it's a quick way to progress public rulings. Thanks for starting us off, Fred.

Fred read through the attached document and he couldn't make much sense of it. In fact, he thought it was a complete shambles so he rang Miles to ascertain what they had done.

"Hans was keen to workshop the document and we effectively started over. We had hoped to complete the process and polish it up, but we didn't get very far," Miles said. "Why don't you contact Hans?"

Before Fred had the chance to contact Hans, he received a call from Hoa.

"Welcome back," Hoa said.

"Thanks Hoa, it's really great to be back," Fred stated sarcastically.

"Hans organised a workshop and asked a couple of us to join in. I don't really have any background in international tax. I was basically keying in on the laptop whatever they said," Hoa admitted.

Fred then contacted Hans and before he could say much, Hans began mouthing off.

"I'm trying to organise a workshop for next week to finish your public ruling," Hans stated.

"I don't see how we could possibly complete the document next week," Fred said. "I'm having a lot of trouble reviewing the document in its present state."

"Listen Fred, you need to be at the workshop. If one is organised next week then you'll be expected to be there!" Hans warned in a stern voice.

"If a workshop is organised I expect that I will attend," Fred responded in an equally stern voice. "However, I don't see how we will be able to complete a quality, technical product at a workshop next week!"

"Well, I'm arranging Betty and Perry to be at the workshop and if they are prepared to sign off on the document then you shouldn't have any problems with it," Hans contended.

"What?" Fred queried. "I shouldn't have a problem even if it's technically wrong?"

Hans ignored the question, repeated his decree and hung up.

Fred was pleased that the workshop didn't get off the ground due to budgetary pressures that restricted travel; however, two days of meetings were scheduled via telephone hook-up. The documents to be examined were the three public rulings of Milton, Theo and Fred.

The hook-up went ahead, where Milton went through his public ruling and received few comments.

The group moved on to Fred's public ruling, where he was required to use the version that was reworked during his absence.

The group was having difficulty with the document and it was then decided to start from scratch.

Fred was called upon to commence a new document using Microsoft Communicator. The group went through every one of the legislative provisions and listed the provisions as they went.

"Excuse me," Fred interrupted. "We are listing every provision, but not every one of these provisions requires an interpretative view that would usually warrant an explanation in a ruling."

"That's okay," Miles said. "We can always take them out later."

The group proceeded to list all the main provisions and Fred was instructed to rewrite the public ruling, adopting this new approach.

"What do you think about that?" Hans enquired.

"Well, to be perfectly honest, I'm effectively being required to rewrite the ruling in a manner that I'm not comfortable with so I'm not happy," Fred admitted. "However, if this is the approach that I am directed to take, then so be it."

The final document that the group considered was Theo's public ruling. The consensus was that the document needed redrafting, but no-one provided any meaningful comments. Fred had a number of ideas, but he wasn't prepared to air them to people who were most likely not able to appreciate or understand them.

Penny Farthing eventually broke the silence. "The precise wording of the document can be worked out later," she suggested.

Fred took the comment as an admission by Penny that she had no idea, but it did give Fred a lead-in. "Okay, I'll work with Theo to redraft the document," he said.

After a couple of weeks, Fred and Theo sent around their respective rewritten public rulings for comments. They reviewed the comments as they came through and made minor changes.

Fred then sent Miles an email, where he attached the latest version of his public ruling and forwarded Theo's public ruling. Fred noted: "Once you've had a chance to digest the documents Theo and I would be happy to discuss. I don't expect that it will be this year. Happy holidays!"

Chapter 56 – In the Year 2014

The new year was met with a hive of activity by the team leaders and technical leaders as they jockeyed for position with their proposals for a restructure of the Techo Group.

Fred further developed his public ruling, while Milton and Theo fine-tuned theirs. They were then required to present them at a workshop to be attended by a number of senior executives and a consultant named Hazel Nutt. Hazel was quick to admit that she did not have a background in international tax.

Milton, Theo and Fred presented their documents, with the document given the most attention being Fred's.

A number of senior executives made comments that Fred considered to have little legislative foundation; however, he bit his tongue and remained silent.

Hazel was then called upon to express her views. "I would like to make a number of observations," she stated and proceeded to make a number of points that Fred considered to be trivial or innocuous.

Hazel then made a sweeping statement, which Fred absorbed, but this time he could not contain himself. Fred tried to explain, in the most delicate way he could, that he considered the statement to be absurd. However, Hazel simply repeated her statement. Fred then tried to rephrase his response, again in the most delicate way he could, in an effort to explain how he thought that the statement was utterly idiotic.

"I heard your response," Hazel said, frowning. "I hope I don't have to repeat my statement again."

"No," Fred replied, finally appreciating that Hazel was not interested in hearing feedback on the merits of her comments. She was only there to impart her observations, regardless of how ridiculous they may be.

The authors left the workshop with the task of considering the feedback and revising their documents once again. Fred sent an email attaching the latest version of his public ruling as well as an Executive Summary to Betty Mason and Perry White, copied to Mark Higgins,

Milton and Theo.

Fred then noticed two Tax Office emails. The first was for managers to support the initiative of voluntary redundancies and the second was to employees seeking expressions of interest in a voluntary redundancy.

There was much excitement by some employees about the opportunity to depart the organisation and Fred was one of them. He proceeded to print out all the attached information and brought it home to absorb over the weekend.

As Fred sifted through the information at home, he wondered how he would feel if he were given an opportunity for an early separation from the Tax Office and he broke into song with the words of *Que Sera, Sera (Whatever will be, will be)*.

Returning to work on Monday, Fred mulled over the application he had drafted for a voluntary redundancy. The application required two ratings to support the case for his position to be made excess—a position assessment and a personal assessment.

I'll sleep on it one more night and consider whether it requires editing, Fred thought.

First thing the following morning, Fred registered on the system and commenced the voluntary redundancy process. At 11.00 am, he received an email confirming his registration. He then got caught up with work on his public ruling.

The next day, Fred finalised his application for a voluntary redundancy and submitted it on the computer system. At 2.00 pm, he received an email confirming that his application had been submitted.

Fred examined the public ruling documents that had been forwarded to the secretariat of the Rulings Panel and noted that there were a number of changes made by the approving officers. He considered most of the changes to be unnecessary, some inappropriate and some incorrect.

Fred then received an email concerning nominations for a Management Program. The program was compulsory for all managers at the Executive Levels 1 and 2; however, the initial rollout was targeted for priority staff. Fred was not going to nominate, but Roman Cox had other ideas.

"Have you nominated?" Roman asked.

"No, I have no intention of nominating, as the email makes a request for priority nominations and, as a manager of two experienced staff, I hardly consider this warrants a priority nomination," Fred responded.

"We have an allocation of a couple of places for the Techo Group. Since no-one else is nominating, other than me, you should nominate," Roman stated. "In any case, everyone will have to do the course at some stage."

"I'm prepared to do the course when I have to, but I don't want to do it now," Fred replied.

Roman shook his head. "I'm going to nominate to do it and I'm going to nominate you as well."

Fred was hoping that Roman was joking until he was copied into Roman's email nominating both of them. Fred was properly pissed off.

Later that day, Theo and Fred were having discussions with David Meaney, the Business Manager, who expressed criticism of the work practices. "As executive level officers in the Techo Group, you guys should only be engaged on cases to undertake specific tasks on technical issues and then disengage," David stated.

"The Techo Group was set up as part of a restructure to change the culture from one of escalation to one of engagement," Fred explained. "An important part of this change was to break down the barriers so that we as technical specialists could be engaged on a more flexible basis. Once we are engaged on a case, we take an ongoing role until the case is concluded."

David was uncompromising with his reaction. "Yeah, I know all about the reasons for the restructure; however, the Techo Group has limited capacity and should only be engaged on cases to provide technical specialist advice. When the Techo Group has completed their discrete task, that's it: they should disengage."

"The problem is that the Techo Group has never had any guidelines or even as much as an indication of the work we are supposed to be doing other than to assist with technical work. We have queried this very point a number of times but management have never sought to address it," Fred advised. "That is why we have been referred anything and everything with an obligation to do it as we have no basis upon which to reject the work."

"David was unsympathetic. "All this requires is a level of judgement and I'm sure your team leaders would instruct you in the type of work you should be doing based on the priorities of the area."

The moment that David mentioned what the team leaders should be doing, Roman Cox popped his head up from his workstation partition.

"Yeah, the team leaders are aware of the priorities and provide guidance on the type of work we should be doing," Roman said. "There's also flexibility and judgement required in these matters."

Fred was unimpressed with Roman's comments as he was well aware that Roman tended to allocate every international case to him, even when other team leaders were of the opinion that Techo Group involvement was not required.

The Techo Group officers were soon advised that the restructure had been set in stone. Paul Peters and Fred would no longer report to Roman Cox; instead, they would now be reporting to Duke Box. With the team leaders having less staff reporting to them, there were two officers who seemed particularly happy with the changes—Roman and Duke.

The restructure of the Techo Group also accommodated a new Executive Level 1 officer, Zara Majid, who was a breath of fresh air with her friendly nature and cheery personality.

Fred received an email that provided a progress update on the expressions of interest in a voluntary redundancy, detailing the process steps. Fred noted the final step in the process, being the notice of termination for employees who had accepted a voluntary redundancy prior to 30 June 2014. He gazed into space, contemplating the potential significance of the statement and his face developed a large grin.

Fred fronted the Rulings Panel, where there were three external panel members and nine Tax Office representatives who progressively took a seat. Hooking up via telephone were Miles and Hans. Fred was asked to go through his public ruling. As the document was examined, various topics were taken up for discussion and the external members provided a number of suggestions.

The panel meeting had reached the scheduled time for discussion on the document to end and the chairperson recommended that the public ruling could proceed subject to the agreed changes. Fred was reasonably pleased with the outcome, particularly as most of the changes related to the additions made by the approving officers.

* * *

Nathan Witt visited the Techo Group, sporting a smile.

"What's up?" Cas asked.

"You know the Interpretative View that you guys developed and then had to withdraw? Well, they've finally issued a public ruling," Nathan said as he provided a copy and left.

The document was handed around and, one by one, the officers had a similar reaction of incredulity.

"This is bullshit!" said Paul.

"I can't believe it!" Fred responded. "This would have to be the worst piece of crap I have ever read."

"How can they get away with this sort of stuff?" Theo asked.

"It's because they have the direction of senior executives and guys who mindlessly sign off on such rubbish," Fred replied.

* * *

Roman conducted Fred's mid-year review where, as usual, he wasn't interested in going over Fred's work; he was only interested in parroting the corporate messages and noting them down on the standard forms. Fred wasn't fussed about the process and was happy to hear Roman's passing, final comment.

"So I think you've satisfied the corporate requirements and I'm prepared to give you a fully effective rating."

* * *

On Friday 14 March, officers who had placed an expression of interest for a voluntary redundancy were being contacted and advised whether they had been successful.

"I need to have a word with you," Duke Box whispered to Fred.

Duke and Fred found a vacant meeting room and Duke went through the corporate messages before he advised the outcome.

"Fred, you have been categorised to be in a position that cannot be determined as excess, which means that you will not be progressing in the process."

Fred was silent for a moment to absorb the disappointing news. Not only had he been unsuccessful, he had no hope of getting a voluntary redundancy as part of the process.

"That's okay," Fred replied with resignation and solemnly returned to his workstation.

Harry Rice and Jim Zissis, formerly from the Quality Control Unit, were soon to send emails to Charlie Ambrose and Fred to boast of their success in gaining voluntary redundancies. Charlie and Fred responded separately that they had also applied, but were unsuccessful. It was an occasion that warranted Harry and Jim shouting Charlie and Fred some drinks.

On 31 March, Fred was required to commence the Management Course.

"Where have you been, Fred?" Roman asked during the lunch break.

"I'm attending the Management Course; you know, the one that you nominated me for," Fred responded sarcastically.

Chapter 57 – A Public Ruling Goes Public

Fred revised his public ruling and passed it on to Miles for review.

"You should be happy with the outcome of the Rulings Panel," Miles suggested.

"It's encouraging," Fred replied. "But I'll only be happy when the product is actually published as a final ruling."

"There'll be many more products to be developed," said Miles.

"I'm well aware of that, but I wouldn't be interested in repeating this saga," said Fred. "In any case, I'm just praying to score a voluntary redundancy."

"What? You're too young to be leaving, aren't you?" Miles asked.

"I'm actually quite ancient," Fred responded with a smile. "Even though I really enjoy the work, I'm fed up with all the politics and the deadheads I have to deal with. Yes, I'd be quite happy to leave, thank you."

"I think I know what you mean. This place gets to me as well," Miles admitted.

Miles reviewed Fred's public ruling and escalated the document to Betty and Perry. Betty returned the document with the approved changes the day before the deadline.

While Fred was putting the finishing touches on the document, an email was sent around from Aaron Lincoln. With only a day to complete the document, Aaron took it upon himself to review it and then to rewrite it.

Fred was stunned. He took some deep breaths and did a little thinking before he sent an email to Betty and Perry, where he wrote: "I plan to read through Aaron's suggested changes and make a call on effecting changes that I consider appropriate".

Within half an hour of sending the email, Fred received a telephone call from Perry. "Don't worry about reviewing Aaron's suggested changes," he said. "I've just been on the phone to Aaron and I explained that I'd go through the document and make a call as to what is deemed necessary to change. It's only a draft so we can consider Aaron's suggestions in more detail at a later date."

Fred was forwarded the changes from Perry and spent the day incorporating them into the final document. As he proceeded to effect the changes, he was cursing many of them. He then received a call from Miles.

"Some of these changes are utterly ridiculous," said Fred.

"Just change them back," Miles suggested.

"No way, I'm not doing that," Fred replied. "I have accepted my place in the world and I'm resigned to the fact that I should just take direction from the senior executives, no questions asked."

Miles reacted with shock. "Fred, I'd never thought I'd hear you say that."

"Neither did I," Fred stated. "But now I see how there's no use arguing against the senior executives. Right or wrong, they're always going to get their way and resistance is futile."

When Fred finalised the document, he sent it through for final sign off.

On Monday 7 April 2014, Errol Jonaitis returned from long-term leave and sounded downbeat as he telephoned Fred. "I applied for a voluntary redundancy, but I was unsuccessful," he advised.

"Well, join the club," Fred replied. "Although the rumours are that there are going to be more as part of the process so hang in there and you might still be successful."

"I don't know whether I can wait," Errol divulged. "There's a lot of pressure by the senior executives and they're even instructing me to put staff on performance management. I'm just fed up with all this crap."

"I can't believe what I'm hearing," Fred commented. "You used to enjoy coming into work and now you can't stand the place. What's with the huge turnaround?"

"I must admit, after everything you've been through and your comments about this place, my time away from the office really made me reflect. Now I believe that there's much more to life," Errol said. "I also think about the people around my age who have had health issues and that has also made me reflect on my life."

"Well, I appreciate that a decision to finish a lifetime career may be a tough one for some people," Fred said. "But it's absolutely no problem for me. I can hardly wait to get out of this shithole."

Fred's public ruling was finally published as a draft. He grit his teeth and shook his head as he picked up on the typos and the wording added in by the senior executives. He then prepared himself to be on stand-by to field the telephone enquiries and for the written submissions.

Fred was required to attend the next two days of sessions for the Management Course. At lunchtime on the first day, Roman asked Fred where he had been.

"I'm doing the Management Course," Fred advised. "You know, the one you nominated me for."

"I'm doing it as well and I'm finding it a real pain," Roman complained.

Chapter 58 – Budget 2014

The Budget was handed down on the evening of 13 May 2014. It was reported that there would be a reduction of 16 500 public service staff. Fred got on his computer and scoured the internet for more details.

There was a section in the Budget papers noting the staff reduction in the Tax Office. Fred was not impressed to read that the numbers were the same as those earmarked by the previous government.

Fred felt deflated by the figures until he read that the numbers for the 2015–2016 year were to be brought forward to the 2014–2015 year. *The current year staff reduction is 900. Next financial year, the staff reduction will now total 2 100. This means we're looking at a total of 3 000 staff reductions when there had been only 2 500 expressions of interest,* he thought. *Could I be so lucky?*

Arriving at work the next day, there was much chatter about the Budget. Staff had been sent an email, which confirmed the Budget figures, and Fred was now entertaining the possibility that he might escape the Tax Office. It gave him a glimmer of hope.

The Tax Office conducted a series of post-Budget speeches by various senior executives and Fred was unimpressed by the messages as managers encouraged as many staff as possible to nominate for voluntary redundancies.

"Although the current figures indicate there will be additional redundancies in a couple of years, things can easily change and you can't count on this to actually happen," the senior executives warned. "You should apply for a voluntary redundancy now."

There was a change in mood with staff, as an atmosphere of fear seemed to be taking over. Officers who previously stated that they weren't interested in a voluntary redundancy were now thinking about throwing their hats into the ring.

"I didn't think I'd be applying; however, I don't like what I'm hearing about what it's going to be like for those left behind," Robert Romano advised. "My manager is suggesting that most of the work and decision-making will be pushed down to the Executive Level 1 officers, which means that I'll be expected to carry the team. I don't like this prospect so I think I'll go for a package."

Robert's sentiments were being echoed by others and, even though all the predictions were that the numbers for voluntary redundancies would be undersubscribed, Fred was fearful that the numbers might now be oversubscribed.

One afternoon, Duke Box visited his staff in Melbourne office.

"How's it going?" Duke asked Fred.

"The situation regarding the voluntary redundancies has been occupying my mind and I was wondering whether you know anything about my rating?" Fred queried.

"I don't know about your rating," Duke said. "I was contacted and was just asked a few questions. I can assure you that I responded in a manner to support your wish for a redundancy."

Duke then departed.

"You'd be comforted to know that Duke is supporting you," Sarah Boo commented.

"I don't feel comforted at all," Fred replied. "Based on my past experiences in this place, I don't trust any of the managers."

Tax Office employees received an email advising that the expressions of interest in the new process for a voluntary redundancy were now open. This was followed by an email to staff who had previously applied. Fred read through the instructions before he discussed the process with Sarah.

"I'm going to put in my application today," he informed her.

"I might think about it a little more and put mine in next week," she said.

Fred updated his application and crossed his fingers before lodging it.

*   *   *

The Docklands office held sessions on the transformation of Big Business. Fred attended one of the sessions, absorbing various comments concerning the challenge to deal with the future direction in line with the Commissioner's messages.

During the session, the senior executives were communicating messages from the Commissioner for the need to do more with less, to cut red tape, to enhance the client experience and to be less risk averse.

Be less risk averse? You've got to be joking! Fred thought. *How can an officer be anything but risk averse when the Tax Office has developed a culture where they give you no support and target you even when you have gone by the book and done nothing wrong?*

"We should be willing to take decisions without the need to rely on Tax Office guidance," one excited attendee suggested. "The speeches made by the Commissioner should be sufficient support for us to be empowered to take on this responsibility!"

Fred could not believe his ears. *Years earlier I was unfairly subjected to false allegations of breaching code of conduct for not applying Tax Office guidance and not undertaking processes in line with a senior executive's view of the world and it is now being suggested that staff should make their own decisions without guidance and expect that management are going to support them. How ridiculous!*

The audience left the session and there was much discussion when they returned to their workstations.

"I couldn't believe some of those suggestions," said Kasin.

"Those suggestions just confirm to me that I'm desperately in need of a voluntary redundancy," Sarah remarked.

"The future of the Tax Office appears to be to allow staff to make decisions that basically give big business taxpayers what they want. This seems to be what the Tax Office means by enhancing the client experience," Fred suggested. "I wouldn't be comfortable in that sort of cretin environment so bring on a voluntary redundancy for me too please!"

Chapter 59 – On the Brink

Rumours were spreading with many conflicting comments concerning the voluntary redundancies. There were unofficial reports that the Tax Office had already received the required number of applications and it was anticipated that the numbers would balloon. Sarah and Fred looked at each other with expressions of concern.

The next Friday, several people on Fred's floor were offered voluntary redundancies from the first round, which further upset him. Later that day, Fred received a series of external submissions on his public ruling and he sent out acknowledgements before he departed the office at 6.30 pm.

First thing Monday morning, Fred was burdened with the requirement to attend the next stage of the Management Course; the course that he always referred to as the one Roman Cox nominated him for.

Roman was buzzing around trying to capture the gossip on the voluntary redundancies even though he was very discreet in divulging what he knew. He managed to catch Fred during a break in the course.

"You shouldn't have any worries about the voluntary redundancies," Roman commented sarcastically.

"If the Tax Office has achieved in excess of the numbers they require for the voluntary redundancies then there will be some people who miss out. So why would you say that I shouldn't have any worries?" Fred asked.

Roman didn't respond and appeared very upbeat as he began humming.

The following week, a person named Ray Cardus, an International officer, contacted Fred by telephone. "I've been asked an administrative question on international tax and I was wondering if you could take a look at it," Ray said.

"I haven't been involved in any of that work," Fred advised. "However, I'm prepared to look at the query and provide any thoughts I might have to you later in the day."

Ray sent through the query and Fred noted that the issue had been in the Tax Office for almost a month. He also noted that the query had been referred by the very people who had been undertaking that work. He was unimpressed but began to look into it.

While Fred was conducting his research, he received a subsequent email from Ray. Attached to the email were associated documents.

Fred spoke to Duke Box on the telephone and mentioned the matter. Duke expressed his desire to be involved.

Fred examined the associated documentation and noted that the matter had already been signed off by senior executives but had not been published on the Tax Office website.

In the early afternoon, Fred was looking into the matter when he was copied into another email. It was from Ray to the senior executives involved. It read: "Hello. Fred said that he would provide me with a written response by tomorrow".

Fred could not believe what he was reading. He forwarded the email to Duke and included a note: "Duke, this has just come through. It completely misrepresents the basis of my discussion with Ray".

Philip Latio was at his workstation during the time of Fred's distress, singing and whistling. Fred attempted to ignore him; however, the escalation of the matter, which seemed to harmonise with the escalation in Philip's singing and whistling, was getting to him.

Fred was then hit by another email from Ray, copied to Duke and various senior executives. Ray wrote: "Hi Fred. I forgot that I am on annual leave tomorrow. I've spoken to the person who made the enquiry and she is keen to get the advice tomorrow rather than wait for me to provide it to her next week so I told her that you would do it. Please send it to her directly and copy me in".

Fred was stunned by Ray's audacity, and was amazed that Ray considered it appropriate to send such an email to all the senior executives involved.

"I can't believe these unprofessional and useless people," Fred exclaimed. "I have the overwhelming urge to just walk out!"

"Oh no, don't do that," Philip impulsively stated.

Fred had no intention of actually walking out, but the unsympathetic nature of Philip's reaction further upset him.

Fred had done as much background work as he could and thought he would sleep on the matter before drafting a response. He reflected on the case and why information that had been cleared by senior executives had not been published on the Tax Office website. This point was plaguing Fred's mind as he left the office at 7.00 pm.

The first thing Fred did on Friday morning was to check the Tax Office website. Even though the information was not there the day before, like magic, the information appeared before him. He drafted an email to Duke where he wrote:

> I've checked the Tax Office website this morning and it appears that the relevant information has now been published, which essentially provides the information sought by the enquiry. I suggest that this obviates the need to respond to the query. The person can simply be advised of the publication.

Duke contacted Fred by telephone. "I agree with your suggestion; however, I still want to send a message that the Techo Group should not be used as a dumping ground for matters that are the responsibility of other areas," Duke advised.

Fred received a copy of an email sent by Duke to Ray, which was also copied to the various senior executives. Duke gave an account of the issue, how it was resolved and criticised the referral, although he offered to be involved and render assistance in the future.

Duke's quest to come across as omniscient is never-ending, Fred thought. *He simply can't help always taking credit for the work of others to big-note himself.*

Fred was starting to experience chest congestion, a sore throat and severe headaches. He visited Dr Wells, who prescribed antibiotics. The doctor also took his blood pressure and noted that it was elevated at 150 over 90.

"Work may be affecting your health so you may wish to take a break," Dr Wells suggested.

"There are a few issues with my work and the voluntary redundancies that are causing me some concern. I've been struggling for a while but I think I can continue on," Fred stated.

Fred struggled to complete the review of the external submissions on his public ruling. He found the environment at work, with the uncertainty of the voluntary redundancies and the unsympathetic attitude of the managers, to be making life difficult for him. His ill health was aggravating the situation. Fred was feeling so bad that he rang the counselling service and made an appointment.

The next week, Fred drafted an email to Duke to advise him of his appointment with the counsellor. When he went to send it, he found that he simply couldn't hit the "send" button. Instead, he hit "delete". He contacted the counselling service and cancelled the appointment. He then just continued to struggle on.

The authoring team for the international tax rulings was advised that draft compendiums were required by the end of July in order to be ready in time for the Rulings Panel. Fred was progressing well and was confident of meeting the deadline. Penny then called a meeting with Theo and Fred.

"The draft compendiums may be required for a possible early release so we will need them next week," Penny advised.

Theo and Fred looked at each other and were silent.

"We really don't have much choice about this," Penny added.

"I'm confident I'll be able to get something to you by the middle of next week," Fred stated defiantly, but Theo was quiet.

"What about you, Theo?" Penny asked.

"Well, I can only do what I can," Theo said, his face stony.

"Okay gents, if you can leave me now, I need to make a call to Milton Hustler to let him know," Penny said.

Fred was feeling uneasy regarding the voluntary redundancies as other officers were being told of their ratings and had the opportunity to make representations about them, with some of the ratings subsequently being changed. However, Duke and Roman consistently said that they knew nothing about them.

Given the inconsistent information regarding the ratings, Fred decided to check with the union and sent an enquiry email to John Lazarus.

As Fred sent off his enquiry email, he received an email from Milton Hustler, which he had sent to the project team. Milton wrote:

> I have serious concerns about the international tax project. On a number of occasions, deadlines have been brought forward that were impossible for me to meet. However, I was told that I had to meet them. I cancelled leave more than once to meet these changed deadlines. Penny has now advised that the deadline for the compendiums have been brought forward three weeks. I had planned to spend time with my family, but I have now cancelled this leave. If this goes on, I do not feel that I can continue on the project.

Fred read the email, which upset him. He then heard comments that management was not at all sympathetic to Milton's situation, which upset him further and prompted him to send his own email. He wrote: "To whom it may concern. For the record, I wholeheartedly agree with the sentiments echoed by Milton".

Working hard to complete the compendium, Fred drafted detailed responses to every issue raised in the external submissions. He provided full explanations and analysis to support his recommendations and submitted it in an email. He wrote:

> I attach a draft compendium based on the submissions for the public ruling. This version has been written for the Rulings Panel where I have attempted to provide background and context to support my suggested recommendations. It would need to be reviewed and appropriately edited for any other release.

Tony Robbins, a senior executive signing off on other rulings, was quickly on the phone to Fred. "You make reference to some other release for the draft compendium. I believe that we should only be releasing the draft compendium as per standard processes," Tony said.

"I am very much in agreement with you," Fred advised. "A possible early release was communicated to me by Penny Farthing and I am merely operating under this direction."

"I don't agree with this course of action and it won't be happening with the compendium to my public ruling," Tony confirmed.

Fred had a very rough night without getting any sleep before he arrived at work the next day. He was feeling sick with continued headaches, a sore throat and chest pains. He read an email from Perry White, where he had written: "Thanks for sending through the draft compendium, Fred. I haven't read it, but I noted that it was 48 pages long. Do you think you could edit the document to reduce the number of pages?"

After taking a deep breath, Fred mulled over the fact that Perry was most probably asking for an abridged version of the document to accommodate a possible early release—something that should have been completely unnecessary.

As a joke, Fred fleetingly flirted with the idea of simply reducing the font size of the document to reduce the number of pages. Instead, he drafted an email to Perry, copied to the other internal stakeholders, where he wrote:

> I have drafted the compendium in a manner to provide the Rulings Panel with as much information as necessary to assist them to make fully informed decisions. It is consistent with the approach I have

taken in previous public rulings I have authored and which was considered appropriate.

Fred sent the email and momentarily sat back in his chair when he received a telephone call from Ferris Wheal.

"I completely agree with your email and I have taken a similar approach with my compendium," Ferris said. "Tony Robbins is comfortable with this approach."

"Thanks for your words of support, Ferris," Fred stated. "It's a pity that Tony isn't signing off on all the international tax products as I'm sure it would have resulted in a lot more plain sailing and a lot less pain."

When Fred got off the phone, he remembered that he needed to take his antibiotics. Sarah observed him taking his pills and looked over at him.

"You really don't look too good," she commented.

"I really don't feel too good," he responded. "I think I might visit my doctor."

Fred tried to ring Duke, but got his voicemail so he left a message. He followed this up with an email advising that he wasn't feeling well and was going to visit his doctor.

As Fred sat in the doctor's waiting room, he was overwhelmed with a feeling of grief. *Life really doesn't have to be this difficult*, he thought. When Dr Wells called out his name, he walked deliberately into the doctor's office.

Dr Wells seemed to sense Fred's situation as he automatically commenced to take his blood pressure. The doctor was engaging Fred in conversation when he wrote something on Fred's record. Fred peered over and saw the figures: 174 over 110.

"So what's happening at work at the moment?" Dr Wells asked.

Fred had to swallow his spit before he forced a response. "It's a critical time for a public ruling," he advised. He stopped and took a breath before he recommenced his response. "I've been struggling on with my work and I've been upset with the process taking place with the voluntary redundancies. I'm not very hopeful of getting one given the rumours going around."

Fred looked over when Dr Wells wrote down the next set of numbers: 179 over 114.

"I think you should take a break from work as it seems to be affecting your health," the doctor recommended.

It was at this point that Fred broke down. "I really wanted to be at work over the next couple of weeks to complete my tasks and be there for the notification of the voluntary redundancies," he said.

Fred felt his chest tightening and an accentuated pulse in his left arm where the blood pressure cuff was placed.

"I can give you a certificate to take two weeks off, which will give you a break from work," the doctor said.

Fred was emotional and eked out a reply. "Okay."

"That's good. Now do you have a pair of sunglasses with you?" Dr Wells asked.

"Yes, I do," Fred responded, confused by the question.

"I want you to put on those sunglasses and leave my office. Don't worry about signing the form," the doctor instructed.

"But I want to do the right thing by you," Fred replied.

"This requirement is not necessary in exceptional circumstances," the doctor advised. "You just get yourself home."

"Thank you, Doctor," Fred stated as they shook hands.

When Fred arrived home, he sent an email to Duke Box. He wrote:

> I visited my doctor and he has certified that I will be unfit for work until 24 July 2014. Please find attached the medical certificate.

Fred then sent another email to John Lazarus, where he wrote:

> Please be advised that if you need to send any correspondence to me over the next couple of weeks, it would be appreciated if you could send it to my personal email address. I visited my doctor this afternoon and he has given me a medical certificate for two weeks.

Fred sat back in his chair and then noticed that he had received an email from John Lazarus. John wrote:

> I was advised that managers had to consult about the voluntary redundancy rating. The manager should have recommended a rating to the delegate. You should be told the rating and the reasons for it. You should then be entitled to make submissions if you disagree. If your manager does not agree to provide you with this information, an industrial relations executive has agreed to contact your manager to advise of the obligation.

Fred was infuriated to learn that he'd been given the run-around and sent an email to John advising that he would take it up with his manager when he returned to work.

Convalescing at home, Fred received a telephone call from a private number and he answered.

"Hello, Fred. It's senior executive Karen Carney here and I'm ringing to confirm whether you wish to progress with a voluntary redundancy."

Fred caught his breath. "I'm sorry, but are you saying that the Tax Office is offering me a voluntary redundancy?" he asked in hope.

"That's if you want one," Karen replied.

"Of course I want one," Fred confirmed.

"You'll have to be prepared to leave the office by 29 August 2014," Karen added.

"I'll take anything I can get," Fred replied.

"Okay then," Karen said.

"You've just made my day," Fred remarked.

"Well, it's good to know that I've made someone happy today," Karen commented.

Fred hung up the phone and took a few moments to absorb the information before he stood up, walked outside and screamed out, "Yeahhhh!"

Chapter 60 – Voluntary Redundancies

Returning to work on 25 July 2014, Fred was pleased to hear that Sarah was also successful in gaining a voluntary redundancy. Upon checking his voicemail, he found a message from Penny.

"As soon as you are back at work, I'd like to explain what Betty, Perry and I are looking for in terms of editing the compendium," Penny said.

Fred shook his head as he knew exactly what they were looking for. They wanted to sanitise the document in case there was to be an early release to ensure that they didn't expose themselves.

The next thing Fred did was to review his emails. The first one he read was from Duke, who had replied to his email where he had informed Duke that he was going to visit his doctor. Duke had written:

> If you are going to visit your doctor now, Penny has asked me to tell you that she wants to talk with you about the compendium when you return.

The two weeks Fred had been away from the office resulted in him being relieved of the job of editing the draft compendium. Miles had been given this responsibility and he had been sent a copy.

Fred reviewed the document, which he considered to be absurd. *They've simply summarised each issue raised. They've taken out all the supporting information and analysis, which makes the document virtually useless.*

*   *   *

Roman approached Fred. "So what do you want in terms of a send-off?" Roman asked.

Fred was quick to respond. "I don't want anything."

"Oh Fred, you have to have something," Roman stated condescendingly.

"No, I don't have to have something," Fred asserted.

"Fred, Fred, Fred, you've been in the office for over 30 years, you have to have something," Roman insisted.

"Roman, I've previously spoken to Duke, who happens to be my manager, and I mentioned to him that I wished to go quietly and he respected my wishes," Fred advised. "I hope that you can respect my wishes as well."

"Now, I've spoken to both Tina Colomba and Sarah Boo and they are both happy to have a combined lunch. You should also join them in a lunch," Roman suggested.

"I don't mind joining them for their lunch," Fred said, "but I don't want anything for me."

"They are only looking at having a small gathering with just the team in Melbourne. Why don't you think about it?" Roman asked.

"Okay, I'll think about it," Fred responded.

"You might also want to think about anyone else you may wish to invite," Roman added.

"Okay, I've just thought about it and I don't want to invite anyone else," Fred immediately replied.

"Now Fred, you really should think about inviting your manager," Roman persisted.

"Duke's in another office and if I invite him then that creates issues with the other people in the other offices," Fred pointed out.

"I'm just asking you to think about it," Roman said. He walked off.

Sarah made an appearance and Fred raised the issue of the send-off for her.

"I don't want a send-off," said Sarah. "I only told Roman that I would be prepared to attend a lunch for you and Tina but I definitely didn't agree to a lunch for me."

"Well, what you are telling me contradicts what Roman told me," Fred stated. "It may be something that we need to clarify with him."

Sarah went off and soon returned. "I came across Roman. I clarified that I didn't want anything and he accepted this," Sarah advised.

"He accepted this?" Fred asked.

"Yes, he did," said Sarah.

"Well, I'd be surprised if Roman has really accepted this. Knowing him, I bet he raises the issue again," said Fred.

The following Monday morning, Roman escorted Tina to Sarah's and Fred's workstations. "Okay you three, I just wanted to confirm what you guys wanted to do regarding a send-off," Roman said.

"I don't want anything," Fred was first to reply.

"Neither do I," Sarah quickly followed.

All eyes turned to Tina.

"I'm having a morning tea next Thursday because my last day is next Friday," Tina advised. "I'd be prepared to come in for a lunch but I'm not fussed."

"Okay then," Roman stated in a matter-of-fact way. "Fred started in the office in 19… well, when Fred?" Roman queried.

"What are you going on about?" Fred replied.

"You started in the office in 19…" Roman repeated.

"Sorry, Roman, I don't know what you're on about," Fred said.

"Fred doesn't know what I'm on about. Fred, Fred, Fred," Roman stated patronisingly.

"Do you know what he's on about?" Fred asked Sarah.

She shook her head.

"You're not thinking of putting some words together about me for the purposes of a speech, I hope," said Fred. "I thought we just agreed that I wasn't having anything."

"Fred, Fred, Fred," Roman repeated and it sounded like an echo as he walked off.

*   *   *

Miles sent out an invitation for an international tax workshop to be held in Melbourne over three days to cover the compendiums and the final public ruling documents. Fred was at a total loss to understand why there was any need for a workshop.

The workshop was attended by Miles Long, Betty Mason, Perry White, Penny Farthing, Hoa Lu and Fred. Theo wasn't available to attend as he was on leave.

"I'm amazed that you've turned up for the workshop, Fred," Perry commented with a smile.

"The ruling has been my baby so why wouldn't I attend?" Fred asked.

"Well, when some of the officers I know were notified of their voluntary redundancy, the only thing that they seem to have time for is organising their departure lunches," Perry stated. He laughed and the others joined in, except for Fred.

Miles was facilitating the workshop where Betty and Perry were putting forward some new thinking concerning a new approach to Theo's ruling. Fred argued against just about every point being raised and his resistance appeared to be enough to sway the others, as they eventually seemed to accept his views.

After three exhausting days, the attendees reached agreement on the way ahead. Miles took on the role of redrafting Theo's ruling and Fred was to make the agreed changes to his ruling.

Early the next week, Miles and Fred exchanged the updated versions of the respective documents. Fred made few changes to his ruling; however, Miles had extensively redrafted Theo's ruling. To Fred's surprise, Miles also took the liberty of contradicting much of what he thought had been agreed on in the workshop.

There were further hook-ups arranged to discuss Fred's and Theo's rulings. Fred's ruling had a relatively easy passage; however, there were robust discussions on Theo's ruling, with Betty and Perry locking horns with Fred. Theo was caught in the middle. In the end, Betty and Perry made the final calls on Theo's ruling, which Miles volunteered to amend.

Within a couple of days, Miles rang Fred. "I find it difficult to just add some words to Theo's ruling," Miles advised. "I find the need to rewrite various sections."

Fred didn't like what he was hearing. He was getting the feeling that Miles was embarking on another redraft.

"Based on what was agreed on in the last meeting, you should only be making minimal changes," Fred suggested. "I have limited time to dedicate to this in my last couple of days as I have many other matters to attend to before I leave the office. You may wish to discuss your points with the others on the project team."

The following morning, Fred checked his emails and noted two from Miles, which was also sent to the project team. The first contained the final version of Fred's ruling document. He scrolled through the document and observed few changes. The second email contained an updated version of Theo's ruling, which he didn't even bother opening.

Fred then commenced his clean up of his electronic and hard copy files. He got to his electronic folder on the Management Course he was undertaking and he smiled with relief that he didn't have to complete it. He then shook his head when he considered the taxpayers' money that was wasted because Philip had nominated him.

When it came to the end of the day, although Fred had made a lot of headway, he still had a lot more to do. He left the office, saying goodbye to the few staff remaining in attendance.

Fronting up to work on his last day, Fred was confronted with a group of people milling around his workstation. There was a cheer as he was noticed.

"Congratulations, Fred!" Roman said and he handed Fred a framed certificate. It was a Certificate of Recognition awarded to Fred Campari in recognition of 32 years of service to the public service upon separation from the Tax Office.

After Fred read it, he looked at Sarah, who was also holding a framed certificate.

"I got one too," Sarah confirmed.

The group slowly dispersed and Roman mentioned that the team was going for morning tea break at 10.00 am.

"That would be good," Fred said.

Fred then began to complete his final tasks when he received an email from Duke:

> I'm having trouble putting through your certificate of separation on the system. You apparently have national office files in your possession that you need to hand over. You also need to provide a job number for your deregistration from Unix.

"What in the blazes is he going on about?" Fred cursed.

Fred got on the phone to Duke and, while on the phone, the team indicated that they were heading off to morning tea. Fred placed his hand over the receiver. "I can't go now," Fred advised. "I might meet you there." He returned to the phone call. "Duke, I haven't had national office files for years," he advised, "and I have no idea about a job number for Unix deregistration."

"I need to be off soon as it's also Otto Palo's last day and I've arranged to meet with him for handover matters," Duke advised. "I suggest you try to find out why the national office files are still marked in your name and arrange to get the job number for Unix deregistration, as Otto included a job number on his form."

Fred rang numerous people in an effort to resolve the issues; however, the consistent reply was that they would have to get back to him. He would have liked to have asked other staff who had completed the voluntary redundancy forms what they did but they were all out to morning tea. He eventually made contact on the phone with a male computer systems officer who was able to look into his network profile.

"I can't see that you have any attributes that would indicate that you need to deregister from the Unix system," the officer advised.

"There's another person in our group who apparently did have to deregister," Fred advised.

"So what?" the officer replied. "That doesn't establish that you necessarily have the same profile that requires you to deregister."

The staff returned from morning tea and Fred bombarded them with questions.

"I didn't have to get any job number for Unix deregistration," Sarah replied.

"I put through Sarah's separation forms and I didn't have any trouble," Roman stated. "I don't know what your problem is, Fred. I didn't bother with all the questions, I just put 'yes' to everything."

Fred got back on the phone to Duke and briefed him with what he had found out.

"Well, I wouldn't want to hold you up on your last day," Duke said. "I might just put 'yes' to everything."

Fred shook his head as he got on to finalising his tasks prior to his scheduled departure at midday. He went off to the photocopying room to deposit some confidential documents in the security bin and, when he walked by Roman's workstation, he overheard Roman on the phone with Duke. They were clearly making fun of Fred and laughing out loud.

Fred ignored the antics and gathered his belongings. As he was walking out, he was confronted by a group of people who had gathered to meet him.

"We were just wondering whether you might want to have lunch with us," Theo said.

Fred looked around the small group. Their names popped into his head as he saw each one: Sarah Boo, Zara Majid, Cas Boer, Paul Peters and Theo Onassis.

"It'd be my pleasure to have lunch with you," he said.

They were making their way out of the building when Roman came scurrying after them. "I have to collect your building pass when you leave," his voice echoed.

Fred went through the security doors, handed Roman his pass and they shook hands. Fred then proceeded down the stairs and on to the footpath. He turned around, looked back to the Tax Office building and jokingly performed a final victory salute, à la Richard Nixon.

After an enjoyable lunch, the small group strolled down Bourke

Street until they came to the crossroad with Village Street. It was at this juncture that Fred was to part ways. Sarah had to go back to the Tax Office to complete her last day and the rest of the group had to return to the Tax Office to complete the rest of their careers. Fred kissed Sarah and Zara on the cheek and shook hands with Cas, Paul and Theo.

Fred continued walking down Bourke Street and, even though the pollution was typical that day, he took a deep breath and considered that the air had never felt fresher. It was an air of freedom.

www.ingramcontent.com/pod-product-compliance
Lightning Source LLC
Chambersburg PA
CBHW060954120726
47910CB00002B/627